D0745984

STORM & FURY

A STORM & FURY ADVENTURES COLLECTION

GAIL Z. MARTIN
LARRY N. MARTIN

SOL

CONTENTS

STORM & FURY

A STORM & FURY ADVENTURES
COLLECTION

by Gail Z. Martin & Larry N. Martin

ISBN: 978-1-939704-66-5
Copyright © 2018 by Gail Z. Martin and Larry N. Martin
All rights reserved.

The right of the author to be identified as the author of this work has been asserted in accordance with the Copyright, Designs and Patents Act 1988.

All rights reserved. No part of this publication may be reproduced, stored in a retrieval system, or transmitted, in any form or by any means, electronic, mechanical, photocopying, recording or otherwise, without the prior permission of the copyright owners.

This is a work of fiction. Any resemblance to actual persons (living or dead), locales and incidents are either coincidental or used fictitiously. Any trademarks used belong to their owners. No infringement is intended.

Airship Down © 2014 Resurrection Day © 2015, Lagniappe © 2015, Grave Voices © 2015, Ruin Creek © 2015, The Hunt © 2016, Rogue © 2016, Ghost Wolf © 2015, The Patented Troll © 2015, Iron & Blood © 2015.

Cover art by Lou Harper.
SOL Publishing is an imprint of DreamSpinner Communications, LLC

To our readers - because you read, we write.

INTRODUCTION

WELCOME TO OUR world. This is a collection of short stories and novellas from the *Iron & Blood: A Jake Desmet Adventure* universe, set in the late 1890s in an alternate history Pittsburgh. Enjoy the adventures of Department of Supernatural Investigation agents Mitch Storm and Jacob Drangosavich as they fight to keep the world safe from occult and paranormal threats.

AIRSHIP DOWN

AIRSHIP DOWN

"THREE ORBS AT THREE O'CLOCK, over the Homestead Works." Mitch Storm's voice carried over the hum of the dirigible's engines.

"I see them." Jacob Drangosavich leaned over to speak to the airship pilot, who veered their craft like a black ghost over the Monongahela River. "Get in close," he said to the pilot. "I want to get as close to the sons of bitches as we can."

"They match the description of what they sent us out to find," Mitch replied. "Too far away to see detail. Is the camera working?"

Jacob checked over the camera controls. The Department had outfitted the airship with the best new, secret technology the folks in Rochester could come up with, small cameras that ran on a remote switch, something the agents could operate from the bridge of their airship. "They're set, if they work," he sighed.

"And there go the lights," Mitch said, pointing. As if on cue, the Edison lights that illuminated Carnegie Steel's flagship factory dimmed to brown, flickering out several times before struggling back to their original glow.

"Same as the other times," Jacob said, scribbling in his journal with a Waterman safety pen and still managing to get ink on his fingers.

Mitch sighed and shook his head. "I don't know why you bother," he said, resignation coloring his voice. "No one will be able to read that chicken scratch."

"I will," Jacob replied. "You think it's bad in English; even my mother can't read my Croatian."

"Sir," the pilot, Captain Nowak said. "The lights are moving."

Mitch and Jacob dropped their banter and scrambled back to the observation window. "Keep them in view," Mitch ordered. "Don't lose them." Dark-haired and dark-eyed with a five o'clock shadow that showed up at three, Mitch Storm looked like what an adventure-book illustrator would come up with for an army captain and sharpshooter. Mitch was a few inches shorter than Jacob, but what he lacked in height he made up for in attitude. He had a pugilist's build, all-muscle, and a gleam in his eyes that promised mischief.

"I'm on it," Nowak replied. He was a good ten years older than either Storm or Drangosavich, with a little gray starting to show in his brown hair around the temples. To Jacob's eye, Nowak looked more like he belonged at the prow of one of the river barges than high in an airship. He had the rumpled, lived-in look of a man who has spent his life in one cramped ship or another, either on the Oder River in his native Poland, or navigating the traffic on one of New Pittsburgh's famed three rivers. Instead, a stint in the Navy had landed him in the nascent airship corps, and the Department had snapped him up for their own uses.

The airship's engines whined as Nowak increased the power, steering their ship above the black ribbon that was the mighty Monongahela River, or as New Pittsburgh locals liked to call it, the Mon. Behind them, the Monongahela and the Allegheny Rivers joined to become the powerful Ohio, which in turn found its way into the Mississippi. Beneath them, the burn-off flares from the Jones and Laughlin steel mill on the south banks of the river reflected off thick clouds of coal smoke from factories that churned out coke and steel around the clock.

"What'd that reporter say it looked like?" Mitch asked. "Hell with the lid off? He got that right."

Their airship, the *Onyx Shadow*, glided above the city. From here, the Mon seemed to be illuminated by torchlight, as up and down the river Mitch and Jacob could see the tall flare stacks of one massive steel mill after another.

"Have a care to give those flames a wide berth, or we'll have big trouble," Mitch warned.

"Don't worry. I've got them in my sights," Nowak assured them.

"The orbs are moving faster," Mitch said. "Keep after them!"

Jacob looked down and then thought better of it, gripping the railing white-knuckled. "I hate flying," he muttered. The river bank slipped by rapidly beneath the airship with its rail lines and mill towns, as barges chugged downriver without a care about the excitement in the skies above.

Jacob pushed a stray lock of dark blond hair out of his eyes. He didn't like his hair as short as regulations called for, or nearly as short as Mitch preferred to keep his. With a long thin face and pale blue eyes, Jacob was well aware he looked like the majority of Eastern European immigrants who had flocked to the manufacturing cities of the Northeast to work in the factories of America. The same slight accent that occasionally prompted a dour look from the Brass made him fit right in among the mill hunks and factory workers, as did his ability to speak several Slavic languages like a native. Like those mill workers, Jacob was tall and broad-shouldered, and hard work had put muscles on his lean frame. He seldom started fights, but often finished them.

Nowak maneuvered the *Onyx Shadow* through the ever-present smoke. Visibility from the airship's small bridge waxed and waned, and Jacob fingered his St. Blaise medal, certain they would plow into one of the high brick smokestacks or the steep hillsides that sloped down to the river. The experimental airship moved at top speed, faster than any of the commercial or private dirigibles, thanks to the Department's top-secret technology and design. It was even faster than the *Flying Scotsman* locomotive in its best race. That didn't bear dwelling on, in Jacob's opinion.

"They're damn fast," Nowak said, leaning forward as if it would help the airship gain momentum.

"Can you keep up?" Mitch urged. Jacob had seen that light in his partner's eyes before, usually just before the two of them created a calamity that tended to include explosions and which required lengthy explanations to their superiors.

"I can try," Nowak said, his expression set in grim resolve. "We're still working out the bugs. Not completely sure yet what this baby can do."

"Do it." Mitch moved as far forward as the airship bridge allowed, staring at the flying orbs as if willpower alone would narrow the gap.

"They're heading upriver, like as not toward the Edgar Thomson Works," Nowak said as he managed the instruments and checked the gauges. Their reconnaissance ship held a crew of five, including Mitch and Jacob. Compared to the bigger zeppelins, the *Onyx Shadow* was fast, light, and classified, using a combination of rotorcraft and a much smaller gas envelope than the typical airships.

"I've got 'er opened wide up," Nowak said. "With a little luck and a tailwind, we'll keep them in sight."

Jacob was torn between heady exhilaration and sheer terror, a common feeling when he and Mitch were in the field. The bridge was humming from the sound of the straining engines, and without feeling or hearing the sound of the wind whistling by them, a glance down made Jacob think that the moving scenery far below them was nothing more than scenes from a praxinoscope projection.

"We're gaining on them," Mitch said, with the same raw competitiveness that had made him the Department's top crack shot three years in a row. He held a portable version of the airship's cameras and had it pressed against the glass, muttering as he tried to hold it still enough to get a shot of the glowing orbs that danced through the sky.

"I can't hold this speed forever," Nowak snapped. "This airship wasn't tested for this. It's fragile."

"Just a little longer," Mitch said, never taking his eyes off the orbs. "We've nearly got them."

Jacob could hear the airship's engines protesting. "Mitch, this isn't a train. Push a locomotive too hard, and you stop rolling. Push this too far, and we fall out of the sky. Those rotors need to spin to keep us in the air."

"Almost there," Mitch said, in a tone that let Jacob know that Mitch hadn't heard a word he or Novak had said.

The orbs dipped and swirled toward the massive Thomson Works mill, moving fast. They aligned over top of the mill, and the factory lights and all the street lamps dimmed and flickered, casting the Braddock riverside into near-darkness before the power came back.

"There they go again!" Mitch said, carefully snapping another picture as the orbs began to move again.

Nowak opened his mouth to protest, but before he could say anything, there were two loud bangs from the direction of the engines.

"Abandon ship!" a man's panicked voice shouted from the speaking tube on the bridge. "Repeat, engines failing, rotors two and three both down, abandon ship!"

"Not again," Jacob muttered.

Mitch grabbed his parachute and tossed chutes to Jacob and Nowak. He strapped his on almost without looking, then made sure he secured his precious camera inside his leather jacket before heading to the emergency hatch. Jacob grabbed his journal and shoved it into his jacket and zipped it up.

"*Wariat*! You're insane," Nowak shouted. "You're bloody insane!"

"Get ready to jump," Mitch said as if he had not even noticed Nowak's outburst. He yanked open the emergency hatch, and cold wind ripped through the bridge, scattering papers and howling in their ears. The airship was no longer level, slowly sinking toward the river as the two remaining rotors fought gravity. Nowak struggled with the controls, trying to slow the airship's rate of descent and level it out as much as possible for everyone to clear safely.

"Come on!" Mitch said, grabbing the pilot by the arm and shoving him toward the hatch. "Jump!"

Nowak had the same training Mitch and Jacob had taken, but Jacob bet that the pilot hadn't needed to use his as often. He went out the hatch pale with terror.

"Jacob—jump!" Mitch shouted, holding tightly to the railing to keep from being pulled out of the airship.

"*Magarac*," Jacob muttered under his breath, not bothering to translate. He had called his partner a jackass often enough that Mitch knew at least one word in Croatian. He dove from the hatch, counted silently and pulled the cord, feeling his heart in his throat until the black silk billowed into the sky above him. To his left, he spotted the two men from the engine room, gliding down with their parachutes. He saw Mitch a little ways over, his dark clothes nearly invisible against the night sky, but his face alight with the thrill of the jump.

The *Onyx Shadow* nosed toward the river, its engines sputtering and three of its rotors now in flames. They had dimmed its running lights to avoid notice, but even so, it would be difficult to imagine that no one was going to notice a large flaming object falling out of the sky and into the swift waters of the Mon. Once or twice, this kind of thing could be explained away with tales of weather balloons or atmospheric disturbances. Too often, and they'd have to call in help to clean things up. Jacob sighed. He should have known the night was going to end this way.

Jacob brought his chute down on a barren strip of land by the railway, not far from where Nowak and Mitch had landed. They wrapped up their chutes, weighted them with rocks and sank them in the river. Jacob shook his head. He had way too much experience with this sort of thing.

Nowak, still cursing in Polish, had gone in search of his crewmen. Mitch already had his camera out. "Come on," he said. "We'll track them on foot."

Jacob opened his mouth to argue and shut it again with a sigh of resignation. There was no reasoning with Mitch when he was like this. The best he could do was to try and keep the damage to a minimum, if it wasn't already too late for that. Mitch could explain it to the higher-ups. He always did.

"Damn." Mitch struggled to the top of the embankment, where he had a good view of the massive steel mill. The orbs were gone.

Jacob removed a cigar from his pocket and lit it. "Put that out!" Mitch said. "Someone will see us."

Jacob shrugged and shoved his hands into his wrinkled canvas jacket. "See what?" he said out of one side of his mouth. "Two jokers walking by the river? We sent the chutes to the bottom, along with the airship. Tomorrow, a barge with no markings will come along and dredge this area, and take out some odd-shaped thing under a tarpaulin. Colonel Falken will hand us our asses when he finds out, you'll sweet-talk our way out of it, we'll end up on probation—again—and next week, just to let us know they're annoyed, they'll send us out to the Rockies to find that big furry guy—again."

"I thought we made a deal with him that we'd leave him alone if he didn't bother the railroad workers?" Mitch said, looking genuinely confused.

Jacob took a drag on his stogie and sent the smoke in Mitch's direction just to watch him cough and swat the air. "Right now, I'm going down to Birmingham since we're on the south side of the river and get some decent pierogies," he said. He said it the way the locals did, "sah side."

"And a beer?" Mitch asked with a knowingly raised eyebrow.

Jacob grinned. "This is New Pittsburgh. A shot-and-a-beer. Iron City." He took another puff. "See how many people are talking about strange doings over the Mon," he said, and his accent, usually nearly non-existent, grew more and more Slavic. "Need to know how much damage control is needed. Before we stir up more."

"You don't care what I'm going to do?" Mitch retorted.

"Nope," Jacob said. "Because you're going to hang around here and get some pictures, telling everyone you're a newspaper man. Then tomorrow, you're going to wake me up early and drag me out to Tesla-Westinghouse to see if that boy-genius had anything to do with the orbs," Jacob added, his gravelly voice carrying even though he did not turn his head.

"You're angry about the crash," Mitch said.

Jacob shrugged and kept on walking.

Mitch jammed his hands in his pockets and glared at him. "Who insisted on having parachutes on the airship?" he said. "Me, that's who."

"And who made us need to use the parachutes?" Jacob replied drily. "You, that's who. See you at the house, Mitch. If I win a few hands of cards, I might bring you a bucket of beer." With that, he sauntered off down the riverside.

At first, he could hear Mitch fuming behind him, but it was all for show. He and Mitch had been partners since the Johnson County Wars out West, only back then, they were green recruits, still wet behind the ears, newly signed up for the adventure of being in the U.S. Cavalry. He took another long drag from his stogie and let it out slowly. *Adventure. That's what they called it. Nearly got our asses shot off. Still have some lead in my leg from that one.*

By the time Jacob reached the safe house in Shadyside, it was after midnight. The lights were out, and no one responded to his quiet knock. Jacob picked the lock and let himself in, then crept up the back stairs.

"About time you got back," Mitch said. He had hooded the room's only lamp so that it could not be seen burning from the street. "I waited to send our report until you came back."

On the table in front of him sat a clockwork carrier pigeon. It was a mechanical marvel, designed with the ability to fly long distances and return to its home base just like its living counterpart. What set the Department's "pigeon" apart was the hidden compartment on its steel back into which small objects could be placed.

"I developed the pictures we shot earlier," Mitch said. "Got in a good photo or two. I had to make them small to fit the bird, but it's enough to give Falken an idea of what we're seeing." Mitch stared at the photos for a few minutes before maneuvering them into the hidden compartment. On the table nearby lay a mobile telegraph switch, and Jacob saw a wire snaking out of the window to the pole outside.

"I think we need to show these to the wunderkind over at Tesla-Westinghouse. You printed extras, right?" Jacob asked.

"Yup," Mitch said. "Oh, and Falken telegraphed. We're on probation—again."

Jacob muttered under his breath in Croatian. "I hear Idaho is lovely this time of year. We might as well buy a cabin."

"Not a bad idea," Mitch replied. He turned off the light, opened a window and released the clockwork bird into the night sky with the sound of the rustle of brass wings.

———

JACOB GROANED AS sunlight streamed through the window, hitting him full in the face. "Get up, lazy ass!" Mitch's voice sounded far too chipper given the late night they had put in. "The carriage is coming for us. I brought up a cup of coffee and a roll for you, but you need to get dressed."

Jacob had barely pulled on his clothing and gulped his coffee before the driver arrived. He grabbed the roll, biting off chunks as he followed Mitch down the steep steps. "No cross words from Mrs. Hanson about last night?" he asked with a mouthful of bread.

Mitch chuckled. "She's got nothing to complain about. The Department paid to patch up the holes from the last time. You can hardly see where the fire was."

Hans, their driver, waited with the carriage in the street, a second cowled man beside him. Hans had his cap pulled low over his face, shading his features. Most people wouldn't look twice at a carriage driver, but if they did, one glance would have made it clear he had been modified.

Half his face was metal, with a mechanical eye and exposed gears —results of a bad explosion a few years back. Likewise, his companion kept his visage equally hidden. Hans was still obviously human, but the second man was clearly a mechanical, one of the latest generation of *werkmen* the Department had begun to deploy. They were loyal, trustworthy, did exactly as ordered, and they did not require hazard pay.

"Hello, Hans," Jacob said as he and Mitch climbed into the open carriage door.

Hans nodded curtly. "Good day, sir," he replied, with the odd whirring and clicking that accompanied his voice when he spoke.

"Tesla-Westinghouse—you know the way," Mitch said when they were settled.

"Very good, sir," Hans replied, climbing back up into the driver's seat beside the guard.

The carriage wound through the crowded New Pittsburgh streets. Jacob glanced out the window. Most of the damage of the Conflagration of 1868 and the Great Pittsburgh Flood of 1869 had been repaired, although the devastation had changed the city's destiny forever, especially after the Quake of 1872. The catastrophes had leveled buildings, changed the topography, opened up rich natural resources and made or destroyed fortunes. And for once, the Department hadn't had a thing to do with it.

"You really think Wunderkind can help with the orbs?" Jacob asked, drawing himself out of his thoughts.

Mitch grinned. "If he doesn't, he can figure out how to get what we need. He's as good as his reputation—maybe even better."

The carriage brought them across the Monongahela to Wilmerding, where the main Tesla-Westinghouse labs were housed. The carriage pulled up to "The Castle," the elaborate, turreted Renaissance Revival/Romanesque building that housed the company headquarters. A fire two years ago had leveled the structure, and the rebuilding not only restored the grand structure but added a new set of secret laboratories beneath it.

"Stay with the carriage, Hans," Mitch said as he and Jacob disembarked. "Keep your ears open—I'll transmit if we need you."

Mitch and Jacob each wore a wide-banded "watch" that was one of the Department's latest toys, since it included among its many functions a short-range Morse transmitter. The receiver was concealed in a rather large lapel pin. Jacob had no reason to expect danger, but he had grown accustomed to being surprised.

Mitch flashed his Department badge at the agent on duty. "Hi, Grace," he said with a grin and a wink.

Special Agent Grace Palmatier gave him a coolly appraising

glance. "Captain Storm," she replied. "And Captain Drangosavich. Nice to see you again. Please try to leave the building—and our vehicles—intact, this time. Your last visit was expensive."

Mitch gave her his best "aw shucks" look, but she shook her head, and Jacob chuckled. "I think she's got you figured out, Mitch," Jacob said as they took the stairs to the basement, then entered the left elevator, where Lars, another *werkman*, was dressed as an elevator operator.

"Good day, sirs," Lars said with mechanical stiffness.

"Minus three," Mitch said. "We're expected."

"Very good, sirs." The elevator buttons only showed the upper levels. Lars flipped a switch, revealing a secret control panel, with the subterranean levels that were home to Tesla-Westinghouse's confidential and experimental projects.

When the doors opened, a tall, skinny young man in a lab coat was waiting for them. A mop of straight, sandy brown hair fell into his eyes, over wire-rimmed glasses that appeared to be smudged. "Wunderkind," otherwise known as Adam Farber, stood several inches taller than either Jacob or Mitch but looked as if he skipped regular meals. He was gawky and rail-thin, all of maybe twenty-two years old, and one of the most brilliant inventors on the Eastern seaboard.

"Come on back," Adam said, dispensing with formalities. "Coffee?" He was as twitchy as a squirrel, making Jacob think the man had probably consumed more than enough caffeine, even though the morning was still young.

"No thanks," Mitch replied. "But we're hoping you can help us with a new project."

Adam poured another cup of black coffee for himself and took a seat at a cluttered table, gesturing for Mitch and Jacob to join him. "What do you make of these?" Mitch asked, laying out several photographs of the orbs.

"Who wants to know—and why?" Adam asked. His eyes suddenly appeared much older, wary from the time he had already spent navigating the push and pull of competing powers who wanted to ransack his intellect for their own purposes.

Mitch rolled his eyes. "The Department of Supernatural Investigation—who else? We chased these damned things up the Mon last night, lost one of our new recon airships doing it. We think they're behind the power failures, and I thought there was an off chance you might know something about them."

Adam studied his coffee for a moment, then grabbed a pastry and took a few bites. "We don't know for sure," he said with a full mouth. "No government is claiming them, and we haven't had direct contact. We refer to them as 'the visitors.'"

He paused to swallow and wash the pastry down with more coffee. "They showed up right after the first time I tested one of my larger inventions," he said. "Highly classified. Works on Mr. Tesla's designs for something that could shoot a beam of energy a long distance." He grimaced. "It may have gone a bit farther than we originally thought."

"Meaning that you shot something off into space like an invitation to a family reunion and some long-lost galactic cousins showed up?" Mitch asked incredulously.

"I wouldn't have put it that way, but that's the basic idea." Adam shrugged. "Could be a coincidence." He paused. "Then again, big power-drains happen when the 'ships' are sighted."

"So they're sucking up the power from the biggest factories and using it for fuel?" Mitch pressed.

Adam shrugged. "Maybe. Just conjecture."

"If you see them again, and they're hostile, Colonel Falken said I could give you these." Adam opened a small metal box to reveal several odd clockwork cartridges, about the same size as a shotgun shell. "They attach to whatever they hit, and you can track them using this controller." He indicated a large piece of equipment.

Mitch regarded Adam skeptically. "Come on. You're holding out on us."

Adam grimaced. "Sorry, that's as much as I can tell you —classified."

Mitch looked like he was going to say something Jacob would regret. "Thanks for your time," Jacob said quickly, grabbing Mitch by the arm and taking the cartridges and the controller. "We're due for a meeting with Falken. Keep up the good work."

Mitch kept silent until they were back in the carriage. "Well, that was interesting," he said. "I hate it when he pulls out the 'classified' card—hell, we're the ones who are supposed to keep secrets."

———

"WELL IF IT isn't *Sturm und Drang*, the storm and fury boys," Colonel Kurt Falken said as Mitch and Jacob entered his office. "I noticed that your message omitted the loss of *another* prototype recon airship." He paused. "Good thing Captain Nowak makes a *complete* report.

"Of all the dimwitted, reckless, irresponsible things you have ever done, losing the *Onyx Shadow* has got to be the worst yet." Falken's glare could melt ice. "I can't bury this," he ranted. "That airship cost as much as a private railcar—maybe two. I've already had a telegram from HQ wanting a report. And do you know what I had to report to them? That you burned and sank their goddamn airship!"

Mitch wasn't having any of it. "Farber says any other details on the orbs are classified. Is that true?" Mitch demanded.

Falken muttered a curse. "Sit down. That's an order Storm. You too, Drangosavich."

"We damn near pitched into the river going after those orbs. Do we keep chasing them?" Jacob asked.

"Absolutely," Falken replied. "I'm not convinced these orbs are alien—at least, not alien from space. There's some unrest going on in Europe. They could be using these orbs to test our responses, maybe even keep us under surveillance." He glared at them. "I got you a new ship. Ironically enough, it's the *Phoenix*. I want this one returned in working order. I mean it, Storm. If there's a scratch, I'll have you and Drangosavich working off the cost of repairs in Leavenworth, so help me God." He paused as if counting to ten. "I'm counting on the two of you to figure it out," thrusting the mechanical carrier pigeon at Jacob. "Without too much additional damage. Now get out."

The door shut loudly behind them. "Damn, that was more painful than usual," Mitch said in a sulk. "Okay, okay, show's over. Go back to work." Mitch added loudly, looking around the large office where everyone was staring open-mouthed at the two agents.

"I feel like my flesh has been flayed from my body," Jacob muttered. "I told you there'd be hell to pay. Probation again." Jacob groaned.

"Look at the bright side. We got a new ship, and we're still on the case!" Mitch encouraged.

"One toe out of line and we're investigating Bigfoot again."

Mitch grinned. "Not this time. We're on the right track. We'll head back out to the Thomson works. If the pattern runs true, they'll be back," he said with confidence as he and Jacob climbed back in the carriage.

————

A FEW HOURS later, after darkness fell, Mitch and Jacob stood outside the rear door of the rooming house, and Jacob shook his head. "Where the hell did you get those things?"

Mitch grinned, resting his hand with pride on one of the two steam-bikes outfitted with brass boilers, unusual tubes, and a dangerous looking mechanism right behind the rider's seat. "It's a velocipede," Mitch said. "With some modifications courtesy of Wunderkind."

Jacob eyed the unwieldy contraptions. "Are you sure Adam isn't just trying to kill you?"

Mitch slapped him on the shoulder. "So little faith. They run on water, they're small enough to slip around traffic, and at top speed, they move as fast as a horse at full canter."

Jacob paled. "Why not just get horses? They run on water, too."

Mitch rolled his eyes. "Horses get spooked around machinery, and there's no telling how they'd react around the orbs." His steam-cycle had two leather saddlebags strapped on the back, from which Mitch produced a pair of unlikely-looking guns.

"Here. Take this."

Jacob grimaced. "More presents from Wunderkind?"

Mitch grinned. "I told you, he likes us." Mitch held up the gun.

"Adam's been experimenting with elastic materials. Think of these as new-model harpoons." The grip and trigger resembled that of a large handgun, while in the front, an iron grappling hook was connected to a length of strange-looking braided rope. The rope was coiled on one side of each of their bikes, attached to the top of the grappling hook, which had an iron shank that disappeared into the barrel of the gun.

"Didn't know we were chasing whales," Jacob observed.

"Big, glowing sky-whales," Mitch replied, excitement alight in his eyes. "Orbs, my friend."

"Let me get this straight," Jacob said. "You want to ride over there on these contraptions, chase down the orbs, and then harpoon them?"

"Yep."

"And then what? Are you going to hang on while they take you into outer space?"

Mitch sighed. "The cords are heavy elastic—another one of Wunderkind's new inventions for us to try. We shoot one hook into the ground, the other into the orbs, and the orbs go nowhere. Then we figure out how to take them down."

Jacob gave him a skeptical look, but Mitch already swung one leg over the velocipede and gave it a kick. The engine started up with an awful racket that drew glares from the neighbors and more than a few curious stares.

So much for covert operations, dammit. Jacob thought. Mitch was already speeding toward the street before Jacob had gotten his bike started, then he drew a deep breath, kicked the starter, and sputtered off behind Mitch.

Night traffic was light. Their steambikes spooked cart horses as Mitch and Jacob sped across bridges and down New Pittsburgh's nearly deserted streets, heading for the Edgar Thomson Works. Jacob cursed under his breath whenever the bikes hit brick streets, jarring unmercifully with the thinly padded bike seats. Mitch was undeterred, and kept the bike's regulator full-open, forcing Jacob to do the same to keep up.

They thundered over the West Braddock Bridge, a narrow trolley bridge that was the only way over to the far side of the Mon for miles, except for the railroad trestle Port Perry Bridge just below the steel-works. The steambikes clattered over the bridge's wooden bed, and Jacob was convinced his teeth were going to rattle out of his head.

"I think they'll hear us coming," Jacob groused.

"I slipped the night guard a couple of bills," Mitch replied, ignoring Jacob. "Enough to guarantee he'll keep their goons off us." He looked up at the night sky. "Now we just wait for visitors."

Coal smoke billowed from the stacks, and the gas flares lit the night without a need for moonlight. The Edgar Thomson ran all day and all night. Mitch and Jacob stayed in the shadows, still astride their steambikes, watching.

"You got the tracker?" Jacob asked.

Mitch nodded, patting the pocket of his jacket. "Loaded it into a Very pistol. That way I can shoot with one hand and keep the bike on the road with the other." He dug into his saddlebag and handed a second Very pistol to Jacob. "That leaves us a couple more devices for later, if we need them."

If we survive, Jacob added silently.

Just after two in the morning, three dancing lights dropped toward the mill. "Get them!" Mitch shouted, gunning his bike to life. He and Jacob roared from their hiding place, surprising a couple of tired workers who leaped out of the way with shouted curses.

Jacob hunched low over his bike, as much to help him hang on as to increase his speed, as Mitch veered crazily in and out of open spaces in the cluttered mill yard, swerving around piles of steel bars and concrete blocks, weaving past wagons and handcarts.

The cold air stung Jacob's face. The orbs seemed closer than ever tonight. They hung like rogue stars over the mill, and Mitch skidded to a stop, pulling his Very pistol. Jacob did the same, and they fired nearly in unison. Two tracking devices soared into the night sky. Mitch's shot fell short, but Jacob's hit and stuck.

"They're onto us!" Mitch said as the orbs rose and began to retreat. "After them!"

The steel mill lot was not designed for racing. Twice, Jacob nearly spun out on gravel. Mitch was determined to follow the orbs by the most direct path, which meant cutting through the train yards next to the mill.

"Watch out!" Jacob shouted as men rolled a car onto a siding just at Mitch veered in that direction at top speed.

Mitch gunned the bike and made for the narrowing gap between the moving car and the rest of the parked train. Workmen gestured and shouted, then threw themselves out of the way. Mitch's bike shot through the gap just before the couplings were close enough to touch. Jacob veered right, taking advantage of the irate workmen's distraction to hurtle past. He gritted his teeth as the bike crossed a set of tracks, sure he would lose his manhood to the hard seat. Mitch was ahead of him, his bike streaking down the center pavement between a narrow-gauge set of tracks.

"Of all the pig-headed, stupid, dare-devil stunts—" Jacob muttered as he tried to coax a bit more life from his overtaxed bike.

They were heading away from the heart of the mill complex, out into the far reaches of the vast train yard, filled with cars waiting to be unloaded or loaded. It was a dangerous place to walk, let alone flying through it at top speed. Not that such a thought would hold Mitch back in the slightest, Jacob knew.

"Hey! You're not supposed to be here!" Two mill guards came running. Whoever Mitch paid off obviously hadn't gotten the word to everyone. The guards took up positions, firing their revolvers at the two speeding figures.

One bullet grazed Jacob's left arm, and he made a sharp turn to the right, pushing the bike to its limit as he veered to one side and then the other. Three more shots whizzed by, too close for comfort.

Alarms sounded, and across the darkened mill yard, searchlights began to light up the sky, flooding the area nearest the main buildings with light. Jacob dared a glance toward the tall light towers along the riverbank, braced for them to blind him at any second, waiting for a bullet to take him in the back.

The mill's guards ran after them, shooting as they went, following the bikes through the maze of equipment and materials.

Smoke stung Jacob's eyes, and his back ached from hunching

forward. Other parts, not mentionable in polite company, were going to be sore for a while, too. Shots fired overhead, far too close for comfort. Jacob longed for goggles as he tried to keep Mitch's dark, darting form in sight. Above them, the orbs glowed brightly, like stars fallen too close to Earth.

"No, no, no, no!" Jacob muttered as the orbs changed direction, heading out over the Monongahela River. Mitch never slowed down, taking a sharp turn to the right and zooming after his quarry across the trains-only Port Perry Bridge. The wooden bridge bed felt like a washboard under the steambike's tires. The guards did not stop until they reached the edge of the bridge, firing off more shots, the muzzles of their guns sparking in the night.

Beneath Mitch and Jacob, the dark waters of the Mon slid past, deep and swift. Barges slipped beneath the bridge, heedless of the drama unfolding overhead. Up and down the river, gas flares blazed high in the sky from the mills along both sides, and in the distance, Jacob could hear the whistle of a freight train. The nighttime glory that was the sprawling city of New Pittsburgh spread before them.

The train whistle sounded again, closer now. Jacob swallowed hard, glancing behind him and trying to make out whether there was movement on the tracks that ran alongside the river on both banks. Trains ran all day and night in New Pittsburgh, and the tracks to the mills were among the busiest in the bustling industrial city. The eerie, lonesome sound of train whistles echoed from the steep hillsides, but to Jacob's ear, the howl was definitely closer.

Halfway across, too far to turn back even if there weren't armed men waiting for them. Mitch was focused on the orbs, dodging and weaving overhead. Mitch put on a burst of speed, trying to close the gap with the closest orb, his "harpoon" already in hand. Swearing mightily, Jacob readied his harpoon-gun, wondering if the grappling hook could possibly find purchase in whatever the glittering orbs were made of.

He caught up to Mitch, who had stopped his bike in the center of the bridge. Mitch had tied off the end of his elastic rope to one of the main bridge supports, and just as Jacob pulled alongside, Mitch raised the gun and fired. The grappling hook sailed into the night sky, and to Jacob's astonishment, he heard a clang as metal tore into metal. The line uncoiled fast as the orb headed away.

The train whistle sounded again, much closer. This time, a blinding light accompanied it, down at the far end of the bridge, rapidly growing closer.

"Mitch! Train!" Jacob shouted, too terrified to be angry. The bridge shook with the might of the steam locomotive that hurtled toward them, closing the distance with every second. The rhythm of the pistons was a death knell. Even if going back didn't mean a chest full of lead, their steambikes could never outrun the train. Jacob eyed the dark water beneath them, a drop of at least fifty feet into the icy current.

"You've got your gun?" Mitch asked, eyeing the train.

"Here." Jacob shoved the gun to his partner. *There won't be enough left of me for Last Rites,* Jacob thought as the train thundered closer.

"Give it to me, and let me drive!" Mitch shouted, climbing onto the bike in front of Jacob. Since death was inevitable, Jacob didn't feel like arguing. Mitch handed him the back end of the second elastic rope.

"Tie this around us. Hurry." And with that, Mitch kicked the bike to life, riding straight for the oncoming train.

Soldiers keep moving when the brain freezes in terror. Jacob's training took over, and he wound the end of the rope around their chests, under their arms, knotting it securely. *It won't matter. There won't be enough left of us to identify.*

Behind them, the orb Mitch had hooked with his shot strained against the rope, pulling it tight, jerking the orb back and down.

"Here. We. Go!" Mitch shouted.

The train was close enough for Jacob to read the manufacturer's plate on the front. He heard the second harpoon gun discharge, then Mitch tore the steambike to the right, hitting the rail at full speed and vaulting over the side. They were falling in darkness, toward the pitiless waters of the Mon River. Mitch kicked the bike away from them. Sheer panic made them hang on to each other like drowning men.

Overhead, the train hurtled past, as the orb gave a mechanical shriek and fell out of the sky, colliding with the train's engine. An explosion rent the night as the train and the orb became a massive fireball, thundering toward calamity when the freight train reached the rail yard.

Jacob was muttering the words of the Hail Mary as they plummeted. Mitch was bellowing the tune of a drinking song. Five feet above the inky waters, the elastic rope caught with a force Jacob thought would rip his arms off. Caught—and held.

He had only an instant to process not-dying before the elastic jerked them back into the air, then dropped them again so close to the water that Jacob might have been able to touch the rippling surface had he been head-down and not holding on for dear life to his partner, who had just as tight a death grip in return.

Five times they bounced, as overhead, the sound of ripping metal and the screams of panicked men filled the air. A series of bone-jarring crashes told Jacob that the train had missed its turn, and its cars were piling up near where the guards had squeezed off their last shots.

Finally, their momentum spent, the elastic rope left them dangling in the cold night air.

"I hate you," Jacob said.

"Wouldn't have it any other way," Mitch said. His wide grin and the light in his eyes told Jacob that Mitch had enjoyed the evening far too much.

"Now what?"

Mitch whipped a knife out of a sheath at his belt and severed the cord before Jacob could protest. They dropped like stones into the cold water, fighting the current to make it to the opposite shore.

Jacob sputtered as he pulled himself out of the river and onto the bank. "That's the second time you've nearly drowned me in as many days," Jacob growled, wringing the water from his sodden clothing.

"We're alive."

Jacob glared at him. "We lost the bikes."

Mitch shrugged. "Adam knew it was a risk when he gave them to us." He grinned. "Come on. Let's get back to the room. I think one of the trackers stuck."

"We just crashed a freight train into the Edgar Thomson Works," Jacob pointed out, holding onto his anger because it was his last, slipping link to sanity. "They shoot saboteurs for less!"

Mitch started walking. "Good thing, then, that we're on the other side of the river, huh?"

———

NOT ENOUGH REMAINED of the wrecked train or the orb that collided with it to find any trace of the tracking device. Disguised in stolen police uniforms, Jacob and Mitch heard the railroad inspector exclaim over the unusually hot fire from the explosion, and had gotten close enough to the wreckage to assure that nothing of the orb had survived.

Late the next night, Jacob watched from the ground as Mitch climbed to the top of the tallest brick smokestack towering over the Jones and Laughlin steel mill. They had left the car down the road, and Hans and the werkman were taking opposite circuits, roaming the night to make sure they did not get disturbed.

The guard at the gate had appreciated the beer Jacob had brought him, until his eyes had rolled back in his head and he had slumped to the floor of his gatehouse. Once he awoke, he'd have a nasty headache, but no memory of how he had gotten there and no lasting after-effects.

The muted tapping of Morse Code sounded close to Jacob's ear from the receiver on his coat collar. Mitch was in place. Jacob chewed his unlit cigar, wishing he was sitting in Mirko's Bar, drinking beer and smoking his stogie down to the stub.

Jacob maneuvered himself in to position. He was next to the main power line coming into the plant, and he had tapped in with one of the Department's gadgets so that he could watch any fluctuations in the electricity and send a warning to Mitch. Up on the tower, Mitch had a shotgun ready, loaded not with bullets, but with a gadget of his own making. The Very pistol shot from the other night had hit but not stuck, leaving them with no tracking information to show for their trouble.

The dial in Jacob's hand spun wildly. *This is it*, Jacob thought, chomping down on his cigar. He tapped out 'go' on his wrist piece, signaling Mitch to be ready to shoot. He looked up, but he couldn't see Mitch against the darkness.

Overhead, two orbs danced against the night sky as the mill's lights dimmed until they were almost dark.

Jacob heard the crack of the shotgun. A heartbeat later, an explosion rocked the ground. Fire blossomed where the orbs had been. Jacob thought he saw a shadow fall from the tower. The shockwave shattered windows in the mill, spraying the area with broken glass. The explosion rocked the ground and made the steel roof groan. Its force sent Jacob sprawling, and for a heart-stopping moment, he thought he saw the tall brick tower sway before the whole world went dark and silent. Slowly the sound returned. He heard alarm bells clamoring, and men shouting, whistles shrieking and footsteps pounding closer. The mill was dark, but his eyes were now adjusting to the moonlight.

If we get caught, they'll assume we're saboteurs, and the Department will probably let us hang, Jacob thought.

"You need to get out of here now, sir." Hans had come up behind Jacob without a sound.

"Not without Mitch," Jacob said. "He was up on that tower, but I don't know how he could have kept his hold with that blast."

"The *Werkman* is retrieving him. I'll keep watch." Hans usually went to great lengths to hide his adaptations but now, his clockwork additions propelled him across the short distance to the tower faster than any Olympic sprinter. Jacob saw Hans connect with the *werkman* as they circled the tower, then the *werkman* went up the tower like a mechanical spider, scaling it without a living being's regard for pain or fatigue. Jacob squinted, trying to follow his movement, but it was too dark. He had seen a shadowy figure fall when the explosion hit, and his gut clenched. The tower was far too high for anyone to survive a drop like that.

"You there! Stop!" A guard shouted in heavily-accented English.

"I just came out to take a piss," Jacob said in Polish, before he clocked the guard with a roundhouse punch. "Sorry about that," he added under his breath.

"Run!" Hans yelled. "We've got him." Jacob glimpsed that the *werkman* carried a body in his arms and his throat tightened.

"Get Mitch to the carriage," Jacob ordered. "We've got to see what kind of debris that thing left behind. I've got false papers, just in case. I'll be fine. Go!"

Hans and the *werkman* melted into the darkness with the faint hum and click of gears. Jacob dragged the unfortunate guard into the shadows and lit his cigar.

"Stop, or I'll shoot!" The speaker wore a guard's uniform, but the voice sounded like it had barely reached puberty.

"Will you now, lad?" Jacob replied, his voice heavy with an Irish brogue. "Don't make more trouble for yourself than you're already in with the Inspector." At that, Jacob flashed the badge in his pocket.

"Pinkertons, Special Agent Cavanaugh," he snapped. "And put that damn gun down, boy, before I shoot it out of your hand."

"There was an explosion… Anarchists…" The young guard was pale with fright, and the gun in his grip trembled so hard Jacob feared he might get shot by accident.

"The gun," Jacob ordered. "Put it down, lad. I'm on your side, and I'm here to help."

The guard lowered the gun but seemed rooted to his spot. "Come with me," Jacob said, puffing on his cigar and striding toward the darkened mill. In the moonlight, he could see the millworkers standing in small groups, talking in hushed voices in a babble of languages from across Europe's poorer nations.

"What did you see?" Jacob asked briskly. Between the guard's fright over the explosion and his terror of being in trouble with the Inspector, the young man nearly fell over himself to clear the way for Jacob and maneuver them through the onlookers with official prerogative.

"I was walking my rounds, sir, and I saw those damned orbs in the sky, the ones that show up before the lights dim," the guard replied, his voice reedy and tremulous.

"And then?" Jacob snapped, knowing that the more he kept the guard off-balance, the less likely it was for the man to question his authority.

"I thought I heard a shot, and then the sky lit up, and I got knocked flat on my ass," the guard replied. "Sir."

"You heard a shot?" Jacob countered. "Are you sure? Could it have been a weather balloon popping?"

The guard looked doubtful and scared. "Maybe. I guess so, sir."

Jacob nodded. "I thought so," he said, and let out a string of curses. "Damned government Weather Service. Send those flimsy balloons up to look for storms, and they drift loose and something like this happens." He gestured with his cigar. "Your boss should send in a bill to the government for all the lost production time, that's what he ought to do," he grumbled.

"What are we looking for, sir?" the guard asked as Jacob began to stride up and down along the side of the building nearest the blast. He could see where a section of the sheet metal in the roof had bowed with the force and several of the air vents on the roof peak canted to the side. Shards of glass littered the ground.

"Bits of weather balloon, strange pieces of metal, anything that doesn't belong," Jacob replied tersely. "Find some, and you'll be a hero for your boss. I imagine with proof like that—after the Pinkertons validate it, of course—he wouldn't have any trouble at all getting damages back from the government."

Jacob tried to hold off the thoughts that crowded into his mind. *Mitch wasn't moving. He must have fallen. Dammit! He's dead, and the least I can do is get the goods on whatever it was that put off that blast. Damn.*

Near the base of the brick tower, Jacob spotted a spent shotgun shell and pocketed it before his helper could see. But nowhere were other debris in evidence, other than the obvious damage to the steel mill. No canvas skin for an airship or a weather balloon, no bits of metal from the engine or frame, nothing that seemed odd, out of place or even slightly alien in any sense of the word.

"How could they just vanish like that without leaving debris?" the young guard wondered aloud.

Jacob puffed on his cigar. "That's the thing with these weather balloons nowadays, built so flimsy that it probably burned up completely in that fireball." He gave the boy a look. "Be glad it wasn't one of those big airships raining fiery bits down on everyone."

He made a show of scribbling in an otherwise empty notebook, then snapped the pad shut and slipped it into his pocket. "Looks like we're done here. I'll file a report and make sure I put in a good word for you," he said. "You've been a good lad; maybe there's a promotion in it for you."

"Thank you, sir. Kind of you, sir. Is there anything else I can do to help, sir?" the young guard asked, looking like a hungry puppy, eager to please.

Jacob gave a curt shake of his head. "No, I think I've got everything I need. If they find something, make sure your boss knows to send it in for a claim to the government. You deserve to be compensated."

"I will, sir. Thank you, sir."

As they had talked, Jacob had maneuvered them back along the building until they were near the fence. "That's it then." He paused. "You'd better go see what's going on," he said, pointing along the back of the mill, far removed from where the rest of the action was. "I just saw a man in a supervisor's hat waving to you."

The young guard peered into the shadows, but saw nothing. "Go on," Jacob urged. "You don't want to keep him waiting. I can find my way out." He waited until the guard had turned the corner before he headed off at a brisk walk for the hole in the fence they had used to enter. There was enough commotion near the front of the plant that Jacob's exit went unnoticed, and he soon made his way back to where Hans and the *werkman* had hidden the carriage.

"I was about to come looking for you, sir," Hans informed him.

"I'm here," Jacob said. His mood had soured considerably on the walk, now that the reality of what happened had sunk in. *Falken will have my head, and I don't care. I lost a good partner. Those are hard to come by. What a stupid way to die.*

27

"Tell him to get his *dupa* in the carriage so we can get going." Mitch's voice was strained, but there was no mistaking the speaker.

Jacob climbed in, utterly bewildered. Mitch sat on the other side of the compartment, stiffly positioned against the cushions. One eye was well on its way to swelling closed, and his shoulder looked oddly askew. Mitch's clothes were torn, and from his shallow breathing, Jacob guessed he had cracked a couple of ribs. "What the hell?" Jacob said as Hans got the carriage in motion.

Mitch's eyes widened in pain as the carriage bumped down the rutted access road, and he went pale. "You don't happen to have a flask on you, do you?" he asked, his voice thin.

Jacob chuckled and pulled one from his boot. He cranked off the cap and handed it across. Mitch took a hearty swig. "I saw you fall," Jacob said, still reeling from the turn of events.

Mitch let out a ragged breath. "I did. But I'd used a safety cable—my father built some bridges in his time, and it was something he always did in high places. I figured the recoil might put me off balance—never figured on blowing the damn thing up." He gave a chuckle that sounded as if it hurt.

"The *werkman* found me dangling and unconscious. I swung when I fell and hit the side of the tower hard enough to knock me out and break a few bones. He and Hans got me down."

"Damn, you gave me a scare," Jacob admitted.

"Me, too," Mitch replied. "Did you find anything?"

Jacob shook his head. "Just your shell casing, which I've got. No other debris, which there should have been if it had been an airship."

"Check the instruments, sir," Hans said. Mitch pointed to a bulky receiver on the seat next to Jacob.

"What do you—" Mitch started to say, but gasped in pain at the effort and fell back, looking as if he were going to pass out.

"I'll have a look." Jacob waved Mitch silent and took over. It was a rare turn of events and usually happened only when Mitch was bleeding.

"The tracker appears to have connected with its target," Jacob mused. "And it's headed east, toward the ocean."

"Told you!" Mitch's exultation was dimmed considerably by his broken ribs.

"But this can't be right. It's moving too fast—and rising quickly." Jacob shook his head, staring at the rapidly fluctuating dial. "I don't know of any experimental craft that can go that fast or that high—wait!" He gently jiggled the indicator, and then looked up, mystified. "It's gone. The dials are all at zero."

"So what was it?" Mitch asked between gritted teeth. "European spies? Or Farber's 'visitors?'"

Jacob was still staring at the indicators as if they might suddenly reveal the answer, but they remained lifeless. "I don't know," he said quietly.

He opened his flask, took a swig, and passed it to Mitch. "Let's get you to a doctor," Jacob added, leaning forward to give instructions to Hans. He settled into his seat. "We need to get you patched up. Because I bet they'll be back. Especially now that you've shot down two of them."

"And how do we write up this one for the Department?" Mitch wheezed.

"Like always. Supernatural phenomenon, source unknown…"

RESURRECTION DAY

RESURRECTION DAY

"DAMN GRAVE ROBBERS." Agent Mitch Storm stood looking down into an empty hole.

The mortuary safe, a latticework of iron bars designed to keep out body thieves, had been pried open like the rib cage of an autopsy victim. An expensive maple coffin had been torn into with enough force that its lid lay separate from its base. The tufted satin interior was empty.

"You don't think it could be premature burial?" Mitch mused. He pointed to a nearby tomb with a bell on a rod. Inside, a cord went down to the corpse in the casket, just in case the dearly departed hadn't actually been dead and gone. Similar bells dotted the cemetery, between the carved urns and elaborate angels.

"Nah," Jacob replied. "No one calls in federal agents for that. At least it's pretty clear that someone was trying to get in, instead of getting out." Agent Jacob Drangosavich, Storm's partner, swept his gaze across the rolling hills of New Pittsburgh's Allegheny Cemetery as if he expected to spot the resurrectionists making off with their prize.

"How do you figure?" Mitch asked.

Jacob nodded toward the lid, which lay upturned a few feet away from the casket. "No evidence of scratching against the lining, and an outward-bound force wouldn't have taken off the lid so neatly. You've seen what it looks like when they rise on their own. I don't care whether they're ghouls, vampires, or wraiths, they make a mess of it."

Jacob Drangosavich and Mitch Storm were a study in contrasts. Their badges from the Department of Supernatural Investigation were one of the few things they had in common. Storm was shorter, with an athlete's build. He had dark hair and dark eyes, along with a five o'clock shadow that started at three. Mitch still had the cocky assurance that had made him one of the Army's best sharpshooters, along with a rules-are-for-other-people attitude that continued to get him into trouble.

Jacob, on the other hand, was tall and blond, blue-eyed with Eastern European features that let him easily fit in among the new immigrants working the city's mines and mills. And although Jacob favored deliberation before action, somehow his caution did not seem to keep the pair out of trouble.

"Question is," Jacob said, "who's the body snatcher, and why do the snatchers want corpses?"

"It's not the medical students this time," Mitch said. "They've finally got legitimate ways to get study stiffs."

Jacob was about to reply when he heard a clockwork click and hum. "Get down!" he yelled, diving to the ground as a shot rang out. He scrambled to his feet, but Mitch was nowhere to be seen. Jacob's gun was ready in his hand, and he ran for the copse of trees where the shot had originated.

"Federal agents—come out with your hands up!" he shouted.

A figure darted from behind the trees. It looked human but moved all wrong. Metal glinted in the sun from places on the figure's form, and Jacob heard the click and whine of meshing gears. It was dressed like a man, but it moved stiffly, without the grace of a real person. *Whatever it is, it moves fast*, Jacob thought, sprinting after it.

"Halt! Police!" he shouted again. He put on a burst of speed, but the attacker paused long enough to squeeze off another shot that sent Jacob dodging, then took off again at a full run.

The stranger was too far ahead of him to catch and running for one of the carriage roads. Jacob's long legs carried him quickly over the uneven terrain of the old cemetery, but the shooter was faster.

Jacob's lungs burned, and he knew he would tire long before he reached the carriage road. Catching up with their attacker was not going to happen. The hiss and thump of an engine sounded behind Jacob, and Mitch let out a whoop as he roared by on one of the department's experimental steambikes.

"Be careful with that thing!" Jacob shouted, but by that time, Mitch was too far ahead to hear him.

Mitch rode the bike like he was jumping hurdles with a stallion. The cemetery's rolling terrain gave him just what he needed to send the bike airborne, vaulting over several granite headstones and barely missing the wings of a mourning angel sculpture.

The bike came down hard, but Mitch stayed with it, pulling it out of a slew and barely remaining upright. He gunned the engine, and it popped and hissed in protest, but the bike took off again, with Mitch weaving between and around the stone obelisks intent on his quarry.

The shooter was fast, but Mitch's bike was faster, and the gap between the two narrowed. The runner veered left, and Mitch cut off the corner to intercept. The distance between them went from yards to mere feet. Mitch steered straight for the runner, closing in, intending to run the assassin down.

A muffled explosion echoed off the field of monuments and mausoleums with a sickening wet thud. The runner exploded, just a few feet in front of Mitch's bike, sending a rain of skin, hair, bone, and clothing falling through the air. Mitch skidded to a stop, covered in gore, staring in complete horror at the spot where the would-be assassin had detonated.

Jacob jogged up a few minutes later, winded and sweating. "What the hell just happened?"

Mitch for once was speechless. "I almost had him," he said, staring at the burned patch of ground where the bomb had gone off. "And then he just... boom—"

"You're sure it was a man?" Jacob tried to catch his breath and wrinkled his nose at the distinctly unpleasant smell.

"It looked like a man," Mitch replied. "But it didn't move like one. It was jerky and awkward, and way too fast. There was something really strange about him."

Jacob frowned and moved into the blast range, sniffing the air and then kneeling to look closer at the chunks of flesh that littered the grass. "There's no blood."

"What do you mean, there's no blood?" Mitch demanded. "Didn't you see him blow up right in front of me? How can there not be blood?"

Jacob shook his head. "I don't know how, but there isn't. Look," he said, pointing. "I think we've answered one question, why the mystery man moved strangely. He was already dead."

"You saw him run. He shot at us. Dead men don't do that," Mitch argued.

Jacob pointed to the spray of gore. "Look at the flesh, Mitch. It's not bleeding. It's not the right color. Smell the air. Formaldehyde and rotting meat." He gestured toward some brass bits that caught the sunlight and shimmered. "Bits of metal. Where did they come from? They had to be in with the skin and bone."

Mitch sat back down on his steambike with a worried look. "You think someone finally managed to do it? Create a clockwork creature?"

Jacob spread his hands and shook his head. "More like clockwork abomination… I don't know much about that kind of thing. But I can think of someone who might."

———

INSIDE THE HUGE Romanesque Revival building locals called "The Castle," down in the hidden laboratories of the secret subterranean floors, Adam Farber poked the charred and twisted metal pieces with a wooden pointer as Mitch and Jacob told a highly edited version of their brush with a clockwork assassin.

"Maybe," Adam said to the question Mitch posed. Adam Farber was the boy genius of the Tesla-Westinghouse Company, a gawky, too-skinny young man in his twenties with stick-straight light-brown hair, wire-rimmed spectacles, and angular features. A nearby table was littered with used coffee cups, and it was clear Adam had already drunk enough caffeine that he nearly vibrated.

"Maybe what?" Mitch pressed.

Adam chewed on his lip as he tilted his head from one side to the other to examine the bits of metal Jacob and Mitch had retrieved from the cemetery bombing. "Maybe someone could build one. I mean, theoretically," Adam replied.

"Could you?"

Adam's gaze slid up to meet Mitch's eyes, and Jacob saw a glint of irritation. "If you are trying to ask 'did I,' the answer is no," Adam replied tersely. "Could I?" He gave an off-hand shrug. "I don't know because I wouldn't try. We've been successful with the *werkman*. Why would anyone want to work with dead, rotting bodies?"

"What Mitch was trying to ask with his characteristic charm is, could it be done?" Jacob interceded. Mitch glared at him but did not contradict.

Another shrug. "Theoretically, yes," Adam said. "But it would take a lot more than using gears for joints." He shook his head. "Sweet heavens. You saw what we did for Hans, after his accident. There are a few others like him. It's not easy replacing damaged parts on a living person. It can be done—but it's expensive, and there's a better than fifty-fifty chance it won't work."

"Oh?" Mitch asked.

Adam nodded. "Sometimes, the damage is just too bad to fix. Or the flesh fights the metal and gangrene sets in. That's why we haven't gone public with the process. Think of all the war injuries, the factory accidents." He grimaced. "People would clamor for the process, and it's not ready for that kind of scale yet." He sighed. "On the other hand, replace joints with gears on a corpse, and all you have is a metal-bound corpse."

Adam looked up to meet their gaze. "You saw it run?"

Mitch and Jacob both nodded. "Then what made it move?" Adam challenged. He straightened and ran a hand back through his straw-colored hair. "It would be much easier to create a mechanical man from scratch than hinge and joint a corpse. Unless—"

"What?"

Adam shook his head. "Unless someone's discovered how to raise the dead, or at least animate them. I mean, there are stories, sure. Fables meant to be told around a campfire. Zombies from the islands under the spell of a conjurer. That Shelley woman's awful mad scientist tale. But that's all just fiction." He waved his hand at the metal bits. "That's crazy talk!"

As if on cue, a man made of metal lumbered out of the laboratory's small kitchen carrying a tray with a fresh pot of coffee, a china creamer, and three porcelain cups. The mechanical marvel, one of Adam's prototype *werkmen*, moved with the creak and hum of gears and steam like a ghostly suit of armor. Jacob and Mitch had seen Adam's *werkmen* before. The Department had procured several of the prototypes.

"Your coffee, sir." The *werkman's* voice had the metallic, scratchy quality of an Edison cylinder.

"Thank you, Lars," Adam said. Lars the *werkman* gave a short bow and returned to the kitchen. Adam poured a cup for himself and then remembered to offer some to Mitch and Jacob, who declined.

"The idea's been around for a while," Adam said after he had tinkered with the cream and sugar for his drink as if it were a precise lab experiment. "Adding machines to men. Using corpses as puppets. Fixing cripples. Enhancing warriors."

He said the last comment off-handedly, but there was an edge of bitterness to Adam's voice that made Jacob wonder if the inventor had been approached by others on the subject. Maybe even by the Department and its competitors.

"Who else could have a hand in this?" Jacob asked. "Who might have the interest—or the skill—to even come close to making a clockwork corpse?"

Adam's eyes turned flat and hard. "When it comes to snake oil, one man always comes to mind first. Francis Tumblety, king of the charlatans."

Tumblety was a name Mitch and Jacob recognized. A quack physician and failed spiritualist, Tumblety revelled in the dubious notoriety of having been investigated—and dismissed—as a suspect in the Ripper murders in London. He had passed through New Pittsburgh on more than one occasion, always leaving in a forced hurry.

Mitch's lip curled in disgust. "Yeah, I could figure Tumblety for having something to do with this, even if it was just thieving the bodies."

"No idea whether he's back in town, but he's the first person I'd go looking for if I were you," Adam said. "Now that I think of it, there is one more thing I heard about, from one of my materials suppliers. There've been thefts over on the North Side from a chemical warehouse. Not sure what was taken, but that would be Tumblety's style."

"We're on it. Thanks," Mitch said.

"You're welcome. Get the Department to throw some more money my way. My lab could use some more equipment," Farber replied.

Outside The Castle, their carriage was waiting for them. Hans, their driver, opened the door for them with all the aplomb of a well-trained coachman, although his skills lay more in combat and munitions. He kept his cap down over his face, hiding the metal plate, clockwork jaw and mechanical eye Adam had crafted for him. Beneath his driver's uniform, there were other replacements. Mitch gave him directions, and Hans nodded.

"North Side," Mitch said to Hans as they settled in. He turned to Jacob. "Sound familiar?"

Jacob nodded with a dour expression. "Same area where all those poisonings happened and half a dozen people disappeared from their own wakes."

"Yeah."

The carriage stopped in the alley behind the jail in downtown New Pittsburgh. The jail was a massive stone structure with a turret and a bridge that crossed over the street like Venice's bridge of sighs. Across the street, Dr. Zebulon Sheffield presided over the city's coroner office, grim territory that Sheffield ran like his own private fiefdom.

"Well, well," Sheffield said as Mitch and Jacob entered. "If it's not the Storm and Fury boys." Sheffield wasn't the first to match their last names up to *"sturm und drang,"* and the allusion made him chuckle every time.

"Good to see you, too," Mitch replied. He glanced at a black armband around Sheffield's left arm. "Are condolences in order?"

Sheffield sighed. "My uncle died. He lived with us. Ninety years old and full of piss and vinegar, but the years finally caught up with him. We're holding the wake tonight and tomorrow; then he'll be buried over at Union Cemetery. New mausoleum. Pretty fancy. Can't cross the street it seems without seeing an advertisement for them."

"My sympathies," Mitch replied, and Jacob nodded.

Sheffield eyed them warily. "If you're here, then there's a shit storm coming," Sheffield said. "Always seems to work like that. What is it this time?"

Mitch jumped up to sit on the edge of one of the clean stainless steel autopsy tables. Jacob leaned against the wall, arms crossed, trying not to let the overwhelming smells of sanitized death make him throw up.

"Stolen bodies," Mitch replied more cheerfully than the subject warranted. "Maybe even someone who wants to create mechanized, clockwork corpses."

Sheffield looked from one of them to the other. "Seriously? You're talking about zombies?"

Jacob shrugged. "There's a word for the living dead because people have tried it before," he said. "The guys in the legends used magic. Everything's scientific nowadays. Figures that someone is going to try sooner or later."

Sheffield looked up from the papers he was shuffling on his desk. "Huh. You think they actually made it work?"

"Well enough for someone—or something—to take a shot at us over at Allegheny Cemetery yesterday," Mitch replied.

"What have you heard?" Jacob asked. "You're in the body business."

Sheffield snorted. "Never heard it called that before. But yes, I do know a lot of the embalmers in town, and the cemetery managers. We run in the same professional circles."

"And?" Mitch probed.

Sheffield looked away. "There's been talk." He picked up a now-cold cup of coffee and leaned back in his chair. "You heard about the robbery at the mortuary supply on the North Side and the missing chemicals?"

Mitch nodded.

"Do you know what kinds of chemicals went missing?" Sheffield asked. "Formaldehyde. Embalming fluid. I found out because I and many of my colleagues had orders in that now can't be filled."

Mitch and Jacob exchanged a glance. "We're back to mad scientist territory," Jacob muttered.

"You hear any theories about who took the chemicals?" Mitch asked.

Sheffield shrugged. "Rumors. Could be jealous competitors."

Jacob raised an eyebrow. "Sometimes rumors are right in spite of themselves."

Sheffield sighed. "I'm hearing a lot of griping about a new embalmer in town. He's been doing quite a bit of business lately, underpricing the long-time players, moving in on neighborhoods they considered their territory."

"Name?"

"David Congeliere," Sheffield replied. "Showed up about six months ago and yes, that was just a little bit before the spate of grave robbings, but so was Christmas and the full moon and I don't think they had anything to do with the missing corpses. Sometimes, timing is just a coincidence."

Mitch jumped down off the autopsy table. "Maybe in your business," he said. "Not in ours." He tipped his hat. "Where can we find him?"

"Over on Ridge Avenue."

"Thanks for the information," Jacob said.

Sheffield frowned. "These zombies, think you can take them?"

Mitch grinned. "Sure. With one hand tied behind my back. It's the living you've got to watch out for."

"We'll be in touch," Jacob said, heading for the door.

"Don't rush," Sheffield replied. "The last time you guys showed up, you wanted me to store a vampire in my mortuary drawer."

"It was just for the day," Jacob replied. "It's not like you were using it."

"I used to sleep at night, before I met you two," Sheffield replied. "Back when I thought things like vampires were fairy tales."

"Um, doc, about those fairies—"

"I don't want to know!" Sheffield snapped and covered his ears with his hands. "Out! Out!"

———

THE CARRIAGE HAD not gone two blocks from the coroner's office before Hans gave three sharp raps to the sliding glass panel between the driver's bench and the carriage.

"We're being followed," Mitch interpreted, and both he and Jacob drew their guns.

New Pittsburgh's streets were full of black carriages, but the one behind them looked more ominous than most. It wasn't a hearse, but it had a funereal sense about it, from the cloaked driver whose face was hidden beneath the shadow of his hat to the black plumes that adorned the horses' bridles. And despite the crush of pedestrians, carriages, and trolleys, that one particular carriage stayed close behind them even though Hans made a series of turns designed to lose a casual follower.

Thump-thump. Thump-thump.

Mitch and Jacob hit the floor of the coach as bullets thudded into the doors at close range. Suppressors on the guns hid the sound amidst the mid-day bustle. Steel plates kept the bullets from coming through. Mitch lurched to the bullet-proof glass window but saw only well-dressed pedestrians walking past.

"Anything?" Jacob asked, warily looking out on his side.

Mitch swore. "No one who looks like an assassin."

Jacob glanced out of the back window. The funeral carriage was gone.

"I think we've just been sent a message," Mitch said, straightening his jacket but not bothering to holster his gun.

Jacob sighed. "And as usual, we're going to ignore it."

The rest of the ride over to Manchester was thankfully quiet. They left the factories on The Point, the triangle where three mighty rivers converged, and crossed the river into the city of Allegheny with its ethnic neighborhoods and workingmen's houses along the riverfront, while elegant brownstones and wealthy neighborhoods settled comfortably farther inland. The brick walls were painted with advertisements for tobacco and gum, milliner shops and dressmakers. There was even an ad for modern hygienic burial vaults at Union Cemetery.

"They'll advertise anything nowadays," Jacob muttered. "Where are we meeting Fletcher?"

"Mihilov's. And let's hope he's got some information worth paying for," Mitch replied.

Mihilov's Bar was nothing special. A battered wooden sign hung over the door, which had seen a lot of use. The windows were set high in the walls of the narrow room, which held a bar along one side and a few tables with chairs along the other. The air smelled of whiskey, cigarette smoke, and fried fish.

The tired men who hunched over the bar were mostly mill workers, stopping for a shot and a beer before heading home. Eddie Mihilov, a balding man in his fifties, nodded curtly as Mitch and Jacob entered. Drostan Fletcher, private investigator, waited at a table in the back with a glass of whiskey.

"How's business?" Mitch said as he shook Drostan's hand in greeting.

Drostan shrugged. "Enough to keep me in rent and scotch," he replied and gestured for them to sit down. Mitch went to the bar and came back with ale for Jacob and himself.

"I got your note," Drostan said. He was a tall, strongly built man with red hair and the faintest trace of a Scottish burr to his voice,

43

perhaps ten years older than Mitch and Jacob. "How did Washington get interested in this?"

Mitch grinned. "Washington isn't. The Department, on the other hand, finds this sort of thing fascinating."

Drostan took a sip of his scotch and leaned back in his chair. "You've heard Tumblety's back in town?"

Jacob nodded. "Heard he might be connected to David Congeliere."

Drostan raised an eyebrow. "Congeliere's made a lot of enemies."

"How?"

"Undercutting the competition. Running advertisements in the paper for his services that people find in poor taste. Adding a discount at that new mausoleum if he gets the embalming job." He shook his head. "Rumor has it he pays doctors to be tipped off on who's dying so he can get to the family first."

Mitch and Jacob exchanged glances. "What's his connection to the cemetery?"

Fletcher scowled. "That's where it gets strange. The cemetery is completely legitimate. And maybe the mausoleum is, too, but they advertise like Beeman's gum." He took another sip of his drink. "Adolph Brunrichter gave a large sum of money to have the mausoleum built."

"I don't recognize that name," Mitch replied.

"The guy is a bad penny," Fletcher said. "Plenty of rumors: hanky-panky with female patients, botched surgeries, questionable experiments." He shrugged. "But nothing seems to stick to him."

"If they're behind the clockwork corpses, do you know where they're doing the work?" Mitch asked.

"Congeliere travels all over the city and embalms corpses at their homes," Fletcher replied. "A day or two later, after the wakes, his hearse traces the same path and picks up the bodies for interment. Since he offers a discount on the new mausoleum, a lot of his 'clients' end up over there."

"Interesting," Jacob said and took a long pull on his ale.

"Tumblety and Brunrichter seem to spend most of their time at the house on Ridge Avenue," Drostan added. "So if Congeliere really is stealing bodies, he's probably making the clockwork zombies there."

"And just so you know, I've had two people take a shot at me since I've been looking into this for you," Drostan said with a pointed look at Mitch. "The first was a warning. The second meant to hit me, but I dodged it. I don't want a third." He drew out a rolled-up blueprint.

"I got my hands on the floor plans to Congeliere's house," Drostan added. "Thought you might want them."

"Let me have a look at those," Mitch said, reaching for the plans. "I've got an idea."

————

"This has got to be the worst thing you have ever dragged me into, Storm." Dr. Sheffield muttered.

"It's for a good cause," Mitch replied smoothly. "Think of it as your uncle's final service to his fellow man."

They stood in the front parlor of Sheffield's house. The mourners had departed, and Sheffield's family was in bed, believing that he and his friends would sit vigil with Uncle Frederick.

"What happens if someone goes into the loft of the carriage shed and finds him up there?" Sheffield demanded sotto voce. "I could lose my job."

"Does anyone go up to the loft in the carriage shed?" Mitch asked. "He's embalmed. We'll have him back where he belongs tomorrow at the latest."

Sheffield glowered at him but said nothing. The casket lay empty on a makeshift bier constructed from boards and sawhorses, covered with a dark tablecloth. In the dining room, some of the leftovers remained from food brought by well-wishers, along with ample bottles of whiskey for the comfort of the mourners.

"It'll be easy," Mitch said in a cajoling tone. "Drostan is going to sit up outside, just in case. We'll be in here. Congeliere's hearse is due to come later tonight. Right before they get here, Jacob jumps in the casket, and Hans, Drostan, and I follow the hearse. Once we get wherever they take the bodies, we throw them a little surprise party."

"Be glad I hadn't arranged for a cremation," Sheffield groused.

Jacob climbed into the empty coffin. He could not get his long legs into the box without his knees sticking up. "This isn't going to work."

Jacob climbed out and eyed Mitch's shorter frame. "Oh no," Mitch said, backing up a step. "No. Not even for flag and country. No. I'm not doing it."

"We're not going to have another chance like this," Jacob said in a practical tone.

"No."

"The casket has an air tube," Sheffield offered. "Uncle Frederick was obsessed with Edgar Allan Poe's 'The Premature Burial.'"

"No."

Jacob sighed. "All right, Mitch. But I'm not sure how quickly we can get the goods on Congeliere and the others. There could be more poisonings."

"That's not fair," Mitch said, glaring at Jacob.

"It's true. We have a golden opportunity to get into the middle of their operation. Drostan, Hans, and I will be right behind you," Jacob promised.

"What if you're not?"

"We will be."

Mitch folded his arms across his chest. "I want weapons."

"You can have what I was going to use. A sawed-off shotgun. A Colt 45. One of Farber's Morse Code watches. I'll have the receiver, so you'll be in contact with me the whole time," Jacob said. "And you got that listening device from him the last time we saw him. Works on aetheric waves. So I can hear what you hear."

"You knew this was going to happen," Mitch muttered.

Jacob chuckled. "No, I didn't. But sometimes the universe is amazingly just."

The clatter of hooves in the street outside ended the conversation. "He's here!" Jacob said. "Get in the box!"

Mitch checked the wide leather strap on his left wrist that had

Adam Farber's telegraph mechanism and the odd brass contraption that looked like a cross between a speaking tube and a miniature Edison cylinder, the aetheric wave transmitter. His shotgun was already in the casket, and his Peacemaker was holstered on his hip. With a sigh, Mitch climbed in the coffin.

"Don't forget to come after me," he muttered.

"Sure, Mitch. Right after breakfast," Jacob said, trying to lighten the mood. "Just remember—you were very optimistic when I was going to be the one in the box."

"That's because it was you. This is me," Mitch grumbled, but he got into the casket and pulled the lid shut.

————

"HERE WE GO," Jacob muttered under his breath. He had slipped out the back of Sheffield's house when Congeliere's men carried the casket out the front. Hans was driving the carriage and pulled out of the side street a discreet distance behind the hearse.

Drostan Fletcher had been watching the house from a thicket on the other side of the street. He slipped from cover on a bicycle, requiring only a leisurely pace to stay well behind the hearse and its two black carriage horses.

Jacob rode one of the Department's steambikes. It was loud enough that he had to hang well back, but if something went wrong, he could move faster than Drostan's bicycle and maneuver better than Hans's carriage.

The streets of New Pittsburgh were nearly empty. The shops and businesses were closed; there was little reason for anyone to be abroad given the hour. Few were except for cops walking their beats and tired millworkers trudging home from the night shift.

Congeliere's hearse moved quickly, at the upper limits of decorum, making its way through the shadowed streets like the driver had a schedule to keep. The carriage made two more stops, sliding additional caskets in beside the coffin that held Mitch, before turning toward the Allegheny River.

Once the hearse was out of the residential neighborhoods of Shady-side and approaching the warehouses of the Strip District, Jacob heard a carriage closing behind him. He glanced back, and cold terror ran down his spine.

Damn. Congeliere suspected something. It's a trap—and Mitch is stuck in a coffin.

The driver wore a black cloak and a top hat. The turned-up collar of the cloak hid the man's face. But nothing could hide the sunken flesh and protruding ribs of the dead horses that drew the carriage through the night, or the click and hum of the metal joints that moved their dead limbs as their hooves clattered against the paving stones.

Jacob choked back a cry of terror. He did not dare push the steam-bike for more speed without tipping his hand to the driver of the hearse. Drostan's bike was almost invisible in the darkness, keeping to the sidewalks and the shadows. With luck, Jacob's pursuer would not notice Drostan, and Jacob could draw the intruder off.

Hans must have spotted the intruders, because he stuck to the plan, taking a left turn at the nearest intersection, able to find the hearse again with one of Adam Farber's tracking devices, clipped to the waist-band of Mitch's trousers. Jacob turned right, and the carriage with its clockwork corpse steeds followed him, more intent on the oddity of a steambike than suspicious of an unmarked carriage. No one seemed to notice the bicycle.

Jacob's elation that he had drawn off the pursuers faded as he realized that he was now the sole quarry. The warehouse district was deserted at this hour, too late for regular deliveries and too early for the wagons that would come in the wee hours of the morning. The hum of his steambike vied with the relentless rhythm of the zombie horses, dead steeds that could keep up their pursuit without tiring.

Here in the empty streets, Jacob feared being caught or trampled more than he worried about odd looks at his government-prototype steambike. He depressed the pedal, and the gap between him and the ghostly carriage widened. His tire hit a loose paving stone, nearly throwing him, and he veered crazily, trying to regain control of his bike.

Echoing from the deserted side streets, Jacob heard the howl of dogs. Feral packs were spotted now and again down by the docks. But the howls sounded wrong, strained and unnatural. Up ahead, Jacob saw one cur then another slink from the cover of the shadows, eyeing him with the dead glare of their taxidermy glass eyes.

"Shit!" Jacob muttered, and gunned his bike. The dogs took after him, and Jacob heard the familiar click and hum of clockwork gears. Only four dogs, but they were big, and they moved fast for being dead. Jacob could not spare attention to get a good look, but what he glimpsed made him shudder.

Like the horses, the zombie dogs would never pass for living beings. Their dirty, matted fur hung against visible ribs. Patches of fur were missing, exposing putrefying flesh. *They can't last long like that,* the thinking part of Jacob's brain observed, as the rest of his brain argued for survival. *Were they experiments? Or can Congeliere and his buddies put these damned things together fast enough to make them disposable?*

He didn't have time to ponder. The dogs were stalking him, moving to close off his escape from the carriage and its hell-horses behind him. Veering right would put him in the river. Turning left would require trying to climb one of the steeply inclined streets for which New Pittsburgh was famous. Even if the bike could chug its way to the top, he would slow enough that the dogs could take him, or the carriage could ride him down. The uneven paving stones beneath his tires made it impossible to even think of shifting his grip to pull his gun.

What good is shooting them? They're already dead.

Mitch was stuck in a casket headed for a crazy resurrectionist's lair, and there was nothing Jacob could do to help. Despair warred with terror, sending a sheen of cold sweat down Jacob's back.

The clockwork curs were close enough for Jacob to hear their mechanical howls and the snick of their teeth, fangs that looked even larger protruding from blackened, dead gums. The undead stallions were closing on him; hoof beats deafening in the still night air.

Ahead, Jacob saw barricades of lumber and stone closing off the street for construction. There was nowhere to go. His luck had run out.

Jacob skidded the bike around so that his back was to the barricade and stopped. He flipped up a protective cover and pressed down on a button to activate the steambike's small Gatling gun. Nothing happened. *Jammed,* he thought, cursing under his breath.

Jacob drew out his pistol and pumped a shot into each of the approaching zombie curs, but the dead animals kept on coming, even though the bullets tore into their embalmed flesh. Their glassy eyes full of torment and madness fixed on him, and the pack gathered for the kill as the carriage and its wretched horses thundered toward him.

Light flared, and an explosion beneath one of the curs threw the zombie dog into the air and out of the way. Explosion after explosion rang through the night, echoing from the warehouses and the street, rumbling down the thoroughfare.

"Take that!" Drostan Fletcher shouted, riding his bicycle as if the Devil himself were after him, using the steep incline of the side street to increase his speed to a suicidal pace. He rode straight at the dogs, scattering them and making the corpse-horses shy back, then retreated just out of reach long enough to light fuses. Drostan hurled a long string of lit fireworks toward the dogs. The fuses glowed in the night, then exploded in a deafening roar as if all the artillery of the old Fort Pitt Foundry were going up at once. Jacob pumped his last two shots at the remaining mechanical curs, putting them out of commission and, he hoped, out of their misery.

Pounding hoof beats sounded behind the clockwork zombie carriage. Jacob glimpsed another black carriage closing on his attacker, heard the snort and snuffle of living horses. Hans drove his team at a reckless pace, intent on his quarry. A long metal tube telescoped between the two carriage horses, and with a roar and a flare of sparks, an egg-shaped projectile flew toward the zombie coach.

Jacob dove to the ground with his arms over his head as the Ketchum grenade exploded.

The explosion sent the zombie coach into the air along with its undead steeds, careening toward the solid brick wall of a nearby warehouse. Fletcher scrambled out of the way, ducking behind a wall to miss the worst of the flaming debris.

Bits of dead flesh and twisted clockwork mechanisms rained down on the street, filling the night air with the smell of a charnel house. For a moment, everything was quiet. Jacob climbed to his feet, righting his steambike, which was still running.

A low growl made Jacob pivot as the lone remaining clockwork cur sprang, teeth bared, a garbled mechanical growl coming from its dead throat, malice in its glass eyes.

It never saw the steambike coming. Jacob let go of the handlebars, and the bike lurched forward, knocking the zombie cur out of the way with enough force that it did not rise.

A plume of dark smoke rose from the ruins of the corpse horse carriage. For a moment, the street was still.

Jacob reached into his satchel and pulled out a department beacon. He planted it near the wreckage and clicked it on. The Department would have to see to clean up — no telling what stories the locals would tell if they saw the carnage in the light of day. That's when Jacob heard the clicking coming from the receiver pinned to his collar. Three short blips, three longer clicks, three short blips.

"Mitch is in trouble," he said. "Time to go."

Drostan threw his bicycle in the carriage and swung up to ride beside Hans. Jacob took off on the steambike, adjusting his steering for the damage the machine had suffered in the fight.

Mitch also had the aether wave transmitter. The range was limited, and Adam hadn't worked out all of the flaws yet, but the closer Jacob got to Congeliere's Manchester shop and home, the more often he could pick up a few words. Enough to know Mitch had been caught.

"… you were sniffing around at the Coroner's office…" a voice said. Jacob was still too far away to hear clearly, but this voice sounded nasal and whiny.

"… should have finished the job at the cemetery. Your friends are already dead." The second voice was low, heavy with a German accent.

"… just playing a prank—" Whatever Mitch was going to say was cut off with a resounding crack that sounded like a fist hitting bone.

"Federal agent… needs to disappear…" The third voice sounded unruffled as if whatever was going on was all in a day's work. It was his calm efficiency that chilled Jacob to the core.

"… making a mistake—" Again, Mitch was silenced with a bone-jarring thud that made Jacob wince and tighten his grip on the handle-bars of the bike. He had opened the bike's throttle up to its maximum speed, but the way the conversation was going, it might not be fast enough to get him there in time.

The steambike hissed and rumbled over the uneven paving stones of the New Pittsburgh streets, jarring Jacob's teeth together and assuring him he would ache in every bone and sinew. He fairly flew across the Seventh Street Bridge and headed for Ridge Avenue, hunched over his bike with Hans and Drostan hot on his heels.

"… just the beginning…," the man with the German accent said, from what Jacob could pick up over the wind roaring in his ears and the sound of the steambike.

"… limitless army of the dead…," the whiny-voiced man added.

"… valuable cannon-fodder…" the confident man said with a cold-ness that stoked Jacob's anger.

That was the motive behind the scheme Tumblety, Brunrichter, and Congeliere had cooked up, Jacob thought. Corpse shock troops, drawn from military and civilian dead. Cheap labor for mines and mills that needed no pay, food or shelter, unable to protest even the most brutal conditions.

"… you'll make a valuable addition," the German man said. A shot rang out at close range to the transmitter, and after that, all Jacob heard was static.

That would have been me, if I'd have fit in the box, Jacob thought, feeling as if the bottom had dropped out of his stomach. *They shot Mitch. Shit.*

A few blocks from the house, Jacob pulled over to the side of the street, and Hans pulled the carriage up beside him. He told them what he had heard, omitting what he feared. From the look on Drostan's face, he guessed they put the pieces together for themselves.

"Odds are good they're in the basement," Jacob said. "I'll need a diversion to go in after them."

"I'll handle it," Hans said.

"I'll come with you," Drostan volunteered. "You're going to need back-up." He had retrieved one of the extra sawed-off shotguns Hans had stocked in the carriage. Jacob did the same, reloading his revolver as well.

"What's the plan?" Drostan asked.

"Ride the steambike at full speed into the back door and hit the ground shooting," Jacob replied.

"No, seriously," Drostan said. "What's the plan?"

When Jacob just stared at him, Drostan cursed fluently, his Scottish burr becoming much more pronounced. "You've been hanging about with Mitch Storm too much if you think that's a plan," he said.

"Got a better one?"

Drostan sighed. "No. Come on. We've got work to do."

Hans took the carriage around to the front of the house on Ridge Avenue. Jacob took the steambike around to the back, and Drostan stood on the other side of the alley.

"What's the signal?" Drostan asked.

A high-pitched whistle split the air, followed by the thud of metal against wood and seconds later, the front of the Congeliere house exploded with a Ketchum grenade.

"That." Jacob revved the bike and ran it at full speed at the wooden basement door. Its tires jumped the small doorstep, and then it splintered the door, landing on the brick floor without the benefit of the two concrete steps. The impact threw Jacob forward, and as he struggled to keep his seat and his grip, his palm hit the Gatling gun button.

It was no longer stuck.

The bike's magazine was small in comparison to a full-size Gatling gun, but it shot off a hundred rounds in a matter of seconds.

By the time the shooting was done, Jacob stood with the shotgun in one hand and the revolver in the other. Drostan was behind him, similarly armed.

It was a good thing. The clockwork zombies hit them hard.

Waxy, embalmed skin hung in shreds from the mechanized corpses' emaciated bodies. The Gatling gun's bullets had torn into bone and joint, but the undead creatures lurched forward, a human shield between Jacob and their makers.

The blast from Jacob's shotgun blew away most of the closest zombie's head. Drostan's shot followed a second later, tearing a hole in the second zombie's chest big enough to fit his fist through.

Jacob caught a glimpse of the room through the firefight. Five metal autopsy tables filled half of the room, along with an embalmer's tank. On one of the tables lay a woman's severed head, and on another, the body from which the head had come. Other bodies lay in various stages of "enhancement," with steel pins protruding from bone and joint or clockwork mechanisms in the process of being fused with flesh and sinew. A rack of surgical and mortuary instruments hung against one wall. Floor to ceiling shelves held row upon row of glass containers filled with dusky fluid, preserved pieces of once-living things.

Smoke wafted down from the main house, much of which was no longer there, thanks to Hans. Glowing embers straggled through the air like shooting stars. At least four of the clockwork zombies lay in pieces on the floor, ones that had borne the brunt of the Gatling gun's punishment.

"Where's Mitch?" Jacob demanded. He brought his revolver to bear on the survivors of the blast.

Three men were crowded against the far end of the room, and Jacob matched them to the voices he had heard. He guessed the tall man with blond hair and hawk-like Aryan features to be Brunrichter. Congeliere, the ambitious embalmer, was likely to be the scholarly-looking dark-haired man in the white coat slumped against the wall, a bullet hole between his sightless eyes. That left Tumblety, who was easy to recognize with his huge mustache. Epaulettes and brass buttons gave his tailored jacket a quasi-military flair Jacob was willing to bet the charlatan doctor had earned as much as his bogus medical degree.

On the left side of the room, bloodied and still, he saw Mitch. Mitch lay with his hands behind his back, and from his torn clothes and the blood, it looked as if his captors had worked him over.

"You've ruined everything!" Brunrichter snarled. He leveled his

Smith and Wesson at Jacob in the same instant Jacob drew down on him.

Jacob dodged to one side, avoiding the bullet, but it sent his aim wild. His shot hit one of the big glass specimen jars, shattering it and sending a cascade of foul-smelling formaldehyde into the room.

A third shot rang out from the left side of the room, clipping Brunrichter in the arm. Jacob saw Mitch out of the corner of his eye, one arm flung wide, holding a Derringer he had somehow managed to conceal from his captors. At just that moment, Drostan lobbed a handful of lit firecrackers into the room and took a shot at Brunrichter.

Jacob remembered one of the few things he knew about chemistry.

Formaldehyde is flammable.

The right side of the basement exploded in a shower of broken glass. Bits of preserved and pickled human organs rained down on them along with burning embers from overhead. The beams holding up the ceiling groaned as one of the upstairs walls collapsed. Smoke filled the basement, choking them and making it nearly impossible to see.

With a deafening crack, the ceiling at the opposite end of the basement collapsed, falling in a torrent of burning wood and debris between Jacob and the clockwork zombie masters.

"Cover me!" Jacob shouted. "I'm going after Mitch."

Choking and wheezing from the smoke, Jacob lumbered toward where he had last seen his partner. Mitch was trying to get to his feet, hobbled by the stout rope that bound his ankles.

"Thank me later," Jacob muttered, grabbing Mitch by the waist and heaving him over his shoulder. Mitch was dead weight, one arm still fastened behind him. Eyes streaming tears from the acrid smoke, lungs protesting the stench of chemicals and decomposing corpses, Jacob hurled himself through the doorway with Drostan following a heartbeat later.

They had barely reached the alley before the entire house went up with a bang.

The explosion rocked the ground under their feet and shattered windows in nearby houses. Dogs howled, and babies screamed. The blast threw Jacob to his knees, knocking Mitch from his grasp to roll several times before ending in the gutter on the far side of the street. Drostan staggered but did not fall, backing away from the house, his gun still trained on the conflagration.

"What about Tumblety and the others?" Drostan asked in a strangled voice.

Jacob ignored his bloodied knees and bruised palms, managing to get to his feet. "I lost sight of them after the ceiling came down," he said, coughing and choking on his words. "But if they're still in there, they're toast." He stared at the Congeliere house as it burned. Not much was going to be left except for a charred crater.

"I could use a hand." Mitch's voice was strained and gravelly, but he still managed to sound impudent.

Jacob sighed and drew out a knife from a sheath on his belt. He righted Mitch to sit on the curb, then cut the rope around his ankles and freed his left arm. One eye was swelling shut, and half of Mitch's face was purpling with a bruise. He had a split lip and a broken nose, and it looked as if he had taken a beating. Jacob guessed that the sound he heard on the transmitter was the bullet that had grazed Mitch's arm.

"You've looked better," Jacob observed.

"You took your sweet time."

"We ran into complications on the way," Drostan said, still warily watching the flaming wreckage, his gun fixed on the ruins.

"Complications!" Mitch croaked. "I was trapped in an ever-lovin' coffin and attacked by mad scientists and zombies."

"Stand in line," Jacob said drily. "We got chased by hellhounds and Dracula's coachman."

"I know the cops in this part of town," Drostan said, still keeping a wary eye on the flames. "We'd better be gone when they get here."

Hans brought the carriage around, emerging from the billowing smoke like a dark avenging angel. "I trust the distraction was sufficient?" he asked as Jacob and Drostan helped Mitch into the carriage.

"Not exactly subtle, but it did the trick," Jacob said. "Thanks."

Hans managed a crooked smile. "If you'll pardon my saying, sir. I had a stake in this fight. What had been done to those creatures made a mockery of what Mr. Farber did for me. I couldn't stand for it."

Jacob nodded. "You and me both, Hans. Now get us out of here, before we all end up in the clink. That fire should keep the cops at bay until our boys show up."

"Capital idea, sir."

Mitch stared at the burning remnants of the house on Ridge Avenue. "Do you think they're dead?" he asked.

"Congeliere is. One of us put a bullet between his eyes," Jacob replied, pretending not to notice that Mitch was shaking.

"What about the others?"

Jacob guessed that the horrors Mitch had seen, and how close he had come to joining Brunrichter's army of clockwork zombies, would haunt Mitch's dreams for a long time. He heard the unspoken need for certainty, for vengeance, and for a closed case. But that confirmation was something Jacob couldn't give.

"Presumed dead," Jacob said. "The Department may find evidence in the wreckage. Maybe not."

"Nobody could survive a fire like that," Mitch said as the carriage turned the corner and headed in the opposite direction of the clanging fire bells.

They had given New Pittsburgh's firemen a busy night, Jacob thought. *Give us a few more hours, and we'll burn down the whole damn place.*

"Not if they were in the blaze, no." Drostan was watching Mitch with a look that said he knew something about combat shock. "But they're both slippery, and they've stayed alive and out of jail by being hard to catch. If they had a secret exit and time to get to it—"

"If they come back, we'll be ready for them," Jacob said. "And hey, you'll probably get a commendation for bravery out of this—or at least, a few of the black marks taken off your record."

A shadow of Mitch's rakish grin spread across his face. "Think so? Just make sure to tell them, I got in that shot with one hand tied behind my back."

LAGNIAPPE

LAGNIAPPE

"I've got to catch that train!" Agent Jacob Drangosavich of the Department of Supernatural Investigation opened the throttle on his steam-powered experimental velocipede, pushing the steambike to its limits as he raced to catch up with the locomotive.

All of his attention was focused on the train, and he willed himself to go faster, closing the distance between himself and the speeding locomotive.

Mitch Storm, his partner, was aboard that train, and he was counting on Jacob to back him up. The sound of a gunshot in the train's sole passenger car doubled Jacob's resolve.

That's got to be Mitch, Jacob thought. *Question is, was Mitch doing the shooting or getting shot?*

Jacob coaxed a bit more speed from the velocipede, despite its straining engine. He was gaining on the locomotive, close enough now to see the automaton in the cab, a metal man taking the place of a human railroad engineer at the controls of the train. The *click-clack* of the train on the rails drowned out the roar of Jacob's steambike, and the clouds of smoke belched from the locomotive's stack drifted between him and his quarry, partially hiding him from view.

"Come on, come on," he muttered to himself, pushing the velocipede for every bit of power its engine could muster.

Jacob had a Peacemaker in a shoulder holster and another, less conventional weapon holstered at his hip. The Department paid the best scientists in the country a premium to supply them with top-secret, often one-of-a-kind weapons, tools, and gadgets that made the stories of Jules Verne pale by comparison.

"Just a little more," Jacob muttered, crouching low over the velocipede's handlebars to reduce the wind resistance. The steambike edged nearer to the train, and Jacob grabbed his second gun, an odd contraption with a bulbous grip and a metal tube in the center of a coil of wires. Jacob veered his bike a few crucial inches closer, leveled his weapon at the copper-faced *werkman* at the train's controls, and fired.

The gun emitted an earsplitting whine, growing high-pitched and louder in a matter of seconds. Just at the moment when Jacob was sure his ears were about to bleed, the weapon fired and an invisible blast of force hit the automaton through the open window of the locomotive cab, putting a large dent in his metal head and slamming the mechanical man forward with enough impact to twist his frame.

"Damn!" Jacob gunned the velocipede one more time and gave a mighty leap, grabbing one of the handholds on the side of the engine and swinging up to the platform between cars. The riderless steambike veered off into a gully, sending up a puff of steam and a dark belch of smoke.

The downed automaton had fallen forward, keeping the train's deadman switch active while the train hurtled down the track. Except for his smooth, expressionless face and his mechanical body, the metal man resembled a real person in form and shape. "First things first," Jacob muttered to himself, keeping his gun in one hand as he approached the *werkman*. "Now, if this is one of Farber's fantastic creations, the kill switch should be... here," he muttered to himself, opening a plate on the automaton's neck.

"Uh oh." Just as Jacob spoke, the metal man shuddered, and the boxy metal head turned to fix Jacob with a glassy stare.

The automaton stood a foot taller than Jacob and wider by half. It would have been a giant of a man, ham-fisted, like Casey Jones or Joe Magarac, the workingmen of legend. The metal man towered over

Jacob as it regained its sense of purpose, and glowered at him with red-lit eyes.

Whoosh. One huge metal fist swung and missed. Jacob dodged, fast as a first-night boxer. He felt the breeze through his hair and cringed at the sound of metal groaning with the impact.

Whoosh. Strike two from the other side grazed Jacob's face and sent him reeling, his head ringing and his left eye beginning to swell.

Metal Man was on his feet now, fiery gaze focused on Jacob, winding up for another try. *I won't survive another hit,* Jacob thought, desperately working to clear his thoughts as the *werkman* took a menacing step forward.

Jacob still clutched the force gun. He had no idea what discharging it at such close range would do since the gun hadn't been fully tested in the field. Yet as he watched the hulking metallic creature begin to rise, and took a second look at the powerful metal hands the size of melons, Jacob decided to take his chances on the gun.

"Nothing personal," he muttered, pulling the trigger.

The ear-splitting whine sounded again, right before a ripple of energy surged from the gun. The energy blast threw the automaton into the steel wall of the cab and out the other side, hurling him off the train to bounce along the rocky ground beside the rails until the metal man clanged to a stop in a dented heap. Jacob flew in the other direction, thrown against the opposite side of the cab so hard that his vision swam and the breath was knocked out of him. He sank to the floor, winded, ribs aching. *That's going to bruise,* he thought ruefully.

Jacob climbed to his feet, moving over to the engineer's position, careful to stay clear of the ragged-edged hole where the *werkman* had been thrown clear. He peered down the track ahead of them, looked at the map of the rail route tucked into a corner of the engineer's cab, and nodded to himself. "Going in the right direction," he muttered.

"On second thought, maybe I won't drive," he said to himself, unfastening his suspenders and using them to keep the lever pushed forward so that the dead man's switch did not bring the train to a halt. "Carry on," he said, patting his rigged contraption before he prepared to make his way back to the passenger car. He made sure his guns were secure and began the climb over the coal car. As he reached the roof, he drew the Peacemaker and swung the door open to the passenger car.

Two shots rang out, one zipping so close to Jacob's ear that he let out a yelp and dropped to the floor. Before anyone could fire again, he dove into the nearest row of velvet-flocked seats for cover.

"Mitch?" he shouted, daring to peer above the seat long enough to see who was shooting. His partner, Mitch Storm, was hunkered down, crouched in the aisle of the passenger car where he could dodge behind the seats for cover. A man in a dark coat with a scarf wrapped around his face was standing near the back of the car. The man saw Jacob's head rise above the seat and shot. Jacob threw himself onto the floor, hearing the bullet hit where his head had been a second before.

"Took you long enough!" Mitch retorted.

"One-two?" Jacob yelled back.

"Gotcha!"

With that, Jacob stood up and began to shoot as fast as his Peacemaker could chamber the rounds, pinning down their assailant with steady fire. As he shot, Mitch dove over two rows of seats and hurtled down the aisle toward the dark-clad man, who had to choose between returning Jacob's relentless fire or defending himself against the madman charging at him with a gun.

At the last second, the man turned as Mitch dove toward him, squeezing off a bullet that nearly parted Mitch's hair. Mitch leaped for the assailant and missed as the man stepped back through the door onto the open platform and touched the lapel on his coat.

With a muffled snap, a white parachute bloomed behind their attacker, jerking him back and upward as the chute caught the air. The gunman waved an ironic good-bye as he was snatched away and out of reach.

Mitch scrambled to his feet and ran onto the platform, spreading his feet wide and bracing his gun arm to shoot at their assailant, although the man was too far away to see whether the shots hit or not.

"I'm losing my touch," Mitch said in disgust, watching as the man's figure receded against the light blue sky.

"Did your training include having to shoot at parachute targets from moving trains?" Jacob asked, raising an eyebrow.

"No," Mitch snapped, holstering his gun impatiently.

"Well then," Jacob replied with a shrug. "There you have it. Exceptional circumstances. Even so, you winged him."

"Yeah, well," Mitch grumbled, then looked at Jacob. "If you're here, who's driving the train?"

"Shit! My suspenders..." Jacob ran back toward the cab and over the coal car. The firefight had temporarily taken his attention away from the fact that the train was still rumbling at full speed down the track without an engineer. Mitch joined Jacob in the cab just as Jacob ripped away his makeshift tether on the dead-man's switch.

"Suspenders?" Mitch asked incredulously. His hair, usually meticulously plastered with Macassar oil, was awry from the fight and climb over the coal car. There was also a rip where a bullet had torn through the outer edge of his coat's shoulder. "We've trusted our lives to a train run by a pair of suspenders?" He turned to look at Jacob and frowned. For the first time, he noticed Jacob's injuries.

"What the hell happened to you?"

"Just a little disagreement with the engineer," Jacob said and pulled on the lever with all his might. "You should have seen the other guy," he said with a nod toward the gaping hole in the side of the engineer's cab.

The engine slowed, grinding to a halt. Jacob let out a long breath and drew his sleeve across his brow to mop the sweat. Mitch bent over to examine the twisted steel where the automaton had torn through. "One of Adam Farber's creations?" he asked.

Jacob shrugged. "A poor copy, more likely. You know what they say. Imitation is the sincerest form of flattery."

Mitch gave him a level glare. "Unless someone is imitating a *wunderkind* boy genius and his mechanical marvels," he replied. "Then imitation is the shortest route to the nearest cemetery."

Jacob slapped Mitch on the shoulder. "Lighten up. We made it this far, didn't we?"

Mitch and Jacob had been friends since their Army days back

during the Johnson County rancher wars. They could not have been more different. Mitch Storm was a few inches shorter than Jacob with a compact, athlete's build and a five o'clock shadow that started at three. An Army sharpshooter, Mitch's cockiness was rivaled only by his ability, and his uncanny talent for annoying authority figures.

Jacob Drangosavich was tall and blond, with a long face and hound dog eyes. He spoke most of the languages of Eastern Europe fluently and had a talent for blending in that made him a perfect choice for undercover work. After a stint in the Army, both men had been recruited by the Department of Supernatural Investigation, a secret branch of the intelligence community dedicated to investigating the threats and unusual occurrences that defied rational explanation.

"Did you get what we came for?" Jacob asked, turning to Mitch.

"Didn't really have a chance to look—getting shot at and all," Mitch replied drolly.

"Someone's bound to show up sooner or later, and we'd better be gone when they do," Jacob replied. "Let's get going."

Mitch swung the door open to the passenger car, noting the bullet holes with a grimace. "There wasn't anyone else on the train," he said. "Just the engineer, and Mr. Personality," he added, referring to his adversary.

"Was it Dallinger?" Jacob asked.

Mitch shook his head. "No. I got a good look at the shooter's face. Too young, wrong build—not the kind of thing you could fake, even with talent." He looked around the empty, damaged passenger compartment. The Pullman car was opulent, with burgundy velvet upholstery, brass fittings and flourishes, and rich wooden inlaid panels on the sides of the car. It was the type of accommodation only the very wealthy could afford, men like Horace Dallinger, who made his fortune in patent medicines and a series of risky, questionable, and borderline illegal business schemes.

"Do you even know what we're looking for?" Jacob asked as Mitch led the way into the ruined passenger car.

"Not exactly," Mitch admitted, though the admission did not signal a lack of confidence. "It's here. Dallinger sent his personal train to pick up the Morrigan treasure."

Bart "Blackflag" Morrigan had been the most successful blockade runner of the Civil War. His mad risk-taking, close scrapes, and fearless defiance of the Union Navy running illegal cargo into and out of the Confederate states were legendary and grew with the telling.

"Ah ha!" Mitch spotted a small wooden crate on the rearmost row of seats.

Jacob frowned. "That's it? Looks rather small, don't you think?"

Mitch grinned. "If it's filled with gold, it doesn't have to be large." He went to see how heavy the crate was and looked utterly flabbergasted when he lifted the box easily.

"Not gold," Jacob observed. "Or else someone already stole what we came for."

Mitch set the box down and shook his head. "I don't get it. Our intelligence was dead certain that Dallinger was moving the treasure." He sighed. "Let's open it up and see what we've got, since we wrecked a train—"

"—and another velocipede—" Jacob supplied.

"—and another velocipede," Mitch repeated, "to get it." He went back to the cab and returned in a minute with a small crowbar, prying the wooden lid open. Inside was an oak chest battered with time and darkened from exposure to the elements. He and Jacob peered at the chest.

"Looks old enough to be the real thing," Jacob said.

Mitch nodded. "Let's see what's inside." He lifted the chest out of the crate and picked up the crowbar to break the lock, but the lid opened easily and fell back to reveal a tattered satin lining.

"No doubloons," Jacob observed.

Mitch frowned, reaching into the box and removing the items one at a time. "One stack of old letters, tied with a ribbon," Mitch reported. "A nice opal necklace, ring, and set of earrings, a fancy corset, and a steamboat ticket," he said, staring at the chest in disappointment as if it were coal in a Christmas stocking.

"What if that's not the treasure?" Jacob mused.

Mitch glared at him. "Of course it's not the treasure! It's a bunch of junk! We are going to be in so much trouble with Headquarters—"

"You didn't let me finish," Jacob replied laconically, used to Mitch's outbursts. "What if it's a clue to find the treasure? What if Morrigan wanted to hide his map in plain sight, and we have to figure out a puzzle of some sort, with these objects, to get to his money?"

Mitch took a deep breath and slowly nodded. "Could be. Maybe. Everyone said Morrigan was a crafty bastard, and more than a few stories say he learned black magic down in the Caribbean."

"I heard that too," Jacob said, eyeing the objects as if they might bite. "Folks said black magic gave him his good luck—until his final run."

Blackflag Morrigan ran his own version of the "triangle trade" during the war, and charged exorbitant prices to compensate for the insane risks he took. A desperate Confederacy gathered jewelry and silver place settings plus all the cotton it could spare to raise money and entrusted the cargo to blockade runners. Morrigan and the others like him ran small, fast ships past the Union naval blockade to sympathizers in Nassau, Bermuda, and Havana. On the return trip, the blockade runners brought the guns, coal, cloth, gunpowder, blasting caps, sugar, and rum that were in short supply in the Confederacy. It was a lucrative business, but fraught with dangers, and most blockade runners ended up in prison or at the bottom of the Atlantic.

"Gather it up and let's get out of here. Kennedy's going to be here any minute," Jacob said.

Mitch grabbed the chest, leaving the larger crate behind, and the two men made their way to the rear of the car. Jacob poked his head out, gun drawn, in case Mr. Personality had doubled back, but he saw nothing but Louisiana scrubland, stretching to the horizon. "Clear," he reported, as Mitch emerged with the chest.

Right on time, a small airship was heading their way, gliding above the ground, casting a cigar-shaped shadow like a steam-powered ghost. The name *Bienville* was clear on her rudder. Jacob waved his arm, the all-clear signal, and the airship gradually descended until it was about thirty feet off the ground. A rope ladder dropped out of the cargo bay, along with another rope and a net bag for the chest. Jacob and Mitch secured the chest and then climbed up, and the airship began to rise as soon as they and their prize were onboard, with the cargo hatch closing automatically.

"Nothing blew up. You boys are slacking." Agent Della Kennedy strode back to the bay to meet them.

"Who's flying the airship?" Jacob asked, skeptical after their run-in with the automaton on the train.

"At the moment, that difference engine your *wunderkind* inventor gave us," Della said off-handedly.

"You mean there's no one on the bridge?" Mitch said.

Della shrugged. "I wasn't planning on staying for a round of poker. Just making sure you made it in without bleeding all over my ship." Della Kennedy was just an inch or two shorter than Mitch, with the piercing blue eyes and dark hair of her Black Irish heritage. The daughter of a general and the only girl in a family with nine boys, Della did not take guff from anyone. Since she could out-shoot almost everyone on the force, and out-fly them as well, most of the agents had made their peace with her presence, and those who harbored any resentment knew better than to say anything, especially if Mitch and Jacob were around.

"Get us out of here," Mitch said. "We can figure this out once we're back on solid ground."

Della gave him a devil-may-care grin. "Next stop, New Orleans," she said, heading back toward the bridge.

The triumph was short-lived. "We've got company, boys," Della shouted back to them a few minutes later. "Either of you feel like riding shotgun?"

Mitch and Jacob scrambled up to the airship cockpit. The *Bienville* was small and fast, not unlike the blockade runner ships Morrigan and his privateer friends had favored, and the Cutter-class airships like the *Bienville* were put to much the same uses as Morrigan's ship, the *Siren*, a generation before. DSI used the quick, less noticeable Cutters for reconnaissance, night raids, limited pursuit, and picking up or dropping off agents to hot-spot locations.

"I thought these ships had a crew," Jacob said as they reached the bridge.

"We do," Della snapped. "Oscar is down in the engine room. Clyde's my First Mate, and he's normally up here with me, but the boilers have been persnickety lately, and he's down helping Oscar."

"I'll do the shooting," Mitch volunteered, opening a hatch and dropping down into a glass-and-steel gunner's bubble. He strapped into the swivel-mounted seat and grasped the handles to the modified Gatling gun.

"Jacob—I need extra eyes," Della ordered. "There are two air sloops dodging in and out of the clouds, and I'd bet a month's pay they're after us."

Jacob nodded and grabbed the spyglass from the First Mate's station. "I'm on it," he said, going to his post.

The air sloops were even smaller than the *Bienville*, designed for one- or two-person crews, often launched from a larger ship for patrols. The sloops had limited range, but they were wickedly good at short pursuit and carried plenty of firepower. "Hang on," Della warned. "This isn't going to be the smoothest flight."

"You've got one coming in at ten o'clock," Jacob reported, working at keeping his voice impassive even though sweat beaded on his forehead. He had never gotten used to these new-fangled airships and preferred to have his feet firmly on the ground, or at least, in a good set of stirrups on a fast horse. "And another at three o'clock."

"Do not engage unless fired upon," Della snapped. "That's an order, Storm." She set her jaw. "I'd like to try to get out of here with my ship intact for once, if I can."

Della changed course, giving the sloops the opportunity to pass by without incident. When the two ships shifted their course to pursue, the game was on. "All right Storm," she said. "Give 'em hell."

Jacob muttered a curse in Croatian under his breath, grabbing belatedly for a handrail as Della slewed the ship around to face their attackers, making their pursuers the pursued. "Are you crazy?" he yelped, nearly losing his balance as the airship rocked.

"Probably," Della agreed. "But I am not running from gnats. Storm —take them out!"

Mitch opened fire, raking the air with the sharp *rat-tat-tat-tat* of Gatling fire. The sloops shot back, and Della put the *Bienville* through a series of tight turns and altitude changes that left Jacob struggling not to lose his lunch.

"Shoot the ships, not the clouds!" Della shouted. Mitch muttered something in reply that Jacob did not quite catch, probably for the best. A stray bullet from the attackers cracked one of the bullet-proof glass panels in the airship bridge, and Jacob gave a startled yelp.

"Sloop One is going high," Jacob reported. "Sloop Two is going low."

Della pulled back hard on the controls so that the *Bienville's* tail swung around to set the airship on a perpendicular course away from the pursuing sloops. "I don't have to play the game by your rules, buster," she said addressing their pursuers, a look of fierce determination on her face. Mitch swiveled so that he kept Sloop Two in his sights, and bursts of gunfire vied with the whine of the *Bienville's* straining engines.

"What in the Sam Hill are you doing up there?" Oscar's voice carried through the speaking tube from the engine room. "Are you trying to kill us all?"

"Just keep those boilers boiling," Della called back. "Give me all you've got."

"The *Bienville* wasn't really built—"

"I don't care what she's built for. You've got to get us a little more speed."

"This is as fast as she'll go," Oscar argued.

"Then get out and push," Della said, hunching over the controls determinedly. Once again, the pursuing craft had to make a last-minute adjustment to keep up with Della's changing course, and it brought the sloops perilously close to each other, nearly causing a collision.

"Yes!" Mitch exulted, as a burst of Gatling fire tore through the tail of the lower sloop, sending it veering away and out of control. Beneath them stretched swamps and the bayou, with its Cypress trees and black water. The enemy sloop dove for the ground and Jacob lost sight of the craft as it crashed through the canopy below.

Mitch's triumph vanished as a more gunfire sounded, zinging close to the *Bienville's* bridge and the underslung gunner's mount where Mitch hung suspended in mid-air. "Sloop Two is gaining on us," Jacob reported.

"Take us up—now!" Mitch shouted. Della pulled back on the controls with all her might, and the *Bienville* nosed upward, giving Mitch a perfect shot at Sloop Two's hydrogen-inflated main balloon envelope.

The explosion rattled the glass in the *Bienville*, as Sloop Two became a fireball. The outer skin peeled back from the melting steel skeleton, raining flaming debris into the swampland below. "Got them!" Mitch yelled, as if anyone could have missed the conflagration.

"HQ is going to have my guts for garters," Della muttered. "We were not supposed to do anything high profile on this run."

Jacob sighed. "Seriously? Did they know Mitch was assigned? It's been relatively quiet, compared to the last time we went on a job."

Della raised an eyebrow. "The Department is still cleaning up the debris from that, and paying off witnesses," she replied archly. "I've been told that incident is going into the training manuals as a cautionary tale."

"And yet, here we are," Mitch said, climbing out of the gunner's mount. "So for all the gnashing of teeth back at HQ, they keep sending us out because we get the job done."

"Just get one thing straight," Della said, pulling herself up to her full height and looking Mitch in the eyes. "My airship is not expendable."

"Of course not," Mitch said with a smile that sank a thousand ships. "Who else would rescue us?"

Della turned away, muttering something highly un-ladylike under her breath, and Jacob rubbed his eyes. Mitch was smart, talented, and aggravating, not necessarily in that order, and Jacob had grown accustomed to the headaches—literal and metaphorical—his partner caused on a daily basis. He only hoped that the success of their mission would be spectacular enough to win them a pass—again—on disciplinary measures.

Della docked the *Bienville* at a field just outside of New Orleans, leaving Oscar and Clyde to see to the ship's maintenance. She joined Mitch and Jacob in the ship's small passenger area to have a look at the chest that had caused them so much trouble.

"That's it?" she asked, clearly skeptical that the item was worth the gunfight it had taken to get it.

"We think it might be a series of clues," Mitch replied defensively.

Jacob rolled his eyes. "Maybe. We're not sure. But that's more hopeful than assuming we've been snookered."

Della peered into the chest and examined the contents. "We'll have to have a look at these letters, and see if there's a connection to the ticket," she mused. Jacob knew Della would be champing at the bit to dig in, since she was a fiend for puzzles and often liked to have a try at working ciphers. She looked at the opal jewelry and frowned. "Pretty opals, but the settings aren't remarkable," she said, holding them up to the light. "Not the best gift, considering some folks think opals bring bad luck. Curious."

Della lifted the corset and let out a whistle. "Someone spent a pretty penny on this," she said, examining the fabric. "Whalebone stays, French lace, Chinese silk." She chewed on her lip as she thought. "Funny—why would someone spend a lot on a corset, which no one sees—except perhaps for Morrigan and his lover—and so little on the jewelry? Usually, people like to show off their money with their gems, not their underwear."

"You'd better hope that Jacob's right about all of this having something to do with Morrigan's treasure, because I don't want to explain a firefight over a corset to HQ," Mitch grumbled.

"Captain Kennedy, the ship checks out," Oscar's voice filtered through the speaker tube. "We're cleared to go ashore. Clyde and I will run the pre-flight maintenance, restock the boilers, and be ready to shove off anytime you want."

"Acknowledged," Della replied. She put her hands on her hips.

"Well, boys? What say we have a stroll down Bourbon Street and figure this out?"

———

WHILE ONBOARD THE *Bienville*, Della had favored practical attire like modified bicycle bloomers and a jacket, but a more conventional traveling suit was required in public, even with New Orleans' *laissez bon temps rouler* attitude and even on the infamous Bourbon Street. It did not take much for Mitch to slip into his cover as a riverboat gambler, or for Jacob to assume the persona of an Eastern European gentleman. But, as usual, Della was vocal about her guise.

"Why do I always have to be the whore?" she groused as the three of them sashayed down Bourbon Street's crowded sidewalks. "Why can't Mitch take a turn? He's pretty."

Mitch choked, and Jacob chuckled. "I'd rather not see Mitch in a dress, if it's all the same to you," he replied.

Della snorted. "There are all kinds of whores," she replied, and managed to bring a flush to Mitch's cheeks. "Personally, I think I could pull off the riverboat gambler look in a trice." Slim and athletic, with dark hair a bit shorter than fashion dictated, Della could probably pass for a young man, given the right suit of clothes, Jacob allowed. He avoided looking in Mitch's direction, unable to keep from laughing.

"First of all, our lodging is above a brothel," Mitch retorted, straightening his tie in an attempt to reclaim his dignity. "Since it's the one place that would permit us all to be alone together without raising eyebrows. And secondly, even here, it's the only cover that lets you have more freedom of movement than the 'respectable' ladies."

Della was about to reply when an inebriated well-heeled wastrel made a lewd comment as he passed by. Before either Jacob or Mitch could react, Della had grabbed the drunk, wheeled him up against the nearest storefront, and pressed a hidden dagger against his groin. "Say it again, and you'll be singing with the girls' choir," she hissed.

"Beggin' your pardon, miss," the man slurred. "No harm intended. Just don't rob me of my family jewels."

"Ix-nay on the iolence-vay," Mitch murmured as he and Jacob formed a human screen between Della, her victim, and the passers-by.

Della turned the man loose with a shove that was a little more forceful than flirtatious, sending him reeling into the street. "Just having a little *tête-à-tête*," she replied. She glowered at Mitch. "It's what 'us' whore-types do."

The Department's idea of "hiding in plain sight" was to keep a room in Mahogany Hall, the well-known brothel in New Orleans's Storyville, run by the famed madam, Lulu White. The women of Mahogany Hall were famous for their beauty, and Jacob had to admit that the tales did not do them justice. Tall and short, light, dark, and in-between, White, Asian, Creole, African, and Islander, the working women of Storyville's most prestigious brothel even included two curvaceous automaton prostitutes, for the adventurous.

Mitch was playing his role to the hilt, and a disconcerting number of Miss Lulu's girls greeted him by name as they entered. Jacob had the good graces to blush, just a little, and Della increased her swagger, lifting her head high as if in challenge.

Miss Lulu herself met them inside the parlor, a handsome, mocha-skinned woman with dark hair and blue eyes. She wore a glittering necklace of sapphires and diamonds, and diamond teardrops dangled from her ears. "Oh, my lands! Look at you. You look so good, I could just eat you up!" she said loudly, taking Mitch's arm and leading them out of the public parlor into her private office in the back of the house.

Once the door was closed, she dropped Mitch's arm and sat on the corner of her desk. "Well if it's not Storm and Fury, the *Sturm und Drang* boys," she said, making a play on their last names. "Tell DSI they're late with their rent," she snapped. "I could sell that room of theirs several times a night."

"My apologies," Mitch replied, still charming although he had eased back on the riverboat rogue act. "I assume we were on time with your pay?"

Miss Lulu's eyes narrowed. Jacob and Della knew the madam had been on the DSI payroll as an informant for years, with ready access to some of the wealthiest, most powerful men in Louisiana. "Yes, my pay was on time," she growled.

"Then our credit should still be good," Mitch said with a smile. "Now, what do you know about Blackflag Morrigan?"

Miss Lulu raised an eyebrow. "Now there's a name. Bart Morrigan was trouble with a capital 'T,'" Miss Lulu replied. "But he was also quite a gentleman, and he treated me and my girls like royalty."

"He was a patron?" Mitch asked.

Miss Lulu gave a throaty laugh. "Can't tell all my secrets; you know that. But I did know Bart—how don't matter none. Why do you ask?"

The last thing they needed was a massive hunt for whatever treasure Morrigan left behind. "The Department thinks he stole some of their equipment, and they want it back," Mitch replied.

That was true, to a point. Morrigan did a little piracy around the edges of his blockade running business, and one of the ships he boarded had belonged to a Department operative. The Department figured Morrigan either died with the plans he stole, or that he had sold the plans and so they deserved a chunk of his treasure in compensation.

Miss Lulu gave a knowing chuckle that sounded like whiskey and wet dreams. "You want his treasure? You'll have to get in line, boys. Everyone went looking for Blackflag's Booty when he died. So far as I know, he put one over on everyone. That was just like him. He probably started the rumor just to have everyone looking for something that didn't exist."

Jacob leaned toward Miss Lulu's views, but Mitch believed there was something to the treasure rumors. "We'll stay out of your hair," Mitch promised. "Just send up our meals and a little whiskey to wash it down with, and you won't know we're here."

"Humph," Miss Lulu replied giving him a gimlet-eyed stare. "You're full of promises, Mitch Storm. I had to have the whole room redone after your last visit, and we still haven't gotten the smell of smoke out completely." She wagged a finger at him. "It costs me business when we have to evacuate in the middle of the night. Some of

those men can't go back to what they were doing when they get inter-
rupted, if you know what I mean."

Della snickered. Mitch rolled his eyes. "I've got no intentions of
blowing anything up this time," he said.

"You never do," Jacob muttered, just low enough for Mitch to hear.
Mitch glared at him, then returned his attention to their hostess. "And
when we get back to HQ, I'll get my friend in the office to speed up
your paperwork."

Miss Lulu gave a nod. "All right then. Your room is ready, and I'll
send up dinner when it's done." She paused. "One more thing—Old
Blackflag Bart had a Creole woman he kept company with, don't know
whether they were married or not, but she was his lady. She died when
he was out on one of his runs, and he never got over it. Folks said they
would see him, out at St. Louis Cemetery Number One, talkin' to her
grave at all hours of the night."

"Thank you," Jacob said. "Do you happen to know her name?"

"Marie Doucet," Miss Lulu replied. "Her father had cane planta-
tions down in the islands, and everyone said he bankrolled old Blackflag to do his blockade runnin', back during the War."

They thanked Miss Lulu again and headed for their room. Like the
rest of Mahogany Hall, the room was lavishly appointed, as opulent as
Hotel Monteleone in the French Quarter. True to its name, the mansion
had mahogany wainscoting around the lower part of the walls, and
watermarked green silk above, with molded plaster ceilings and a
disturbing number of large mirrors. A four-poster bed—also mahogany
—commanded much of the room, but there was also a sitting area with
a red velvet couch, two brocade-upholstered wing chairs, and a small
table for taking private meals. A crystal chandelier glistened with
gaslight, as did two light sconces that dripped with faceted glass
teardrops.

"Nothing but the best!" Mitch said, pouring them each a finger of
Four Roses bourbon in Baccarat crystal glasses before dropping into
one of the chairs. Della set the contents of Morrigan's chest on the
table and accepted the drink, pulling up the other chair so she could

study the items. Jacob sat on the straight-backed couch and joined Della in handling the items.

"Hand me the letters," Della said, and leaned back, sipping her bourbon, as she perused the stack of yellowed papers. She scanned one after another of the old letters, muttering under her breath, then rose and walked over to the ornate inlaid desk, spreading the letters out beneath the glow of the gas lamp. She plucked a pen from the inkwell and a piece of the scented stationery from the blotter, talking to herself in a whisper as she worked.

"Do you know what she's doing?" Mitch asked.

Jacob shrugged. "Code stuff," he replied, and sipped his bourbon. "I figure she'll tell us something when she's figured it out."

After an hour, Della set the papers aside with a triumphant smile. "Got it!"

Mitch raised an eyebrow. "You figured out the letters?"

Della shook her head. "No, but I figured out the codes. It's a Caesar shift cypher with steganography to make it more complicated. The steganography key is in the oldest letter by postmark," she said with a grin. "Tiny little dots that look like pinpricks of ink are under twenty-six letters. Their order gives us the outer ring on the Caesar shift cypher key. Plug in the regular letters they correspond to, and we get the message,"

"Which is?" Jacob prompted.

"Opals and bay leaf, dress to kill, coins in the basement. Strong spirits open door."

Mitch gave her a skeptical look. "Are you sure that's what the code says? Sounds like gibberish to me."

"I'm sure," Della replied with a tone that said she was willing to fight about it. She riffled through the box to find the opal jewelry and the corset. "Now if you'll excuse me, I'm going to try these on, just because."

She shrugged out of the jacket to her traveling suit and sauntered over to one of the large mirrors that was nearly the size of the room's door. Della slipped on the opal necklace, adding the pendant earrings and the silver and opal ring. Then she held the corset up, turning to admire it from one side and another, then laced it loosely up the back and pulled it closed, tugging to fasten the hooks.

Della looked into the mirror and gasped. "Oh my God," she murmured. "Mitch, Jacob—do you see what I'm seeing?"

Mitch started to make a smart comment until he saw the stranger looking at them through the glass. "I see it," he said slowly. "Not sure I believe it."

Jacob crossed himself and touched the silver medallion that hung from a chain around his neck. "I see it," he said in a low voice. "Do you think that's Marie Doucet?"

"Strong spirits open the door," Della quoted. "Maybe Morrigan didn't mean liquor. Maybe he meant ghosts."

"Now you're talking crazy," Mitch said, but his voice lacked certainty.

Jacob stared at the woman in the mirror. She wore a dress that was at least twenty years out of date, and her center-parted dark hair was pinned up in the back with ringlet curls around her face, a style from a past era. She regarded Della quizzically, then turned to look at Mitch and Jacob, all the while giving Jacob the sense that the ghost was truly interacting and not merely a bit of stray memory, trapped in the aether. Before Della could react, the ghost reached out of the looking glass and her fingers touched the corset. The fabric ripped between the stays like a thin sheet of paper. With that, the ghost vanished.

Della was shaking. She went to the desk, downed the last of her bourbon, and sat staring at the mirror in shock. Her hands trembled as she unhooked the antique corset. The thin silk was shredded, revealing the whalebone stays that provided its structure. One of the stays fell out of the cloth into Della's hand, and her eyes widened.

"Scrimshaw," she said, staring at the narrow, yellowed piece of whalebone.

"What?" Jacob asked, moving quickly to stand beside her.

Della was already recovering from her shock. She had turned back to the desk and was tearing the old corset apart to pull its narrow, ivory-colored stays from their places. "Look," she said pointing to the stays laid out on the desk.

Dark India ink-stained scratches on the stays making scrimshaw, the artwork of seagoing men for hundreds of years. Etched into the whalebone were scratches that on each individual piece were unintelligible, but when the pieces were placed together, looked wholly different. "It's a map," Mitch said with surprise.

Just then, one of the servants arrived with their dinner. Bowls of fragrant étouffée in a dark brown roux, rich with fresh-caught crab and shrimp over rice, a bottle of red wine, and a pile of fresh, hot beignets covered with powdered sugar along with a pot of strong coffee with chicory made for a mouthwatering meal. As they ate, Della noticed a bay leaf in her étouffée and pulled it out with her spoon, dabbing it dry with her napkin.

"I wonder," she said, folding the bay leaf around the opal ring she still wore from the chest.

"Holy shit!" Mitch sounded shaken. "What the hell just happened?"

"Della?" Jacob called. "Della?"

Della looked at them as if they had both lost their minds. "What is wrong with you?" she asked. "I'm right here."

Mitch paled. "Are you? Because we can't see you."

Della unwrapped the leaf from around the ring. Just as suddenly, she reappeared exactly where she had been sitting before she vanished. "Okay," she said, drawing the syllables out and staring at the ring as if it might bite. "That was freaky."

"Black magic from the islands," Mitch murmured. "Maybe it was truer than people thought."

"The code!" Della said, and ran to the desk to grab the piece of paper where she had written the cryptic words. "Opals and bay leaf, dress to kill, coins in the basement. Strong spirits open door," she repeated. "Well, we know what happens with the first two," she said, giving a sidelong glare at the bay leaf by her plate.

"Dress to kill," Mitch mused. "I've heard of women hiding a shiv in their corset, even a Derringer. And the whales are killed for their bone. The corset?"

Jacob nodded. "Strong spirits open door," he said thoughtfully.

"Well, we've met a spirit, maybe of Marie Doucet. But what door does she open?"

"She ripped the corset to show us the scrimshaw stays," Della replied, more curious now than concerned. "Maybe if we find out where the map on the stays leads, we'll know more about the rest of the coded message—and what the number on the ticket means."

Together, they hunched over the desk as Della moved the scrimshaw stays around to recreate the map she had formed earlier, though the streets were not any Mitch recognized from New Orleans-proper. "Alley Number 24," he said, perplexed, searching a map of the city. "It doesn't exist."

"Here's another one: Alley Number 11," Jacob pointed out.

"Hold your horses!" Della said, pointing to another section of the inked stays. "Here's one at the bottom that says Conti Alley, and one at the top that's St. Louis Alley." Her eyes widened with excitement. "You're looking in the wrong place, Mitch. This isn't a map of the city of New Orleans. It's a map of a city of the dead—and I'll bet you all the beignets at Café Du Monde that it's Saint Louis Number One."

"So the number on the ticket, it's not a house number," Jacob said, not liking the direction the revelations were taking.

"Want to bet it's Marie Doucet's tomb?" Mitch's voice held a mixture of curiosity and horror.

"Coins in the basement," Jacob said, meeting their gaze. "There's only one kind of basement in a New Orleans cemetery, and that's a *caveau*."

The thought made Jacob shudder, and by the look of it, Mitch and Della were squeamish as well. New Orleans was famed for its above-ground family tombs. Most resembled small mausoleums, one drawer wide and two drawers high. A family would inter a loved one, allow the body to naturally cremate in the stifling heat, and when another family member died, the first body, now mostly dust and bone bits, would be pushed to the back, where it would fall down below the drawers into a small cave-like holding area—the *caveau*.

Della fixed him with a deadly glare. "You're telling me that we have to go to a cemetery and look for a treasure inside an old tomb?" she asked incredulously.

"With a ghost," Jacob added. "Remember—strong spirits open the door."

Della threw her hands into the air. "Seriously? You're really going to go through with this?"

Mitch shrugged, recovering some of his bravado. "The Department wants Morrigan's treasure since it was earned by ill-gotten gains. And they'll forgive us our little dust-up on the way here if we deliver what we were sent to get."

Della sighed, knowing when to give up a lost cause. "All right," she said. "Let's make a plan."

"THIS IS YOUR idea of a plan?" Della said as she struggled to keep up with Mitch and Jacob along the deserted sidewalk. The items from Morrigan's chest were tucked in a small bag she carried beneath her arm. There was no fixing the corset, but they brought all the pieces, especially the scrimshaw-covered stays, which Mitch had managed to affix to a piece of paper with flour-and-water glue. The opal jewelry was in the bag as well, no doubt intended by Morrigan as a gift for his Marie, a gift she did not live long enough to receive.

"Yep," Mitch replied, now firmly back in charge despite any misgivings he might have felt. Jacob listened to the two of them argue, but he watched the night, concerned that the darkness might not be as empty as it seemed.

Mitch and Jacob both carried Peacemakers and Adam Farber's experimental force guns. Della carried a Winchester rifle and what Mitch called a "Swedenborg Meter," a gadget that detected fluctuations in the aether common to ghostly sightings, named for the famed spiritualist. The contraption looked like a combination Edison cylinder and zoopraxiscope, and had a thick wire that led to a headset much like that of a telegraph operator, through which Della could hear the variations in pitch that supposedly indicated spectral activity.

Mitch picked the gate lock and gestured for them to hurry. "The Archdiocese is not going to be happy with that," Jacob observed, slipping through the iron gate.

"You never know. They've done business with the Department. We're all in this together," Mitch replied off-handedly, closing but not locking the gate behind them. Earlier that night, they had retrieved the velocipede Mitch left hidden beneath tarpaulins in the shed behind Mahogany Hall, and they had squeezed onto it for the short ride to Saint Louis Cemetery Number One.

"We're not alone." Jacob nodded toward where gaslights burned on one side of the cemetery, not far from where the scrimshaw map directed them.

"Let's see who's here," Mitch murmured. They made their way through the shadows, moving along the narrow gravel paths between the tombs. Some had elaborate wrought iron fences or were adorned with vases of fresh flowers, while other tombs were crumbling from neglect. Yellow Fever, Cholera, Malaria, they all left their mark, filling the tombs of New Orleans's cemeteries.

"Well, well," Jacob said quietly, inclining his head toward the group crowded around one of the tombs farther up the pathway. Banks of lit candles flickered in the darkness, and flowers, single and in bunches, were strewn in front of the tomb, which had been marked over and over again with the letter "X." Even at a distance, Jacob could see that gifts littered the edges of the tomb, and the small crowd of people who sang, chanted and danced ecstatically to the beat of drums were less like revelers and more like devout worshippers.

"Marie Laveau, the Voodoo Queen," Mitch said quietly. "Still has quite a following it appears." He gestured for them to slip down a parallel pathway, counting the tombs until they reached tomb number three hundred, fifty-eight.

"Here we are," Della said in a whisper, nervously rocking back and forth onto her toes. "Marie Doucet's resting place." She adjusted the dials on the Swedenborg Meter. Listening intently, she nodded. "According to this, the place is lousy with ghosts."

"We only need one spirit," Mitch said. "Let's do this and get out of here."

Della nodded and took the jewelry from the bag she carried, handing the meter over to Jacob, who held it in his left hand so he could keep a gun in his right. She clasped the opal necklace around her throat, clipped on the earrings and put the ring on her finger. She gasped, and Jacob looked at her with alarm.

"There's something about the opals," Della said. "A connection with Marie Doucet's spirit. Like she knows the jewelry was for her."

"Can you see her?" Jacob asked. "Because this meter is going totally nuts."

"Yes," Della said, moving toward the tomb. "But how do we get her to open the door?"

Della had no sooner spoken than a gray shape appeared in front of the tomb, growing more and more solid into the shape of a woman. Before anyone could move, the woman grabbed at Della's jewelry, and the bricked-up and stucco-covered door to the lower tomb drawer shattered, revealing an empty niche.

Mitch dove for the niche, digging frantically in the gray dust and unnamed hard bits. The gray ghost's fingers tore at Della's necklace, snapping the chain, and an instant later, yanked the earrings from her lobes with enough force that Della cried out in pain. Jacob dropped the meter, since the ghost was clear to the naked eye, and leveled his force gun at the revenant.

"Leave her alone!" he commanded.

Mitch sat up, emerging from the tomb streaked with dirt but victorious, holding a small metal casket that was much heavier than its size suggested. "Got it!"

"I'll take that." The man's voice sounded behind Jacob. "Drop the gun," he ordered, poking the barrel of his six-gun between Jacob's shoulders. "You, too," he said to Mitch.

"Mr. Personality returns," Mitch said acidly. "Who do you work for? Dallinger?"

"None of your business," the stranger snapped. "I just came for the box. No one has to die."

Della vanished into thin air. Marie Doucet's ghost shrieked like a nightmare come true, speeding toward the attacker, hands outstretched. Jacob's gun rose by itself, hovering without visible means of support, and squeezed off a shot that caught Mr. Personality in the right elbow, forcing him to drop his weapon.

Marie Doucet's spirit was in a frenzy, attacking the newcomer with fury. Ghostly hands tore at his hair and clothing, opening long scratches on his face and neck. Mitch grabbed his force gun, but he had no idea whether it would temper the wild ghost's rage, or whether once Marie Doucet was done with Mr. Personality, she would avenge herself on them.

"Be still, my child." The voice came from behind Mitch this time, and Jacob looked up to see a dark-skinned woman standing just behind his partner. She wore her hair wrapped in block-printed cloth after the African fashion, a shawl around her shoulders and large gold hoops in her earlobes. A sense of power and peacefulness radiated from the figure, and as Mr. Personality dropped to the ground in a terrified, bloodied heap, the ghost slowly withdrew her vengeful attention from her victim and turned to look at the woman in the shawl.

"Your lover brought you a final gift," the dark-skinned woman said. "It's time for you to go to the gods child, and rest."

Marie Doucet's ghost nodded, and Jacob saw that somehow, the ghost now wore the opal necklace and earrings it had ripped from Della. Della was still invisible, using her bay leaf and the opal ring to hide herself, in case their new savior turned out to have ulterior motives.

"Take your treasure," the woman in the shawl said, her voice contemptuous, addressing Mitch. "It has troubled this place for too long. Take it and leave us in peace." She turned to the empty air next to Jacob. "Do not become fond of that bit of magic, girl-child," she said to Della. "It is dark power, and it cursed the one who wrought it. Leave it here, and be free of it."

Jacob blinked, and Della was visible once more. Moving slowly, she walked over to Marie Doucet's tomb and placed the ring just inside the open doorway. Jacob had already moved to secure Mr. Personality, in case fear of capture won over fear of the dead. Mitch rose to his feet, keeping a watchful eye on the woman with the shawl.

"Thank you," he said. "*Merci.*"

The woman inclined her head, and then turned and walked back toward the dancing crowd near the candle-lit tomb. The crowd, intent on their revelry, paid them no mind. As Jacob watched, the woman's shape grew indistinct, and then faded altogether before she reached the row of candles.

"You don't think—" he stammered.

"Was that who I think it was?" Mitch asked.

"We've got an airship waiting," Della said, glancing overhead as a dark shadow glided past the moonlit clouds. "We got what we came for, and captured a prisoner—a bonus. Consider that a *lagniappe*, a little something extra. Let's go home."

GRAVE VOICES

1 / GRAVE VOICES | MONSTERS

New Pittsburgh, 1898

"THE STREETS OF New Pittsburgh aren't safe for decent people anymore!" The speaker shouted as he strode back and forth the steps to the courthouse. He had worked up a sweat that made his shirt cling to his muscled body. A crowd gathered, muttering their agreement as he spoke. The hand-lettered sign leaning against the bottom step proclaimed "Edmund Luss, Monster Hunter." Nearby, a reporter was busy scribbling notes on a tablet as a photographer's flash powder made the crowd blink when he took a photo.

"It's not bad enough that the pickpockets and petty thieves lurk down the alleys, preying on hard-working men and women!" the man added, and the crowd nodded. "Not bad enough that feral dogs snatch meat from butchers' carts and fresh fish from the fishmonger. But now, there's a new horror—the police are too afraid to admit it's lurking out there—and ladies and gentlemen, you know I'm telling the truth because you've heard it from your friends and neighbors. There are monsters, monsters I say, roaming the dark alleys of New Pittsburgh and I am here to drive them back to the fires of Hell where they belong!"

A cry went up from the crowd, cheering and whistling. The speaker stood triumphantly with his hands on his hips, letting the crowd go wild.

"Can you do it? Can you send the monsters away for good?" a man in the front of the crowd shouted.

"How do we know you've actually fought real monsters?" a skeptic asked.

The speaker nodded as if he had anticipated the questions. "To the first question—yes! I can do it. I can rid New Pittsburgh of the monster scourge. And to the second question—very wise, very prudent of you, sir, to be so careful—again I say yes! I have fought real, actual monsters. Fought them with my bare hands and with weapons too terrible to mention, in fights I cannot describe with ladies present! But I can show you—the monsters gave me these!" And with that, he stepped closer to the crowd and held out both arms to show long, jagged scars that might have been made by the claws of a beast.

"That's how close I got to the monsters! That's how I know that I can defeat those terrifying beasts! And ladies and gentlemen, I came away with the best of the deal by far! Because while I will bear the scars of those monsters until my dying day, I dealt out unwavering justice to those infernal, abominable creatures. Behold!" And with a flourish, he held up a black, shaggy pelt matted in places by what might have been blood.

The crowd gasped. Two women in the back swooned and might have fallen had their companions not eased them to a seat on the stone courthouse steps, where they fanned themselves until someone went to fetch them water.

"Don't let the evidence alarm you!" the speaker cried, working the crowd to a frenzied pitch. "I am willing to take on the risks of hunting these beasts, these monsters, in order to guarantee the safety of the good people of New Pittsburgh!"

The crowd went wild once again, cheering, screaming, and stomping their approval. "When can you start?" a man yelled.

The monster hunter shrugged. "That all depends on the vote by your City Council," he said. "I have given them my modest proposal, modest indeed considering the great risk of bodily harm involved. They are considering that proposal as we speak, weighing the safety of the people of New Pittsburgh against the paltry sum I request to exterminate, once and for all, the monstrous vermin that prowl the streets of this fine town. They may be waiting to hear from the people of the city. So if you want me to drive out the monsters, if you want to sleep secure in your beds at night and rest assured that your children and your wives can go about their business without harm, if you want peace and safety for the city of New Pittsburgh, then I ask you, I *beg* of you, let your voices be heard!"

The resulting racket was impressive. Men and women shouted their assent, and some waved fists in the air for good measure. Ear-splitting whistles echoed down Grant Street along with thunderous applause. The monster hunter stood silently, hands clasped in front of him, just the hint of a satisfied smile touching his lips.

He did not seem to notice the three people watching his rally from across the street. Mitch Storm, Jacob Drangosavich, and Della Kennedy stood where they could hear what the monster hunter was shouting to the crowd, and observe both him and his audience.

"That's him," Mitch said. "Edmund Luss, aka Edward Lustig. Con man, snake oil salesman, huckster extraordinaire."

"Do we nab him?" Jacob raised an eyebrow.

Mitch shook his head. "He hasn't done anything illegal—yet. Although I'd bet anything that 'monster' pelt is just a dyed goat skin, or maybe monkey fur."

"Interesting timing for his little rally," Della said. "Nice way to let the Council know he's got supporters—and make it uncomfortable for them to turn him down, no matter what fee he's charging."

Mitch nodded. "Lucky for them, we're here." He turned to go. "We've seen enough. Time to plan a little 'monster hunt' of our own."

A few blocks down Grant Street, a street preacher stood on an overturned fruit crate. "The end of the world is nigh!" he proclaimed with fevered passion. "Monsters roam among us. Surely that is a sign of the end of the world!" The preacher had gathered almost as large a crowd as the monster hunter, and more people continued to join the group as the man's voice rose. He was dressed better than the monster hunter, with a vest over slacks and a starched white shirt, and he waved a worn Bible in one hand as he shouted to the crowd.

"Monsters! Demons! Abominations! Right here in New Pittsburgh, come to kill our children and taint our souls!" He was already sweating and mopped his brow with a handkerchief. "But we can fight that evil! Yes, we can. Do you believe that we can fight the evil?"

The solemn crowd nodded, and a few "amens" sounded from the gathering. Mitch, Della, and Jacob drifted closer, and Mitch's eyes narrowed. Jacob bet his partner was thinking the same thing: that the two speakers were very likely working together. That suspicion grew stronger when he saw the table of patent medicine bottles and protective medallions next to the street preacher's make-shift stage. The name painted on to the suitcase displaying the items for sale read *"Reverend Joe Sherril."*

"The Lord can save your soul, and I can save your life," the preacher continued. "The Lord has sent us a warrior, sent us Edmund Luss, a fearless man who can hunt down the abominations and drive them from our city. But he has also given me a vision, a vision that may save your lives." He turned toward the bottles and medallions on the table.

"The Good Lord helps them who help themselves," Sherril continued. "Now we're not all called to fight monsters. But you can protect yourself, your loved ones, even your horses and pets with these fine items." He lifted one of the bottles, and the liquid inside was the color of pond scum.

"I received a message in a dream to protect the good people of New Pittsburgh with these potions and medals," Sherril continued, eyes alight. "These medals have been blessed by every type of church in this city. They are inscribed with a prayer in Latin that drives away monsters. If you wear one of these, no monster will come within five feet of you," he promised.

"What do the potions do?" someone called from the crowd.

"I'm glad you asked!" Sherril said. "These fine potions and elixirs let you protect your house, your chicken coop, your garden, and carriage shed from the unholy monsters terrorizing our city."

He clutched one hand over his heart. "I'm not here to make money from misfortune. No, indeed. That's why the price is so very low. I am here in the interest of public safety, doing the work of the Lord," he added with a brief glance skyward. "But I have to tell you; these are the last bottles and medals available."

At that, the crowd surged forward. "I want one!" a voice cried

"Give me two of each!" someone else yelled.

"Hey, one to a customer!" another person protested. The onlookers surged forward, throwing coins and bills at Sherril as they nearly trampled each other to get the bottles and medals.

"Pretty slick," Della observed, as they watched from a distance. "Think he and the monster hunter are in it together?"

Mitch nodded. "Certain. 'Reverend Sherril' is a fake. That's Shifty Joe Shurlman. He's as much of a con man as Lustig. But if we bust him, Lustig will know we're on to them. Let's go."

The building that housed the New Pittsburgh office of the Department of Supernatural Investigation was intentionally shabby. A pawn shop—operated as cover for the Department—took the street-level Liberty Avenue storefront, while DSI occupied the upper floors. Blinds covered the windows, hiding DSI's facilities. A few minutes later, the three agents were in the briefing room. Mitch and Jacob had laid their jackets aside, and Della was seated primly in a chair that allowed room for the bustle of her skirt.

"We've had four reports in as many weeks of people seeing 'monsters.'" Mitch slapped his pointer against the map of the city that hung on one wall of the briefing room. "And during every sighting and chase, a break-in or robbery."

"You think Lustig and Shurlman, aka Sherrill, are behind it?" Della asked, sipping a cup of tea.

"It fits with what they've done in other cities," Jacob replied, leaning back and stretching his legs. Jacob was tall, with a long face, blond hair and hound dog eyes. His Eastern European heritage was clear in his features. That made it easy for him to move unnoticed among New Pittsburgh's newly-immigrated population, especially since Jacob spoke a number of languages.

His Department partners were a study in contrast. Mitch stood a few inches shorter, but he was compact and muscular, with dark hair and a five o'clock shadow that showed up at three. He looked like the epitome of what every dime novel writer pictured as an army sharp-shooter or secret agent. Della had dark hair and piercing blue eyes. She was the daughter of a general and the only girl in a family of nine boys, making her ideally suited to help Jacob rein in Mitch's more outlandish schemes. Della was also one of the best airship pilots in the entire Department.

"What's Lustig using for monsters?" Della wondered, tapping the toe of her high-button boots as she thought.

"In Des Moines, we're pretty sure he had a trained bear that he shaved. It looked very, very strange," Mitch replied. "In Chicago, our sources think he put a costume on a trick riding horse. In each city, he stages several frightening sightings of 'monsters,' shows up and presents the Town Fathers with a contract to rid the town of its prob-lem, pockets a big fat check, and moves on to the next bunch of suckers."

"He's a con man, pure and simple," Jacob agreed. "He was an animal trainer with the circus before they threw him out for petty theft. Shurlman, the fake Reverend Sherrill, was a doctor before he lost his license for selling fake patent medicines. Looks like they've upped their game."

Della set her teacup aside and went to study the map. "Do you have a drawing compass?" she asked. Mitch dug in a drawer and handed one to her. She jabbed the point into the wall, then drew a series of concen-tric circles that cut through all four of the sighting-dots.

"Clever," she said, standing back to view the map. "Lustig's engi-neered sightings in every part of the city—including Shadyside, so the upper crust can't just dismiss the beasts as being someone else's prob-lem. But all of the 'monsters' have appeared within a five miles or so of the warehouses out on Liberty Avenue," she said, tracing the circles she had drawn in pencil again with her finger. "Not a bad place to hide, especially if he's using trained animals."

Jacob nodded. "Big buildings, lots of empty space, people coming and going at odd hours, so no one pays attention. It's worth checking into."

Mitch stared at the map, thinking. "It wouldn't be difficult for him to load a trained bear into a wagon, and minus the 'costume,' a horse is just another horse. No one would notice."

Della turned to Mitch. "Lustig is going to stage another monster sighting, either to pressure the Council in to hiring him, or to prove he's doing his job. Do you have a hunch about where he'll turn up next?"

Mitch grinned. "Oh, yeah. And when he does, we're going to hunt the monster hunter."

Later that night, Mitch and Jacob waited in the shadows of the Liberty Avenue warehouses. Thanks to genius inventor Adam Farber, both men wore headsets that connected to an aetheric wave transmitter, allowing them to receive signals from Della in the airship overhead.

"Everything set?" Mitch said into his mouthpiece.

"Set," Della confirmed. Jacob glanced skyward. Della's ship, the *Bienville*, ghosted through the night sky above them. The airship's large inflated envelope was black, and its lights were muted. Anyone who wasn't looking for it might take the lights for the twinkle of stars.

"See anything?" Jacob asked. Tonight, Della and her crew were their eyes in the sky, and the *Bienville* flew lower than usual so the airship lookouts could spot Lustig when he made his move.

"I've got something," Della warned. "There's a wagon parked two blocks from Smallman Street, and it doesn't look like a regular delivery vehicle."

"We're on it," Mitch said, and with a nod to Jacob, he gunned his steambike, and the two agents headed toward the area locals called the "Strip District."

Mitch and Jacob both wore goggles that Farber had created just for the Department, outfitted with more of his experimental technology to help them see better at night. The steambikes were Farber's creations, too, though the inventor preferred to call them "velocipedes."

The Strip District earned its name from being a strip of land along the Allegheny River. The area came alive between midnight and dawn, since its produce markets, fishmongers, butchers, and bakers supplied the city's restaurants, merchants, cooks, and housekeepers who came looking for fresh food. *What's the good of defeating a monster if no one sees you do it?* Jacob mused. Lustig would need a fresh scare to get the Council on his side, but so many of the city's residents were afraid that evening programs had been cancelled. The Strip was certain to have an audience.

A glance skyward reassured Jacob that the *Bienville* was still their eye in the sky. Tonight, Mitch had a rifle slung over one shoulder and his revolver in a holster on his belt. Jacob carried a shotgun with special ammunition, his Peacemaker, and a few "surprises" Farber had created for them. Both steambikes incorporated weapons as well, including a small Gatling gun and some Ketchum grenades. Mitch and Jacob were ready for whatever Lustig the monster hunter had planned.

Mitch gave the signal, and they throttled down, coasting toward the intersection, waiting in the shadow of St. Stanislaus Kostka church. Jacob strained to see with his night-vision goggles. Smallman Street bustled with activity. Longshoremen unloaded crates of produce. Fishermen brought in their catch and haggled over the price with the store owners who would display those fish on ice in a few hours for eager buyers. The air smelled of freshly-baked bread, fresh fish, and coal smoke.

"Uh oh," Jacob muttered. A commotion was brewing down near the foot of Smallman Street Jacob heard men shouting and the clatter of carts and wagons scrambling to clear the road.

"Got a visual on the monster," Della said over the headset. "Large figure moving toward Smallman two blocks down from you. Looked like it came out of the wagon. Someone's waiting with the horse for a quick get-away."

"I see it," Mitch growled.

A terrifying howl sounded in the night. In the distance, a creature emerged from a side street, standing in the shadows between street-lights. At first, it walked on all fours like an ape, then stood on its hind feet, revealing a large hump in the middle of its back. It was too big to be a man, and it looked like it was covered by the same dark, shaggy pelt Lustig had waved at his frightened audience. The thing lurched forward, toward the nightshift workers who had begun to stop to look in the direction of the commotion.

The stevedores and fishermen saw it too. No doubt they were supposed to, given how much noise it was making. That made Jacob more certain the whole thing was a fraud. Mitch and Jacob had fought their share of real monsters, human and otherwise. *Predators that mean business don't announce themselves caterwauling at the top of their lungs. The first—and last—thing you hear is the snick of their teeth,* Jacob thought.

Startled shouts and frightened yells went up from the men on the loading docks. They pointed and swore, but none of them made a move toward the beast. Jacob saw several men reach for knives, brass knuck-les, and pistols. Night work was dangerous, even when there weren't monsters running amok. The men stole furtive glances at one another as if they were each waiting for someone else to go first.

A new figure appeared from the shadows of a side street. Lustig made his entrance with the crack of a bullwhip, moving into the glow of the streetlight so that everyone got a good look at him. He snaked the whip toward the monster again, and the creature bellowed, an unnatural, distorted sound.

"Stand back!" Lustig warned, projecting like a trained thespian. "Let me handle this."

The men unloading trucks and boats were happy to oblige. They fell back but made sure they still had a good view. The laborers were scared, but there was a sense of excitement too, as if they realized they had front-row seats at the ring to the match of the century. Jacob saw a short guy in the back moving from man to man and figured he was taking bets.

Lustig had his whip in one hand, and a revolver in the other. "Back!" he shouted at the monster. "Leave these good men alone!"

Jacob rolled his eyes. Lustig's delivery was like a bad vaudeville skit, but the longshoremen who stared wide-eyed at the monster in the shadows seemed to be eating it up. The monster roared again, and its whole frame shuddered, long arms shaking. Lustig cracked his whip, snapping it inches from the monster's face, a sound that reverberated like a gunshot.

The monster roared again and started toward Lustig. The onlookers murmured and drew back a few steps. They were enjoying the show, but no one wanted to be part of the fight.

Lustig stood his ground. Jacob noticed that, not coincidentally, Lustig made his stand in the pool of light from the streetlamp, his own personal spotlight in the drama he had so carefully choreographed. That left the monster in the shadows where it was the most frightening, a menacing silhouette. *He's a showman, all right.*

Lustig's first shot made the longshoremen jump. The monster heaved closer. From where Jacob watched, it looked as if the creature swung a long, thick arm at Lustig, which the monster hunter barely dodged. Lustig and the creature circled each other. The monster swung again, slamming a fist into Lustig's left shoulder, sending him rolling across the cobblestones. A gasp went up from the men who watched from the safe distance.

Lustig came up shooting. The creature lunged at him, and Lustig and the monster grappled before Lustig tore free and squeezed off two more shots.

"They're dancing, not fighting," Mitch observed.

"Want to bet he's shooting blanks?" Jacob replied. He and Mitch had seen their share of gunfights, both as DSI agents and before that, in the army. To a practiced eye, Lustig's moves seemed designed to make the monster look more menacing, when it was really doing very little except bellowing.

Lustig moved left. The monster moved right. The monster clubbed him again with its beefy fist, and Lustig staggered. He snapped his whip, but the creature absorbed the blow, tangling the long tail of braided leather around its arm. With one move, the monster jerked the whip from Lustig's hand and thrust out its arm.

Lustig went sprawling, and the monster loomed over him, arms raised menacingly.

"Down, spawn of Satan!" Lustig cried, and shot again at point-blank range. This time, the monster roared and fell back, his huge body shaking fearsomely. The creature sagged to its knees and roared one last time, then collapsed to the paving stones.

A cheer went up from the longshoremen and onlookers. Lustig staggered to his feet, making a show of reloading his revolver and keeping a wary eye on the downed beast.

"Thank you," Lustig shouted. "No applause necessary. Just doing my work, as the City Fathers and The Lord Above ordained. But stay back!" he commanded as the curious crowd started forward for a better look.

"These creatures are tricky," he warned. "My associate and I will see to it that this beast never troubles New Pittsburgh again."

On cue, a man dressed like a monk in a cassock and a cowl that shaded his face emerged from one of the side streets with the enclosed delivery wagon Della had spotted from the air. Given the other man's build, Jacob was certain it was Shurlman in disguise. Together, the two men hefted the monster into the wagon. They closed the doors and threw the bolt; then the "monk" went around to climb into the driver's seat.

Lustig turned to address the crowd once again. "What you've seen here tonight took years of training with master fighters," he said gravely. "Please, if you see a monster such as this loose elsewhere in the city, I beg of you, do not try to fight it yourself. I would much rather you call for me, and let me handle it. For your safety."

Another cheer went up from the dockworkers, and Lustig stood by for a moment, modestly inclining his head before he joined the monk in the wagon. With another wave, they headed away from town.

"Moving," Mitch muttered into his headset.

"We see him," Della confirmed from the airship. He's turning left on Liberty." She paused. "I've got a wagon on its way."

"We're on it," Mitch acknowledged. With a nod to Jacob, Mitch went left, and Jacob went right. The longshoremen startled at the rumble of the steambikes. They pointed and stared at the unfamiliar vehicles as their horses shied away. Jacob opened up the throttle, anxious to get behind Lustig's wagon and cut off his retreat before the noise of the steambikes gave them away.

Mitch was already out of sight. The side streets were steep, and Jacob's velocipede strained, but Farber's ingenious design gave the bike the power it required to scale New Pittsburgh's challenging slopes. Jacob barely missed a baker's wagon and swung wide, ignoring the curses the man yelled after him.

Lustig's wagon was moving quickly. "You'd better move on him as fast as you can," Della warned through the earpiece. "There aren't as many streetlights in the direction he's heading. I'll lose him soon."

"Got it," Jacob muttered. He sped up and kept the bike steady with his left hand while he drew his shotgun from over his shoulder and chambered a round. He fired, and his shot hit the right rear wheel of the fleeing wagon, breaking it at the axel. A second later, Mitch's rifle sounded, two shots in quick succession that broke through the tongue of the wagon, sending its horse fleeing in panic as the wagon careened to one side.

Lustig had his revolver out, though Jacob doubted the monster hunter had time to replace the blanks with bullets. "What's the meaning of this!" he blustered.

Mitch flashed his DSI badge. "Government agents. Stay where you are and keep your hands where I can see them," coming around to level his rifle at the two men in the driver's seat. Jacob went to the back of the wagon.

"Stay clear of there!" Lustig yelled. "There's a dangerous beast inside!"

Jacob chambered another round and slammed the bolt open. He waited, just in case Lustig's creature was still alive, then moved to angle the headlamp of his steambike into the rear of the delivery wagon. The monster lay still, a lump of dark, shaggy fur.

"Drag it into the light," Mitch commanded with a twitch of his rifle barrel.

"You can't just—"

"Or we can wait until the police get here and see what they think of your monster," Jacob replied.

Cursing, Lustig and his partner climbed down. The monk's cowl fell back, exposing Shurlman's face. Lustig and Shurlman hauled the monster to the back of the wagon, and the body made a scraping noise against the wooden floorboards.

Mitch kept his rifle trained on the two men and motioned for them to step aside as Jacob approached the beast. He prodded the body with the barrel of his shotgun and heard a dull thud as the poke hit something hard beneath the fur. Jacob took a knife from his belt and knelt next to the creature.

"Hey! That's my property!" Lustig protested.

Jacob ignored him and cut a long gash in the fur. He pulled the pelt aside. "Metal," he reported. He shifted to examine the hump on the creature's back and cut through the fur to expose a large metal key. "Well, well," Jacob said.

The clatter of hooves made Jacob turn, and he leveled his shotgun at the street behind him before he realized it was a DSI paddywagon. The back door swung open and more agents jumped out. "Take these two in for questioning," Mitch said, indicating Lustig and Shurlman. "We've got them on fraud, probably more. There's a body in the back, too."

Jacob climbed down and let the four DSI men do their work, keeping an eye out should the police show up. This late at night, the warehouse district was nearly deserted, but he still had no desire to answer uncomfortable questions.

"So?" Mitch asked as Jacob joined him.

"Mechanical, like we thought," Jacob replied. "Looks like the Dollmaker is back in business."

2 / GRAVE VOICES | MISSING BODIES

"Been worse than usual, lately." Mr. Henry, the old gravedigger, leaned on his shovel and gave a nod toward the rows of markers in Allegheny Cemetery. Jacob could see where a dozen or so graves had recently been disturbed. Those with mortsafes had managed to trap their desperate undead residents in the ground, instead of keeping grave robbers out. Rotting corpses lay beneath the cage of iron bars sunk into the ground over the graves. Most still twitched, or groaned unsettlingly.

"How about the ones that didn't dig themselves out?" Mitch asked, pointing to a few graves that definitely appeared to have been opened by the living.

The gravedigger shrugged. "No idea. Seems kinda strange, picking odd ones here and there. But they're gone," he added. "Took the whole casket. Didn't make a mess of things."

"The graves that were dug out by someone else, did they have anything in common?" Mitch pressed.

Again, Mr. Henry shrugged. "Not that I can see. Weren't related, if that's what you mean. Have a look for yourself at the headstones. I've got to clean all this up." He sighed. "Old Mr. Kemmer is up for the third time in as many weeks."

Mitch thanked the Mr. Henry, then he and Jacob began to walk across the cemetery's rolling hills. Jacob wrinkled his nose. The stench of decay was unmistakable. "Got a theory?"

Mitch shook his head. "Nothing yet. Just observations. I'm willing to bet we've got two different forces at work here, and we don't know enough to guess whether they're working together or not."

Jacob nodded. "Grave robbers, and a necromancer."

Mitch grimaced, catching a particularly strong whiff of sun-warmed zombie. "Necromancer, dark warlock, or maybe something else—I heard the Romanians were working on an energy projector that could force the dead to speak. We don't know what we're up against, and that drives me crazy."

"Why would a necromancer call up zombies that couldn't get out of their graves?" Jacob mused. "Not very effective. Alerts everyone to the fact that you're around, but doesn't get you any evil undead minions."

"And if you can make the dead dig themselves out, why send people to rob the grave?" Mitch asked as they walked up to one of the plots that had been disturbed. "Seems more risky to send people in to do the work if you can just get the dead to bring themselves to wherever you are."

"Thomas Bakewell," Jacob said, looking at the tombstone. "Not a recent death. Eighteen sixty-six. Can't imagine he was in great shape after all that time."

Mitch frowned. "And he's one the grave robbers took. Maybe that's why. Maybe he couldn't get out by himself. But why him?" Mitch took a small tablet out of his coat pocket and began to make notes as they surveyed the damaged graves. Jacob read off the names and dates of death, and Mitch wrote them down, as well as any unique epitaphs. They cataloged six more sites where the departed had dug themselves out, as well as a mausoleum where the zombie had tried and failed to bend the iron door to escape.

"Bernard Lauth," Jacob said as they came up to another robbed grave. "He's pretty recent. Eighteen ninety-four."

"That name rings a bell, but I can't place it," Mitch said. "Anyone else?" Their inventory of the newly undead had taken them deep into the large cemetery, toward a large stretch of forest that ran along one side of the cemetery.

"One more—another robbery," Jacob said. "George Ferris. He's also recent—just two years ago."

"Ferris? Like the Ferris wheel?" Mitch asked.

Jacob shrugged. "Maybe. Adam Farber would know."

Mitch started to answer when a low, feral growl came from the darkness of the trees. He and Jacob exchanged a warning glance, and both agents drew their guns at the same time, leveling them at the stretch of forest. In the next breath, a dozen rotting corpses broke from the tree line, heading straight for them. Some of the zombies were well-preserved. They moved the fastest. Others were ravaged by time or poor embalming, cheeks sunken, eyes hollow, clothing from decades in the past. They shambled, as if whatever propelled them could barely make their badly decomposed bodies function.

Mitch and Jacob opened fire. Jacob's shotgun caught the well-dressed corpse of an old man full in the chest, blowing a hole through his rib cage. The zombie fell back a step from the blast, then kept on coming.

Mitch's rifle shot hit another zombie in the middle of its forehead, taking off half of its skull when the bullet exited. The zombie fell to the ground, quivering.

Jacob's next shot caught a zombie square in the pelvis, blowing the legs off the rotting body. Mitch shot again, going for the kneecaps of a fourth, walking corpse. None of the downed creatures stopped moving, quivering where they lay or trying to claw their way forward on the lawn.

"This isn't working too well!" Jacob yelled above the gunfire.

"Beats hand-to-hand combat," Mitch snapped back, and his rifle shot dropped a fifth zombie as Jacob's shotgun blast felled the sixth.

"They might not be destroyed, but they're not going anywhere fast," Jacob said, watching the twitching zombies and keeping an eye on the tree line in case any more walking corpses emerged. He spared a glance toward Mitch.

"I hope you've got a theory about this."

For once, Mitch lacked a sarcastic reply. "I've got nothing," he admitted. "We're going to have to pull in Renate Thalberg as well as Adam Farber and do some research."

"Uh oh," Jacob said. "Trouble."

Mitch raised his rifle, only to see Mr. Henry striding across the lawn scowling. "Stay away from the forest!" Mr. Henry shouted. "You'll only make them angry."

Jacob stared at the gravedigger. "You mean the zombies? You know about them?"

Mr. Henry rolled his eyes and spat to one side. "Of course I know about them. Hard to miss, aren't they? We've got a truce, sort of. They keep the rats away, and I don't go hunting them."

Jacob cleared his throat. "Are there always zombies in the forest? And you didn't think to mention this when we asked about the graves?"

Mr. Henry looked at him as if he had gone daft. "Lately, yes. They don't usually last long before they fall apart, but then something brings up a new batch, and it starts all over again."

"Has this been going on long?" Mitch asked, frowning.

"It's always been an on-and-off thing," Mr. Henry replied. "Lately, last month or so, more than usual." He swore. "Gets so that I can hardly bury the new dead before they pop up again. Wastes my time burying them two or three times. I don't get paid for that."

Mitch and Jacob exchanged glances. "Grave robbers, zombies, and mechanical monsters," Mitch said. "There's got to be a connection. And we'd better find it soon, before things really get out of hand."

————

"It's a pretty interesting mechanism, once you clean away all the fur and whatnot." Adam Farber looked down at the clockwork remains of Lustig's monster, which lay partially disassembled on a worktable in his basement laboratory at Tesla-Westinghouse's headquarters. The skinny inventor wore a stained lab coat. His wire glasses were askew and slightly smudged, and his sandy brown hair was falling into his eyes.

"What's so interesting about it?" Jacob asked. He and Mitch had come straight to Tesla-Westinghouse's "Castle" in Wilmerding after they left Allegheny Cemetery.

Adam pointed toward the monster's mechanical innards. "It's really a big wind-up doll, but more sophisticated than any toy I've seen. On the other hand, it's not nearly as complicated as the *werkmen* I've built." He gave a nod toward Lars, a brass and chrome metal man wearing the uniform of an elevator operator.

"Any idea who made it?" Jacob asked. He and Mitch had their suspicions, but he wasn't ready to rule anything out, not yet.

Adam grabbed a cup of coffee from the workbench and finished it off. He set the empty cup off to the side with half a dozen others. "I suspect any good clockmaker could put something like this together. It can move its legs to walk, raise and lower its arms, and swing them from side to side, and shake. Not all that different from a toy that hops or dances. But it's got an Edison cylinder for a voice. That's odd."

"That's how it was able to roar?" Mitch asked, leaning closer for a better look. With the old fur pelts stripped away, the body of the monster was plain and crude, a metal barrel with jointed cylinders for its arms and legs and a round metal head with a clockwork jaw. The inside of the chest area was full of gears and pulleys, along with a dark waxy object set in a metal case.

"So someone recorded that noise, and stored it on a cylinder," Jacob said, looking more closely. Edison cylinders were pretty new and rather remarkable. A machine etched markings onto a hard wax tube to record sounds, and another machine played them back. The machines were touchy and expensive, but the involvement of genius inventor Thomas Edison made their ultimate success likely.

Adam nodded. "Yeah. Easier said than done, especially in a mechanism that moves and jostles so much. But making 'monsters' like this would be pretty expensive. I don't think you've got to worry about someone unleashing hordes of these things on an unsuspecting population."

Jacob sighed. "Lustig didn't need hordes of them. Just one, enough for him to get paid plenty of money to 'kill' the beast and for his accomplice to sell worthless amulets and monster repellent."

A smile quirked at the corner of Adam's mouth. "Really? Monster repellent?" he chuckled. "Mr. Barnum was right about there being one born every minute." He poked a tool into the mechanical man's chest. The creature's left arm came up fast, hitting Adam in the chest hard enough to knock the thin inventor onto his ass and slide him across the floor.

"I need to study some of the connections further," Adam said, dusting himself off as he climbed to his feet. "The gears are primitive but intriguing. That was amazing!" Jacob had never seen Adam happier than when he was either taking something apart or building a new contraption. Right now, Adam's face beamed with the joy of a puzzle to unravel.

"So you don't see a threat in something like this, a way it could be used as a weapon?" Mitch pressed.

Adam frowned, taking another close look at the dismantled clock-work mechanism. "It would be a lot cheaper to put men in armor on the front line than a row of these," he said, shaking his head. "They're time-consuming to make, limited in ability, easily broken, and difficult to transport. And expensive as hell to construct."

"We interrogated Lustig and Shurlman," Jacob said. "They admitted that the other part of their scheme was creating a distraction for break-ins. But that's where it goes a little murky. They claimed the thefts were for a single buyer, but they said they never met him in person. Everything was set up with messages carried back and forth by a mechanical carrier pigeon."

Adam crossed his arms and frowned. "I really hate it when the bad guys steal the concepts from my inventions. I gave the Department clockwork carrier pigeons ages ago!" He paused. "You're afraid the Dollmaker is back, aren't you?"

Mitch and Jacob exchanged a look. "What do you know about the Dollmaker? That's supposed to be classified."

Adam snorted. "Yeah, and so's everything in this lab. But people talk. Word gets out. Inventors like to be acknowledged, especially the evil genius kind like Dollmaker." He shrugged. "Phineas Sheldon used to make the rounds of all the engineering and academic meetings," he went on. "Had some good ideas, but they weren't quite as brilliant as he thought they were, and he got annoyed when we didn't elect him leader-of-everything. He was always fascinated with artificial life. Taxidermy. Dioramas. Dolls, mechanical men, clockworks. I wouldn't be surprised to find out he veered into resurrectionist territory."

"Did he have any magic?" Jacob asked.

Adam poured himself another cup of coffee from the pot on a nearby Bunsen burner and gulped it down black. "Magic? Not to my knowledge. He was more of a watchmaker with dreams of creating a really important invention and retiring rich." He sighed. "I think that's what rankled the other inventors and scientists about him. It was never science or learning for the sheer thrill of discovery. With Sheldon, it was always first and foremost about the money."

Mitch and Jacob thanked Adam, promised him first chance to examine any more unusual equipment they found, and Lars, the *werkman*, escorted them out. Hans, their coachman, was waiting by their carriage.

"Is Mr. Farber doing well?" Hans asked. "I do hope you passed along my best wishes to him." Hans kept his hat pulled down low, and his collar turned up to hide his features from curious passers-by, but up close, Jacob could see where metal parts had replaced flesh and bone too damaged to repair. Adam's inventions had enabled Hans to return to work after a catastrophic accident, and Hans remained deeply grateful.

"Fine and dandy," Mitch said as he and Jacob climbed into the coach.

"There has been a slight change of plans," Hans said, leaning into the coach. He lightly tapped a hidden earpiece that enabled him to receive telegraph messages. "Agent Kennedy insisted I was to bring you to the Conservatory. She says it's of utmost importance."

Jacob chuckled. "I have a feeling Della's been doing some legwork of her own while we're off shooting zombies and picking Adam's brain."

Mitch nodded. "Let's hope she's found a few more answers. I have a feeling there's a lot more going on than a couple of third-rate hucksters and their mechanical monster."

Hans drove the carriage to Oakland, where the soaring white metal spires and arches of the ornate Phipps Conservatory gleamed in the sun. The metal and glass conservatory was a marvel, an elaborate greenhouse displaying exotic plants and rare flowers from all over the world.

"Did Agent Kennedy say where we should look for her?" Mitch asked as he and Jacob alighted.

Hans held the door for them. "No, sir. She said they would find you."

Mitch and Jacob exchanged a glance as they headed into the man-made jungle. Only a few steps into the humid atmosphere of the artificial rainforest made Jacob tug at his stiff, starched shirt collar. Mitch was trying to act as if the heat didn't bother him, but sweat beaded on his forehead.

"I don't much care for hide and seek," Mitch grumbled. Jacob shared his sentiment. The thick vegetation made the Conservatory an ideal hiding place, and like Mitch, he kept a hand near his gun, while trying not to alarm the ladies and gentlemen out for a stroll amid the pretty flowers.

"Who's hiding?" Della stepped out from behind one of the huge philodendrons. She wore a blue traveling suit with a short jacket that nipped in at the waist, accentuating both her slim figure and the skirt's moderate bustle in the back.

"You decided we needed an outing? Why did you have us meet you here?" Mitch asked, a touch of annoyance in his tone.

"She didn't. I did." The second voice seemed to come from thin air. Then the air shimmered and the illusion faded. A slim, almost ethereal woman with light brown hair stood near Della, a hint of a smile on her finely-featured face. Renate Thalberg, absinthe witch, seer, and very well-connected member of New Pittsburgh's powerful, hidden magic community.

"Hello, Renate," Mitch said, as he and Jacob gave a nod in greeting to each of the women. "To what do we owe the honor?"

"I wanted to warn you," Renate replied. "You haven't found all the monsters. Andreas and I are doing what we can, but there's something big going on, and I think it's got a foot in both our worlds."

They walked together through the winding paths of the conservatory. Plants overhung their raised beds, dripping tendrils, and runners into the aisles that brushed the tops of their heads. Lush greens, vibrantly colored flowers, rare orchids, and plump succulents vied for space, mounding in their rich soil beds. Mitch walked with Renate, while Jacob and Della walked behind, guns hidden by close at hand, on guard. The air was heavy with the perfume of dozens of tropical flowers, the smell of fresh vegetation, and the scent of loam and moist earth.

"What do you mean?" Della asked. "What other monsters?"

"Man-like creatures have been spotted in several neighborhoods," Renate replied, keeping her voice low. "Not living men. They have the form of men, but they're not normal. Faster, stronger. So far, we haven't been able to capture them."

"Automatons?" Mitch speculated. "Like the *werkmen* the Department uses sometimes?"

Renate shook her head. "No. There's a taint of magic to them, but so far, they've gotten away before we could capture one. The descriptions vary. Some say the figures have no faces, and others say they looked like giant puppets."

Jacob sighed. "That last part sounds like the Dollmaker. But why? What do the 'monsters' do?"

Renate glanced around to assure herself that they were alone. Jacob suspected she had magical means of making certain they were not overheard as well. "Several different things, if the stories we've heard are true," she said. "Sometimes, they created a distraction while a nearby place was robbed. In other cases, they chased people. Some of the people got away; some didn't."

"Lustig and his assistant are in custody," Mitch said. "His monsters won't be terrorizing anyone anymore."

Renate shook her head. "He was the least of the problems. Just another con man. These other monsters took advantage of the distraction Lustig presented. We need to work together on this. Whoever's out there is using the supernatural *and* the scientific. Bad magic, and powerful technology—it's a dangerous mix."

The conservatory changed the themes of its displays throughout the year, hoping to entice patrons to visit for each new exhibit. As they walked along the paths, Jacob noted the current "Town and Country" theme, complete with topiaries made in the shape of furnishings or farm animals, and small tableaus of rural and city life.

Figures of people made from terracotta were posed in a variety of settings. Clay figures of a man and woman sat at a table with teacups in the midst of a rose garden, while a few steps away, two more clay mannequins looked like they were out for a hike among a display of wildflowers. Three figures dressed for safari were situated in a room full of jungle plants, while another three of the mannequins in the desert room appeared to be gold miners amid the cactus. The terracotta people looked a bit like garden pots put together to make rough human forms, and Jacob could not decide whether they were whimsical or unnerving.

"Can you trace the magic back to the one who cast it?' Jacob asked, returning his attention to the conversation.

Renate sighed. "It's rarely as simple as that. Not when the one doing the magic is good at the Craft. Whoever it is has power, and the residue stinks of death magic."

"A necromancer?" Mitch asked. Quickly, he filled Renate in on the stolen bodies and animated corpses. She listened quietly, her expression concerned.

"There are different kinds of death magic," Renate replied. "Not all who practice it are necromancers. But from what you tell me, the most likely suspect would be Sandor Kasmir." She paused. "That's who I'd bet is either behind it or has a hand in the mess somewhere. He has some skill with necromancy, but he is fascinated with technology. He is sure that he can find the intersection of science and magic."

"I've already sent word to Father Matija and the *Logonje* about the restless dead," Della added. "To see if they can help keep the corpses from being tormented by whatever's making them rise." The *Logonje* were a secret group of Orthodox Polish priests who worked outside of normal church channels and used relics and holy objects to fight supernatural threats. Matija and his priests occasionally crossed paths with the Department.

"Lustig's beast was completely mechanical," Jacob said. "But those zombies at the cemetery certainly weren't. Could the Dollmaker and Kasmir be working separately, toward different goals?"

Conversation halted as a group of older ladies who looked like they were from a Shadyside garden club maneuvered past. Only a handful of other visitors walked the Conservatory paths at this hour.

Renate frowned. "Maybe," she replied with the garden ladies were out of earshot. "But there's another piece you need to know. Several women with strong clairvoyant abilities have gone missing in the last two weeks."

"Witches?" Mitch asked quietly.

Renate shook her head. "No. Mediums. People with a genuine talent for speaking with the spirits of the dead."

"That makes Kasmir a more likely suspect," Della said.

"Did the mediums have anything else in common, other than their talent?"

Renate shrugged. "Not that Andreas and I have been able to figure out. But the magical community is frightened. There are rumors that the police are behind the disappearances, or even the Department."

"You know that isn't true," Mitch retorted.

Renate fixed him with a look. "What I know doesn't matter. It's what the others think. If I'd have believed DSI had anything to do with it, I wouldn't have agreed to meet you here."

Just then, an odd clanking sound made them stop in their tracks. Della and Jacob drew their guns, and Mitch went for his revolver. Renate went very still, her face composed, eyes distant, and Jacob knew she was calling on her magic to look for the source of the noise.

More clanking, and the sound of a footstep on gravel. Jacob and Della turned so that they were back to back with Mitch and Renate. No other visitors were in sight. They had a clear view of the longest path in the Conservatory, and there was no one visible.

The clay man from the garden tea tableau burst from among the ferns and palm trees, arms outstretched, his manner unmistakably menacing.

Mitch's quick reflexes put a hole through the clay man's chest. The revolver bullet tore through the figure's clothing and shattered the terra cotta, revealing an empty oval torso. The mannequin kept on coming, undeterred by the gaping opening in his clay body.

"How the hell is that possible?" Mitch grated.

Another figure lumbered through the center display of plantings. This time, it was the woman from the tea scene. Della fired, shattering the clay head, and the rest of the pottery body clattered to the ground and lay still. A moment later, Mitch's shot exploded the man-figure's clay skull, and the creature fell to the path with the sound of breaking crockery.

"Shoot for the head!" Della snapped, angling for another shot as two more of the clay figures pushed past fronds and large, broad leaves, their flat terracotta feet smashing flowers and plantings. The three miners from the cactus exhibit closed from one side, while the jungle explorers headed toward them from the other direction.

One window of the glass-walled Conservatory smashed into fragments as two more creatures joined the attack from elsewhere in the large greenhouse. Mitch fired at the safari figures, dropping each with a bullet to the head. Della turned her fire on the newcomers that were crashing their way through the glass wall, while Jacob took careful aim and shot down the clay figures dressed like miners.

From the sound of it, more of the figures were rousing from where they had been displayed elsewhere in the Conservatory. On the other side of the central row of thick plantings, screams rose from the garden ladies.

"Renate! Can you stop them?" Mitch asked.

Renate's face was taut with concentration. "It's magic, but not necromancy. Something very strange. I can't get a fix on where the person is who is making them move. It's as if the magic's been activated and now they're moving on their own."

"Where's the puppeteer?" Jacob asked, as his shotgun blew the head and shoulders off a clay figure dressed as a gardener.

"That's what I'm saying," Renate snapped. "They're animating themselves!" She murmured under her breath, her hands tracing patterns in the air. A shimmering veil of light, like a curtain made of fireflies, appeared and surrounded the four of them.

"I can hold them off, but not forever," Renate warned.

"Can we fire through whatever that is, or will the bullets bounce back?" Della questioned.

"You can fire through. But they can't get in," Renate assured her.

"Doesn't help the other people in the greenhouse," Jacob said. "We're going to need to take these things down." He pumped his shotgun and fired, smashing the head of another crockery monster in a garden party dress and wide-brimmed ladies' hat.

Renate's curtain of golden light kept the creatures at bay. Mitch, Della, and Jacob fired again and again, until all of the terra cotta attackers lay shattered on the floor. By that time, sirens sounded in the distance. Several moments passed, and no new monsters emerged from the vegetation. Renate dropped the protective warding, though they all stood on alert.

Renate knelt next to one of the clay creatures. She let her right hand hover over its empty pottery chest. The thing's head was shattered, but Renate frowned and withdrew a pair of tweezers from her purse, then reached among the shards to pick up a ripped bit of parchment covered with strange writing.

"Not puppets," she said, eyes widening as she realized what the paper meant. "They're golems."

"Is that a kind of doll?" Mitch asked. Jacob kept watch in one direction as Della remained on alert facing the opposite way, as much to fend off curious onlookers or keep Conservatory staff away as to avoid another attack.

"Not the usual kind," Renate replied, tucking the paper into a silk drawstring pouch in her purse. Della pointed to several more of the paper slips amid the wreckage, and Renate gathered them as well. "It's old magic. The spell that animates the golem is placed in its mouth. The creature has its instructions and enough magic to make it move, and it carries out its orders without the person controlling it needing to be nearby."

"Fill us in later. You'd better get clear," Mitch said to Renate. "We've got badges." Renate gave a curt nod and headed outside the building through the shattered glass windows. Footsteps were rushing toward them, and across the divide of trees and vegetation, Jacob could hear the garden club ladies recounting their experience to the police.

"No one could have expected that we would come here," Della said, kicking at the bits of crockery with the toe of her shoe. "So the monsters weren't meant for us. Then why were they here? Who were they after?"

Mitch looked down at the broken pottery creatures. "Or were they just to supposed to cause a scare?" he asked. "The way Lustig's 'monsters' frightened people out of their money?"

"We'd better find out before more of those things show up," Jacob warned. "And we also need to discover what happened to those missing mediums. Someone's got a plan behind all this, and we need to shut that person down—permanently."

"You're certain you can speak to my brother's spirit?" The woman spoke softly, eyes lowered. Her somber dove gray traveling suit suggested that her loss was still fresh. A solidly-built man watched her solicitously, as if she might collapse.

"I'm sure of it." Clare Monihan was a thin woman with sharp features and intelligent eyes. Her red hair was pulled up into a prim bun atop her head, accenting her angular features to give her a bird-like profile. "I've had the gift of 'Sight' all my life, and I assure you, I can carry your message to the Beyond and bring back a reply." She paused. "What was his name?"

"Simon," Della said, her voice just shy of a sob as she acted her part. "Simon Markham. We lost him so young—"

Della Kennedy staggered as if overcome by grief. Mitch Storm took her arm to steady her. Della gave a wan smile of thanks. "What will it require?" Della asked.

"I need to prepare, but you've come at a good time of day to speak to the spirits," Clare replied. "If you're willing to wait for a few minutes in the parlor, I can get the séance room ready, and we can call to your brother tonight. Would you like that?" Clare's voice was comforting, her manner direct, and her gray eyes shrewd.

"Oh, yes." Della fingered a necklace made of dark, woven hair, a piece of funeral jewelry made from a lock taken from the dearly departed. "It's just that... I miss him so much." Once again, she might have swooned if her companion had not steadied her and guided her to one of the flocked velvet chairs in the darkened, comfortable parlor.

Clare nodded. "Well then, I'll get everything ready. Please, make yourselves at home. There's a pot of water and everything you need for tea on the table. I'll come for you when we're ready to begin."

Della reached out and took Clare's hand in both of her own. "Thank you," she said earnestly. "You can't imagine what this means to me."

Clare gave a sympathetic smile. "I've lost loved ones myself, Miss Kennedy," she said reassuringly. "And so have my clients. I am sorry for your grief, and I hope I can make things a bit better." With that, she left them, closing the door to the hallway behind her.

A moment after the door latched, Della was on her knees, searching beneath the chair and the fainting couch next to it for hidden wires or gadgets. "Watch the door!" she hissed. Mitch didn't need to be told. He already stood where he could block the door from opening.

"Hurry. We don't know how long we've got until she comes back," Mitch warned in a whisper.

Della checked the undersides of the other furnishings. "Nothing," she muttered after a few moments. The parlor was a shabby version of the most popular styles: dark woods, claret velvet upholsteries, and gas lamps with painted globes or faceted crystal dangles. Cheap paintings of storms at sea or moody landscapes hung on the walls. Della opened the drawers on the mahogany writing desk, smoothed her hands down the heavy velvet draperies, and pulled the large framed mirror away from the wall far enough to get a look behind it.

Finally, after she had even looked under the slightly threadbare rug in the center of the room, Della put her hands on her hips and glared around the room, as if it were a child keeping secrets from her. "Nothing," she repeated in an exasperated whisper. "No wires. No cameras or equipment. No switches or peepholes. If she's a fake, there's nothing to prove it here."

Mitch grinned. "It was worth it just to watch you 'swoon,'" he teased. "Did you have to practice in the mirror to get it right?"

Della glared at him. Nothing about Della's stance suggested the likelihood of swooning, and Mitch was sure she had one gun and maybe more hidden in her long skirt. Mitch and Della had worked together on a number of cases. This wasn't the first time they had posed as a couple.

Just as Della was about to reply, the white porcelain doorknob rattled. Immediately, Della slumped into a chair looking beside herself with grief, and Mitch came to stand behind her attentively.

"Everything is prepared," Clare announced. "Please, follow me."

Clare led the way down a hallway lined with framed photographs of dour ancestors. Their bleak eyes seemed to follow Mitch and Della down the corridor.

"Here," Clare said, ushering them into a room that was decorated in a fashion Mitch could only describe as gypsy-Victorian. Ruby-colored fringed lampshades cast the room in an unsettling crimson glow. Swags of fabric were draped to each corner from a central point in the ceiling, suggesting a Roma fortune-teller's tent. The smell of sage and sandalwood rose from burning incense. Pillar candles in a variety of sizes and heights flickered all around the room, and the gas lamps were turned down low. A round mahogany table sat in the center of the room, and three chairs waited for them.

"Please, be seated." Clare had changed clothes. Instead of the waistcoat and bustle ensemble she had worn to welcome Mitch and Della, she now wore a flowing silk gown. It reminded Mitch of the Voodoo mambos in New Orleans, though Clare did not appear to share their heritage.

Mitch pulled out the chair for Della and took his seat, making sure their backs were to the wall. That left Clare with her back to the door. "Take my hand," Clare said, offering each of them her outstretched palms.

Mitch and Della complied, and Clare raised her face to the ceiling and closed her eyes. "Spirits from beyond," she intoned. "Hear me."

As soon as Clare's eyes were closed, Mitch and Della dropped their clasped hands and readied their guns on their laps, just in case.

"Spirits! I call to you! Give me a signal that you hear me!"

Although he was expecting it, Mitch still struggled not to flinch as the peal of a bell rang mournfully out of nowhere. Such gimmicks were common with the sham mediums the Department often pursued for fraud. Mitch suspected that a search of this room for wires and tricks might turn up very different results than they found in the parlor.

"Thank you, gracious spirits," Clare said, eyes still closed. Her body swayed back and forth, and her expression suggested that she was caught up in a rapturous trance.

"Kind spirits," Clare entreated. "Send to me Simon Markham. His beloved sister wishes to know that his spirit is content." Mitch heard strains of distant music, distorted and faint.

"Do you hear that?" Clare asked, still not opening her eyes. "The spirits acknowledge our request. Oh, we are very lucky today!" She moved in her chair, her head turning as if addressing an invisible audience on the other side of the room. "Spirit guides! My trusted friends! If Simon Markham is among you, send me a sign!"

Since Clare wasn't looking, Mitch rolled his eyes at the dramatic presentation. Della gave him a reproving glare. They were on high alert, watching for trouble.

Three hard taps, as if someone were knocking on a door, sounded from somewhere in the room. Mitch reined in his impatience. So far, everything he had seen was unremarkable as fake clairvoyants went. Mitch had seen more than his share of hucksters willing to cheat the bereaved out of their money for a chance to say a last goodbye to a loved one.

"Yes! Yes!" Clare cried out. "The spirit of Simon Markham is present. Simon, use me as your vessel to speak to your loving sister."

A scratching noise drew Mitch's attention. He frowned and glanced at Della, who gave a nod to indicate that she had also heard the sound.

"I am Simon Markham." The voice that came from Clare's mouth was not her own. It was deeper and masculine, and something about it sent a cold chill down Mitch's back. Della's eyes widened. "And I don't have a sister."

The door behind Clare burst open. A man's rotting corpse stood in the doorway, and it lurched toward Clare, arms outstretched. Mitch's sharpshooter training kicked in, and he sent a bullet past Clare's head close enough to take off a few stray hairs that stuck out from her bun. The bullet caught the zombie square in the forehead and blew away a chunk of its skull. With an unnerving death rattle, the corpse collapsed.

"You're not going to make me disappear like the other ones!" Clare yelped. She tried to raise a derringer of her own against Mitch, but Della upended the table against Clare just as Clare's eyes took on the unfocused look of a trance once again. From her expression, this possession was entirely unwanted.

"I won't let you hurt my friends." Simon's voice came from Clare's lips, as the medium struggled against the influence of the spirit she had summoned. Della was already on her feet, with a gun pointed at Clare. Mitch circled, keeping his Peacemaker trained on the rotting zombie on the floor.

Clare looked as if she were fighting an internal struggle between her own desires and the wishes of Simon Markham's spirit. Simon was winning, at least for the moment, and Della lost no time cuffing Clare to the chair, fearing that Simon would lose his influence at any second.

"Thank you, Simon," Della said. The slight tremor in her voice told Mitch that Della was as freaked out as he was that Clare had actually been able to summon the spirit of their late fellow agent, a brother in arms if not a brother in fact.

"Not much has changed, I see," Simon replied, sounding wistful. "I miss you and Jacob," he said to Della, "and sometimes, even Mitch." Clare's mouth twitched in a smile that was pure Simon. "I have to go now. Take care." With that, Clare slumped forward, completely herself again. And was she ever angry.

"How dare you!" Clare struggled against the cuffs. "I am not going to go quietly!"

Mitch knelt next to the corpse on the floor. He was trying not to breathe since the body was old and decomposition was far along. "This corpse has been shot before—recently. As in, since he's been dead."

Clare sighed. "Sometimes, I don't know my own strength."

Della seemed to have recovered from the shock of actually encountering Simon's spirit. "So you're the real thing?" she asked, giving Clare and appraising look. "If that's true, why all the falderol?" Della gestured to indicate the gypsy trappings and nudged the wires that were apparent on the underside of the overturned séance table.

"Yes, I actually can summon spirits from Beyond," Clare said, glaring at Della. "Occasionally, I get more than I bargain for," she added with a nod toward the corpse. "As for the decorations and the spooky effects, it's the show customers want for their money. I can call up grandma's ghost and pass on a legitimate message, but without the scary extras, my clients don't believe it's real." She gave an ironic half-smile. "They think the real stuff is fake, unless I give them a good performance."

"Who's the stiff?" Mitch looked up, still keeping his gun trained on the sorry-looking corpse in case it moved again.

"I don't know," Clare admitted. "He was buried in the basement. This is the third time he's been shot. He keeps popping back up."

Mitch raised an eyebrow. Clare grimaced. "I really am a medium. I've been able to see and talk to ghosts for as long as I can remember, and in the last couple of years, I learned to channel their spirits. But if I focus too hard, I guess I send out too strong a signal or something, and they show up in person."

"What's this about being afraid we were going to make you disappear?" Della asked. She kept her gun on Clare, but Mitch could tell from Della's posture that his fellow agent did not anticipate a threat.

"Who are you two—really?" Clare countered. "I've told you too much already."

Mitch reached into his pocket and pulled out a badge. "Agent Mitch Storm and Agent Della Kennedy, Department of Supernatural Investigation," he said. "We got called in after there were reports of body snatchers operating near here."

Clare rolled her eyes. "If you're talking about the problem last week over at Allegheny Cemetery, it wasn't on purpose. I didn't realize my client's house was so close to the graveyard."

"So—who did you think we were and why did you think we were after you?" Della prodded.

"Three other mediums have disappeared in the last couple of weeks," Clare replied. "We all know each other, whether we're legit or frauds. And right now, we're scared."

"If you thought we might hurt you, why did you agree to meet with us?" Mitch asked. He poked the dead body with his gun, but it did not move. Warily, he rose to his feet and moved away, still keeping his eye on the corpse. *If she could raise it once, she can probably do it again,* Mitch thought. *I don't need to be clobbered by a dead man.*

"A girl's gotta eat," Clare said with a sigh. "This is how I make my living. And I thought you seemed okay, until the ghost ratted on you. Who was Simon, anyhow?"

"Simon was a fellow agent," Della said. "And a good friend. We lost him in the line of duty last year." Mitch could see the pain that lingered in Della's eyes.

"Do you know who might be behind the disappearances?" Mitch asked.

Clare shook her head. "No. But whoever it is only takes the people with real talent, the ones who can actually talk to the spirits. So far, none of the frauds have been kidnapped."

"And there've been no demands for ransom, no notes—nothing?" Della frowned, thinking through what Clare had told them.

"Not that I've heard," Clare said. "Look, if you're government agents, do you have one of those black airships? Can you protect me?"

Mitch gave a crooked grin. "Yes, and yes," he said. Then he turned to look at the corpse and sighed. "But first, we need to drag this poor guy back to the basement."

4 / GRAVE VOICES | HAUNTED DOLLHOUSE

LIFE-SIZE DOLLS, like wooden corpses, littered the workroom. Agent Jacob Drangosavich moved slowly, gun ready, careful not to make a sound. His partners Mitch and Della had gone after another quarry this evening, and Jacob went to check out a site the Department's sources said had been a hotbed of strange energy fluctuations. The whole place gave him the creeps.

The assembly area was in the back of an old shop on the south side of New Pittsburgh. Its display windows were filled with dolls of every size—wooden marionettes, porcelain babies that looked eerily real, wind-up mechanical figures, and hand-sewn ragdolls. Some of the life-size dolls were made for dry goods shop mannequins or for theater props. Rumor had it that poppets of another sort were sold from beneath the counter, custom-made to be the likeness of a living person, cursed or blessed to suit the desires of the purchaser.

Most educated people in New Pittsburgh would have scoffed at the idea of a Voodoo doll. Jacob's years working with the Department of Supernatural Investigation assured him there were many strange things that modern science could not fully understand. Still, science could help a great deal. Jacob was happy to have brought along several new gadgets from Adam Farber, genius inventor and *wunderkind*, firmly believing that in a fair fight, technology could kick magic's ass. Unfortunately, fights were seldom fair.

The workroom was dimly lit, just the glow of the street gaslights through the dirty windows. Weighing the danger of being ambushed in the dark against the risk of discovery, Jacob erred on the side of caution and lit one of the overhead kerosene lamps, turning the wick down low. Jacob consulted the metal box in his left hand, one of Farber's latest creations. The box was an EMF reader, able to sense the presence of the electromagnetic energy of ghosts. Jacob didn't pretend to understand how it worked, but he had seen enough of Farber's wild inventions to trust its readings. And right now, the dial on the "ghost-finder" box was pegging the meter. Another piece of equipment also hung from his belt. Farber called it a "Maxwell box," and it could attract or repel ghosts using something to do with energy frequency. Jacob hoped he wasn't going to need to use it, doubly so since he hadn't yet tried out the new gadget.

This isn't good. Not good at all. Jacob muttered a curse in his native Croatian, and was glad he had worn his saint's medal. He inched forward. The dolls were just shadows and silhouettes in the dim light, far too much like people. It would be so easy for someone to hide among them. The faint glow of the gaslight glimmered on the glass eyes of the dolls as he passed among them. He glanced down at the meter again, saw the needle fluctuating like a tree in a gale-force wind, and repressed a shiver.

Headquarters thought the Dollmaker might be smuggling stolen inventions from Europe in the crates of dolls and materials. Mitch and Della wondered if the dolls hid other contraband, like plans for the kind of gee-whiz inventions Farber dreamed up, contraptions that could change the balance of power in a fight—or in a war. Whatever the Dollmaker was up to, Jacob was certain it wasn't child's play.

He heard something creak, saw the shadows shift, and bit back a yelp as one of the large dolls tipped off a shelf right behind him. For a moment, Jacob stood with his gun trained on the doll, which was the size of a small child. He was breathing rapidly, pulse pounding, and the

EMF box meter was hitting so hard on the red side of the dial that Jacob could hear the needle clicking against the side. The doll did not move, and after a moment, Jacob took a deep breath and forced himself to relax.

Jacob turned back toward the main workroom and froze. The dolls were not arranged as they had been just a moment ago. He was certain of it. The shadows had shifted subtly, enough for him to sense the change. A chill went down his spine. Forcing his mind back to business, Jacob took a few more steps toward the center of the workroom. Long tables filled the center of the room. Some held cloth and batting for the ragdolls and the soft bodies of the porcelain-headed dolls. Others held an assortment of carpenter's tools for the wooden dolls. The third table looked more like it belonged in a laboratory than a doll shop. Odd wax cylinders, delicate copper wiring, unfamiliar mechanisms and small metal boxes littered the work surface.

After another wary glance at the EMF reader, Jacob clipped the meter to his belt and picked up one of the cylinders with his left hand, keeping his gun ready in his right. It reminded him of a recording cylinder, the kind newfangled machines Thomas Edison had created to record and play back music and speeches.

Odd. Perhaps the Dollmaker is recording voices? A darker possibility presented itself. *If Headquarters is right, maybe "voices" are what he's smuggling. Voices with code words and classified information, hidden inside the dolls.*

Jacob glanced around the workshop, and once again, the dolls had moved slightly. This time, he knew it was no accident. He had intentionally noted the position of a few memorable dolls, and now they were seated differently. He swallowed hard, reminding himself he had shot far more terrifying monsters, and continued his search.

Jacob came to another workstation near the far side of the room. One table held an array of gears and hinges, perfect for the articulated joints of the mechanical dolls. The other table held a selection of life-size doll heads made from painted earthenware. Notes written on scraps of parchment littered the work surface. Compared to the fine features of the porcelain dolls or the carefully carved faces of the wooden marionettes, these heads were crude, barely human, without even paint to soften their appearance. The earthenware heads were skull-like with a separate lower jaw attached with twine.

Just like the golems at the Conservatory Jacob thought. *So even if the Dollmaker doesn't have the magic to animate them, he's making the bodies for whoever can.* Nearby stood life-size hollow wooden bodies, the front halves and the back halves neatly separated, with the same rough articulated joints. Jacob wished he could use the new-fangled small spy camera Farber had given him, but the light was far too dim for the camera's limited abilities, and Jacob had no desire to call attention to himself by setting off flash powder to get a good image.

Whatever the Dollmaker was up to, Jacob didn't want to linger in the dark workroom any longer than necessary. He opened the rucksack he carried on his back and grabbed several of the mechanical pieces, including one of the wax cylinders. On impulse, he looked around and stuffed one of the small dolls into the backpack as well, tying it closed.

A shuffling sound made him freeze again. The dolls had done more than shift position this time. Perhaps, their subtle movements had been a warning. Now, more than a dozen of the large dolls stood up, their movement jerky, their malice unmistakable.

Jacob was surrounded.

There goes any chance of sneaking out without leaving a trace, he thought. The door was on the opposite side of the room. In between were dozens of dolls. Most of them hadn't moved—yet. The others were clearly oriented on Jacob, meaning their sudden activity wasn't a fluke. He heard the *whirr* of gears and the *clunk* of wooden feet against the floor. The dolls raised their arms, hands outstretched. This wasn't a trick of the light, or a puppet master hiding in the rafters. Jacob was close enough to his opponents to see that no strings moved their bodies.

The dolls came after him.

Jacob fired, blowing a hole in the wooden chest of the nearest life-size doll. It knocked the mannequin backward, taking out half a dozen of the other figures, but the rest kept coming. A second shot tore through the metal of a wind-up doll which rattled and shuddered, then kept on moving. Six shots in his revolver, but dozens of dolls. Jacob had a second gun in a shoulder holster, but it would take a Gatling gun to mow down all the dolls that shambled toward him. He had no desire to find out what they intended to do if they caught him.

Click, whirr, clunk. Closer now, the dolls leered at him with their painted faces and garish features. Some had real human hair, increasing their resemblance to walking corpses. Glass eyes glimmered fixed and staring in the light of the single kerosene lantern. The wind-up dolls marched stiffly, like toy soldiers, while the wooden mannequins flopped with their hinged joints. Jacob got in four more shots, stuffed his revolver through his belt and grabbed for the nearest animated rag doll. The doll squirmed and twisted in his hand, tearing at his flesh with straight pins that poked through its mitten-shaped fingers like claws. Jacob ignored the pain and blood.

"Get back!" he warned, and held the rag doll up near the flame of the kerosene lantern. A few yarn hairs singed, and the smell of burn string carried in the musty air. The attacking dolls hesitated, though the rag doll in Jacob's hand stabbed him with the pins, and he had to keep his hand turned to keep the attack from opening the veins in his wrist.

Thuds and muted cries came from the direction of a door Jacob assumed led to a storage closet. He hoped the lock held; the odds were already in the dolls' favor without them gaining reinforcements. If the Dollmaker had other creations that even he felt necessary to lock up, Jacob had no desire to meet them.

Jacob thrust the vicious doll into the flame, igniting its cloth head. Whatever animated the poppet let out an unholy shriek. Wielding the writhing doll like a torch, Jacob forced the other dolls to back away, clearing a path toward the door. He expected his shots to bring someone bursting in at any moment, either police or the Dollmaker himself. He saw ruin impending either way.

Jacob ran for the door, and his left hand went to the Maxwell box that hung from his belt, banging against his leg. He found the switch and turned the box on, and spun the knob to the left, desperately hoping he had remembered the instructions correctly. *Right to call the ghosts, left to push them back,* Farber had said, though why anyone sane would want to attract spirits was more than he could fathom.

A sudden, piercing wail went up from the attacking dolls, and they fell back, twisting as if in pain. Some of the dolls fell to the floor, their porcelain heads cracking with the impact like ruined crockery, while others backed away so hurriedly that they knocked over other mannequins in their clumsy retreat, ending up in a tangle on the ground. The small doll he had imprisoned in his rucksack howled and bucked, trying to tear its way out of the backpack.

Jacob didn't stop to watch. The rag doll had nearly burned out, and he tossed what was left onto the pile of fallen mannequins and bolted out the door. As soon as he was out in the street, he ripped the rucksack from his shoulder and fired a single shot into it, stilling the vicious poppet inside.

Sirens sounded in the distance. Jacob holstered his gun, grabbed his damaged rucksack, and ran, keeping to the shadows. He did not turn off the Maxwell box until he was blocks away, and even then, his hands shook as he worked the switch. Jacob's left hand looked like it had been scratched by a wildcat, and his fingers blistered from the heat of the burning rag doll. He leaned against a brick wall in the shelter of a dark alley, certain that any mugger lurking there could not possibly be as terrifying as what he had just escaped.

What the hell is the Dollmaker up to? Considering the dramatic effect the Maxwell box had on the menacing dolls, Jacob had no doubt that ghosts were somehow involved. *Are the mannequins haunted or possessed? How did they get that way? The Dollmaker's never been more than a smuggler and courier. Whatever's going on, he's got to have a partner, someone who's pretty damn good with dark magic and clockworks, too.*

A few names came to mind, ambitious criminals or remorseless men who were willing to kill to get what they wanted. As Jacob headed for the rendezvous site, he eliminated one suspect after another. One was known to be out of the country, another was in prison, and a third lacked the financial backing to manage the clockwork inventions Jacob had seen. The few possibilities that remained were the worst of the bunch.

We haven't seen the last of the Dollmaker. He'll know we're onto him now.

"TELL ME AGAIN why we're freezing our butts off down here by the riverfront?" Jacob muttered. Della grumbled in agreement, her face hidden by the fur ruff around the hood of her heavy coat.

"Because we got a tip that there were 'monsters' down along the docks," Mitch returned under his breath.

"How good of a tip?" Jacob returned.

"Very good, I'd say." Drostan Fletcher sauntered out of the shadows beneath the huge steel bridge over their heads. His Scottish burr was clear in his voice, and with his collar turned up on his Macintosh coat, he looked the part of a private investigator.

He chuckled at Jacob's raised eyebrow. "Yes, Mitch brought me in for extra eyes," Drostan said. "And the truth is, there have been stories for a couple of weeks now about strange people down by the river. Some people swear the drowned men of the rivers are returning home."

Jacob repressed a shiver. Three rivers met at the triangle of land locals called "The Point," the Allegheny River, the Monongahela River, and the Ohio River. Boats of all kind traveled these waters, including plenty of barges, steamboats, fishing vessels, and cargo ships. The swift waters and strong current made for sometimes dangerous navigation, and changes in depth meant navigating the dozens of wicket dams that helped keep ships from running aground.

Sometimes, even experience and caution could not prevent tragedy. The river bottoms were littered with the wrecks of unlucky crafts, and their waters were the final resting place of their dead crewmen.

This stretch of river was between the big docks, and near the waterfront. The hulking steel skeletons of a passenger bridge and a railroad bridge shadowed the banks, making it nearly impossible for travelers to see what might be going on beneath them, even if they had cared to look.

"Smuggling?" Mitch asked, watching the riverbank for movement.

"Doubtful," Della replied. "Smugglers have their pick of anywhere along the rivers to unload. They wouldn't choose the busiest part of the waterway."

"Isn't this the stretch they call The Cemetery?" Jacob glanced up and down the river. Few boats were in sight this late, and the water looked black, its rippling surface barely reflecting the glow of street-lamps far above. "Because so many ships have sunk here over the years?"

"Yes, it is," Drostan said. "And that's why we're here. I've been working on a case for a shipping company that was having problems with thefts in this stretch. I found the ring of thieves and busted them, but along the way, I saw something else that seemed odd—men coming up out of the river late at night. I didn't think too much about it until Mitch contacted me. Now, I have a suspicion what I saw might be connected to your case."

"Shh!" Della warned. "Something's going on near the water's edge!" For tonight's work, Della had forsaken her long skirts for bicycle bloomers, which her coat covered should anyone notice. She carried a rucksack with additional weapons and supplies over one shoulder, along with two pistols and a rifle in a back holster.

They pulled back to the shadows and waited. The surface of the black water rippled and then a man's head rose, silhouetted against the lights from the far side of the river. He moved like a man in armor, with jerky, stiff motions, and he looked like he was wearing a jointed suit. The wind shifted, and an awful stench hit Jacob hard enough he nearly gagged. Not the smell of dead fish or the effluvia of the river;

no, this was the smell of meat gone bad in the sun. That's when Jacob realized something else wrong about the riverman. For having been completely submerged, he wore no diving suit.

Two more bedraggled men climbed onto the riverbank, and then three others. The smell was enough to make his gorge rise, but Jacob swallowed down his urge to vomit and kept his shotgun ready.

"Stop!" Mitch shouted. With a hiss and a roar, Della and Drostan lit kerosene torches, illuminating the area under the bridge. In the torch-light, Jacob could see that the men were all carrying objects that were encrusted with mud and muck from the river bottom.

It was also very clear that they were jointed wooden life-size dolls.

Ten of the figures now stood along the riverbank. They paused briefly at Mitch's shout, then began to walk forward at a steady pace. Their glass eyes did not blink, and the carved features showed no emotion. Water coursed from their joints, making Jacob wonder if the suits were hollow. The wet slap of their feet echoed from the stone bridge supports.

"Government agents! Stop now, or we shoot!" Mitch shouted. He held the torch in his left hand and his revolver in his right hand. His rifle was slung across his back, just in case. The flickering flames of the kerosene torch gave the area a hellish glow.

The wooden men kept on walking. Drostan and Jacob opened fire, followed a second later by Della and Mitch. They shot for the head, after their experience with the golems, and Jacob expected to shatter a hollow sphere of wood. Their bullets burst open the wooden shell of the man-sized dolls and splattered the concrete with decaying flesh and bone shards.

"They're hollow! Wooden dolls with corpses inside!" Drostan yelped, but the shock did not slow his fire or make his aim waver.

Della muttered something decidedly unladylike as she took off the top of one wooden doll's head, then braved the shower of gore to thrust her flaming kerosene torch at two more of the creatures, waving it between them and forcing them to a stop. "I will never get the smell out of this coat!" she growled, and spent her pique on the nearest two wooden men.

Ten shots, ten kills, and the bodies of ten broken dolls. What leaked from the ruined wooden heads and the real skulls inside them smelled of embalming fluid and rot. Drostan stood guard over the riverfront, playing his torchlight across the swift, dark water in case more of the abominations rose from the waves. Jacob watched the roadway, sure that even at this hour their fusillade would draw unwanted police attention. Della and Mitch bent to examine the fallen wooden soldiers and the corpses inside of them.

"They didn't drown inside those wooden doll shells," Della murmured. She poked at one of the corpses with a stick. "Not fresh dead."

"More damn zombies," Mitch said. "Just like at the cemetery."

Della frowned and picked up what the fallen doll-man had dropped. "Interesting," she said, holding it up in the glow of the torch. "A silver platter." She brushed a hand across the engraving, trying to read it. "*The Ariella*," she made out.

"That was a steamboat," Drostan said over his shoulder. "Went down in this area several years ago. Passenger ship headed from Pittsburgh down the Ohio River. Pretty swanky."

"This one's got a bunch of odds and ends," Mitch said, gingerly opening a canvas bag and spilling out its contents. Out poured a collection of old coins, some dirt-encrusted jewelry, silver flatware, and other oddments.

"The ones back here were more ambitious," Della said, moving to examine the next row of felled zombies. One carried a small, rusted safe, like the kind found in the captain's cabin of a ship. Another carried a wooden crate that was in good enough condition it must have come from a recent wreck. A third carried a single gold bar. So did several of the others.

"Well look at that," Mitch said quietly, and let out a low whistle. "Not a bad haul for a night's work, especially when you don't have to pay the help."

"The gold bars are likely from the *Fortunato*," Drostan supplied. "Alfonso Luigi Russo was a bigwig in the South Side Mafia. Ran a lot of the gambling, dog fights, and horse betting. Made a lot of money.

Then he disappeared. Word on the street was that he didn't pay his percentages to the bosses and someone found out. He ran for it one night in his boat, which suddenly exploded. Rumor had it; he took his gold to the bottom with him."

"Guess someone finally found it," Jacob replied. Anything else he might have said was cut off as a gunshot from the darkness narrowly missed his shoulder. Mitch and Della immediately cut the fuel to their torches, abandoning them among the corpses as they dodged for shelter. The fading orange glow of the still-hot wires and burning rags was barely enough for them to make out shapes in the darkness.

Drostan clung to a steel girder atop a massive stone bridge pylon and swung out to shoot in the direction of the attack. An answering bullet clanged against the steel just an inch away from his head. Della had pistols in both hands, and she answered the shot with two of her own, though the only clue to the position of the shooter was the spark from the muzzle of his gun.

Mitch signaled Jacob and slipped through the darkness to circle around behind their attacker. Jacob dove from cover and fired off a stream of shots he hoped would keep their enemy from noticing Mitch's absence.

Even with their torches dark, the reflected light from the river put them at a disadvantage compared to the assailant in the deep shadows beneath the bridge. And in that dim light, Jacob saw a sight that made his stomach churn. Like obedient puppets, the savaged doll-zombies struggled to their feet.

"Oh hell no," Della muttered. "Cover me!" she shouted to Jacob a second before she dove and rolled, coming up in front of the two kerosene torches. She sloshed something toward the row of staggering figures from a small can, and the smell of kerosene vied with the stench of decay. Flames surged from the wands as Della opened up the feed full blast, setting the spilled kerosene alight. Wet as the doll-zombies were, the kerosene-fueled flames rose like a bonfire, engulfing them.

Jacob and Drostan were firing shot after shot to keep their unknown attacker from easily sighting on Della, silhouetted by the flames. Shots cracked into the stone and concrete, sending up a shower of slivers. Della flattened herself against the riverbank and crawled for cover, as a few of the bullets tore through the hem of her coat and grazed the fur ruff of her hood.

For an awful moment, the corpse-dolls shuddered and crackled in the wall of flames, and then fell to the ground. The smell of burnt wood and rotted meat was overwhelming. Behind them in the shadows, Jacob heard a single rifle shot, then the clatter of horse hooves and wagon wheels, followed a moment later by the rumble of Mitch's steambike.

When no other shots came, Drostan swung down from his perch, joining Jacob and Della. The charred figures on the riverbank bore little resemblance to men. Parts of the hollow wooden shells had been burned away, revealing the corpses inside. The last of the kerosene flames sputtered out. Della retrieved one of the torches and gave them enough light to appraise the damage.

"No doubts anymore that the Dollmaker is working with Kasmir, is there?" Jacob asked.

"And now we know why. Salvage," Drostan added.

Jacob shook his head. "That's part of it, but I don't think we know the whole story yet."

"What now?" Della asked.

Jacob tapped a code into the odd bulky wristwatch he wore, a Morse Code transmitter/receiver that carried its signal through the aetheric waves. Like the steambike and so much of their gear, it was another fine invention from Adam Farber. "Hans should be here in a few moments with the wagon," Jacob said.

Just then, Mitch slewed his steambike to a stop at the edge of the carnage. "Lost him," Mitch said, muttering a few curses before he remembered Della was present and mumbling an apology. She rolled her eyes.

"I'll let you know when I hear something new," she replied. "Seriously boys—we shoot up a bunch of corpses, and you think I'll be shocked by your *language*?"

At the sound of a carriage approaching, all four of them leveled their guns at the opening beneath the bridge, and Jacob let out his breath once he recognized Hans in the driver's seat of the black, unmarked wagon.

"Let's load what we can into the back," Mitch said. "Farber should take a look at this." He glanced up at Hans. "I hope you brought shovels."

———

"No wires." Adam Farber straightened up from the corpse-doll he was examining. Adam had laid out the creature on one of his lab worktables like a makeshift morgue. Pieces of the clay golems lay on another table. "Seriously. There's nothing mechanical about either of these… abominations," he said. Long rubber lab gloves covered his hands to the elbows, and a welder's apron made do instead of an autopsy room smock.

"At least we know what some of the doll pieces I saw at the Dollmaker's lab were for," Jacob said with a sigh. He had gone with Mitch and Drostan directly to the doll shop after the encounter at the riverbank, only to find that the workspace had been emptied and abandoned. "And why the Maxwell box had such an effect on the dolls."

Jacob paused, frowning as something occurred to him. "Hold on. We could smell the 'drowned' men as soon as they came out of the water. There wasn't a smell like that at the Dollmaker's workshop. I would have remembered," he added, wrinkling his nose. "But the dolls still came after me. And some of them were solid wood. I know: I shot them. Some were wind-up mechanicals, and that one I brought back with me was stuffed."

"The one you shot?" Mitch asked, good-natured needling clear in his voice.

Jacob fixed him with a look. "That *thing* was trying to get at my throat. It was a reasonable reaction."

Della made no attempt to stifle a chuckle. Adam was too absorbed in the puzzle of the corpse-dolls to reply, and Jacob wondered if the inventor had even heard their banter.

"Renate told me that there's a long magical tradition of poppets," Della said. "Voodoo dolls. Ventriloquist dummies that speak by themselves. Marionettes that move around theaters when no one is around. She also said different kinds of magic could make the dolls do specific things. So it might be Sandor Kasmir and his necromancy—or someone else entirely."

Mitch shook his head. "I think Kasmir and the Dollmaker are working together, on at least some of this," he replied. He looked to Adam. "You said the Dollmaker is greedy. Well, the 'drowned men' would certainly feed his need for money. Ditto the break-ins when Lustig and Shurlman provided a distraction. I'm sure Kasmir can always use money. But it doesn't seem like a grand enough scheme for him, and it doesn't explain the kidnapped mediums."

"Dead inventors." Everyone turned to look at Adam. He had stripped off his gloves and apron, and walked over to another table where the bits and pieces lay that Jacob had taken from the Dollmaker's workshop. On the way, he had grabbed one of his many half-finished cups of cold coffee and downed what remained.

"Excuse me?" Mitch asked.

Adam looked up brightly. "The names of the bodies that were dug up. Ferris, Lauth, Bakewell. All inventors. Held a bunch of patents. Several of them, especially Ferris, died young."

"And?" Jacob encouraged, with a gesture that indicated "get to the point."

Adam pointed to a mechanical box on the worktable with a large fluted horn to carry sound. The Edison wax cylinder Jacob had taken from the Dollmaker's lair was connected on a spindle. "Listen to this," he said and cranked up the player. A needle skimmed across the rotating cylinder, transforming vibration into sound. Amid static, an eerie, sepulchral voice echoed from the horn, sending a chill down Jacob's back. From the look on the others' faces, Jacob guessed they were affected in the same way. Adam lifted the needle, and the awful, ghostly voice stopped.

"What is that?" Della asked, sounding shaken.

"Thomas Edison's device for recording the voices of the dead,"

Adam replied. "Really, the man is an amazing genius." High praise, coming from Adam, whose talents were hardly shabby. "He wasn't the first to try. Alexander Graham Bell, Guglielmo Marconi, they both tried to create machines either to contact the dead or to let them contact us."

Mitch frowned. "I figured the cylinders Jacob picked up just made the dolls talk."

Adam shook his head. "So did I, until I listened to the one Jacob brought back. That's George Ferris's voice. I know; I was at several meetings with him, just a few years ago."

"Did you actually listen to the whole recording?" Della asked, her expression making it clear that her estimation of the inventor's bravery had just risen.

"Yeah," Adam replied. "Even though it was pretty creepy. And here's the thing. Not only is it Ferris's voice, but he was talking about an invention that isn't among his patents." He looked at them as if they were slow to follow his meaning. "He's inventing things from beyond the grave. Things that someone else will make lots of money from."

"Son of a bitch," Mitch muttered. "That's the link. That's what Kasmir is up to—and why he kidnapped the mediums."

Just then, the telegraph key on Adam's desk began to tap out a message. "It's your office," Adam said, after listening for a moment. He went back to toying with the odd objects Jacob had retrieved.

Mitch, Jacob, and Della walked closer, silent as they decoded the message mentally. When the clatter of the key fell silent, Mitch looked back at Drostan and Adam. "It's Clare Monihan, the medium. She says she's got an urgent message from Simon Markham's ghost. He knows where the mediums are, and he's got a plan to rescue them."

6 / GRAVE VOICES | TUNNEL TO HELL

"FIRST TIME I'VE been on a mission run by a ghost," Jacob muttered. A day of hurried preparations had passed since they had received Simon Markham's telegraph. It had taken time to assemble their team and gather the resources they needed to make a stand against Kasmir and the Dollmaker.

"I'm not runnin' this mission. That's Mitch's job. I'm just advising." Simon's voice and inflection were spot on, though it was Clare Monihan who spoke.

"I still don't think you should be here," Jacob murmured, meaning Clare.

"She says to tell you that it's her friends who have gone missing, and she aims to help. So bugger off," Simon replied. There was a pause. "I'm to tell you that Miss Monihan most definitely did not phrase her statement in that way." Clare gave a lop-sided grin that was all Simon. "But that's what she meant," he added.

The telegraph watch on Jacob's wrist sounded with two clicks, then with three. "They're in position," he murmured to Drostan.

The small railway station sat on a disused set of tracks leading into what remained of a partially caved-in tunnel in the middle of nowhere, a few miles north of New Pittsburgh. Since the railroad re-routed its service, the area around the station went into decline. A few abandoned

139

warehouses and defunct shops remained. Grass encroached on the road, and in a few more years, it would be difficult to see where the roadbed had been. Rocky foothills sat behind the station, while beyond the abandoned buildings lay an empty field covered with tufted mounds of grass.

Della was overhead in the *Bienville*, ghosting along in the night sky. An earpiece and more of Adam Farber's technology made it possible for Jacob and Mitch to stay in contact. Drostan and Jacob kept watch on the station along with Clare, who was channeling Simon's ghost. Mitch and Renate were near the train tunnel, along with allies they had brought along for back-up. Hans, the coachman, was on look-out, farther up the abandoned lane.

"Your intelligence had better be good," Jacob whispered to Simon.

"Never better. The kidnapped mediums asked the ghosts to warn the other clairvoyants, and when I heard about it, I followed up. Geez. Just because I'm dead doesn't mean I stopped being an agent," Simon pouted. Jacob doubted he would get used to addressing Clare and getting Simon in response, so he decided to stop thinking about it.

"What's the meter say?" Jacob asked Drostan, who glanced at the EMF reader in his hand. It detected the energy of ghostly manifestations, and the needle on the gauge was in the red zone.

"Busy night," Drostan replied.

"Let's just hope that the Maxwell box doesn't mess up Simon's connection to Clare if Mitch has to use it," Jacob said.

Four clicks sounded from Jacob's telegraph-watch, Mitch's signal to move. "Showtime," Jacob muttered.

A moment later, fireworks exploded in the empty field in a cacophony of bangs, booms, and bright lights. "And there's Mitch's idea of a distraction," Drostan said with a sigh.

"Go!" Simon urged.

Clare, Jacob, and Drostan ran toward the station, while more of the fireworks blasted from the field. Simon's ghostly reconnaissance had informed them that the missing mediums were being held in the conductor's office at one end of the old train station, which the Doll-maker had claimed as his new workroom. Jacob went to cover her, while Drostan slipped around the back, ready to plant charges to detonate the Dollmaker's works in progress and destroy his dangerous creations.

Clare moved with Simon's sure-footed stealth. She popped her head up at the office window, which glowed with the dim light of a lantern. Jacob crouched beside her, gun at the ready, watching for an ambush.

"They're in there!" Clare's enthusiasm colored Simon's usually droll delivery. She gave three quiet raps on the glass, which drew the attention of the four women inside. The prisoners rushed to the window excitedly when they recognized Clare, then looked puzzled as she set to prying the casement open with a crowbar.

The window locks snapped, and the window opened. Clare gestured for the trapped women to follow, leery of speaking because Simon's inflection might make her voice unfamiliar.

"I'm a government agent, and I'm here to get you to safety," Jacob said. "There's a carriage waiting. You've got to hurry."

More fireworks meant Mitch was doing his best to keep Kasmir and the Dollmaker focused elsewhere, but Jacob knew that could change at any moment.

Drostan joined them just as the last of the mediums crawled out of the window. "Charges are planted," he said. "We've got to get clear before we blow the explosives."

"Watch out!" Simon's warning came an instant too late. A shot from the darkness clipped Jacob in the left arm. He bit back a cry of pain and fired back, as Drostan also took a shot at their assailant. The four mediums huddled against the station wall, terrified. Clare took in the situation with Simon's experienced, unruffled calm.

"It's the Dollmaker, and he's moving left," Clare reported, as Simon tapped into the network of ghosts that gathered around the mediums.

Blood stained Jacob's left sleeve, but he ignored the pain and adjusted his aim, then he and Drostan shot where Simon directed, and the sharp curses suggested they had hit the Dollmaker, or that their bullets had been near misses.

"Get them to the carriage. We'll cover you," Drostan hissed. Clare nodded and motioned for the other mediums to follow her, grabbing their arms and pulling them along when they were frozen by fear.

The *whirr* of gears and the clatter of wooden-jointed limbs made Jacob's heart sink. As the Dollmaker fired again, life-size metal and wooden dolls emerged from the shadows, cutting off the escape path to the carriage.

Three wind-up metal soldiers marched stiffly from their hiding places, with the buzz and hum of their springs and gears. With horror, Jacob realized that their arms were Gatling guns. Wooden warriors with metal swords flanked them, and their herky-jerky movements did not reduce the danger of the weapons in their hands.

"Down!" Jacob warned as the metal men's guns blazed. Clare and the mediums barely had time to hide behind a short stone wall as the bullets flew. Drostan did his best to pick off the malevolent dolls, but while his bullets dented metal and splintered wood, they could not stop the magic that animated them.

Simon, whose ghost still possessed Clare, took matters into his own hands the instant the Gatling guns went quiet. "Call the ghosts!" Clare ordered the frightened mediums, then she dodged above her hiding place, animated by Simon's daring and experience, and lobbed a rock with a pitch worthy of a baseball player that hit the nearest wooden doll right in the face. She swung the crowbar with both hands, and slammed the heavy iron bar into the wrist of a nearby doll, tearing its gun from its body.

Jacob was still trading shots with the shadowy figure of the Doll-maker, trying to keep him away from the mediums until they could get to safety. He tapped a code to Hans for back-up and tried to go to Clare's defense, but the Dollmaker's shots were too close for comfort and Jacob had yet to get a good enough bead on his target to hit the mark.

Drostan's carefully planted explosives could blow the station sky-high, but not until they had gotten far enough away to survive the blast. The malevolent doll-soldiers were no longer firing, but they continued to advance toward the stone wall.

"Come on!" Clare shouted to the frightened mediums. "Show them what we're made of!" It was Clare's voice but Simon's mannerisms. Before the other clairvoyants could object, Clare scrambled over the wall, setting about with the crowbar, taking advantage of the doll's exhausted weapons. Emboldened by her brazen example, the others roused to their defense, sending a hail of rocks flying that pelted the dolls, driving them back.

"Can you shut down the ghosts that are powering the dolls?" Jacob yelled to Clare.

"Tried that," one of the mediums yelled back. "They're under some kind of control. But we can bring in some friends to even the score."

"Call in the reinforcements!" Clare shouted to her fellow mediums. A moment later, the air around the station grew much colder, cold enough for them to see their breath. A thick fog rolled toward the station from the empty field across the way, and Jacob realized belatedly that the mounds and tufts he had spotted were the markers of an old graveyard.

Fog became ghostly figures, at first featureless and then more defined, farmers and merchants, the townspeople from the village once served by the abandoned station. The ghosts came when the mediums called, and from the look of it, they were angry at the Dollmaker's control of the other spirits. Jacob had heard of poltergeists, but the spirits summoned by the clairvoyants went beyond what he had ever witnessed. The ghosts hurled rocks and shoved the doll-soldiers with impunity, pushing them over so they were easy for Clare and the mediums to bludgeon with stones, sticks, and Clare's crowbar. Drostan's well-aimed shots knocked more of the malevolent dolls off their feet, once he started aiming for the knees.

Jacob had no time to celebrate. The Dollmaker shot again, and the bullet sank into the wooden wall of the station far too close to Jacob for comfort. Jacob traded his empty revolver for his shotgun, and keyed the earpiece. "Della! Can you get some light on us? We're pinned down, and I can't see the shooter."

"Let there be light," she replied with a chuckle. A moment later, a spotlight shone down from the sky, seemingly out of nowhere since the black airship was almost invisible against the night sky. Jacob was ready as the light blinded the Dollmaker for an instant, and his shotgun blast hit the mad inventor square in the chest, knocking him off his feet back into the shadows.

"Good shot!" Della cheered.

The Dollmaker was down, but more of his infernal creations lumbered from the station, and it wouldn't take long before Jacob and the others were surrounded. The *Bienville's* weapons were too imprecise to take out the doll-soldiers without either setting off Drostan's explosive charges or hitting Jacob and their allies. And from the shots being traded from the direction of the tunnel, it sounded like Mitch and his friends were not going to be able to help.

The snap of reins and the pounding of hooves came from the roadway. Hans was driving the carriage like a madman, and the former cavalry horses seemed to be enjoying the action. The horses bowled over the dolls in their way, hitting them from behind and riding them down, trampling the metal and wooden bodies with their heavy hooves. The horses reared as Hans reined them in sharply.

"Get in," he ordered.

Clare ran to open the door for the others, who stepped warily around the broken forms of the killer dolls. From the look on Clare's face, it was clear that Simon was torn about leaving his friends and the fight.

"Go on," Jacob urged. "Get them to safety. You've fought a good fight."

Simon's sly smile spread across Clare's features, and she gave a nod to Jacob as she swung up to the carriage's running boards in a move that was pure Simon. "See you later," she promised in Simon's voice. The door closed, and with a shout and a snap of the reins, Hans headed out at top speed. Some of the new ranks of doll-soldiers emerging from the station fired at the carriage, but its steel-reinforced sides deflected their bullets. The ghosts grew less solid now that the mediums were gone, vanishing into the wind.

Gunfire sounded again from the direction of the tunnel. "Come on. Sounds like Mitch needs some back-up," Jacob said, pausing just long enough for Drostan to tie a piece of cloth around his arm where the Dollmaker's bullet had grazed him.

"What about them?" Drostan said with a jerk of his head toward the new wave of killer dolls clicking and whirring their way out of the station.

"Take them out once we're clear," Jacob replied. "Della, take the ship up," he warned through his headset.

He and Drostan were barely a hundred feet away from the station when the whole building exploded, and flames shot toward the sky. "You could have waited a few more steps!" Jacob protested.

Drostan shrugged. "Seemed like the right time to me."

The burning station provided enough light that Jacob and Drostan could see the fight at the tunnel entrance as clearly as if the airship had trained its lights on the scene. "Della, keep an eye out for anything circling behind us. It looks like Kasmir's got a whole army of golem soldiers stashed in that tunnel, and by the smell of it, more of his corpse-dolls, too."

"I could blow up the whole tunnel from here," she offered.

"Negative. Mitch and the others are too close. Don't worry; you'll get your shot," Jacob replied.

"You're going to take out the whole tunnel?" Drostan asked, raising an eyebrow.

Jacob's voice was choppy as they ran to catch up to the fighting. "Maybe. But if Kasmir really does have recordings of new ideas from dead inventors, that's too valuable to bury in a hillside. We'll get them out—and *then* blow things up."

Mitch was nowhere to be seen as Jacob and Drostan sprinted up. Renate Thalberg the absinthe witch was doing her best to hold off a dozen of the corpse dolls and clay golems that were part of the army streaming from the mouth of the tunnel. She stood inside a warded circle, and a shimmering green curtain of energy kept the creatures attacking her at bay as she struck at them with balls of conjured fire and emerald streaks of lightning. Every one of her strikes smashed a golem or incinerated a zombie-doll, but there were too many of the monsters, and it was clear Renate was likely to tire before the onslaught slowed.

To one side, dozens of zombie-dolls advanced on three men with the black cassocks and long beards of Polish priests who were chanting in Latin. Jacob recognized Father Matija and his *Logonje*. The priests held up golden boxes, reliquaries that focused the power of the Divine. Blinding white light and a powerful force wave blasted from the relics, flattening rows of corpse-dolls as it freed their enslaved spirits, but there were still more of the creatures behind those that fell.

On the other side, a short, bearded man in a dark suit stared down rows of golems. A yarmulke nestled in his dark hair. *Rabbi Loew, the Kabbalist,* Jacob thought. *Welcome to the party.* Loew's low, steady voice recited the Psalms in Hebrew, and the rabbi paused now and again to spit three times, a warding against evil. As he spoke words of power from the Scriptures, the golems in the front row staggered and fell, but more of the unholy creatures emerged to take their place.

"You go to the left; I'll take the right," Jacob shouted. Drostan took up a firing stance, blasting away at a row of golems emerging from the tunnel, smashing their heads like sharpshooting targets at the county fair. Jacob aimed at the corpse-dolls, putting bullet after bullet between their eyes, switching guns when he ran out of bullets. It was clear that there were more monsters than he had bullets. The Dollmaker had far more golems and doll-soldiers stockpiled than Jacob had seen in his workshop. Some were corpse-dolls, some the empty shells into which spirits were forced, and some were golems, but they surged from the tunnel faster than the allies could take them down.

"Where the hell is Mitch?" Jacob muttered.

The rumble of a steambike echoed from the hillsides. Mitch headed for the tunnel entrance bent like a racer over of the velocipede, with the addition of a long, stout wooden pole lashed to the handlebars so that the pole extended a few feet on either side. Mitch had the Maxwell box clipped to his belt. Clare was behind him riding pillion, but the grin on her face was all Simon.

"Move!" Mitch shouted above the roar of the steambike. He lowered his head and aimed the bike right into the thick of the advancing golems and corpse-dolls. "Now!" he yelled, and Clare threw something into the tunnel.

A brilliant flash of light and a deafening *bang* stopped whatever soldier-dolls had not yet emerged from the tunnel. Mitch drove the bike into the midst of the doll army, mowing down the unwieldy golems and wooden-shelled corpses with enough force to knock them back like dominos.

Mitch slewed to a stop, and Clare scrambled off. "Cover me!" she ordered in a voice very much like Simon's. Jacob moved in to position, and Clare raised her hands, closing her eyes and summoning her psychic abilities. *Mitch said she was more than just a clairvoyant,* Jacob thought. *She accidentally raised the dead. That gives us a necromancer to counter Kasmir.*

"I thought you went with Hans?" Jacob said, worried that Clare was still in danger.

"I made him let me out of the carriage. I can be more use to you here," she replied, in a tone that dared him to argue with her. Jacob had the distinct feeling that it was Clare's stubbornness and not Simon's influence that brought her back to the fight.

A third of the Dollmaker's creations stopped in place, wobbled on their wooden legs, and then toppled to the ground. Jacob and Drostan cheered. Matija and his priests continued their chant. Rabbi Loew kept on reading, and Renate never hesitated in her magical assault.

The steambike circled for another assault. This time, Mitch angled the bike away from his comrades and opened fire on the remaining corpse-dolls and golems with the built-in small Gatling gun that Adam Farber had added for emergencies. The rapid, staccato blast of the machine gun mowed down more of the attackers, though without the precision necessary to blast the golems in the head and stop them permanently. The shattered clay monsters struggled to rise, still animated until Rabbi Loew cancelled the magic that empowered them or one of the others put a bullet in their terra cotta heads.

Matija's priests worked more slowly than bullets, but the zombie-dolls they felled stayed down. Clare stepped up beside them, raising her hands once more and calling on her power, emboldened, no doubt, by Renate's presence to use her magic openly without fear of censure. A dozen more of the dolls animated by enslaved ghosts or corpses collapsed as Clare wrested control from their master. It was clear to Jacob that Kasmir did not have the strength to fight for his creations against so many different levels of resistance, or to do more than send his doll-soldiers forth with more than the most basic instructions.

With the others handling the last of the attacker-dolls and golems, Renate dropped her wardings and ran to join Mitch, Jacob, and Drostan, who stood with their guns trained on the tunnel entrance.

"He's still in there," Mitch said, watching the mouth of the tunnel warily. "I'd be happy to lob a few Ketchum grenades, but we need those Edison cylinders."

"I'll bet you a pint at the pub it's booby-trapped," Drostan said. "He's just waiting for us to rush in there and get slaughtered."

"Then let me shed some light on the subject," Renate said. She murmured a word of power, and a brilliant glowing orb rose to the top of the tunnel's arch, illuminating the entrance.

Mitch grabbed the steambike, walking beside it as it idled on low. The same steam that powered the bike's motor also ran a single electric headlamp. Together with Renate's orb, the light drove back the shadows just as Kasmir's last defenders opened fire.

The *whirr* of wind-up metal dolls buzzed as the row of metal soldiers leveled their Gatling gun arms and laid down a barrage of gunfire. Renate had an instant's notice, barely enough time to raise an iridescent, transparent wall of power to shield Jacob and the others from the lethal spray of bullets. Jacob could see the strain on her face as she struggled to hold the barrier, as sweat glistened on her forehead and she gritted her teeth.

In a few, deadly moments the Gatling guns had spent their fury, and the wind-up soldiers managed a step or two before their springs and gears ground to a halt. Jacob pumped a shotgun shell into one of the metal dolls, blowing apart its steel cylinder body just to make certain the creatures were no longer a threat.

"How do we know there aren't more of those every few yards

down the tunnel?" Drostan asked, eyeing the now-silent mechanical dolls warily.

"This should help." Renate looked tired, but determined as she motioned for the glowing ball of power to move along the tunnel's roof, illuminating the way ahead of them. Mitch moved to the fore, still pushing the steambike with its electric headlamp, dispelling the last of the shadows.

"What the hell is that?" Jacob swore. Row upon row of jointed wooden dolls blocked their way. Garishly painted, with wide clown features and staring, malevolent eyes, the dolls stretched from one side of the tunnel to the other, two rows deep.

Yet as they approached, the dolls made no move to attack, swaying slowly in the draft of air that rushed from the back of the tunnel. "Marionettes," Mitch said, adding a few curses under his breath. "They're all just marionettes, strung up to slow us down."

Mitch went back to retrieve a piece of curved steel that was half of a downed wind-up soldier, steadying it on the handlebars of the steambike and holding it in front of him like a shield as he crouched low and moved through the first row of marionettes. The dolls bobbled and swung unsettlingly, like hanged men no one bothered to cut free of the gallows. Jacob and the others tensed, waiting for shots or worse.

"I'm through it," Mitch shouted. "Clear."

Jacob, Drostan, and Renate pushed their way through the creepy suspended dolls, and the jointed wooden arms and legs clacked like skeletons as they moved among them. Renate's orb illuminated the back of the blocked tunnel. Jacob recognized the tables and doll parts he had seen in the Dollmaker's downtown workshop. An open trunk lay to one side. None of the assembled dolls remained, spent as cannon fodder to defend Sandor Kasmir's last stand. Tools and materials littered the area, but Kasmir himself was notably absent.

"He got out," Mitch said and pointed to a small passageway that had been dug through the debris that blocked the tunnel passage. "He threw everything he had at us to slow us down, while he escaped. Damn!"

Jacob stepped over to the open trunk. "We might have lost Kasmir, but he didn't get the Edison cylinders out through that hole," he said. "Looks like they're in this trunk."

Drostan hauled one of the worktables over to one side and climbed on top. Pulling a knife from his belt, he sliced through the rope that suspended the wooden dolls across the tunnel. "I've got no desire to go back through them if we don't have to."

Drostan kept watch as Mitch and Jacob gathered anything they considered valuable for the investigation. They carried the trunk between them while Renate maneuvered the ball of light and Drostan took point, gun ready, on the walk back to the tunnel mouth.

The clatter of hooves made them draw their weapons as they reached the end of the tunnel. Jacob relaxed as he recognized Hans and their carriage. A crumpled figure slumped in the drivers' seat next to him.

"Missing someone?" Hans called out cheerily. He grabbed the bound and gagged figure by the scruff of its neck and shook the hair out of the man's eyes so they others could get a look at his face. Unconscious and covered with dirt and rock grit, Sandor Kasmir hung limply in Han's grip.

"I dropped off the ladies at the safe house, and then circled back to pick up the Dollmaker," Hans explained. "Found him trying to crawl away. Looks like he had some of the metal plates he used for those wind-up dolls under his shirt, so the bullet winded him, but it didn't kill him." He grinned.

"Rapped him solidly on the head with my gun, and he dropped like a sack of potatoes." Hans gestured with a jerk of his head. "Got him trussed up in the back. Then I remembered that I knew where the old tunnel came out, and I wondered if these two had worked up some mischief at the other end, so I went around back to check it out, and saw this one come out looking like a coal miner!"

"Rapped him on the head with your gun too?" Mitch asked, looking like he was both pleased at the capture and slightly miffed he didn't make the collar himself.

"Seemed prudent," Hans replied. His clockwork-repaired features made it difficult to tell whether he was hiding a smile.

Clare walked over to join them. She looked exhausted, but from the way she moved and the look on her face, Jacob was sure Simon Markham was still sharing her consciousness. "Nice work," Jacob said.

Simon's lopsided smile twisted Clare's mouth. "Haven't had this much fun since before I died," he said. "It felt good to be back in action, even if I had to borrow a ride."

"Nice to have you back, even if it's just for a little while," Mitch said.

"You know," Simon observed, "you might want to recruit Clare and the other mediums. I'm not the only dead agent from the Department floating around. Maybe we could partner up, do some good. It's worth a thought." He gave Mitch a look. "And I've already told her she's entitled to hazard pay at full agent rates for tonight, so don't try to weasel out of it." Mitch glared at him, then rolled his eyes and nodded in agreement.

"Stay in touch, Simon," Jacob said.

"Try to get rid of me, now that I know I can come back!" Simon replied. "But she's getting tired, and I need to go. Make sure Clare gets home okay. She's scrappy. Might make a great agent someday."

With that, Clare shuddered, and when she looked up, she was herself again. "That was amazing," she said tiredly. "But I'm ready to call it a night."

Jacob and Mitch manhandled Kasmir into the back of the wagon with the Dollmaker, while Drostan helped Clare up to the seat beside the driver. Hans and the *Logonje* were busy chucking the remains of the doll-soldiers and corpse-dolls into the mouth of the tunnel. Rabbi Loew moved from one shattered golem to the next, removing the bits of parchment from their mouths. When he had gathered all the papers, he said something in Hebrew that Jacob guessed was a warding against evil, and then lit the stack of parchment with a match. The rabbi continued to recite until the last of the papers were burned to ashes, which he buried beneath handfuls of dirt.

"Well, that's done," he said brightly, dusting off his hands. "Glad I could help. Like the dolls, the golems were ill-used. They're supposed to be protectors, not monsters. Only a bad man would twist their

GAIL Z. MARTIN & LARRY N. MARTIN

natures. Now, they are at rest." He made a sign of blessing over the ashes and turned away. "Send for me if you need me but remember, I don't work weekends." With that, he headed toward the road where he had left his wagon.

Father Matija walked over as the *Logonje* priests and Hans put the last of the dolls and corpses into the tunnel. "The spirits that were forced into those abominations have been freed," he said. "They will go as the Almighty directs, but they are no longer torn from their sleep or bound to corpses." He shook his head. "The problems in the cemeteries should be over. The dead won't be restless any longer."

"Thank you," Mitch said.

Matija managed a rare smile. "We answer to an Authority even higher than your Department," he said. "It's incentive to do good work."

"We can give you a lift into town," Mitch said to Renate as Jacob and Drostan made a last check to assure that nothing of the battle remained outside the tunnel.

Renate raised an eyebrow and glanced toward the steambike. "On that thing? Not likely. But I'll accept a ride in the wagon to the main road. Andreas is waiting for me with a carriage."

Jacob and Drostan climbed into the back of the wagon to keep an eye on the Dollmaker and Kasmir, who were still unconscious. Hans swung up to the driver's seat, as Mitch walked the steambike back to the road. He waited until they were around the bend from the tunnel before he toggled his headset.

"Give 'em hell, Della," he said.

"Thought you'd never ask," she replied.

Rumor had it; the tunnel explosion could be heard all the way to downtown New Pittsburgh.

RUIN CREEK

RUIN CREEK

"ARE YOU SURE ABOUT THE TELEGRAM?" Agent Jacob Drangosavich set his carpetbag down on the platform of the empty train station. "You're certain you read the time right?"

His partner, Mitch Storm, leveled a glare. "Yes, about the telegram. And yes, I can tell time."

"Then there aren't many other people taking the train to Ruin Creek, are there?" Jacob asked drolly. Their horses were stabled near the station, awaiting their return. A single gaslight burned at one end of the wooden platform. Even the ticket agents were gone by this late hour, and no other passengers were in sight.

"Not leaving from here, anyhow." Mitch began to pace. With dark hair, a trim, muscular build and a five o'clock shadow that darkened at three, Mitch looked like every penny-dreadful writer's epitome of an Army sharpshooter and secret government agent. Jacob was tall and raw-boned, with a long face and blue eyes that spoke to his Eastern European background. All things considered, a darkened train station in the middle of Arizona wasn't the strangest place they'd been sent by the Department of Supernatural Investigation.

In the distance, a coyote howled. Moonlight cast the saguaro cactus in strange shadows. Overhead, the stars seemed bright as a lawman's badge, and the darkened ridge of the Superstition Mountains loomed on the horizon.

"It's just strange, having Headquarters send us out without notice," Jacob remarked.

Mitch shrugged. "Not the first time; probably won't be the last. Things come up, especially in our business. A fellow agent calls for assistance, we go."

"If the telegram hadn't had all the right codes, I'd worry we were being set up," Jacob replied.

"You're worrying about that anyhow." Mitch knew his partner. "I triple-checked the codes."

"I don't like getting sent out at the last minute without more information," Jacob groused.

Mitch rolled his eyes. "When has the Department ever worried about telling us everything we needed to know?"

Jacob grunted in grudging assent.

The mournful whistle of an oncoming train echoed across the empty desert landscape. A silver and black train ghosted to a stop at the platform and sent a puff of coal smoke into the air. It was a small train, just two passenger cars and two boxcars behind the engine and coal car. The passenger cars were brightly lit, but as far as Jacob could tell, they were empty.

"All aboard!" A man with a conductor's uniform leaned out of the doorway to the first passenger car. Mitch grabbed his carpetbag and the long duffel that carried their weapons and hopped on before Jacob could utter a word, forcing him to catch up.

"Classy," Mitch said as they entered the Pullman car. The seats were flocked green velvet, and the cars were paneled with mahogany. Brass-shaded lanterns hung from the ceiling.

"Empty," Jacob said, walking to the back of the car to check that no one was hiding on the floor between any of the empty seats. He peered through the glass in the door to the vestibule, looking into the second, equally deserted car. "I don't like this."

Mitch had already selected a seat with his back to the wall where he could watch the entire length of the car. Jacob reluctantly took a seat opposite him where he could see the other door. Mitch had a newspaper on his lap and beneath it, his Colt Peacemaker. He removed a silver flask from his pocket, took a swig, and offered it to Jacob, who shook his head. "Maybe when we get where we're going in one piece," Jacob replied.

The conductor entered from between the two passenger cars and walked toward them as if an empty train in the wee hours of the morning was the most natural thing in the world. "Tickets, please."

Mitch held out the two tickets that had been delivered to their hotel within an hour of the unexpected telegram. The conductor barely glanced at the tickets, then nodded curtly.

"Do you make this run nightly?" Jacob asked.

"Make it when we need to make it," the conductor replied as the engine started with a slight lurch. "Folks need to get to Ruin Creek; we stop here."

"I know it's late," Jacob said in his friendliest tone, "but it's pretty quiet. Where'd you come from?"

The conductor looked at Jacob as if the question didn't register at first. "Down the line a ways," he answered. "Far away. Long haul."

"I'm just surprised that the cars are empty," Jacob continued. "Seems like a lot of effort to run us out to Ruin Creek by ourselves. Isn't there another train going that way in the morning?"

"Don't know about that," the conductor said, turning away. "I just do this route. Make yourselves comfortable. Won't be long. No stops between here and there." With that, he turned away and ambled down the empty car.

"Talkative fellow," Mitch said.

"Have I mentioned that I don't like this?" Jacob said. "There's something fishy going on." In response, Mitch closed his eyes and leaned back against the tufted seat cushions. "I'll wake you up in two hours," Jacob growled, settling in with his gun handy. "Then it's my turn to sleep."

Phoenix, Arizona, where they got on the train, was a wide-open outpost, not yet twenty years old. Anywhere they were headed was likely to be even rougher. Jacob had never heard of a town called Ruin

Creek before the telegram, but the West was full of tiny railroad towns that sprang up and died within a year or two as the railroad workers and their camp followers moved on.

"You don't think Ruin Creek is anywhere near Canyon Diablo, do you?" Jacob asked, ignoring the fact that Mitch was dozing off.

"Canyon Diablo is twelve miles northwest," Mitch grunted, slouching farther in his seat.

"I'm just saying, two government agents riding into a town like Canyon Diablo aren't going to ride back out," Jacob warned. "I heard that town went through eight lawmen in six months. Nothing but saloons and houses of ill repute."

"Sounds like my kind of town," Mitch said, turning away from Jacob.

"We didn't bring enough ammunition to go into a town like that," Jacob continued.

"Speak for yourself."

With a sigh, Jacob settled in for his time on watch. The train was moving fast, streaking through the night as the wheels made a *click-clack* rhythm. Jacob's Remington revolver was where he could draw it quickly and so was a Bowie knife. A shotgun, Mitch's rifle, and an assortment of other weapons were in the duffel bag overhead.

The train pulled into Ruin Creek mid-morning. "Last stop," the conductor said, reappearing just before the train slowed. Jacob peered out of the window. What he could see was unimpressive. The station was just a small shed and an awning over a wooden platform.

"Funny. There's no one here to meet us," Mitch muttered as they walked across the platform. Behind them, the train whistle sounded, and then the locomotive pulled away from the station.

"There's a note," Jacob said, pointing to an envelope pinned up on the board where schedule updates usually were posted. "Department of Supernatural Investigation," the envelope read. Jacob took it down and unfolded a single sheet of paper.

"Sorry I couldn't be here for your arrival," he read aloud. "Cline's Rooming House is expecting you. Leave your bags in the parlor. I'll meet you there and will explain more then. Many thanks. The letter's signed, 'Ahiga Sani.'"

"That's a Navajo name," Mitch observed.

Jacob nodded. "The town is technically on Navajo land. The brass probably had to clear it through a couple of other offices to keep from getting sideways with the tribe before they sent us."

"That, and the fact that the last agent they sent out here disappeared." Eli Bly, the agent who had sent a telegram asking for back up at Ruin Creek, had not been heard from since that brief, urgent message.

"If it were easy, they wouldn't pay us big salaries to figure out what's going on," Jacob said.

Mitch looked askance at him. "They don't pay us big salaries, but we're still the ones who get shot at." He checked his watch. "Almost eleven now. We'd better get going," he added and hefted the duffle bag onto one shoulder, lifting his carpetbag with the other hand.

"We can drop off our carpetbags at the rooming house, but I'll keep this one with us."

While their carpetbags held only clothing, it wouldn't do to have someone poking around the duffle. Not only had Mitch loaded it with weapons, but it contained experimental—and useful—scientific gear from a genius inventor at Tesla Westinghouse in New Pittsburgh. Some of the equipment was sanctioned by the Department. Other pieces were custom-made, off-the-books items that Mitch maintained were need-to-know only. And the Department, in Mitch's opinion, did not need to know.

Ruin Creek had one main street. Hastily erected wooden buildings lined both sides of the thoroughfare, with sidewalks made of rough-hewn planks. Half a dozen saloons, three bordellos, four rooming houses, a dance hall, and a dry goods store sustained the hard-working railroaders and those who had come West to help them spend their money. Behind the main street sat a blacksmith's forge, a stable, and a few dozen houses that were more like shanties.

"Looks like the townsfolk know how to have fun," Mitch observed drily. Faces peered from the windows as they walked the length of the main street. Jacob felt like he and Mitch were being paraded for the town to see, and his hand never strayed far from his gun. The hair on the back of his neck rose, though nothing presented a clear threat. The town was eerily silent except for the rustling of the wind.

"If it's like the other railroad towns we've been in, they're a long way from home doing a hard job, and they take their comfort where they can," Jacob replied.

Cline's Rooming House was a two-story clapboard home at the end of Main Street. Its weathered siding did not look as if it had ever been painted, and dust clouded the windows and covered the front porch. Mitch and Jacob climbed the stairs and gave a knock at the door. No one answered.

They looked at each other and shrugged. Just in case, Jacob drew his gun, but he kept it down at his side as Mitch pushed the door open.

The rooming house kitchen was unremarkable. A battered farmhouse table and chairs were in the center of the room, while a Hoosier cupboard sat along one wall and a cast-iron stove hunkered against the back wall.

"Looks like no one's home, so I guess we'll figure out where our room is later," Mitch said, as Jacob nosed into the parlor and found it empty. "Let's drop off the bags and find someone who can tell us why we're here."

When they headed out a few moments later, a lone man stood on the porch, waiting for them. He had sharp features and tawny skin, and he wore a loose chambray shirt over worn denim pants and scuffed boots, along with a black reservation hat with a woven hat band. The stranger held up his hands. "I mean you no harm." He paused. "Are you from the Department? Thank you for coming."

Mitch wore the same expression he used for poker, flinty-eyed and unreadable. "Maybe. Who are you?"

"My name is Ahiga Sani. This is Navajo land, and I'm the local shaman. I came to greet you, and help you understand your task."

Mitch stepped forward to shake his hand. "Agent Mitch Storm, and this is my partner Jacob Drangosavich," he said, with a smile that didn't reach his eyes. Jacob noticed that before Mitch shook hands with the stranger, his left hand closed around a charm on his watch fob. It was a gift from an absinthe witch, a way to tell if the person being touched had magic. His expression gave nothing away, but Jacob knew his partner well enough to notice a slight flinch. *There's magic afoot,* Jacob thought. *But why?*

"What seems to be the trouble?" Jacob asked. "Contacting the Department means you're requesting a very specific type of help. We're not exactly the Texas Rangers."

"No, you're not," Sani replied. "Ruin Creek has a peculiar kind of trouble, and that requires a particular kind of help."

"We were invited by a man named Eli Bly," Mitch replied. "Have you seen him?"

Sani nodded. "I met Mr. Bly. But he is gone now. As for the reason for the telegram, you are correct about there being 'problems.' Strange airships have flown overhead. A silver ship crashed near here. Pieces of it scattered across the desert. They call to the *chindi*, the bad ghosts. They brought a skinwalker and an outlaw. Bly's message for you was to find the pieces, set the ghosts to rest, and release the spirits."

"Who's the outlaw?" Jacob probed. "And if an airship crashed, what do the pieces have to do with ghosts and monsters? Why would it cause problems for the town?"

"Some things aren't meant to be here," Sani said. "They give off bad energy. Strange power."

"Do you know where the pieces are?" Mitch asked. "Can you lead us to them?"

Sani shook his head. "No. Their power wars with my magic. But the railroad people disturbed the site after the crash, brought things to the surface that should have stayed asleep. No one can rest until it's put right."

That explains why Mitch reacted the way he did. Jacob thought. "So you think the pieces that caused the problem are near where the railroad construction was?" Jacob eyed the stranger warily. Something about the man made the hair on the back of his neck prickle.

"It wasn't a regular airship, was it?" Mitch asked.

Sani shook his head. "It was not meant to be here. What it left behind doesn't belong. Things won't be right until it's gone. You have to find it."

"We're not going to have any problems with the tribe, are we?" Mitch asked. "Because top people signed off on our clearance."

"The tribe is not the problem." Sani led them to where they could see the horizon west of town. "See that rise?" he asked, pointing. "Just over it is a valley. About six months ago, people started seeing strange lights in the sky from over that way. Bright lights that weren't stars, moving too fast to be anything natural. Odd noises, too. Scared off the animals—even the coyotes, and they don't scare easily," he said with a chuckle.

"Then folks saw airships in the sky, day and night, but they didn't look like regular airships," he said. "Too many lights on them, and too much metal."

"Maybe the Army is trying out new equipment," Mitch suggested.

"The Army denied ownership, remember?" Jacob said recalling one of the few pieces of information they were given. *Typical,* Jacob thought. *Try out a bunch of newfangled inventions, scare the locals half to death, and pretend it never happened.*

"There was a crash. Some people from the town disappeared," Sani continued. "Cattle died. Chickens quit laying eggs. Dogs barked at nothing."

Mitch and Jacob exchanged a look. *Now we're getting somewhere,* Jacob thought. *Strange airships and weird occurrences are right up our alley.*

"What about the railroad?" Jacob asked. "That's why the town is here. How much longer will the work last?" He looked around at the deserted streets. "And where is everyone?"

Sani shrugged. "They finished the bridge the townsfolk were here to build about six months ago, right after the crash. The work's dried up, and Ruin Creek dried up with it. But there were a few still doing clean up, moving the last of the supplies. The ones that didn't leave town after the crash, the skinwalker took. All that's left now are the dead, buried out yonder by that big tree," he said with a nod of his head. "But they don't rest easy."

"You never said how you knew about the Department," Mitch said it casually, but Jacob picked up on the caution in his partner's tone. "After all, we're not common knowledge."

"Eli Bly told me to expect you," Sani said. "Then he left."

"Where did he go?" Mitch asked.

Sani shrugged. "Don't know. But he wasn't the only stranger poking around. There's been another man looking around the ridge. Bly said he was an outlaw. He took a shot at me, when I got too close. The spirits don't like him, either."

"What did he look like?" Jacob raised an eyebrow, as a suspicion grew.

"Tall man, thin like a scarecrow. Sharp nose. Hair like straw. Shot his gun left-handed," Sani replied.

Mitch and Jacob exchanged a glance. "Peter Kasby?" Mitch said with a sigh. "He's trouble, all right."

"From what you've said, it makes sense he'd show up here," Jacob added. "Everyone calls him 'The Prospector' because he goes out to sites where there are problems and sees what he can steal."

"He's a dangerous man," Sani agreed. "Be careful. He may still be around."

"We've tangled with Kasby before," Mitch replied. "But thanks for the warning. Now, we need some horses and supplies if we're going to have a look over that ridge."

"You'll find your horses in the stable, ready to go, saddlebags packed with all the equipment you should need," Sani said. "Best you be back here by nightfall. There are worse things than coyotes in the dark. You'll find food in the cupboard for your meals and some to take with you when you ride out to look beyond the ridge. There's a well in the back to fill your canteens and a few bottles of whiskey in the dry sink cabinet. You're the only guests at the rooming house."

"Sounds like you've taken care of everything," Mitch said. "So we'll get to work." He glanced at Sani. "Are you coming out to the ridge with us?"

Sani shook his head. "My magic will not permit me to enter the crater. The power of what the silver ship left behind wars with my abil-

163

ities." He dropped his voice. "I speak with the dead. The spirit of the captain of the silver ship came to me. He told me to find the metal boxes and turn them off so he and his people can finally rest."

"Metal boxes?" Jacob asked. "Equipment?"

Sani sighed. "I am a shaman. I speak with spirits. But sometimes, the spirits can't say plainly what they need. This spirit shared an image with me, of two metal boxes and a silvery oval. I assume they were the equipment he meant. I gathered they were damaged in the crash, and something about those boxes is raising hell. It got worse when someone started digging, bringing them closer to the surface. The sooner you can shut them down, the better." Sani gave them a tip of his hat in farewell and strode off down the street. Mitch and Jacob turned and walked toward the stable.

"You believe him?" Jacob asked under his breath.

"Not completely," Mitch replied. "There's something weird about this place—but that's the point, I guess. The sooner we find out what it is and how to put it right, the faster we can get back to New Pittsburgh or somewhere else that's civilized."

"You think Bly just told him about the Department—and us?"

Mitch shrugged. "Maybe. We don't know how well he knew Sani, and what called him away. And the Department didn't bother to tell us. Typical."

"So is Bly really missing? Or just reassigned?"

"Maybe when we get to the bottom of this, we'll know," Mitch replied.

They found the horses saddled and tied up to the hitching post by the stable. Mitch and Jacob checked the saddlebags and found food, water, and survival equipment: a pickaxe and shovel, compass, tarpaulin, and a few other essentials. Mitch secured the duffel bag, and the two men rode out toward the ridge.

"Ruin Creek isn't the first place to report strange airships," Jacob observed.

"Been a lot of reports this year," Mitch agreed. "Always in some godforsaken corner of the desert where the people who might see something aren't likely to be taken seriously."

"Do you think Sani is telling the truth about Bly?" Jacob asked.

"Don't know what I think about that," Mitch replied. "Bly sent a request for backup. So where is he?"

"The West is a big place," Jacob said. "He could have gotten reassigned by one of the other managers. You know they don't talk to each other. We drew the short straw because we were handy. For all we know, Bly's up in the Yukon, looking for Sasquatch."

"Are those hairy guys causing problems again? I thought we told them to keep it quiet and stay in the woods." They rode in silence for a while. Jacob kept looking over his shoulder, sure they were being watched, but he saw no one. Still, he made certain his duster was out of the way of his holster, in case he needed a fast draw.

"Well, will you look at that?" Mitch murmured as they reached the crest of the rise. Below them spread a wide crater with deep, sloping walls. "Holy Hell."

Jacob raised an eyebrow. "Whatever made a hole like that when it hit had to be big."

The desert stretched as far as the eye could see in every direction. They slipped and slid their way to the bottom of the basin. "Yeah, they were looking for something," Jacob observed. Dozens of holes pockmarked the bottom of the depression. They had clearly been shoveled out, and the work looked recent.

"Sani's story doesn't explain why people disappeared or why there were problems with the livestock," Jacob replied.

"Could be coincidence. Something strange happens, and people blame everything that happens afterward on it, whether the two are related or not," Mitch said with a shrug. "Or maybe they got hit with the ship when it fell. Doesn't take much to set dogs to barking, and chickens go off laying for all kinds of reasons." He pulled out a black box with a silver metal probe connected by a cord and cranked it up, watching the dials and gauges as he swept the probe in an arc around him.

"I'm getting some very strange data," Mitch said. "The EMF readings are pegging the dials."

"Okay," Jacob replied, drawing out the syllables. "That could mean about a dozen or more things."

"Despite what I picked up from Sani, I don't think we're dealing with magic out here." Mitch tucked the meter away and drew out the charm he had been given by the absinthe witch. He held it by a thin silver chain, and to Jacob's eye, the charm did absolutely nothing. "See? It's not glowing or spinning."

"There's magic, and then there's the supernatural," Jacob said. "People call those hills the 'Superstition' Mountains, for a reason. We're on Navajo land. Maybe Renate's charm doesn't pick up on Navajo juju."

Mitch scowled at him and shoved the charm back in his pocket. "There's a new toy Farber built for me—a mineral detector. It's the funny-looking thing in the duffle bag that's not a gun. How about taking a look around with it?"

"What are you going to do?"

Mitch grinned. "Fiddle with the Maxwell box."

Jacob had plenty of experience with Adam Farber's experimental gadgets. The young man was a certifiable genius who impressed even Nikola Tesla with his designs. But often, the first-of-their-kind pieces of equipment Farber built for the Department caused unintended consequences. Jacob had learned to be cautious.

Jacob pulled out a metal contraption that looked like a pole with a few loops of steel tubing at the bottom, and plenty of wires and gauges along the sides. Powered by a Gassner battery, and embellished by Farber, the detector began beeping loudly as soon as Jacob turned it on.

"There's iron scattered all over this lake bed," Jacob said. "Lots of it. Some nickel, too."

Mitch kicked at the ground, then bent down to pick up a handful of blue-white crystals. "Bring that thing over here, will you?" Jacob rolled his eyes but complied.

Mitch flipped a switch on the detector, then ran the crystals beneath the scanner. "Look at this," he said. "Really strange quartz—not like anything I've ever seen before. Even the scanner is saying there's got to be an error."

166

"Maybe the airship crash did something to the rock, especially if there was a lot of heat," Jacob said.

"Maybe." Mitch pulled out a black box with knobs and gauges. "Let's see what kind of ghosts we can call up."

"I really wish you wouldn't," Jacob replied. "We don't have the usual protections."

Mitch made a dismissive gesture. "I'm not going to turn it on full blast. Let's start with the simple stuff."

"Only you would consider ghosts to be 'simple.'"

Mitch glared at him. "All right. Just in case, grab one of the Ketchum grenades in the bag. And there's an icon in that red box from Father Matija."

Jacob grumbled under his breath, but he retrieved the items. Mitch turned the knob on the Maxwell box. They didn't have long to wait.

"Look!" Jacob said, pointing to the ridge. Light shimmered like heat waves coming off the desert all along the lip of the depression. In those shimmering waves, Jacob made out the faces and forms of people, though they were distorted by something that pulled them this way and that, like a column of smoke in a breeze.

"Something's interfering with the Maxwell box," Mitch said. "Something strong enough to repel the ghosts even though I've got the power turned up." He glanced at the gauges. "We're pegging the meter. Plenty of ghosts to go around, but for some reason, they can't pass the crest of the ridge."

"Let them go," Jacob urged. "Bad enough that they're dead. Now we know—this place has the spirits all stirred up, but they don't want to come into the basin."

Mitch nodded and turned down the knob on the Maxwell box. The shimmering line of ghosts winked out. "They're gone," he said, looking up at the now-deserted ridge.

"I still feel like we're being watched," Jacob replied. "You believe Sani about *chindi* and the skinwalker?" he asked as he replaced the grenade in the duffel bag and drew his revolver. The heavy, cold steel was a comfortable certitude.

"I believe that he believes in them," Mitch replied with a shrug.

"But I'm intrigued about these 'missing pieces,' and I really want to know why Kasby—if he's the one—is hanging around."

"Maybe someone else has a wunderkind like Farber coming up with secret inventions," Jacob said. "Only one of theirs didn't work so well. And maybe their 'silver bird' had other off-the-books gadgets onboard that got damaged in the crash and are going haywire." He shrugged. "Imagine an airship crashing with a Maxwell box onboard and having it get stuck turned on full blast."

Mitch repressed a shiver. "I'd rather not, if it's all the same to you."

"What now?" Jacob asked.

"We go looking for the pieces that Mr. Sani told us got dug up in the railroad construction. Find them, and we're closer to fixing the problem."

———

"THERE'S A LOT of nothing out here." Jacob kicked a rock and sent it tumbling through the dust. It was still mid-morning, cool by desert standards. Saguaro and mesquite stretched as far as the eye could see. "And so far, we've seen more rattlesnakes than pieces of strange airships."

"I think Sani was right," Mitch replied, ignoring his comments. "Somebody crashed an experimental ship with gear onboard. Either they couldn't find the missing pieces or no one filed the right paper-work for a recovery team, so it's still here, causing issues."

"You think it's one of ours?" Jacob asked, raising an eyebrow.

"We're pretty far south for it to be the Canadians," Mitch replied, walking a parallel course to the railroad tracks, running the metal detector back and forth. He frowned as the detector beeped, but all he found was the button from a man's jacket. He straightened and looked at the button in the light.

"What if it's other?" Jacob asked.

"European?"

"Farther than that."

Mitch shrugged. "Maybe. It's happened before. Those orbs over

New Pittsburgh. Remember?"

Jacob remembered. The Department of Supernatural Investigation was not limited to problems with rogue magic. Sometimes, the threats came from far away—not just beyond the United States, but beyond Earth. "Yeah, I thought of that. But let's start with the simplest explanation. And that would be someone with enough resources to outfit an experimental airship with off-the-record bells and whistles. That's scary enough, considering the short list of who might be behind a project like that."

Mitch held out the button to Jacob. "What do you make of this?"

Jacob frowned as he examined the stamped brass. "Military issue. One of our folks. Doesn't look like it's been out in the elements too long."

Mitch nodded. "Might be a clue to confirm our hole-digger. Now let's see—treasure hunter, rogue agent, outlaw—sure sounds like someone we know."

Jacob swore. "Yeah, the Prospector. I was hoping it wasn't."

"Well, it all fits. I thought they'd finally locked him up in Fort Leavenworth," Jacob replied.

"Maybe he got out for good behavior. Or escaped. Or paid someone off," Mitch said.

"Think he had anything to do with Bly being here—or his sudden departure?" Jacob's tone made his own opinion clear.

"I think it's very possible. Even likely."

Mitch and Jacob were both on the lookout for danger as they climbed the sloping sides of the basin. Nothing but cactus and rock formations met their gaze as they peered over the rim before scrambling out.

"I set the Maxwell box to its lowest setting," Mitch said, glancing at the device. "Farber assured me that would just monitor whether ghosts were present, but not call them or drive them away."

"And?"

Mitch made a face as he stared at the readings. "There's a lot of activity around the basin. And some weird readings I can't explain."

Mitch gave the Maxwell box to Jacob and took the mineral detector for himself, hefting the duffel bag with their extra weapons over his shoulder. Then they led their horses by the reins over to the railway tracks.

The stretch of railroad tracks ran as far as the eye could see. They agreed to walk for two miles in either direction of the track closest to the crater, then switch sides. Out of the corner of his eye, Jacob glimpsed movement, but when he turned to look, no one was there. *On the other hand, my horse is skittish as a colt,* Jacob thought. *People say horses can see ghosts. So maybe I'm not crazy. I'm certain we're not alone, and I'm positive we're being watched.*

"I'm getting some strange readings," Jacob said.

"Me, too," Mitch agreed.

The toe of Jacob's boot caught an edge of something metallic. "I've got something!"

"What did you find?"

Jacob bent down, kicking at the dirt for a better look. "A bit of silvery metal—not the kind of thing I'd expect from the Atcheson-Topeka."

"Throw it in the bag," Mitch said. "We'll sort it out later."

"And you?"

"Lots of rocks," Mitch replied. "Bits of something my detector recognizes as metallic, but can't identify the composition. We may have to send them to the lab at HQ to get an analysis."

"We can send a telegraph from Ruin Creek," Jacob said.

"Yeah," Mitch replied. "I think that would be a good idea. Something about this whole mission gives me the creeps."

Jacob was glad Mitch admitted being uneasy. He had misgivings since they had been dispatched. The missing folks of Ruin Creek and the mysterious Navajo shaman only deepened his concerns.

"Now that's interesting," Jacob said, bending down for a better look. A smooth, oval-shaped metallic object caught the light. It was no bigger than his palm, and definitely not natural.

"What?"

Jacob let his hand hover over the object and felt a prickle of power. "I'll throw it in the bag," Jacob said. "You find anything?"

"Nothing bigger than a quarter," Mitch replied. "Makes me think our Navajo friend was right, but whatever it was didn't just crash—it exploded."

"Makes you wonder what they had onboard," Jacob said.

They heard the unmistakable crack of a rifle shot, and the bullet barely missed Jacob's shoulder. His horse shied. Mitch had his rifle up and sighted before Jacob could calm his frightened horse, and returned fire, though there was no one in sight.

"Get to cover!" Mitch snapped, and Jacob pulled his mount into the only shelter close at hand, the shadow of three large saguaro cactus. Mitch swung partway up to the saddle, rifle at the ready, as he rode for the scant protection of a rock pile left behind by the railroad construction.

A second shot kicked up dirt just behind Mitch's horse. Jacob returned fire. He could not spot the sniper, but the only likely cover was another pile of dirt from the construction efforts, far enough away to make even a sharpshooter's aim iffy.

"Look!" Jacob called to Mitch, pointing toward a rising dust cloud behind a rapidly retreating man on horseback. "Do you think we can catch him?"

Mitch shook his head. "Too much of a chance he's leading us into an ambush. He'll be back."

"It's not like Kasby to miss," Jacob observed. Mitch was a sharp-shooter, and long ago, Kasby had been part of Mitch's rifle unit. A lot of bad blood separated then from now.

"He missed on purpose," Mitch replied, anger clear in his voice. "He's warning us away from 'his' find. To hell with that."

———

ALL OF THEIR hot, dry hours of work led to a bucketful of bits of odd metal, fused rock, and shiny objects. All the while, Jacob could not shake the feeling that they were being observed.

Movement off to one side caught Mitch's attention. "What was that?"

171

"I don't know," Jacob said warily. "Whatever it is, I don't like it."

Both Jacob and Mitch pulled their guns. This time Jacob caught movement out of the corner of his eye, something cutting them off on the right. "Let's get back to town," he murmured.

"Sounds good to me," Mitch agreed.

A strange, lonesome cry broke the desert silence. Both their mounts spooked at once, whinnying and prancing nervously. When Mitch and Jacob looked up again, a hunched, snaggle-toothed creature with red eyes and sharp fangs blocked the roadway.

"That's a skinwalker," Jacob said quietly. "When it's not wearing a borrowed skin. Saw a drawing in an old book. We're in trouble."

"Get out of the way," Mitch said, drawing his Peacemaker. "We mean you no harm."

The creature glared at him, a crafty, hungry look. It did not move to let them past.

"Stand aside," Jacob said, bringing up his revolver where he was sure the creature could see it.

In response, the creature snarled and lunged straight at them.

Jake and Mitch reined their horses in hard to keep them from bolting. Mitch fired a shot, but the bullet passed right through the skinwalker without harm.

"It's a ghost!" Mitch shouted.

"Yeah, but it's coming right at us!" They took off at a gallop. The ghost followed, snapping at their mounts.

"I have the feeling we're being herded," Mitch called over his shoulder, as he and Jacob tried to outrun the creature. Every time they tried to get back on the road, the ghost snapped and dove at them, driving them around the rim of the crater.

"Yeah. Me too," Jacob admitted. "The question is—why?"

By this time, they were on the opposite side of the huge depression from where they had entered. The ghost hunkered down just far enough away to keep the horses from bolting. Construction crews had dumped dirt and debris on this side of the basin, and windblown mounds stretched for a quarter mile.

Mitch swung down from his horse. "Maybe we're supposed to find something here. Maybe that's the point."

"*Maybe* that shadow has friends, and they're going to eat us," Jacob replied. "Maybe *that's* the point." They were quiet for a few moments, keeping a careful eye on the skinwalker as they looked for debris.

"I think Sani knows more than he's saying."

"Yeah," Jacob said bending down to examine something that was half buried in the sandy soil. "I think you're right."

Mitch picked up on the change of tone. "What did you find?"

"Not sure," Jacob replied. "But it might be what Bly and Kasby were looking for."

———

BY THE TIME they returned to Ruin Creek, the moon had risen. The skinwalker shadowed them back to town but made no further move to attack.

They headed into the rooming house. Lanterns burned in the windows, but the kitchen was quiet. Dried sausage, cheese, dried fruit, and hard bread were in the cupboard just like Sani said, as was the whiskey. Jacob took a bucket and went out to the well, returning with fresh drinking water.

"I think it's time we got some backup," Mitch said. "Let's get a telegram off to Agent Kennedy. I want to make sure she's going to have an airship out here to pick us up, and if she's got any intelligence on weird airship sightings, now's the time to sing out about it."

Jacob gave a curt nod. "Agreed. Right after we eat."

With a skinwalker and a hostile sharpshooter on the loose, Mitch and Jacob went together to send the telegram. Mitch took the duffel bag of weapons and the three most valuable items they had found at the crater with them, in case Kasby had tracked them to the rooming house.

Lights glowed in the windows of the houses, saloons, and brothels. Faint strains of music carried on the night air, and shadows moved behind the curtains.

"I thought Sani said everyone else was gone," Jacob said nervously. "Are you sure the Maxwell box is off?"

"Yeah, I'm sure," Mitch replied. "But I'm starting to wonder just what kind of a trouble Bly's gotten us into."

"There's the railroad station, where the telegraph office should be," Jacob said, with a nod toward the small shed. Dust covered everything in the cramped office. Rumpled, yellowed papers lay scattered across a hard-used desk. Jacob rustled through the papers while Mitch stood guard. "Can't find anything dated more recently than six months ago," Jacob said. He reached for the telegraph key and began to tap out the Department security code. "Damn."

"What?"

"Telegraph isn't working," Jacob said, adding a few choice curse words in his native Croatian for emphasis.

Mitch kept his gun at the ready as he craned for a look out the window. "Well, that would explain why," he said, pointing. Jacob peered over his shoulder. The nearest telegraph pole was down, and it had pulled the wires right out of the wall of the station when it fell.

"Tomorrow, we'll nail down the truth from that shaman," Mitch said. "Let's get back to the rooming house. I don't know what's going on, but I definitely don't like it."

Both of them had their revolvers in hand as they walked back toward town. Their boot steps echoed on the plank sidewalks. Music still came from the saloons and bordellos, and they could see the silhouettes of townsfolk going about their evening routine behind the thin curtains.

The sound of a raucous player piano grew louder as they approached the Brass Pounder saloon, along with a woman's laughter and the muted rumble of men's voices. Mitch pushed open the door into the tavern and found a darkened, abandoned shell.

"Nobody's here," Jacob said.

Mitch glanced down at the Maxwell box. "Oh, they're here. The meter on the box is jumping like catfish on a hot summer day. Sani told us the truth, at least about the dead being restless." He looked up at the dirty mirror behind the dusty, ornate bar. "Isn't that right?"

The mirror cracked loudly enough that for a second, Jacob mistook it for a gunshot, fracturing from the center out, showing the ruined bar like a crazy carnival mirror. Glassware hurled itself off of the shelves, sending a spray of shards into the room. Jacob dug into the duffle and pulled out a strange long gun, like a shotgun wound with wires and tubes. He kept his revolver in one hand and the newfangled weapon in the other, as Mitch and he began to back toward the doorway, one of them facing in each direction.

Footsteps sounded on the stairs from the second floor. The piano music suddenly started up again, though the old upright along one wall was as swaybacked as a knacker's mare. A chair tipped over as if its occupant stood suddenly, but the Brass Pounder's patrons were not visible to anyone but the Maxwell box.

Someone shoved Jacob, hard enough to make him take a step back. It was a move he would have expected from a belligerent drunk looking to start a fight. Out of nowhere, a tattered playing card wafted down in front of Mitch and landed at his feet.

"All bets are off," Mitch muttered. "Let's get the hell out of here."

Back on the sidewalk, some of the lights had gone out. The Brass Pounder's competition remained lit up, as did the brothels, and as soon as Mitch and Jacob started to walk away, the sound of distant music filled the night air once more.

Unsure who was watching them, Mitch and Jacob stayed in the shadows, moving with prudent speed toward the rooming house. As they passed the Rusty Spike, Jacob peered in through the doorway. What had appeared to be a busy tavern seconds before was as empty as the Brass Pounder.

"Hey!" Mitch shouted at a woman who emerged from a doorway up ahead of them. In the moonlight, Jacob could just make out the name over the door as The Parlor, and he could guess its type of business. He and Mitch ran to catch up with the woman.

"Miss! I'd like a word with you!" Mitch called. Just as they closed the distance, the woman turned. Her mouth moved, but no sound followed. It couldn't have, not with the ear-to-ear slice across her throat.

The woman's figure winked out.

A low growl sounded behind them. Mitch and Jacob wheeled to see a huge, misshapen black dog with glowing red eyes standing in the middle of the street. Head down and hackles raised, it drew back its lips to expose sharp, white teeth. This time, the skinwalker was no ghost.

Mitch and Jacob shot simultaneously. Old danger and long practice meant they fought as a team. Mitch put a shot through the creature's forehead, and Jacob's bullet hit it in the chest, but the beast barely rocked on its feet. Two more shots each hit their target, to no effect.

"Get down!" Jacob cautioned, leveling the strange long gun. He braced himself and pulled the trigger. An invisible cone of energy burst from the muzzle, hitting the skinwalker and tossing the monster half a block down the street.

"Run!" Mitch said, and before the creature could gather its wits, they took off at top speed. As Mitch and Jacob ran past the general store, the lanterns in the shopkeeper's apartment overhead sputtered out. So did the lights in the Brass Pounder and The Parlor, the Rusty Spike and the Paris brothel. Ruin Creek was going dark.

Jacob looked up to see Eli Bly gesturing to them from an alleyway. He motioned them toward the rooming house. Before either of them could say a word, Bly ran past them at the skinwalker, which barreled in their direction. The skinwalker stopped in its tracks as Bly advanced on it, and then begin to warily back away.

"How does an old guy with no gun scare something like a skin-walker?" Jacob panted.

"Got a theory, but you aren't going to like it," Mitch said as they jerked open the rooming house door and flung themselves inside.

When Jacob looked back, both Bly and the skinwalker were gone.

Jacob leaned against the locked door, trying to get his breath. Mitch dropped the duffel full of weapons where it was handy and went to dump out their bag of rocks from the crater on the kitchen table. "Ghost?" Jacob asked, meaning Bly.

"Alien?" Mitch replied. "Or maybe competing skinwalkers."

"Aren't you just a ray of sunshine."

"Someone isn't telling us the truth," Mitch said, anger clear in his voice.

"Before we sift through those rocks, I want to make sure no one's upstairs," Jacob said. "We haven't found the sniper. I want to make sure he didn't find us, first."

They lit two more lanterns from the kitchen and headed for the steps to the second floor. Four doors lined a short hallway. One door was open, and the twin beds were made up for company. "Guess that's our room," Jacob said.

Mitch opened the second door and held his lantern aloft. The bedroom was empty. A bed, washstand, and dresser were covered with dust. "Doesn't look like anyone's been in this room for a while," Mitch said, batting away a cobweb.

He opened the doors to the third room and found the same thing. The fourth room had an occupant. "There's someone in the bed," Jacob hissed. He brought his revolver and the force gun up to point at the figure beneath the covers.

Worn boots sat beside the door, and a battered valise lay on a chest at the bottom of the bed. Objects were strewn across the top of the dresser. Mitch laid a hand on the figure's shoulder, turning it toward them, then flinched as the desiccated corpse fell onto its back.

"I think we've found Eli Bly. Let's see what we can find out from his stuff," Mitch said.

Jacob lit the bedside lantern. Mitch gave Bly's corpse a careful once-over. "He had a bad wound to his shoulder," Mitch mused. "Doesn't look like he had a doctor around to treat it, either." He looked up at Jacob. "Want to bet it's a bullet?"

"You think Kasby was cold enough to shoot him in his bed?"

Mitch shrugged. "Doubtful. I'm betting he was nosing around that crater and Kasby winged him. Maybe Kasby didn't even mean to kill him; just scare him away. But at Bly's age, who knows?" Mitch said. "Came out here in the heat, poked around all day without enough water, and got shot—maybe his heart just gave out on him, or maybe the wound went sour."

177

"From the way he's all shriveled up, he didn't just die in the last few days," Jacob said. "Looks like a mummy I saw at the museum."

"Blame the dry air," Mitch replied. "But you're right—it takes time for a body to dry out like that. Long enough that there isn't even a smell left."

Jacob walked over to Bly's valise and looked inside. "Clothing, and a couple of notepads."

"Bring the notepads," Mitch said. He had moved over to look at a wooden crate by the window. "Looks like Bly was picking up rocks from the crater, too." He hefted the small crate. "Let's take this stuff downstairs. I'm pretty sure the answer is in here somewhere."

Jacob had locked the front and back doors before they headed upstairs. He peered from the window. "I'd bet you next week's pay there's something out there."

"Yeah, but is it the skinwalker or Kasby?" Mitch replied. "Or Sani?" He poured a finger of whiskey into each of their glasses. "You take a look at those notebooks. I've got a theory I want to test."

Outside, the wind caught at the screen door, and it thudded against its frame. Jacob heard a few bars of a piano playing saloon songs, and it sent a cold shiver down his spine. A wolf howled in the distance, and an unholy screech answered the wolf. Ghostly faces appeared in the windows, vanishing before Jacob could get a good look at them.

"Bly had terrible handwriting," Jacob said, skimming through the notebooks while Mitch tinkered with his equipment. "What are you doing with those wires?"

"You'll see," Mitch replied. "What's in the notes?"

Jacob scanned the pages. "Looks like Bly came out here on a hunch. He was interested in all the strange airship sightings, and he wanted to see what he could find out."

"More than he bargained for, apparently."

Jacob nodded. "Yeah." He riffled through pages again. "He spent a lot of time out at the crater, picking up pieces from the wreck." He nodded toward the largest item, a second featureless box. "He mentions finding the box and not being able to turn it on or open it up."

"That's because it's already on," Mitch said, wrestling his contraption to secure more wires. "Even if he didn't realize it. The trick is turning it off."

Mitch pointed toward the silvery object Jacob had found, and the heavy gray box they had unearthed that matched the one in Bly's room. "I think these are pieces of equipment from the ship."

"Difference engines?" Jacob said, raising an eyebrow.

Mitch shrugged. "Maybe. Now see what happens when I turn this on," Mitch said. He pulled out the EMF frequency meter. "I tinkered with the settings." He turned the meter on and suddenly, the room around them changed.

A matronly woman bustled around the stove. Two men sat at the table. The door opened, and Eli Bly walked in. He didn't look well. Jacob gathered that Bly was going up to his room to rest. A brown mutt begged scraps under the table.

Mitch turned the meter off. The images disappeared.

"What the hell was that?" Jacob asked, eyes wide.

Mitch grinned. "I can tell you what they weren't: ghosts or magic."

"So what were they?"

"Ever see a Theatre Optique?" Mitch asked. "Projects a series of still images onto a screen fast enough that your brain thinks the images are moving."

"Yeah, I saw one at the vaudeville theater last month."

"It's a machine that stores pictures and projects them to tell a story," Mitch said. "And I think that's just what one—or all—of these pieces of 'equipment' do."

Jacob frowned. "Why would an airship want equipment like that?"

Mitch shrugged. "Maybe it's an advanced camera. Or maybe it was damaged in the crash, and it's not working right." He pulled out the Maxwell box and the metal detector from underneath the table. "I'm going to fiddle with these and see what I can rig up." Mitch cleared away the silvery debris and fused rock into Bly's crate, leaving only the two gray boxes and the oval-shaped smooth metal object. He maneuvered his jury-rigged machine onto the table. "I've got a theory I want to test."

"God help us all," Jacob muttered.

179

"I'm connecting the Maxwell box and the EMF detector, and powering them up with the Gessner battery from the metal detector," Mitch said as he worked. "Crude as hell, but I want to see if I can get any of these pieces to show us more."

Jacob scooted his chair back from the table. Mitch flicked switches and turned dials, as the Gessner battery hummed. And in the blink of an eye, the kitchen of the boarding house disappeared, and Jacob and Mitch found themselves on the bridge of the strangest airship they had ever seen.

"Where are we?" Jacob whispered.

"Right where we were before," Mitch replied. "Remember Theatre Optique? It's all just photographs. With some extra technological mojo."

Unlike the jerky projected images Jacob had seen at the vaudeville theatre, these images moved and looked like real people, three-dimensional, but not solid. "Technological ghosts," Jacob said.

"More like a record of a journey made by explorers who have a leg up on us when it comes to inventions," Mitch answered.

Jacob watched the crew of the strange airship bustle back and forth. They passed straight through him, and through the table and furnishings of the kitchen. The crew's uniforms were unlike those of any airship company or navy Jacob could call to mind, and the sleek, smooth bridge looked advanced beyond anything in the Department's fleet.

"Alien?"

"I'd bet money on it," Mitch said.

They watched the silent images react as something went wrong aboard the airship. The crew rushed back and forth, trying to save their ship as it pitched and then dropped out of the sky. A moment later, the figures of the crew disappeared. But before Mitch could turn off the connection, new images sprang to life. Mrs. Cline, moving around her comfortable kitchen. Eli and the other boarders eating dinner. They watched for several more minutes as the boxes showed the everyday routine, and then Mitch unplugged the equipment.

"What about the ghosts we saw out at the crater?" Jacob said. "The Maxwell box called them."

Mitch nodded. "And something about the crater pushed them away. If an alien airship crashed, there could be other bits of technology still puttering away over there—which would account for the weird EMF readings."

"But did we get what we were sent out to find?" Jacob asked. "After all, we still don't know who Sani really is, or what he needed us to do that he couldn't do for himself. And what about Kasby and the skinwalker?"

A rifle shot crashed through the window, barely missing Mitch's ear and lodging in the wall behind them. Mitch and Jacob dropped to the floor, guns ready. A second shot broke the lock on the door. Jacob and Mitch fired back. The door swung open to reveal an empty porch.

A dark form shattered the window on the opposite side of the kitchen, landed in a crouch and came up firing. Bullets shattered the plaster in the walls, broke the ceramic plates on the rack over the stove, and shot up the Hoosier cabinet. Kasby ducked behind the cast-iron stove, which gave him an angle that kept Mitch and Jacob pinned down.

"Fascinating theories," Kasby gloated. "Hope you don't mind me listening at the window. I'll take it from here. I've got buyers lined up for those boxes—and those crates of rock. They'll pay a lot more than the Department does."

Mitch rolled and shot, coming close enough to drive Kasby back behind the stove. "You killed Eli Bly?"

"Fortunate accident," Kasby replied. "The old man was poking around that crater. I got there first. Thanks to you, that junk is a lot more valuable now that it works."

Outside, a preternatural howl sent shivers down Jacob's spine. He glimpsed a dark shape in the moonlight, hunched and misshapen, though no less fleet of foot for its disfigurement.

"Did you mean to blow the doors open so the skinwalker could eat us, or was that just a bonus?" Jacob snapped.

"Not a bad way to get rid of your bodies," Kasby replied, swinging out to take a few more shots that were too close for comfort. "I didn't call it. The energy from the crash did, just like it energized the ghosts."

Eli Bly's ghost appeared at the bottom of the stairs and gave a soundless howl of rage. The ghost charged at Kasby. Mitch brought his rifle to his shoulder and squeezed off a shot that went right through Bly's translucent form. He hit Kasby square in the chest at the same time that the high-pitched whine from Jacob's force gun let rip and a wave of energy threw Kasby's bloody form out into the street. The skinwalker lunged, sinking its long fangs into Kasby's shoulder. Kasby screamed, thrashing and kicking to get loose, held tight in the monster's maw.

The ghosts of Ruin Creek woke up. Lights went on in every building in town. The music reached a crescendo like a traveling carnival, pianos playing several popular tunes all at once and out of key. The sidewalks filled with townspeople caught in the loop of their past, going about their errands, stopping to talk, just an ordinary day snatched from the collective memories of the dead.

Every pane of glass in the rooming house shook until it shattered, and the shutters banged as if they would rip from their hinges. A noise like claws being drawn across the siding boards raised primal fear deep in Jacob's gut. Corpse-pale faces stared through the windows. The skinwalker gave a high-pitched howl. All hell had broken loose on Saturday night in Ruin Creek.

Abruptly, everything fell silent.

"I think Mr. Sani has some explaining to do," Mitch said. That was when Jacob turned to find their patron standing in the boarding house doorway.

"You knew the boxes from the crash were out there, but your magic won't let you go into the crater or handle them yourself. Why?" Jacob demanded.

"Because somehow, you're connected to the aliens who crashed, aren't you?" Mitch supplied.

The Navajo shaman sighed. "Yes. But for my people to rest in peace, I need your help."

"Your people?" Jacob asked. "Somehow, I don't think you're just referring to the tribe."

Mitch gave Sani a measured glance. "How about you tell us what's really going on, and then we decide whether we help you or not."

"Fair enough."

"That was a real skinwalker that ate Kasby," Jacob said.

"I'm betting the strange equipment called it here," Mitch said with a nod toward the items he had assembled. "Just like it riled the ghosts."

"Yes, the skinwalker came shortly after the crash," Sani said. "What you saw at the crater was a projection from the airship commander to get you to look in the right places."

"What about the people we saw on our way into town?" Jacob asked stubbornly.

"They were either ghosts—real ghosts—or projections from the broken equipment," Sani said, and his expression was sad.

"You've played several parts for us," Mitch said. "The Navajo shaman. That first monster that looked like a skinwalker but wasn't. Who are you, really?"

Sani nodded. "I am a real Navajo shaman—and a spirit medium. When the silver ship crashed, I was one of the first to approach the crater after the skinwalker appeared. That's when the ghost of the airship commander spoke to me—and requested my help. I'd like to let him speak for himself," he said.

Sani was silent for a moment. He closed his eyes, and a subtle change came over him. His stance and expression shifted, and Jacob was certain that someone else was in control when Sani spoke once more. "I was the commander of the airship you saw." The voice came from Sani's lips, but the tone and cadence was different. "We came from very far away. When we crashed, my crew was killed, my ship was destroyed, and the equipment that survived was badly damaged— dangerously so."

He motioned toward the gray boxes. "We use those to record our missions, to play for our commanders when we come back. If things go wrong, they keep a record for the inquiry. That silver object, is a *psych-pod*, and held data about our crew," said the ghost of the commander.

"Including the wavelength of our personal energies. It monitors and protects us on the long journey."

"You're a poltergeist," Mitch said, looking at the alien objects on the table. "When your ship crashed, and your equipment got damaged, something mashed up what the gray boxes and the silver oval thing did, and you're stuck here."

Sani nodded. "So are my people. Our spirits are trapped, still tied to the devices that once protected us. And as you've seen, we disturbed the ghosts of the dead near here." He paused. "The energy that raised them also makes the spirits quick to strike out at anything in their path."

"The *chindi*," Jacob said. "Vengeful ghosts."

"That's where I need your help," the commander's ghost said. "Because the equipment is causing my problem, I can't touch the pieces. And because the energy of the crash site is unstable, Shaman Sani cannot enter the crater or handle the boxes. But with your help, I think we can drain the power from the boxes, and that should set us free." Sani smiled. "You now have everything we need pulled together —I just need your hands to do the work."

"You tried to connect with Bly," Jacob said.

"Yes. That other man injured Bly before he could help," the ghost brought an unmistakable change to Sani's manner, resigned yet in command. "He was one of the first to visit the crater and survive. I had not yet met the shaman, so I was less able to communicate. But I believe Bly suspected what was going on, which is why he telegraphed for help, even though he knew it would arrive too late to save his life."

"That was really Bly, out in the street waving us in," Mitch guessed." And he's the one who charged at Kasby." Sani nodded.

"Come," the ghost said. "If you will be my hands, we can set this matter to rest. We share a desire to go home as quickly as possible."

Out in the town telegraph office, a collection of wire, metal clips, and other odds and ends lay scattered across a scarred wooden table. Jacob brought the silver object, and Mitch hauled the two metal boxes and his bastardized detectors along, just in case.

"I'll talk you through it," the alien commander said through Sani.

184

He glanced at Jacob. "I saw you out here earlier. The telegraph pole outside is down, but the wires still carry current. You should be able to reconnect the equipment to signal your friends."

"Let's get started," Mitch said.

Though the components were scavenged and primitive, physics remained constant. It took half an hour for Mitch and Jacob to put the pieces together and wire the silver data recorder to the two boxes according to the ghost's instructions. "You know, after we turn this off, our bosses are going to want us to turn it back on again," Jacob said.

"That won't be possible," the ghost replied. "What you're about to do to disable the box will permanently destroy it. That's for the best. Our worlds are not yet ready to meet one another."

"Well," Mitch said when they had everything assembled. "Are you ready?"

Sani nodded. "Yes. And I'm grateful. Your world is very pleasant. But if I can't go back to my world, I would rather go... on."

"There are a lot of questions I'd like to ask you," Jacob said. "A lot of knowledge you could share."

Sani shook his head. "Less than you'd think," the ghostly commander said. "I'm just a shadow of my real self, part projection, part ghost. I've already begun to fade since the crash. I'm less and less who I used to be. My memories of before the crash have slipped away. A few more weeks, and I'd probably be like the rest of my crew— conscious, trapped, and unable to do anything about it."

Jacob shivered at the thought. "Then it's time to send you on your way."

Mitch flipped the switch. The makeshift mechanism hummed, and the silver device glowed with an internal light. Sani shuddered, and the ghost stepped away from him looking very real and solid. Then, Mitch reversed the current, draining the power. As the light dimmed, the ghost became translucent.

"Thank you." The last of the glow faded from the silver form, and the commander's ghost vanished. Seconds later, the equipment fell silent.

"You know that the Department will hang our asses out to dry for not bringing him in to be interrogated," Jacob said.

"Ghosts can't be interrogated," Mitch replied.

"And what about the horses? The ones we rode out to the crater? They were real. What happens to them if everyone else left town or died?"

"Forgive the deception," Sani said with a wan smile, back to being himself once more. "I borrowed the horses from the tribe, and have returned them to their owners."

"Then we'd better hope that I can get the telegraph working," Jacob said. "Because it's a long way back to Phoenix." He sighed. "Do you think this means we'll get sent up to the Yukon?"

Mitch shook his head. "For Sasquatch? Nah. We've got a guy we call in now and again from Georgia for that kind of thing. Let him handle it. I'm ready to go home."

———

AGENT KENNEDY STEERED the airship in to position just after noon the next day. That gave Mitch and Jacob time to bury Bly's body. Sani stayed to help and said a blessing over the grave. They gathered up Bly's things along with the alien equipment and Bly's notes and put it all in a small crate, which they sent up to the airship with their carpet bags in a rope net while they climbed a dangling ladder.

"If anyone asks too many questions, we'll present them with the boxes and bargain our way back into their good graces," Mitch said as he and Jacob climbed.

"C'mon, c'mon. We don't have all day!" Agent Kennedy shouted down to them, clearly enjoying having the upper hand. Jacob suspected she would not let them live down needing to be "rescued" for a long time.

"Thanks for coming to get us," Mitch said. The airship rose skyward, and the ghost town of Ruin Creek receded beneath them.

"Glad I was in the area," she replied. "What are friends for? But I still don't understand how you got all the way out here. I checked the schedules. Hasn't been a train out to Ruin Creek in six whole months."

THE HUNT

THE HUNT

"I WISH FALKEN would quit sending us out to look for agents that vanished," Mitch Storm grumbled.

"Maybe he's hoping we'll be the next ones to disappear," Jacob Drangosavich replied. He shifted his tall frame to get more comfortable in his seat as the rail car swayed. "If you hadn't let Kesterson get away, Falken wouldn't have had a reason to send us to the godforsaken far north."

"I had a sighting inside the building, and the dynamite brought the roof down. That should have stopped him cold. How was I supposed to know he'd gotten into the storm drain?"

Mitch Storm was average height, with a trim, muscular build. He had dark hair, dark eyes, and a five o'clock shadow that started at three. Mitch was exactly what a penny-dreadful novelist would imagine a government secret agent and former army sharpshooter would look like.

Jacob, on the other hand, was tall and lanky, with a thin face, blond hair, and blue eyes that spoke of his Eastern European heritage. He and Mitch had been agents for the Department of Supernatural Investigation since they had returned east after the rancher wars.

The *click-clack* of iron wheels on the rails confirmed that they were making good time. Outside, the Adirondack Mountains were covered with snow. "How long do you think Falken will keep us on probation?" Jacob asked.

Mitch shrugged. "It was four months the last time, two the time before that. So I wager we're up to six months."

"Why did you use dynamite?" Jacob asked, in an off-handed tone.

Mitch rolled his eyes. "I was improvising."

"Might it be possible to improvise a little less... enthusiastically next time? Sooner or later, Falken will give up on suspending us and just convene a firing squad."

"The Department doesn't use those anymore," Mitch replied. "I checked."

Jacob thought of a dozen arguments, but he knew Mitch was unlikely to heed them. He dropped back against his seat. "At least we got a sleeper train and a private cabin. Where do you think Kesterson will go next?"

Mitch turned away. "Not really our concern, is it? Falken made that pretty clear." He was quiet for a moment. "But Kesterson had some family in New England. Since we're all the way up here in the New York hinterland, I figured we might poke around a little after we finish our assignment—strictly off the record."

"Uh huh," Jacob replied, unconvinced. "You can't leave well enough alone, can you?"

Mitch flashed a grin. "Never."

"Speaking of the assignment. How in the hell do two teams of agents and a dirigible, as well as a perfectly functional *werkman* just vanish?"

"If we knew that, Falken wouldn't have had an excuse to banish us up here," Mitch answered.

Jacob glanced toward the door to their cabin. Two unorthodox companions accompanied them: Hans, a man with brass and gears prosthetics, and Oscar, a mechanical man cleverly constructed by Tesla-Westinghouse Corporation's *wunderkind*, Adam Farber. Oscar—and much of Mitch and Jacob's equipment—was experimental. Several items were one-of-a-kind, prototype pieces Mitch was "testing" for Farber. Those items were in a large crate in one of the boxcars. Oscar and Hans took turns standing guard or sleeping in one of the servants' berths.

"So what are we going to do differently that lets us live to tell the tale?" Jacob asked.

"Damned if I know. I make these things up as I go."

———

THE MOHAWK AND MALONE rail line ended in Tupper Lake. A coach was waiting to take them and their gear to the Altamont Hotel. By wilderness standards, it was very comfortable.

"I'm not impressed," Mitch said as he put down his carpet bag and looked around his accommodations. Hans and Oscar were downstairs, stowing the rest of their gear.

"You will be, once we head into the woods and you compare this to our tent."

Mitch cleared off the desk and began unrolling their topographical maps. A few minutes later, Mitch had maps, drawings, and related communiqués pinned up on the walls, ignoring Jacob's protests about damaging the wallpaper. Sighing in defeat, Jacob hung a "do not disturb" sign on the doorknob and returned to find Mitch studying the maps like a general planning a campaign.

"Crawford and Mason left word that they were approaching an anomaly along these headings," Mitch said, adding red pins. "HQ lost radio contact *here*." He marked a point in pencil.

"Donohoe and Irwin's last message was that they were going in on a heading that would have put them about here," Mitch continued, plugging in more pins. "And they lost contact with them *here*." He made another mark.

"HQ got its last message from *Invictus* somewhere in this area," Mitch said, circling a small area of the map in pencil to indicate where the airship went missing. He pulled out a drawing compass and jabbed the pin into the wall hard enough to make Jacob cringe.

"So this is the approximate area of the irregularity," Mitch said, making another pencil circle on the map.

Jacob frowned, staring at the marked-up map. "Even by Adirondack standards, it's a remote area. No rail lines through there, and no roads. It's high ground, so most of the trappers and hunters might choose a different path around it." He paused. "I wonder what the locals think of having part of the forest go 'missing?'"

"We're supposed to meet our guide in the bar in about half an hour. We'll have a chance to ask."

"They'll know we're not from here." Jacob and Mitch dressed like rustic gentlemen, complete with jackets, boots, and canvas trousers.

"Tupper Lake is full of resort guests," Mitch replied confidently. "No one will notice us."

Jacob was sure the year-round residents knew the guests from the regulars, regardless of what Mitch said. Oscar stayed with their equipment, and Hans followed at a discreet distance when they headed out.

Weir's Saloon catered to locals, with pine-paneled walls, a smudged mirror behind the bar, and a dozen scarred tables with battered chairs. It was a stark contrast to the bar in the Altamont Hotel, which was full of polished brass and mahogany trim.

"In to do some hunting?" the bartender asked as Mitch ordered drinks.

"I hear it's good this time of year," Mitch replied.

The bartender shrugged. "So I'm told. Have you arranged for a guide? They're in short supply, if you haven't."

"We've already hired Peter Astin," Jacob said.

The barkeeper's gaze slid away, and he turned back to his bottles. "That'll do, I imagine."

"You know him?"

"It's a small town. Spend enough time here, and you know everyone."

"We thought about heading north of Pitchfork Pond," Jacob said.

The bartender paled, then collected himself. "I don't much tell people what to do," he said. "But I think you'll find better places."

"That's why we wanted a local guide," Mitch said as if he had not noticed the barkeeper's reaction. "They say these woods are wild enough people still go missing, if they don't know their way around."

The barkeeper turned around and began to straighten the bottles behind the bar. "City folks hear 'forever wild,' and they think it's some kind of pretty park. It's real wilderness out there, and hunters that aren't careful don't come back."

One of the men at the bar had been listening. "For once, ol' Yankton isn't being dramatic," the man said. He thrust out his hand in greeting. "I'm Ben Saunders. I take fine gentlemen like yourselves out fishing." Mitch and Jacob shook hands with Ben, who ordered a round of drinks for all of them.

"You're right about people going missing," Ben said. "Kids wander off; hunters fall off cliffs, guys drown in the lake. But this year, been more than a few."

"Shut up, Ben," Yankton the barkeeper said, without turning around.

"It's the truth, Yankton. Even if the mayor doesn't want it said out loud. That area north of Pitchfork Pond, I'd avoid it if I were you. There's better hunting elsewhere."

Mitch leaned on the bar and took a sip of his drink. "If I didn't know better, I'd say you were trying to warn us off."

Ben regarded the liquor in his glass for a moment before replying. Jacob was aware of Yankton's stare as if the barkeeper were willing Ben to keep his peace. "I wouldn't go near the place," Ben said after a long, tense pause. "No one with a lick of sense would, not after the last few fellows that headed that direction never came back."

Mitch managed his most charming smile. "Surely enough people come and go here—or hike on to other places—that it's not unusual for folks to move on."

Ben shook his head. "These weren't tender-foot city boys. They were locals, knew the area, had family waiting for them to come home. Disappeared. Never found a trace."

"People 'go missing' all the time," Jacob observed. "Usually turns out there's old debt or a new woman involved."

Yankton slapped his hand down on the bar, sharp as the crack of a bullet. On the far side of the bar, Hans glanced up from the drink he pretended to nurture. Jacob gave a negligible shake of the head, and Hans looked down again.

"Not in this case," Yankton growled. "One of those men was my brother. Didn't owe anyone a dime, loved his wife like a moon-eyed schoolboy. Knew the woods like the back of his hand. They found his boot prints. Had a hound dog follow the trail for a ways, and then his scent and tracks just disappeared. So did the dog—and part of the forest." He stopped, as if suddenly aware that he had said more than he intended. "Not that it's your business," he added with a sullen glare.

A bell over the door jangled and a man walked in. The newcomer was average height with a thin build. He sported a patchy beard, and his brown hair looked as if he had cut it himself. Dark, close-set eyes and a pinched face gave him a feral look.

"There's your guide," Ben said with a jerk of his head, in a tone Jacob took to mean he was glad to be rid of them. "Since you like questions so much, might want to ask him what happened to the last guys he took out hunting."

"Thanks for the drink—and the information," Mitch said, leaving behind a generous tip. "We'll be around."

"Maybe," Yankton muttered, pocketing the money. "Maybe not."

Jacob caught Mitch's arm. "Let it go."

Mitch shook off his hand and glowered, but said nothing else.

Astin was watching them attentively. "You must be Mitch and Jacob."

"Let's talk over here," Mitch said, heading to a table in the far corner. "It's a little crowded at the bar."

Astin tipped his hat to Yankton and nodded to Ben. The two men regarded the guide with icy silence. "I trust your train trip went well?" Astin inquired as they found their seats.

"Unremarkable, except for the scenery," Jacob replied. "Is everything ready for the trip?"

"Yes. Oh, yes."

"We'd like to take a bit of a detour," Mitch said, as if the thought had just occurred to him. "Head over beyond Pitchfork Pond."

Astin frowned, and Jacob saw concern in the guide's eyes. "Pitch-fork Pond?"

"You don't have to take us all the way in, just get us to the pond," Jacob said. "We'll pack in from there."

"Are you sure?" Astin fidgeted with his signet ring. "I can show you where the hunting is much better."

"Probably more hunters, too," Mitch replied. "My Uncle Kurt told me about a good spot north of the pond, and I've got my heart set on seeing it for myself."

"If you're sure," Astin agreed half-heartedly. "But I need to warn you—there have been bear attacks out that way. Mauled a hunter a week ago, and a couple of out-of-towners never came back."

Bears, huh? Jacob thought. *If it was that simple, Ben and Yankton wouldn't have gotten in a twist about it.*

"Oh, and we brought a couple of friends with us, and some equipment," Mitch continued.

"I hope your equipment is portable. The trails are rough, and it's quite a hike."

"We'll manage," Mitch assured him. Hans and Oscar, thanks to their clockwork enhancements, were substantially stronger than a normal man. They could easily haul the two sledges to get the equipment where Mitch and Jacob needed it.

Astin nodded, though apprehension showed in his eyes. "Well... if I can't change your mind, I'll see you at dawn tomorrow." He walked to the bar to pay for his drink and said something to Ben that Jacob couldn't catch.

When Jacob and Mitch left the bar, it was dark. The shops were closed, and lights glowed from the upper windows where the merchants lived above their stores.

"What did you make of all that?" Jacob asked. Despite Hans following a block behind them, Jacob felt uneasy.

"I think they know more than they're telling. Something's got Ben and the others spooked."

Jacob nodded. "Might just be because we're not from here. Locals stick together. Maybe they're afraid that if word got out, it would be bad for business."

The night was cold and crisp, and a light dusting of snow had fallen. Jacob had worked with Mitch long enough to know that Mitch was intentionally putting them on display to flush out anyone looking for them. *I really wish he'd ask before using us as bait,* Jacob thought.

"You think someone here had a hand in Crawford and the rest disappearing?" Jacob asked, keeping his voice low.

"Maybe. If not a hand in causing it, maybe a stake in covering it up."

"Can I go on record that I don't care much for our guide? Gives me the creeps."

"We hired him because Donahoe and Crawford used him as their guide," Mitch replied.

"And look how well it turned out for them," Jacob muttered darkly. "Ben and Yankton didn't seem to think much of him."

Mitch slid him a look. "Small town… could be almost anything."

Jacob caught a glimpse of motion out of the corner of his eye. Mitch saw it, too, and tensed. A shadow figure moved down an alley and Hans followed him. Mitch and Jacob drew their guns. Mitch jerked his head to the right and Jacob veered off to the left.

Hans was fast, and the alley was short, but by the time Mitch and Jacob circled around, they found only their bodyguard, shaking his head. "I saw someone—but he gave me the slip."

"Keep your eyes peeled," Mitch replied. Jacob couldn't shake the feeling that they were being watched as they headed back to the Altamont Hotel.

Mitch glanced into one of the shop windows as they walked. "There's someone tailing Hans," he murmured, and raised his hand, giving their bodyguard a silent signal. Hans peeled off down the next side street, while Jacob and Mitch kept their guns at the ready.

"Might just be someone out for a stroll," Jacob allowed. Hans emerged from the side street, now tailing their follower. The man stopped, realizing he was boxed in.

"Astin," Mitch said when he got close enough to recognize the man's face. "Why are you following us?"

Astin fidgeted. "I wasn't following you. I was heading over to my sister's place. She lives on the far side of the hotel, down a piece."

"Ben said for us to ask you about the last strangers you took out hunting," Mitch said.

"I don't know what he's talking about."

"Ever meet a guy named Fred Crawford?" Jacob asked.

"You're friends of his?"

"Yeah," Mitch replied. "He disappeared. Know anything about that?"

"No! Look, the sheriff asked me all kinds of questions when Crawford and his buddy didn't come back to town. I told them the truth: I took them as far as the trailhead, and that's where they paid me and sent me back. I swear to God."

"You looked a little green in the gills when Mitch and I asked you to take us the same direction," Jacob prodded.

Astin's gaze flitted back and forth between Mitch and Jacob. "I haven't taken anyone toward Pitchfork Pond since Crawford. I don't want no trouble."

"How about Frank Donahoe?" Jacob asked. "Sound familiar?"

"Donahoe. Tall guy? Yeah, he was here a while back, but he didn't go toward Pitchfork Pond."

"It didn't worry you when you never heard from Donohoe after you took him out to his camp?" Jacob pressed.

"Nah. Lots of guys pay me when we get where they're going, I leave them a map, and they take it from there. By the time they come back to town, I might be out with another group." He looked surprised. "He and his buddy run into trouble too?"

Jacob shrugged. "No one's seen or heard from them."

"I didn't have nothing to do with that. They were fine and dandy when I got them to their camps."

"But something spooked you?" Mitch asked.

"That's why I didn't want to take you up near Pitchfork Pond. I've seen a lot of strange things in these woods. There's something *wrong* about that area now. Me and all the boys around these parts, we hunt elsewhere. Plenty of woods up here; no reason to go looking for trouble."

"How about the animals?" Jacob asked. "Do they steer clear of the area too?"

"Maybe. The moose are running farther south than usual this year, and the cougars and the bear are causing more trouble lately." Astin looked scared, but whether it was related to Pitchfork Pond or to possibly losing their business, Jacob wasn't sure.

"We wouldn't have hired you if we didn't think you were a good guide," Mitch said, relaxing his posture to be less intimidating. Hans and Oscar both had compasses built into their mechanics, so "needing a guide" was strictly for the purpose of deciding how much Astin knew, and what part he might have played in the disappearances. "We'll be ready in the morning. See you then."

Astin gave a curt nod and headed on his way. He walked another two blocks, headed up the steps to a house, knocked at the door, and entered. "Maybe he really does have a sister," Jacob said. "He might not have been tailing us." Mitch looked unconvinced.

"I'll check on Oscar and our things, sir," Hans said after he saw them safely to their room. "And have dinner sent up."

"Make sure they include yours as well," Mitch said. "The Department's paying," he added with a grin.

"Very well, sir." Hans headed back downstairs to the storage room where Oscar stood guard over their crates.

Mitch and Jacob opened the door carefully, guns drawn, standing on either side of the doorway in case shots greeted their entry. When nothing happened, Mitch glanced at the undisturbed powder on the floor just inside the door. "No footprints."

They entered quickly, and turned on the gaslight, one going right and the other left, in a well-practiced sweep of the room that included assuring there were no intruders under the bed, in the wardrobe, or hiding in the tub. They repeated the process in Jacob's room. To Jacob's relief, the rooms were empty.

A gunshot crashed through the window, shattering glass. Mitch and Jacob dropped to the floor and crawled to the windows.

"There!" Jacob hissed, "At the corner."

Mitch carefully peered out to see a shadowy figure at the corner across the street. Even with a rifle, it would have been a difficult shot in the dark, and they couldn't be certain the shadow was their assailant.

Hans knocked at the door. "Is everything all right?"

"We're fine," Mitch replied.

Jacob carefully drew the curtains and turned down the lamps, so they were not silhouetted against the light. Mitch dug the bullet out of the wall and cursed. "Could have come from any hunting rifle."

A few minutes later, a sharp rap at the door brought both their guns up, trained on the doorway. "Sheriff. Open up."

Mitch and Jacob exchanged a glance and lowered their weapons. Mitch holstered his beneath his jacket and headed toward the door, while Jacob moved his gun out of sight but kept it in hand.

"What's going on in there?" The speaker was a stocky, middle-aged man in a sheriff's uniform. He looked like he was in a bad mood.

"Thank you for coming so promptly, officer. We were about to call the police ourselves," Mitch replied smoothly. "Someone shot into our room." He handed over the slug he had taken out of the room. "I'm afraid it put a hole in the plaster and broke the window."

"You're the two been asking a lot of questions?"

"Just getting the lay of the land." Mitch was casually blocking the sheriff from moving farther into the room.

"I ought to run the two of you in for disturbing the peace."

"I believe we're the damaged parties," Jacob pointed out. "We were just lucky no one got killed. Perhaps one of the local boys had too much to drink and decided to shoot the place up?"

The sheriff's face reddened. "You've got nerve, coming in here and stirring people up."

"You don't want anyone to find out about all the disappearances," Mitch replied, steel replacing the affability in his tone. "You're afraid tourists will stop coming if word gets out, and your own boys are too scared to go investigate on their own."

"Think you're so smart. You'll wise up after you spend some time cooling off in a cell."

Mitch had his badge in the sheriff's face before the man had stopped speaking. "We're here on *government* business. Asking questions is our job. And interfering with the job of a government agent is a *federal* offense." He gave a cold smile. "You wouldn't want to spend time cooling off down at Sing Sing."

The sheriff looked as if he had swallowed his tongue. "Why are you here?"

"Enough people go missing, and the Department takes an interest. We appreciate the support of local law enforcement. If that's not possible, we appreciate them staying out of the way."

"It appears we got off on the wrong foot, Agent Storm. I'm Sheriff Marston. And you can count on the cooperation of my department—which would be me and my deputy."

"Thank you, Sheriff. You could start by telling us how you happened to get here so quickly."

"I was walking my usual route around town when I heard a shot. I ran toward the sound, and there were people on the sidewalk who had run outside at the noise. I saw the broken window, and asked the front desk whose room it was."

"And you didn't see anything strange after the shot?" Jacob pressed.

Marston shook his head. "Give me a little credit—I would have noticed someone running from the scene. But no. Just the people outside the hotel."

Mitch nodded. "All right. Now you can tell us what you know about the disappearances."

"I don't know anything, except that more men have gone into the woods and not come out this year than usual," he replied with a sigh, as if the admission was a personal failure.

"Anyone go looking to see what happened?" Mitch pressed.

Marston set his jaw and gave a curt nod. "Sure we did. But there's something very strange going on out past Pitchfork Pond. There's a weird, shimmery wall of light. Peters went in—he was ahead of the rest of us, we saw him walk through the light—and then he disappeared. There was a strange sound, then all kinds of crazy bright flares shot out. Fortunately, no one was close enough to get hurt. We hollered, but he never came back, and we didn't try to go in after him."

"Thank you, Sheriff. You've been very helpful. I'm counting on you not to say anything to anyone else."

Jacob closed the door behind Marston and turned to Mitch. "What part of the 'secret' in 'secret agent' don't you understand?"

Mitch rolled his eyes. "Did you want to spend the night in the Tupper Lake jail? Or have Marston and his deputy on our heels?"

"We're supposed to be discreet."

Mitch guffawed. "How long have we been partners? Did you just notice that discretion is not something I do well?"

Jacob gave up. "Now what?"

Mitch edged over to the window, peering out as he stood to one side. "Thanks to the sheriff barging in when he did, I doubt we'll find any trace of our shooter."

"Do you think that's a coincidence?"

Mitch pursed his lips, thinking. "Yeah. It might be. Marston didn't seem to be lying about his part in things. Of course, he also didn't seem to be too disturbed that someone took a shot at us. My money's on Ben or Yankton. They seemed pretty anxious to get us to go away and leave the disappearances alone."

"We're leaving, so they should be happy. Here's hoping they don't decide to follow us."

———

"WHY CAN'T PEOPLE disappear when it's warm out?" Jacob muttered, throwing his duffel onto the wagon before he jumped in the seat beside Astin. Hans and Oscar had loaded the two large crates, the heavy equipment, and the sledges onto the back of the wagon earlier that morning to avoid prying eyes. They climbed into the back to watch for unwelcome followers while Mitch hoisted his duffel bag of weapons and swung up into the back as well. A boy from the village rode with them to bring the wagon back to town.

"The road ends on this side of Pitchfork Pond," Astin said as they headed out. "There's some rough terrain to navigate on the north side of the pond. I'll get you through that, but it's as far as I'm going. You'll have to manage the rest on your own."

Even in full daylight, the thick forest was dark and forbidding. Astin took it slow and steady, so as not to put the wagon in the ditch. Jacob sat with a rifle across his lap. Mitch, Astin, and Hans also had rifles, while Oscar had a shotgun—and several other built-in weapons Jacob hoped they wouldn't have to use.

Jacob watched the snow by the side of the road for tracks. Moose and deer tracks criss-crossed the road. Foxes had followed the road for a while before turning off into the forest. A bloody streak and tufts of rabbit fur accompanied an unmistakable set of cougar prints leading into the shadows. Closer to the tree line, Jacob saw bear tracks and wolf prints. Nothing to indicate people. Despite his heavy coat, hat, and scarf, Jacob shivered. *Plenty of things out here that could kill us, even without a whole piece of forest just vanishing.*

The sun broke through the clouds by the time they reached the southern end of Pitchfork Pond where the road ended. "All right," Astin said, bringing the horses to a stop. "Here's where we unload. Tommy will take the wagon back, so the cougars don't get the horses while we trek on in. You sure you need all this stuff? That's a lot to haul."

"Yup. We're sure," Mitch said, with a grin.

Hans and Oscar unloaded the heavy crates and equipment onto the sledges, making it look a lot easier than it was. Mitch slung the heavy duffel bag over his shoulder, and Jacob had the backpack with additional weapons, emergency equipment, and supplies.

"Come on," Astin said. "I want to be back in town by nightfall."

Under other circumstances, Jacob might have enjoyed the hike, despite the cold. The forest was covered with ankle-deep fresh snow, and the bare twigs and branches shone with ice in the cold morning light. Pitchfork Pond stretched off to one side, and the expanse of forest was broken only by a few rustic hunting cabins near the shore.

Jacob walked in front with Astin, keeping his rifle ready. Hans and Oscar came next, hauling the sledges, and Mitch brought up the rear, alert for any signs they were being followed. There was no sound except for the crunch of their feet on the frozen snow beneath the fresh powder and the clicking of the icy branches in the wind. *Sounds like bones rattling,* Jacob thought.

The sun did little to illuminate the depths of the evergreen forest on either side of the rough logging road. Jacob scanned the tree line, alert for danger. Birds scolded them for invading. Jacob imagined thousands of eyes watching them unseen from the branches and shadows.

"Stay in my tracks," Astin warned. "This whole area is full of places where the ground suddenly drops off. The snow makes it difficult to see the edge. That's why you've got me."

Despite Jacob's misgivings, Astin knew the trail. Several times, Mitch marked the trees so they could find their way back out. Overhead, the sky grew gunmetal gray with the threat of more snow, and the day grew colder. Jacob kept an eye on the woods around them, unable to shake the feeling that they were being followed.

"Looks like the weather isn't going to be in your favor," Astin noted. "I wouldn't stay out here longer than you need to. Hiking out in a few inches of snow isn't bad, but we can get a couple of feet of snow in a few hours."

Jacob kept watching the tree line. "I think there's something out there."

"You're probably right. Lots of bear in these woods; cougars, too. The wolves usually stay farther out."

By noon they were as far as Astin would take them. "I'll take my money and be off now. Don't say I didn't warn you."

Mitch dug out his wallet and paid Astin. "Nice job with the trail. Thank you."

Astin glanced at the four men. "I know you had a rough time back in town, but if you really can figure out why people go missing and make it stop, they'll probably give you the key to the city."

"All in a day's work," Mitch replied.

Astin turned to go, but a loud bellow and the crash of something large coming through the underbrush made them all turn. A huge black bear lunged from the shadows. It swatted Oscar away with one of its massive paws, sending the mechanical *werkman* tumbling. Jacob leveled his rifle and fired, blasting the bear in the shoulder, but the creature barreled past Jacob, knocking him down.

Astin held his ground and fired his rifle as the bear came right at him. None of his shots slowed the bear. It sprang toward Astin with its teeth bared. Mitch and Hans shot, hitting the bear in the side and hindquarters. The bear bellowed in pain and anger, coming down on top of Astin with its whole weight, tearing into the guide with his teeth. Astin screamed. Mitch and Hans fired again. After a few more shots, the bear finally went still.

"Astin!" Jacob yelled as he and Mitch ran to the fallen man.

"Well damn! That sure went bad fast." Mitch put the barrel of the rifle against the bear's skull and pulled the trigger. "I'm not taking any chances with that thing." He and Jacob rolled the dead bear to the side. Astin's body lay beneath it, savaged by teeth and claws, covered in blood. Jacob knelt and felt for a pulse.

"He's gone. Looks like those claws opened up an artery," Jacob said. "Poor bloke. No one deserves to go out like that." He wiped his hands in the snow and stood. "Least we can do is bury him, keep the animals away from the body. Someone from town can come back for him later."

"Damn," Mitch said, eyeing the damage. "Bears don't usually attack without a reason. It shouldn't have taken so many shots to bring him down or scare him off. That thing was totally crazed."

"You thinking rabies?"

"Nah. It wasn't foaming at the mouth. I'm stumped— unless it's part of the effect the missing forest has on animals."

"Astin said the bears were more aggressive since the disappearances started," Jacob said.

"Let's stack some rocks over Astin's body and leave the bear where it is." Mitch turned to pick up a large stone and signaled for Hans to help him.

"At least let me say a prayer for him. The man just got killed trying to help us."

"You do your prayer thing. We'll start gathering rocks."

Half an hour later, with Astin beneath a cairn of rocks, Mitch, Jacob, and the others were ready to head deeper into the forest. Oscar was still functional, though the *werkman's* metal body was dented and he had a tear in the metal where a claw had caught his side. *If he had been human, he'd be dead,* Jacob thought. They had scrubbed off the worst of the blood with snow, though Jacob worried that the scent would still carry, attracting other predators.

"Anything that's hungry has a bear dinner back there," Mitch assured him. "We've got bigger things to worry about."

Hans and Oscar unpacked the heavy wooden crates. Inside were two experimental velocipedes, modified off-road steambikes, outfitted with broad nubby tires suitable to the rough terrain and equipped with a variety of weapons and helpful gadgets. The sledges attached behind the bikes, letting them haul their gear.

"We could have gotten here in half the time if we had used these from the start," Jacob grumbled.

"We wanted time to talk to Astin, find out whether he was in on the disappearances, remember? And the locals didn't need a look at classified equipment."

Mitch climbed onto one of the steambikes, while Jacob took the other. Oscar and Hans rode pillion. The bikes roared to life, sending birds fluttering out of the trees and echoing across the silent forest. Given the noise, Jacob doubted they would have any more difficulty with bears, and suspected the wolves and cougars would head for higher ground.

They dared not open up the bikes to their full speed in the forest, where branches and underbrush provided obstacles at every turn. The bikes were a trade-off: stealth for speed. *At least we'll get out of here faster than we came in,* Jacob thought.

An hour later they came to a small clearing. "We'll make camp here," Mitch said dismounting and shutting down the bike. "From what we saw on the map, it's not far to where the forest 'disappears,' so we go see for ourselves and be back before dark. I'd rather not navigate these rough trails at night—or be too close to the anomaly."

They set up their tents quickly and tossed their bedrolls inside. Oscar gathered firewood, and Hans made a fire pit. "There," Hans said, straightening up and dusting off his hands. "Everything is set for when we get back." Oscar hung a metal case with their food from the branch of a tree a few feet from the campsite, out of reach of prowling bears.

They powered up the bikes and headed deeper into the forest. "Do you feel it?" Jacob shouted above the sound of the steambikes' engines. As they neared where the irregularity had been reported, Jacob felt a growing sense of unease, bordering on dread.

Mitch and Hans nodded. "The electromagnetic field shows unusual fluctuations," Oscar said in a tinny voice. His brain contained a difference engine designed by Farber, and he spoke via an altered Edison cylinder.

"Dangerous?" Jacob asked.

"Insufficient data."

It took all of Jacob's concentration to keep the steambike on the trail and avoid rocks, tree roots, and other hazards. "Keep an eye out," Jacob instructed Oscar. "If you see something watching or following us, let me know."

"I cannot. Too much data to process."

Jacob sighed. That was Oscar's way of saying he couldn't separate out the creatures that belonged in the woods and those that might be dangerous. "Damn," Jacob muttered. He felt jumpy, and while it might be the EMF field of the "vanished" forest making him nervous, his intuition told him they might not have shaken their pursuer from the night before.

Mitch came to an abrupt stop. Jacob skidded to a halt beside him. "Holy shit," Mitch said.

"Amen to that."

An iridescent shimmer rose from the ground, making it impossible to see what lay inside the wall of light.

"How sure are we that aliens couldn't come here and take a chunk of the earth back with them?" Mitch mused.

"We're only relatively certain they haven't done it before. That doesn't prove it couldn't happen."

Mitch swore under his breath. "I figured you'd say something like that."

Jacob turned to Oscar. "Can you get any readings beyond the shimmer?"

Oscar stared at the curtain of light. His makers had outfitted him with a sensory array, enhancing his vision and hearing. "I'm afraid I cannot penetrate the barrier," Oscar said after a few moments. "I can tell you that it extends in a one-mile circle, and rises to a height of five miles while descending to a depth of three miles."

Jacob frowned. "So there's no way to go over it or under it?"

"Apparently not, sir."

Jacob had walked over to examine cuts in the trunks of several nearby trees. "Hey, Mitch! What do you make of these?"

Mitch joined him and bent to examine the markings. The slices were uniform, all between two feet and six feet off the ground, in a circle around the glowing anomaly. He pulled several experimental gadgets from his duffel bag and started walking around the missing area of forest.

"EMF readings are off the meter. And the frequencies aren't anything we've run into before." He pulled out a Maxwell box. After another moment, he looked up. "No ghosts. This isn't a poltergeist situation or a haunting. The box registers absolutely nothing." He drew out a charm on a watch fob from his pocket, letting it dangle near the curtain. It remained inert.

"No magic, either," Mitch said, turning the amulet one way and another. An absinthe witch in New Pittsburgh had gifted him with the charm, and Jacob knew it reliably glowed if magic was active.

"You think the Canadians tried out a new weapon?"

Mitch shook his head. "I don't think it's Canadian—or European, either. This is ahead of anything they've shown us—or that we've found out about through channels. That leaves us with aliens."

207

"Why would aliens want to steal a mile of Adirondack forest?"

"I have an idea."

"Give the rest of us a chance to get to cover." Jacob signaled for Hans and Oscar to find shelter as he ran beyond the range of the tree marks and ducked beneath a fallen trunk. Mitch made sure the steam-bikes were out of range as well before he dodged behind a large tree and then hurled a handful of rocks at the shimmering light.

Staccato bursts rang from inside the iridescent perimeter, blasting out in a lethal circle. Brilliant beams of deadly light flashed from inside the "vanished" forest, cutting into whatever they touched. Jacob shielded his eyes and ducked down low behind the tree trunk that sheltered him, hoping not to die.

The assault lasted only seconds. When Jacob dared to raise his head, fresh cuts scared the trees nearby, still smoking from the energy that had carved into them.

Mitch emerged from his cover, swearing. "What was that?" he demanded, facing Oscar.

"Insufficient data."

Jacob took a deep breath to slow his thudding heart. "That's the first time I've nearly been killed by light."

Mitch studied the new cuts on the trees. "It shot at the rocks, but the sheriff said his man and the tracking dog walked in." He looked to Jacob. "Do you think the barrier is smart enough to tell organic from inorganic matter?"

"You mean, living beings can pass through, but not other things? Maybe. And unless the sheriff's man walked in naked, his clothing might have triggered the firing response." Mitch nodded. "If so, we could get through, but not Oscar, and maybe not Hans with his mechanical repairs."

"The only problem is, there's no way to test the theory, since no one's come back out." Mitch eyed the steambike. "I have another idea. Oscar, can you triangulate the source of those light beams from where they struck?"

"Yes, sir. Give me a moment." He rattled off the bearing a few seconds later.

"Saints preserve us; you're not going to strip down and cross like some wild animal, are you?"

"Of course not." Mitch tinkered with one of the steambikes. "At least, not until we're out of other options. But I think I can jam the controls and tie the handlebars so that the bike can drive straight without a rider—at least for a few feet. And if we line it up to the source Oscar found... I can set bike's defenses on automatic, or to discharge on impact. Maybe we can send a surprise inside and see what happens." Mitch and Oscar worked together, aligning the bike toward the coordinates within the curtain until Oscar was satisfied.

Jacob shook his head. "Wreck another very expensive prototype bike, and they're going to send us to the Yukon— permanently."

Mitch was about to respond when a shot rang out. Jacob grabbed his arm and dropped to the ground, pulling Mitch behind the fallen log with him as he returned fire. Oscar and Hans dodged behind the trees, shooting back in the direction of the attack.

"You think Ben and Yankton hiked up here after us?" Jacob asked, as he checked his bleeding arm. Fortunately, the bullet had only grazed him.

"It sure as hell wasn't Astin, and I doubt Marston would go to the trouble."

He and Jacob split up, using hand signals to communicate. Jacob caught a glimpse of movement in the trees and fired. More shots came from the forest, and Mitch shot back. Hans and Oscar circled in the other direction.

If someone puts a bullet into that curtain of light, it's going to fire back at all of us, Jacob thought.

Jacob heard a rustle in the leaves and felt the cold steel of a rifle prod his back. "Don't move," a voice said from behind him.

"Storm! Put your gun down and tell your mechanical friends to drop their weapons or I blow away your partner!" Billy Kesterson, con man and fugitive, shielded himself behind Jacob and forced him forward.

Mitch froze, then lowered his rifle and laid it on the ground. "Hans, Oscar—do as he says."

Kesterson gripped Jacob's injured arm with one hand and kept the muzzle of his gun against Jacob's back as they moved toward the steambikes.

"You're the one who shot at us at the hotel." Mitch watched Jacob and Kesterson, careful not to move.

"Yeah. You should have taken the hint. I didn't expect you to follow me up here. Couldn't believe it when I saw you walk out of the bar."

I was right: We were being followed—and not just by Astin, Jacob thought.

"Give yourself up," Mitch said. "Right now, you might get off with a light sentence—if we agree not to report the part about firing on us. Shoot a government agent, and you'll die in prison."

"Not if they don't catch me." Kesterson moved to stand next to the bike. "I'm gonna steal this and get far away from here. I figure it'll take a long while before anyone comes looking for your bodies." He lifted his gun against Jacob's head. "Say good-bye."

A shot rang out, deafeningly loud. Kesterson fell backward onto the steambike and got tangled in the equipment. The bike roared to life as his body activated Mitch's altered controls.

Jacob reeled, dazed. Mitch grabbed him and threw him to the ground, dropping beside him as the steambike carried Kesterson's body through the shimmering curtain of light. Jacob had enough presence of mind to throw his arms over his head before the deadly rays of light hummed out from the "vanished" forest. A second later, Jacob heard the *rat-tat-tat* of Gatling gun fire, followed by the *ka-boom* of the bike's Ketchum grenades exploding.

For a few seconds, the iridescent curtain winked in and out before regaining its opaque shimmer. Mitch pulled Jacob to his feet as Jacob shook his head, trying to hear out of his left ear, still astounded he was alive. Mitch had a revolver in one hand.

"You shot him over my shoulder!"

"What matters is that *I* shot *him* so that *he* didn't shoot *you.*"

Jacob bit back a retort and focused on business. "Did you see what the light curtain did?"

"Yeah." Mitch found Jacob's gun in the leaves and returned it to him. "Let's see what's going on."

They advanced, guns drawn. Mitch grabbed his bag of gear and signaled for Jacob to move behind a tree, then joined him and threw rocks at the curtain of light.

Nothing happened. He tried a second time, and again. Silence. Mitch turned to Hans and Oscar. "Just in case, you two stay here. Someone needs to report back if we can't get out."

"I'll go first." Mitch got down on his belly and crawled through the barrier, trying to stay below the line the lights had cut into the trees. Jacob hung back, waiting for a signal.

"Come on," Mitch said, suddenly appearing again and startling Jacob. "Stop as soon as we're through."

The two agents crossed the perimeter, alert for an attack. Ahead, the wreckage of the steambike was twisted around the melted ruins of a machine the likes of which Jacob had never seen. Kesterson's body was charred but recognizable, still tangled on the bike.

"Looks like we found a couple of the missing people," Mitch said pointing. Two partially decomposed bodies lay sprawled several yards beyond the smoking bike, near what appeared to be an oddly configured hut.

"Careful though. Look to the right of that hut. There's another one of those big killer-light machines. And I'll bet we'll find them all along the perimeter, plus the wreckage of the missing airship. Probably find the other missing agents, too."

"I want to get a closer look," Mitch murmured, eyeing the remnants of the light weapon the steambike's grenade had destroyed. He glanced toward the other, potentially functioning weapons, but halted several feet away and pulled out his EMF reader to scan the metallic console, then repeated the scan with two more of the experimental gadgets from his pack. "It isn't registering as any known metal. No known power source. Configuration doesn't match any of the schematics I've seen."

Jacob pulled out a pair of field glasses to read the markings. "It's not any language I've seen before. And look at the height of the

console, and the size and location of the levers. It's not really configured for human use."

"I'm pretty sure humans didn't build it."

"How do we take out the weapon over there?" Jacob nodded to the
next nearest console. "If it can pivot this direction, we'll never make it
to the hut."

"You have another grenade in your pack, right? Just stay farther
away from it than where the bodies are." Mitch replied, and ran
for cover.

Jacob lobbed the Ketchum grenade and dropped to the ground,
throwing his arms over his head. The explosion still made his ears ring.
When he looked back, the second weapon was a smoking, charred
mass.

Jacob stood up and dusted himself off. His eyes burned and his
throat felt scratchy, but he was otherwise unharmed. Mitch threw a
couple of rocks to make sure there were no other "surprises" and gave
an all clear.

Mitch and Jacob advanced slowly, guns drawn. Nothing moved,
and no sounds came from inside the hut. They crept up, one on each
side of the doorway, and Mitch pivoted into position, gun at the ready.

"Looks like we're too late." He lowered his weapon.

Two mummified corpses lay inside. Neither was remotely human.
The bodies were thin and narrowly-built, with elongated arms, legs,
and hands. Big eye sockets made the large, oval-shaped skulls look
monstrous. "Offhand, I'd say they weren't from around here," Jacob
said. "What killed them?"

Mitch took one reading after another with the prototype gadgets.
Jacob walked around the hut, looking for clues to the identity of the
strange creatures, and found only thin slabs of dark glass.

"Doesn't look like much of an invasion," Jacob observed. "Other
than the weapons outside, they don't appear to be heavily armed."

Mitch frowned as he glanced at his instruments. He recalibrated,
and ran another scan, then looked up. "Sulfuric acid," he said,
meeting Jacob's gaze. "I'm picking up extensive damage on the
bodies from acid burns. Their equipment seems to have been badly

damaged as well. The levels are substantially higher inside the curtain."

"Where the hell did it come from?"

Mitch waved a hand. "The air. All those factories down in New Pittsburgh and elsewhere put plenty of smoke into the air, and the winds carry it all up here. Turns into sulfuric acid when it mixes with rain. Farber told me he's worried it will eventually spoil the lakes and trees up here. But as to why it's so much higher inside the curtained area... no idea."

"Why aren't we burned?" Jacob took a closer look at the desiccated corpses. He glimpsed lesions that might have been burns covering much of the aliens' bodies.

"We would be, if we stayed within the perimeter too long. My eyes are stinging something fierce, and my throat's sore, but it wasn't before we came in. Something about the way this area is contained seems to concentrate the acid." Mitch gestured toward the aliens. "That wouldn't do good things for us, even though our skin is tough enough to take the acid levels in the rain outside the perimeter. But if the aliens weren't used to it, the acid would burn their skin, eat away at their lungs, blind them. Damage their equipment, too, if it wasn't built for this kind of environment."

Jacob looked around the hut. "Why do you think they came here? Scouts for an army?"

Mitch shrugged. "My bet is they were explorers, maybe scientists. They just badly underestimated how the pollutants in the air would be affected by their containment system. If their equipment was malfunctioning, it might have made the problem worse."

"If there were more aliens, they haven't shown up to see what the big explosion was all about."

"We'll need to scout around, but it may just be the two of them." Mitch picked up several of the dark glass slabs and turned them back and forth, trying to decipher their function. "Maybe Farber can make something of these back at his lab. Right now, we need to find the source of this shield and get it down."

"What about those light cannon things? Why would scientists have something like that?" Jacob demanded. "Why make the forest disappear?"

"Maybe they just didn't want to be bothered," Mitch said, leading the way outside. Now that Jacob could look closer at the odd bits of equipment, the metal appeared pocked and corroded. "Perhaps that light curtain is their version of camouflage. They might not have expected anyone to notice, here in the wilderness."

He paused, looking around. "You know, if Faber and the slide rule boys can figure out how any of this stuff works, it could jump our technology decades ahead—maybe centuries." His eyes lit up. "Imagine being able to shoot things with light! And if light can be a weapon, maybe it could slice other things, like steel for factories." He gestured back toward the hut. "Those dark glass slabs— what if that's how they stored their information? They had to be much more advanced than we are to get here from another planet. Think about what we could learn from them!"

"I don't see a ship," Jacob observed. "How did they get there?"

"They could have been dropped off."

"So their friends might be coming back for them?"

"Maybe. They won't be sending out a signal, that's for sure. Now that we know what's here, the Department can set a watcher, so if their friends stop in, we can make contact." Mitch sighed, putting his hands on his hips and surveying the area. "Let's search the place. We can come back later to get the aliens wrapped up and loaded on the sledges. We'll eventually need to take all the equipment. I'm sure Farber would have a better chance of figuring out how those weapons work if we can take one back without blowing it up."

"Time to call in some backup?"

"I hate to do it. But yeah. You want to get Hans and Oscar? Set up some markers, so we know where it's safe to come through the barrier. It'd be real sad to get shot when we just made the discovery of a lifetime."

Jacob sent out a signal and set up a beacon. It would take at least a day, maybe two, before help arrived. They found what had to be the containment field generator. Oscar's sensors confirmed that its operation had contributed to the heightened sulfuric acid levels.

"Are you sure that's such a good idea?" Jacob asked as he watched Mitch place small charges around the base of the generator. "Don't you think HQ may want to save it? You know, see how it works? If you blow it up, we'll never get off probation."

"Trust me. I think it's not only generating the light curtain; I think it's powering those guns as well. And if we leave it running, everything in here will corrode faster. Shut it down, and we've still got a treasure trove of alien technology." Mitch straightened and surveyed his handiwork. "Oscar helped me calibrate the charges. They should disrupt its power source without blowing the thing to bits."

Jacob scowled. *I know this is going to come back and bite me. It always does.* "If you're sure…"

"I'm sure." Mitch walked around the generator, admiring it. "Just think of the possibilities. If we could figure out how to use this force field thing, or how to replicate those weapons… you know what a leap that would be for our military?"

"That doesn't scare you? Cause it should." Jacob eyed the alien technology warily. *I'm not sure Earth is ready for this yet.*

"Fire in the hole!" Mitch and the others took cover. The explosion was deafening. The ground shook, and he could see the flash through his eyelids.

"I thought you said the charges would disable it, not vaporize it."

"They were supposed to!" Mitch looked completely bewildered.

"Something obviously went wrong."

The generator was a smoking ruin in a blackened hole. Oscar and Hans moved out from cover, taking readings. "The weapons are down, and so is the light curtain," Oscar reported. Jacob realized he could see the forest all around them, and presumably, the area was no longer "missing" to people outside.

"That's a big crater," Mitch said, still looking shocked at the outcome.

"And you're going to explain this, how?"

Mitch rallied. "What's to explain? We have aliens, weapons, everything but the generator. Oscar got a good scan of it, so we're not exactly empty-handed. I say it's a win. Enough to get us off probation. Obviously, the generator was set on some kind of self-destruct."

"That's as good a story as any."

Mitch nudged him with an elbow. "Cheer up. If we're off probation, Falken might send us out on another case that *isn't* in the wilderness."

"Maybe," Jacob replied with a sigh. "No telling what trouble we'll land in tomorrow."

"That's what I love about this job," Mitch replied. "Come on. Let's get back to camp. We've got company coming."

ROGUE

1 / ROGUE | THE CABIN

"WATCH OUT!" MITCH Storm yelled as he swung around, coming in to a firing position and leveling his rifle. The shot flashed past Jacob, catching a large gray wolf in its shoulder just as the wolf lunged for the kill. The animal yelped in pain and drew back, bleeding but not defeated.

"Behind you!" Jacob Drangosavich blasted his shotgun, aiming at the wolf running toward Mitch. He missed, cursed, and reloaded, but the wolf changed course, escaping the shot.

The wolves were huge and fast—and more aggressive than Mitch or Jacob had ever seen before. They worked as a pack, keeping their would-be prey corralled, striking in teams with uncanny precision. And despite what Jacob had heard about wolves preferring not to engage with humans, these animals seemed to be looking for a fight.

Four government agents. Four man-sized wolves. Jacob liked better odds.

It was supposed to be a routine mission—as much as any assignment was "routine" for the Department of Supernatural Investigation. Reports of strange sightings and unusual kills of deer and farm animals had the locals worried. Theories abounded, ranging from packs of rabid wild dogs to crazed bears. A few old-timers muttered about dark magic and a witch in the forest. DSI sent two agents to investigate. Those agents disappeared.

A man's scream made Jacob wheel around, in time to see a wolf lunge for Keller, one of their fellow agents. Keller wasn't fast enough to get out of the way, and the creature knocked him to the ground, raking him with its claws. A second wolf closed quickly, biting deep into Keller's arm and knocking his rifle out of reach. Keller shouted and struggled to get loose, pinned by wolves that were each as big as he was.

Mitch gave a war cry and ran toward Keller, rifle at the ready. He shot the wolf that had the agent pinned, catching the animal in the chest and knocking it off Keller and onto its side. The second wolf snarled and sprang at Mitch, who barely dodged out of the way of its sharp claws.

A rifle shot cracked. "Got it!" Agent Anna Corbett muttered as the wolf fell over.

"There's another one coming!" Jacob yelled, blasting the third wolf with his shotgun. It yelped and backed off but did not fall, though it was bleeding from where the buckshot had torn into it. Instead, the wolf kept both Mitch and Jacob in its sight, staring them down with its yellow eyes, waiting for a chance to strike.

By some silent signal, the last two wolves attacked. One went for Anna, while the other came at Mitch so fast, he barely had a chance to pull the trigger. Anna's shot went wide. Jacob struggled to get a clear shot without endangering either of his partners. Mitch's rifle shot caught the injured wolf in the belly and dropped him to the ground. Anna fired again, striking the last wolf in the side.

"I'd say that takes care of the wolves," Mitch said, looking around at the four fallen predators.

Jacob and Anna were already heading for Keller. "He's alive," Jacob reported, hefting Keller into his arms. "But we need to get him to a doctor."

Mitch regarded Keller and then glanced at the cabin. "We will. But we may not get another chance to take a look at that house. Let's go. We'll make it quick."

Their objective was an old cabin in the forest. The area was thinly settled, mostly farms, with large tracts of woods. They were two hours out of New Pittsburgh by rail and another hour out by carriage before they used the velocipedes. All four agents had come up the night before and spent the day interviewing locals. Frightened farmers and spooked loggers reported strange lights in the forest, odd, eerie noises, animals acting strangely, and grisly attacks on deer and cattle.

If it weren't for the dead deer and slaughtered cows, Jacob would have dismissed the whole thing as superstition or low-level magic. The deaths were worrisome, and the missing agents more so. Now, after traveling an hour into the forest, they had found the house, only to discover that it was protected by wolves that were singularly focused on keeping them away.

"I'll stand guard," Anna volunteered. "Why don't you two go in and have a look around. I'll keep an eye on Keller. Mind you be quick about it. We need to get him out of here, and those wolves might have friends." Anna pushed a lock of short red hair out of her eyes. She was tall, with an athlete's grace, and a crack shot with her rifle. Her Philadelphia manners made her seem more likely to be in finishing school than on the rifle range, something she often used to her advantage.

Mitch Storm, by contrast, looked like every penny dreadful's idea of a secret agent. He was built like a boxer, with dark hair, dark eyes, and a five o'clock shadow that started at three. Jacob was tall and rangy, with blond hair, blue eyes, and a long face that showed his Eastern European heritage. Mitch and Jacob had fought together in the Army during the rancher wars and had been recruited by DSI shortly after things settled down out West. Mitch's talent as an Army sharpshooter still came in handy, as did Jacob's ability with languages. Anna was particularly good at gaining the confidence of strangers, making her an adept spy and her partner, Keller was a whiz at gadgets and fixing things. They made a good team.

Anna stayed on the cabin's porch, rifle at the ready, while Mitch and Jacob went inside. Mitch kicked the front door open while Jacob did the same at the rear. The door slammed wide, banging against the inside wall. Mitch and Jacob charged in, guns drawn.

"Not much to look at," Mitch muttered.

"Looks like someone was here recently," Jacob observed. "Wonder how they fared with all the wolves."

The cabin was likely an old hunting retreat, now fallen on hard times. Jacob could see where water had leaked through the roof, and where insects had damaged the log walls. It was larger than most cabins, more than just one room and a loft. Mitch entered through the sitting area. Jacob came through a mudroom in the back, designed for boots and coats, that led into a rudimentary kitchen. In between the kitchen and the sitting room were two small bedrooms.

Mitch circled the sitting room. "Whoever holed up here made themselves comfortable," he called out, noting a worn couch, a small table, and a fireplace that had seen heavy use.

"Someone was here recently enough to leave peelings and eggshells in the garbage that haven't gone sour," Jacob reported from the kitchen. "The coal stove looks like it's been used lately, and there's still water in the reservoir.

Guns drawn, Jacob and Mitch converged on the middle rooms. Jacob went left; Mitch went right.

"Someone left in a hurry," Jacob said. "There are blankets and a bedroll." He scouted the rest of the room. "Nothing else—no personal items."

"I found something." Mitch's voice was flat and hard. Jacob knew from experience that meant trouble. He walked across the hall.

"Maybe the farmers were onto something when they said there was a witch in the woods," Mitch said, nodding toward the center of the room.

A pentacle inside a circle took up most of the floor, almost large enough to touch all four walls. The smell of sage, incense, and burned hair hung in the air. Four candles, burned down to nubs, marked the quarters of the circle. In the center was the butchered body of a chicken.

"Offhand, I'd say someone was dabbling with dark magic," Jacob observed.

"The real question is, why?" Mitch mused. He pulled out one of the experimental cameras their inventor friend Adam Farber had supplied them with and took a couple of pictures of the pentacle.

"What's up here worth hexing?" Jacob asked. "Unless it's a witch who can work magic from a distance—someone who can scry, for example, or do divination."

"Whoever it is, they're trouble," Mitch replied. "So where did they go, and what's their next step?"

"Mitch, Jacob—the wolves are back," Anna called from outside.

"More wolves?" Mitch yelled, putting away his camera and grabbing his rifle.

"No." Anna sounded spooked. "The same wolves. They're getting up again."

"Shit," Mitch muttered. He and Jacob ran for the porch. Anna was right: the wolves were staggering to their feet. Wounds that should have been mortal had rapidly healed, and open gashes were closing before their eyes.

"We've got trouble," Jacob said, chambering a round in his shotgun.

"Run!" Mitch said. "Get to the steambikes. I'll give you and Anna a head start."

Mitch was moving before Jacob could object. Jacob hefted Keller onto his shoulder and then he and Anna ran toward where they had left their velocipedes. Mitch had begun shouting and waving his arms to draw off the attention of the recovering wolves, a move that was brave and expedient but made Jacob question his partner's sanity.

"Hey, Rover!" Mitch yelled. "Over here!"

The wolves moved more slowly than before, but considering they had appeared dead minutes before, it seemed plenty fast. The man-sized predators lowered their heads and slowly advanced as Mitch edged in the opposite direction from Jacob and Anna.

"Sit! Bad dog!" Mitch shouted.

"What the hell is he doing?" Anna asked as she and Jacob ran through the brush. Keller was dead weight on Jacob's shoulder, soaking him with blood.

"He's being Mitch," Jacob replied as if that explained everything.

Their steambikes were where they left them, stashed in bushes behind trees a distance from the cabin. They had walked the bikes for the last mile or so when they were heading for the cabin, not wanting to scare off their quarry. Now, noise was a weapon.

"What about Keller? These things don't have sidecars," Anna observed.

"Wait here," Jacob said, already swinging a leg over his velocipede. "I'll be right back." He started the bike with a roar and then looked back. "Oh, and expect loud noises."

Jacob took off, sending up a spray of dirt and leaves. He crouched over the handlebars, doing his best to evade low branches and overhanging bushes. The ride was rough, and Jacob fought to keep control of the bike. It was another piece of Farber's experimental equipment, and Jacob suspected that one reason he and Mitch so often got prototypes was that anything that survived one of their missions had been field tested in the extreme. Jacob had lost count of how many velocipedes they'd "tested" so far.

Just as he expected, Mitch was in the thick of things by the time he got back to the cabin. Mitch had retreated to high ground and was now on the log house's porch roof. Mitch shot one of the wolves, stopping it with a bullet to the chest. He got another in the hindquarters. The other two moved forward, undeterred.

"Stay put!" Jacob shouted as the steambike burst into the clearing. He flicked a switch, and the bike's custom-built Gatling gun opened fire, spraying bullets across the clearing. The wolves fell to the onslaught, though Jacob doubted they would stay down.

"Run!" he yelled as Mitch swung down off the porch roof and landed in a crouch. Mitch sprinted toward the bike.

"Hang on," Jacob ordered, and flicked another switch. *I can't believe I'm doing this. I think I've been around Mitch too long.* There was a *whoosh* as the Ketchum grenade cleared the launcher, and then a few seconds later, an ear-splitting boom echoed through the forest as the cabin exploded. Jacob didn't stop to watch. He gunned the bike into a turn with Mitch riding pillion and headed back to where Anna and Keller waited, going as fast as he dared through the forest.

"I see you found a way to deal with the wolves," Anna observed, raising an eyebrow.

"For now," Mitch replied. "We've got no idea what they can survive, since bullets sure didn't stop them."

"What about him?" Jacob said with a nod toward Keller, who was still unconscious.

Mitch swore. "I'm a little better with the velocipedes than you or Anna; put Keller on behind me and tie him on. It'll have to do. Anna, you ride with Jacob." He glanced behind them, toward the burning house. "Hurry."

They had barely gone another mile before Anna spotted trouble. "More wolves," she yelled above the noise of the steambikes' engines. "Coming in at three o'clock." She paused. "We've got some on the left at nine o'clock."

At the speed they were going, Jacob could spare no more than a second's glance to the side for fear of hitting a root or driving into branches. It was enough to see the large, gray predators running toward them.

"Can we outrun them?" Jacob yelled to Mitch.

"Maybe."

"That's not what I wanted to hear," Jacob returned.

"Bike goes about forty miles an hour, tops," Mitch returned. "Wolves run a little slower."

"But that's without a second rider! How much slower?" Jacob questioned, as the wolves closed fast in his rear-view mirror.

"Depends on the wolf," Mitch hollered back.

Pray for slow wolves, Jacob thought. "Anna! You're going to have to do the shooting. Keep them off our tails."

Jacob let his bike fall back just a bit, allowing Mitch to move ahead of him on the forest trail. He knew there was no way Mitch could shoot and drive the bike with Keller's unbalanced weight on the back. That left Anna to keep the wolves at bay while Jacob maneuvered the bike. *Even if the wolves can match our pace, they can't keep it up forever. We just have to outrun them long enough for them to tire.*

Bang. The gunshot right behind him made Jacob flinch, nearly sending them off the trail. The next shot's recoil jerked the bike. But Anna managed to hang on to him and shoot. Jacob couldn't spend time worrying about it. Navigating the bike at a breakneck speed took all his concentration.

"Duck!" Anna yelled and shot again. It sounded to Jacob like the shot went right past his head. A huge wolf dropped out of the sky directly into the path of their bike, bleeding from a bullet that had torn into its chest.

"Damn!" Jacob swerved, nearly toppling the bike, but managed to right them before they went over. Mitch's bike was swaying crazily with Keller's dead weight on the back. Jacob steered around the wolf, but he could see two more running alongside the trail. Anna wasn't going to be able to shoot them both at once.

"Slew!" Mitch shouted over the noise of the bikes.

"You've got to be kidding!" Jacob yelled back. He knew the maneuver, but the odds of it working here and now, at this speed on the rough forest trail were not in their favor.

"Go!" Mitch yelled as if he hadn't heard Jacob's comment.

Mitch slewed his bike in a half circle to the right. Jacob skid-turned to the left. Both of them opened fire with their Gatling guns, raking the forest in a circle.

The trick is stopping in time, or we shoot each other, Jacob thought as he fought for control of the bike. His steambike fishtailed, threatening to pull out of his grasp. Anna ducked, slinging her rifle over her shoulder and holding on to Jacob for dear life.

Tree trunks splintered. The wolves let out a yelp of fright and pain. Bits of branches, chopped off by the barrage of gunfire, rained down on them. Bullets pocked the ground, sending up a spray of dirt. A flock of birds rose noisily in a black cloud from the branches overhead, jarred loose by the noise and vibration.

Jacob cut the Gatling fire but could not stop the bike from skidding into almost a complete circle, though he and Anna managed not to be thrown. Mitch's bike cornered low, throwing Keller from the improvised restraints, and sending Mitch and the steambike in opposite directions.

Anna had her gun up and ready, scanning the area. "I don't see any more wolves," she said, and Jacob checked the bike for damage and reassured himself that he was still alive.

Mitch stood and dusted himself off. His jacket and pants were torn, there were leaves in his hair and a new bruise on the side of his face, but the look in his eyes told Jacob that Mitch was enjoying every minute of their desperate ride. Mitch walked over to retrieve Keller. "He's still alive," he announced.

"Amazing, with you driving," Jacob returned.

Mitch gave him a sour glance. "Better than leaving him for the wolves," he replied. With Jacob's help, Mitch fastened Keller onto the bike once more. The wounded agent leaned like a drunk. "Let's get back to civilization, and figure this out later."

———

"WAS IT ABSOLUTELY necessary to set the house on fire?" Kurt Falken paced the office. One hand clenched and unclenched behind his back, and Jacob was certain Falken was imagining tightening his grip around Mitch's neck.

"It was the best way to get rid of the wolves, sir." Mitch actually managed to sound apologetic, although the glance at Jacob and the sparkle in his eyes gave him away.

Jacob cleared his throat. "We weren't exactly sure how to deal with resurrecting wolves, sir." *Mitch is never going to let me forget this, I just know it.*

Falken leveled a cold glare at Jacob. "I thought better of you, Drangosavich. I expect problems from Storm. There's a line in the budget for cleaning up his messes."

"Really?" Mitch asked, in a tone that suggested he was flattered.

Jacob elbowed him.

Falken's expression soured. "You'd find it less appealing if it came out of your pay," Falken sighed. "You know, the nickname's caught on. 'The Storm and Fury boys.' It was not intended as a dare to live up to."

227

Falken had made the play on Mitch's name months ago, matching '*sturm und drang*' to its English equivalent.

"We brought back Agent Keller and pictures of the site," Mitch replied, in what passed for his "obedient" voice.

"And despite the use of extreme force, all four agents escaped alive," Jacob pointed out.

Falken looked as if he had swallowed a frog. "For that, the Department is grateful," he acknowledged.

"We think there are two problems," Mitch added. "A dark witch—objectives unknown. And possibly werewolves."

"Werewolves in Western Pennsylvania?" Falken raised an eyebrow.

Jacob nodded. "Once you get north of New Pittsburgh, there's a lot of wooded area. Go farther toward Kane and the Big Woods, and it's quite wild. There's got to be something else going on. Normal wolves don't get up after being shot multiple times."

"The area's good for wolves, not so good for people who turn into wolves," Mitch mused as if Falken was no longer in the room. "Think about it. People who turn into wolves still need to have a job to provide for the human part of their existence. They have to be close enough to towns to be able to earn money, and close enough to the forest to be able to hide what they become."

Jacob nodded. "Good point. And that would describe the area we were in yesterday."

"Except I don't understand why the wolves aren't being more careful," Mitch said, frowning. "The locals were complaining about strange lights and weird happenings and slaughtered cows. Not exactly the best way to act if you want to remain hidden."

"Maybe they're new at being werewolves." Falken's input was so unexpected that both Mitch and Jacob looked taken aback when he interjected himself into their discussion. He barely restrained a smirk. "What if a witch either partnered with werewolves or bound them to his command, but couldn't completely control them. The werewolves might be too new at the game to control themselves. We're just lucky that it's only dead cows and not dead farmers."

Mitch shook his head. "You've got a point. But where did these wolves come from? And how is the witch involved?"

"Why does it matter?" Falken snapped.

"Because we need to know what he, or she, is after," Mitch replied. "And why take up with werewolves in the first place? They're notoriously hard to control."

"And that is what the two of you—plus Agent Corbett—are going to find out," Falken said, interjecting himself into the conversation once more and taking a step to put himself between Mitch and Jacob to make his point. "Agent Kennedy will be on call to provide airship backup, but only in dire circumstances. This is your case now. Track the wolves. Track the witch. Go looking for missing farmers. Just come back with a solid explanation—some proof would be nice—and put a stop to it."

Falken gave them a pointed look. "Caution seems to fall on deaf ears with you two, but I'll repeat myself, at the risk of wasting my breath. Out of all my agents, the two of you are the most expensive to maintain, thanks to Storm's fascination with explosions. Despite your remarkable record of results, those expenses require me to intercede with headquarters much more frequently than I would like. I am only willing to keep sticking my neck out for you so long as you succeed. Don't make me reconsider my support."

Even Mitch had the good grace to look abashed. "Understood, sir."

"What about Agent Corbett, sir?" Jacob asked. "Where is she?"

Falken walked back to his desk. "I've already spoken to her, and to Agent Kennedy. They both know the orders. Right now, Kennedy's got airship reconnaissance duty, and Corbett's guarding Agent Keller over at Mercy Hospital."

"About Keller..." Mitch said. "He was bitten and scratched by those wolves. If they are werewolves, what are the odds of him turning into one?"

Falken let out a long breath and sat down behind his desk. "We don't know," he admitted. "That's one of the things I want the three of you to find out. One of the reasons we sent him to Mercy Hospital is because the Church has a history of dealing with the supernatural. They can be trusted to be discreet."

"And it doesn't hurt that there are priests nearby trained in exorcism," Jacob added in a dry tone.

"While that's true, I'm not sure it would be effective for lycanthropy," Falken replied. "I have been in touch with the *Logonje*, to see if they were aware of any supernatural anarchists in the region. They knew nothing about the wolves, but have agreed to consult on Agent Keller's situation."

Mitch and Jacob had encountered the *Logonje* before, a secret group of very unorthodox Orthodox Polish Catholic priests who hunted down demons and malicious supernatural predators. The Department was known to call in like-minded groups with specialized skills when the situation demanded it. As far as Jacob was concerned, having Father Matija and his *Logonje* priests involved was a step in the right direction.

"Neither of you were wounded by the wolves, were you?" Falken asked, glancing up sharply. Both Mitch and Jacob shook their heads. "Good. Agent Corbett also escaped damage. That's important because until we know if we really are dealing with werewolves, we need to be very careful. If we are, then we've got to find out what kind of werewolves, and what triggers the change—or how the condition takes hold."

"We'll get to the bottom of it," Mitch promised. He and Jacob moved to leave.

"Storm. Drangosavich." Falken's voice stopped them as they reached the door. "Do try to avoid explosions, if at all possible. I'm tired of filling out reports."

2 / ROGUE | THE ASYLUM

"DR. WAKEFIELD. THANK you for seeing us." Mitch shook the hand of the gray-haired gentleman who met them at the door. Mitch and Jacob wore city suits, befitting the roles they played, a change from the military fatigues they wore the night before. Anna had traded in her riding pants, dark shirt, and boots for a nun's habit.

They took the train up to Mercer, where a tip suggested they would find someone with more information about wolves and strange, midnight rituals. That led them here—to the local mental asylum.

"You're welcome, of course," Dr. James Wakefield replied, ushering Mitch, Jacob, and Anna into the building. "It's not often we get visits from New Pittsburgh to the Mercer Sanatorium, except for referrals from the hospitals there."

"You were recommended by some of our associates at Mercy Hospital," Mitch replied. Jacob tried not to cough at the stretched truth.

"Please, come into my office. You'll be more comfortable. Then we can talk." Dr. Wakefield led the way. The Mercer Sanatorium was a large, white two-story building with an annex, along with an additional detached cabin. Dormer windows jutted from the roof, and a wide porch ran the length of the front of the building. Here, thirty-five residents received care for nervous disorders, with access to the asylum's famous water-cure therapeutic baths.

"I'm pleased to see you taking an interest in the Walker case, Dr. Sound," Wakefield continued. "It's an unusual situation."

"My specialty is delusion, especially delusions involving belief in the supernatural," Mitch bluffed. "My colleague, Dr. Fury, has come all the way from Croatia to work with me in this field. And this is Sister Ann, one of the nuns who runs the psychiatric wing at the hospital." Anna shot Mitch a look before managing a somewhat saintly smile and folding her hands in her lap.

"You understand that I don't want this sensationalized," Wakefield warned. "I'm relying on your professionalism to handle this discreetly."

Mitch nodded. "Absolutely. You can count on us. But we do have a deep professional interest in the Walker situation. There have been other patients with similar delusions lately, and we're trying to find a common root."

"Certainly," Wakefield agreed. "One never knows how these things take hold of weak minds. It might be a book or a play, even a bit of song that becomes an obsession, and then expands until it displaces reality."

"Well said," Jacob replied. "What can you tell us about Walker?"

Dr. Wakefield rummaged in a filing cabinet and returned to his desk with a folder. "Benjamin Walker, age forty-six. Profession: farmer," he read from the file. He set the folder down. "He's been here for a little less than a week. Mr. Walker claims he saw someone dressed in a cloak performing some strange ritual that turned people into wolves."

Dr. Wakefield shook his head. "Sad, isn't it? The delusion has taken deep root. Mr. Walker has repeated his statement many times, to several different consulting specialists. We've helped him become less agitated, but he will not budge on what he says he saw."

That's because the poor bastard might have really seen men turn into wolves, Jacob thought. "Did Mr. Walker say how he happened to escape notice?"

Wakefield shrugged. "No. He believes that they were so intent on what they were doing that they did not see him approach or leave. He's a hunter, so it's possible he could move with stealth. But of course, this is all a delusion, so he was hardly in danger."

I wouldn't bet on that, Jacob thought.

"How did Mr. Walker come to be at the sanitarium?" Mitch asked.

Wakefield sighed. "He was quite agitated after his 'encounter.' He told several people about his experience. They attempted to reason with him, but he will not admit that he either made up the story or imagined it. The more others tried to convince him to see his folly, the more upset he became. His family begged us to take him in, for his own safety."

"We'd like to see Mr. Walker, as we arranged," Mitch said.

"Yes, of course, Dr. Sound." Wakefield paused. "Would you like me to post a guard with you? Mr. Walker can become quite... disturbed."

"We'll be fine," Jacob assured him. "We have experience dealing with people when they're upset." All three of them were well-armed, both with revolvers and with some other, more experimental, weapons.

"Very well," Wakefield replied. "But I will ask you not to agitate him needlessly. It's hard on the patients to get worked up, and we dislike sedating them."

"Understood," Mitch said.

Wakefield led them down a hallway of locked doors. Jacob heard voices behind many of the doors. Some were singing to themselves; others were shouting or carrying on conversations. The combination of sounds gave the corridor an eerie feel. Jacob felt a chill go down his back.

"He's in here," Wakefield said, stopping in front of a door. This room was quiet. "Mind what I told you," he warned.

"We'll be careful," Mitch promised.

"I'll be back for you in twenty minutes," Wakefield replied.

Wakefield unlocked the door and opened it for them. Inside, a man looked up from where he sat on his bed. The room was sparsely furnished, with a cot and mattress, washstand, desk, and chair. A few books lay on the desk, and the room was dimly lit by a gaslight far up on the wall where it would be difficult for someone to reach.

"Mr. Walker? I'm Dr. Sound, and we're very interested in your story." Mitch introduced himself. "These are my colleagues, Dr. Fury and Sister Ann. We'd be grateful if you'd talk with us."

Benjamin Walker regarded them for a moment. *He doesn't look crazy,* Jacob thought. *Then again, getting shipped off to a place like this would probably push you over the edge, even if you didn't start out that way.*

"I've told it to a lot of people. None of them believed me," Walker said. "Pardon my rudeness, but I'm not sure why we'd need to go through it again. I saw what I saw."

Mitch walked over, pausing a few paces from Walker. "That's just it. We believe you."

Walker's expression was wary, but Jacob saw hope flash in the man's eyes. "Can you get me out of here?"

"Very likely," Mitch said. "But first, tell us what you saw."

Walker took a deep breath and let it out again, bracing himself for the telling. "It's in my file," he said.

"We'd like to hear it from you directly," Jacob replied.

"If the people who recorded your story didn't believe you, they might not have told it accurately," Anna said. Her presence seemed to calm Walker and reassure him of their intent.

"You were about to tell us what happened that night," Anna prompted.

Walker nodded. "Yeah. I should have just gone back to bed and kept my mouth shut. That way I'd still be on my farm instead of in the looney bin." He sighed. "So I went to bed as usual, probably around nine o'clock. I woke up later and couldn't sleep. I remember hearing the clock strike midnight. I tossed around a bit and thought I'd go make myself some chamomile tea to help me sleep. When I went into the kitchen, I saw lights out in the forest." He looked from Mitch to Jacob and finally to Anna. "There shouldn't have been any lights out there. Certainly not at that hour of the night."

"Go on," Mitch said.

"I grabbed my shotgun, thinking that maybe guys were out poaching deer, or maybe some hobos sneaking off for a drink," Walker continued. "There was a moon, so I didn't need a lantern, and I know that land like the back of my hand. Those are my woods, and I hadn't given anyone permission to be out there, so I figured I'd go put the fear of God into whoever was out there."

He shook his head. "Kinda turned out the other way around. When I got close to the lights, I hid behind some rocks and had a good look."

"What did you see?" Jacob asked.

Walker seemed to brace himself for derision. "I saw a big circle with a star in it dug into the ground in a clearing. I saw orbs of light flying back and forth through the air. There was a person in a robe with a hood in the center of the circle. He seemed to be directing the orbs with gestures, and he kept chanting, saying things I didn't understand. There were people dancing around the outside of the circle."

Walker stopped and reddened, glancing at Anna. "Begging your pardon, Sister, but the people weren't wearing any clothing. And then, sure as there's God above, I saw those same people change into wolves."

"Why didn't they notice you?" Jacob watched Walker closely. Nothing in his manner suggested dishonesty—or madness. *I think this guy's for real. He just should have kept his mouth shut.*

"I know this sounds crazy, but it's true. They didn't notice me because they were so caught up in whatever the robed person was doing, they weren't paying attention to anything else. The wolves were prancing around in a frenzy. I realized that something was really wrong, and I got out of there and went home."

"Why did you tell anyone?" Anna asked. "Didn't you realize how mad the story would sound?"

Walker looked crestfallen. "My wife says I've always been honest to a fault. I didn't know what was going on, but it didn't look like something that either the preacher or the sheriff would approve of. Didn't know what those folks in the woods would do next."

"But the part about people turning into wolves—" Anna pressed.

"I know it sounds crazy, but that's what happened," Walker said, meeting Anna's gaze. "I'm a God-fearing man, Sister. I didn't want anything bad to happen because I was afraid to bear witness to what I saw." He shook his head and looked around his room. "Fat lot of good it did me."

"What about the person in the center?" Mitch asked. "Did you get a look at the face?"

Walker looked up. "As a matter of fact, I did. Right before I ran away, the man lowered his hood. I saw him—and I'm sure I'd recognize him if I saw him again."

"Does anyone own land near you?" Anna asked.

Walker nodded. "Yeah. Absalom Conroy bought the property next to mine, and the one beside it, late last year."

"Who is Absalom Conroy?" Jacob asked. "I don't recognize the name."

Walker snorted. "Then you're not from around these parts. He's one of the Meadville Conroys, pretty much local royalty."

"Was the man in the cape Mr. Conroy?" Anna asked.

"No idea," Walker replied. "I've never met the man. But the place where I saw the wolves was right on the line between his land and mine."

"How many people have you told about the connection with Conroy?" Mitch asked. Jacob guessed his concern. If the scion of a wealthy family really was involved with witchcraft, the situation was unlikely to end well.

Walker gave him a derisive look. "Do I look that dumb? You seem to believe me. Maybe if I help you, you help me?"

Mitch and Jacob exchanged a look. "I do believe you," Mitch replied. "And that means that for the time being, you're safer in here than you are out there, particularly if whoever it was gets wind that there was a witness to his little party in the woods. He wouldn't know what you did or didn't see."

Walker paled. "I hadn't thought of it that way." He buried his head in his hands. "Oh, lordy. I'm done for."

"Have hope," Anna said, playing her role to the hilt. "The good Lord works in mysterious ways. Confiding in us was the best thing you could do."

Mitch reached into his bag and withdrew a revolver, one of his "spare" weapons and checked to make sure the silver ammunition was loaded. "You know how to shoot one of these?" he asked Walker, who nodded, eyes wide.

"Sure. But—"

"You're in danger," Mitch cut him off. "We'll make arrangements to get you someplace safe, but we can't take you with us right now. Keep the gun hidden; don't use it unless someone tries to break in your room. Don't be shy about shooting—those wolves are incredibly hard to kill."

Walker stared at the gun for a moment, then collected himself and slipped it under his pillow. "All right. Anything else?"

"Don't tell your story to anyone else," Jacob instructed. "Don't leave with anyone except us. If they want to believe you're addled, act addled. You'll seem like less of a threat that way."

Walker nodded. "I can do that." His eyes narrowed. "Why are you helping me?"

Mitch smiled. "Let's just say we have a common interest in finding out what's going on with the wolves."

"You're not really doctors, are you?" Walker said.

Jacob shrugged. "Let's just say we're here to help."

Just then, there was a knock on the door. Dr. Wakefield opened the door. Behind him were four large men in suits. "I see you're finished," Wakefield said. "Just in time. It appears Mr. Walker has more visitors."

"Who are they?" Mitch demanded, playing the entitled physician. "I don't advise having Mr. Walker speak with anyone else today. Too taxing on his fragile nature."

"Get out!" One of the newcomers, a muscular man with dark, short-cropped hair, pushed Wakefield out of the way and strode into the room. "You have no business here."

Jacob, Anna, and Mitch formed a cordon in front of Walker. "This excitement is not good for the patient," Mitch repeated. "I advise you to leave." There was no mistaking the warning in his tone. He and Jacob both moved to draw back their suit coats, exposing the guns holstered beneath.

"We're not going anywhere," the dark-haired man replied.

Dr. Wakefield gave a surprised yelp and scurried out of the way. "Gentlemen! What is the meaning of this?"

"Keep your head down, and you won't get hurt," Anna said, holding a revolver that had appeared from beneath her scapular.

"Give us Walker, now." The dark-haired man demanded.

"No." Mitch drew his gun. "Not going to happen."

"I'm sure there's a reasonable alternative—" Wakefield interjected.

"There really isn't," Jacob replied. "Because if they take Walker, they're going to kill him."

"Now or later," the dark-haired man said. "Pretty much the same to us."

"Later," Mitch shot first, putting a bullet into the knee of the dark-haired man who dropped to the ground, writhing in pain. Just to be safe, all three agents had upgraded their bullets to ones tipped with silver. Jacob grabbed Walker from the bed and thrust him toward the wall, where Wakefield cowered. Anna got in another shot, winging the shoulder of a red-haired man with a flattened nose.

A bald man with a thick neck lunged forward and tackled Mitch. The intruder was big, but Mitch played dirty. He brought his gun down hard on the side of the bald man's head and brought his knee up hard in his attacker's groin. Mitch rolled out from under the big man and kicked the gun out of the man's hand, likely breaking a few fingers in the process.

The fourth man figured Anna for an easy target. He dodged toward her, and she swung in to a high kick, aided by the wide, loose skirts of the habit she had appropriated. Her foot caught the attacker, a squat blond man, square in the face, sending him reeling. Jacob finished him with a knee to the chin.

The red-haired man was bleeding from his right shoulder, but he moved his gun to the other hand. "Stop right there," he ordered.

Mitch grabbed the chair and swung it as hard as he could, connecting squarely with his opponent's head and shoulder, knocking him to the floor.

Bang. A shot whizzed by Mitch and hit the dark-haired man squarely between the eyes, just as the lead attacker had brought his gun up for a clear shot at Anna. The large man toppled over and lay still in a pool of blood.

Mitch, Jacob, and Anna turned around to find Walker still in a firing stance, gun raised.

"Oh dear lord, he's got a gun!" Wakefield wailed.

"And damn fine aim," Anna remarked. "Thank you."

Walker was pale, and it took him a moment to react, lowering his gun and then handing it, butt first, back to Mitch. "I never killed a man before," Walker said shakily.

Mitch slipped the extra gun through his belt. "If it's any consolation, I don't think these four are fully human, and I wouldn't count him as dead yet." He toed the unconscious redhead's body. "I suspect they're four of your wolves—come to take you back to their master."

Wakefield had managed to get to his feet, though he looked as if he wanted to throw up. "Then it's true? What he says he saw?"

Mitch gave him a practiced smile. "I'm afraid I can neither confirm nor deny that, Dr. Wakefield."

"Who are you people?" Wakefield demanded, as his fear shifted to anger and he attempted to regain his dignity.

Jacob flipped open his badge. "Department of Supernatural Investigation," he said. "We're here to help."

Wakefield looked around the room. "Blood—everywhere! Men have been shot. I don't know how I'll ever explain this!"

"It's better if you don't try," Anna advised. "We'll take them off your hands—and Walker, too. It's for your own safety."

Wakefield regarded her rumpled nun's habit and the gun that was still in her hand. "So you're not really a Sister?"

Anna grinned. "Not the kind you're thinking of."

"What do I tell the staff? What do I say if Mr. Walker's family asks where he is?" Wakefield looked as if he might sob. *I'm not overly impressed with their security,* Jacob thought. *The guards seem to have all gone in to hiding.*

"Tell them that ruffians broke in and kidnapped him," Mitch suggested.

"I'll be ruined! The hospital will close!" Wakefield wailed.

"Then say that ruffians broke in and were driven off by the patients," Jacob said.

"That's not much of an improvement!"

"Suit yourself," Mitch replied. "But the less you say about this, the better. Those louts may have friends."

Wakefield ran his hands through his hair. "There was gunfire! How do I explain that? Do you have any idea how long it will take to calm down the patients?"

Mitch was busy securing the redhead's hands with his belt. "Blame a bad radiator for all the bangs and pops. Give the patients some whiskey. Works every time." He paused. "Do you happen to have straitjackets?"

Wakefield closed his eyes. "In the closet in the hallway."

Anna smoothed her habit and went to look, returning in a few minutes with an armful of the heavy canvas restraints. Jacob kept his gun at the ready while Mitch and Anna trundled the injured attackers into the jackets and tied them tight.

"What about him?" Wakefield said, pointing at the dark-haired man.

"Anna, put him in a jacket too... just in case. The silver bullet should have worked but let's not take chances." Mitch turned back to Wakefield. "We'll take him with us."

"Sorry about the blood," Jacob added.

Wakefield drew a deep breath and looked up, as if begging for heavenly guidance. "Leave. Go out the back way. Don't come back. Whatever is going on, I don't want to know. I never saw you. Walker escaped. I'll deal with the family. Just... go."

They wrapped the dark-haired man up in Walker's blanket and sheet. Anna found a gurney and Mitch and Jacob hefted the body onto it. Walker obligingly slung the trussed-up redhead over his shoulder, leaving the bald man and the blond for Mitch and Jacob to carry. Mitch had already scouted the exits and had parked their carriage by the back door, just in case. To Jacob's relief, none of the staff came out of hiding, though all the way down the corridor, patients banged on their locked doors and shouted about the noise.

"That went rather well, overall," Mitch said as they slung the corpse onto the floor of the carriage. It was a tight fit with the three prisoners and Jacob to keep an eye on them, leaving Anna to ride up front with Mitch.

"Shut up, Mitch," Jacob replied tiredly.

"What now?" Anna asked, straightening her wimple and fretting about a bloodstain that marred the skirt of her habit.

"Now, we slap some information out of these guys," Mitch said. "And get a telegram off to a friend of mine. If we're going to go hunting for a dark witch, we need some help from a good witch."

————

THE DEPARTMENT'S REMOTE base of operations was a non-descript farmhouse with a large barn outside of Jackson Center, far enough away from neighbors that Mitch was sure they would not be disturbed.

The three toughs were still in their straitjackets, and the fourth had, fortunately, stayed dead. Mitch and Jacob positioned the men on chairs while Anna kept a gun trained on the prisoners. The redhead was bleeding through his jacket. The bald man did his best to remain still, trying not to jostle his broken fingers within the long sleeves of the restraint. Their blond opponent glared balefully at Mitch and Jacob, though he stopped muttering threats when Mitch backhanded him hard enough to knock him off his chair.

"Who sent you?" Mitch paced behind the prisoners, where he could easily grab anyone who got out of hand.

"Go to hell," the bald man snapped.

Mitch cuffed him on the ear. "You're likely to get there first, buddy," he replied. "Now, I'll try again. Who's your boss?"

"You don't get it," the redhead said. "All you can do is kill us. He can magic us."

"Shut up, Kenny." The bald man turned toward him, eyes blazing.

Kenny made an obscene and physically impossible suggestion. "We're going to die, Josiah. You're the least of my worries."

"What did you want with Ben Walker?" Anna asked. She had

changed out of the nun's habit into her riding pants, a shirt, boots, and leather gloves. A gun belt was slung low across her hips.

"We wanted to shut him up," Josiah replied. "Not too hard to figure out."

"Because he saw you in the woods, changing into wolves?" Mitch accused.

Josiah glowered at them. "Because he saw something he shouldn't have seen and didn't keep his mouth shut."

"Are you wolves?" Jacob asked.

"Do we look like wolves?" Kenny retorted.

"Not now," Anna replied. "But we've seen your kind. Killed a bunch of them. Scared off your 'fearless' master." She paused and gave them an evil smile. "Two of you have nice, red rashes. Silver stings, doesn't it?"

Kenny shifted uncomfortably in his seat. Their faces were all that Jacob and the others could see with their torsos bound up in the strait-jackets, but both them had crimson mottling on their faces that looked painful.

"We can get you medical attention," Mitch said. "Take out the bullets and get rid of the silver. Or we can take our time. Up to you."

"He promised us we'd be like gods," Kenny said. "Stronger. Faster. Harder to kill. Wolves."

"Shut up, Kenny," Josiah warned, but Jacob could see that Kenny was close to breaking.

"Is this what you signed up for?" Kenny demanded. "Do you feel like a god? He made us into freaks to do his bidding, and look where it got us."

"Don't, Kenny," the blond man begged. "He'll find out. It'll be bad. For God's sake, shut up!"

"Can you cure us?" Kenny asked, looking from Mitch to Jacob to Anna. "Can you fix it? I don't want to be a wolf anymore. I want out."

"You don't get out," Josiah snapped. "You're in or you're dead. You made your choice."

"Yeah, well I'm making a different one," Kenny said. He was sweating, and the blood stain on his straitjacket was growing larger. "If

I tell you what I know, swear to me you'll get this damned silver out of me, and keep me safe."

"We can remove the silver," Anna said. "And we'll do our best to protect you. But we need to know more about the dark witch and how this wolf business works in order to help you."

Kenny licked his lips. He was close to breaking; Jacob could see it in his eyes. The pain of his wound, the irritation of the silver bullet, and the discomfort of the straitjacket were taking their toll.

"I don't know who the witch is," Kenny said. "He told us to call him 'Shadow.'"

"Nice taste for the dramatic," Anna remarked drily.

"Where did you meet him?" Mitch asked.

"Us four had just gotten out of jail," Kenny replied. "Bunch of stuff. Breaking and entering. Drunk and disorderly. Bar fights. We had a camp out in the woods until we could get money together to go somewhere else. No one would rent us a room."

"Imagine that," Anna murmured.

"One night, this guy finds our camp. He's wearing a big cloak with a hood so we can't see his face. And he asks us if we want to get the law off our backs for good," Kenny said.

Josiah gave Kenny a dark look and then looked away. The blond man looked from the agents to Kenny and back again. Jacob wagered he was considering spilling his guts, depending on what happened to Kenny.

Jacob could imagine the appeal of such an offer, especially to four men whose prospects were otherwise bleak. "What did he tell you to do?" Jacob asked.

"Said to meet him in the woods at a certain time," Kenny replied. "We all figured he was going to go shoot up the jail or something. We went armed."

"And then what?" Mitch prompted.

Kenny hesitated. The other two men gave him a warning glare. After a minute, expediency won out over fear. "We got out to the woods, and there's this strange mark on the ground. I ain't never seen nothing like it. And this guy in a robe standing in the middle with the hood pulled so we can't see his face. I thought it was a joke. That he was pulling our legs."

"What changed your mind?" Jacob asked.

"There was something about that guy; if you saw him, you'd believe," the blond man spoke up.

"Nothing about him seemed familiar?" Mitch pressed.

Josiah refused to answer, but the other two shook their heads. "I'm sure I never seen him before," Kenny replied. "He made you feel... different. Like spiders on your skin or ice down your back. I wanted to run, but I didn't want to look bad to the fellows."

"And?" Jacob prompted.

Kenny let out a long breath. "I stayed. I was scared to stay and more scared to leave. You don't know what he's like. All silent and dark. He told us to put down our guns. And then he said he could make us the best fighters in the world. All we had to do was swear allegiance."

"You didn't ask any other questions?" Anna's voice was incredulous.

"Lady, I never thought he could turn me into a wolf!" Kenny's eyes were wide with fear and pain.

"How did that happen?" Jacob prodded.

The three men exchanged glances. Kenny's cheeks colored. "I didn't know things could happen like that," he said after a long pause. "I was raised church-going, even if I ain't been in a while. They never said even the Devil could turn a man into a wolf. But I seen it. I've *been* it."

"How did Shadow do it? Turn you into wolves?" Mitch's patience was strained.

"I dunno! Cuz he's magic!" Kenny exclaimed.

"I think Agent Storm means, what happened next?" Anna prompted.

"He told us to dance around the fire," Kenny said. "I was ready to turn around right then, figuring it was all a big prank, only I got the feeling I couldn't leave." He looked ashamed. "So I did what he told me to do. I danced."

"What did Shadow do?" Jacob asked.

"He muttered stuff I couldn't understand," Kenny said. "Then he came to us one by one and made us kneel in front of him. He put his hand on my head, and then I felt something stab into my shoulder. He did that to all of us," Kenny added, and the others nodded. "And then he made a bunch of weird motions with his hands. I was sure someone had put him up to a bet, and we were going to find all the guys from the tavern in the woods having a good laugh at us, only I got really spooked. You had to be there."

Kenny looked at her for affirmation, and Anna nodded, favoring him with a slight smile. "I told you about the spidery feeling. It got worse. My skin started to get all tingly, and there was buzzing in my ears. My head felt like I'd had a bottle of whiskey, and I was stone cold sober. Then my bones started to ache. I got scared," he admitted, ducking his head to avoid the glares of his fellow prisoners.

"And then what?" Anna asked gently. Kenny was frightened reliving the experience, but for all their bravado, Josiah and the blond man seemed unnerved as well.

"My hands started to change," Kenny said. He looked up defiantly. "I'll swear on a stack of Bibles it's the truth." He looked ready to fight a challenge. When none came, he went on. "My arms got longer. My gut hurt. And then everything happened at once. I felt like I was being torn apart. My body wasn't mine anymore. It was something else. The next thing I knew, I was looking out of a whole different set of eyes. Wolf's eyes."

"Is that what happened to the rest of you?" Mitch asked. The blond man nodded. Josiah hesitated, and then nodded as well.

"What happened after you turned into wolves?" Anna asked quietly.

"We kept running around the circle," Kenny replied. "I've never felt so strong, so *alive* in my life. I never wanted it to stop."

"But it did—eventually," Jacob said.

Kenny nodded. "By morning, we were us again. I felt sick, like the worst whiskey hangover I'd ever had. We were all lying in the woods when we woke up, without any clothes on." He gave a guilty glance toward Anna, but she nodded permission to go on.

"And then?" Mitch asked.

Kenny shrugged. "We went home. Figured we must have had a bad batch of whiskey. Put us wrong in the head for the night. Only a few nights later, Shadow showed up in my dreams and called me back out to the woods. And the same damn thing happened all over again, 'cept he didn't need to stab me in the shoulder again. He made some motions, and I just changed."

"Did you try to resist him?"

Kenny shook his head. "How? You didn't meet him, or you'd know. He's not the kind you turn down."

"Did Shadow give you any orders?" Jacob asked. "That night, or any other night?"

"He told us we were his soldiers," Kenny replied. "That he expected us to help him win his prize. But we had to prove ourselves. Do everything he said. Show him we were worthy."

"Did you know that night that Walker had seen you?" Jacob asked.

"I didn't. Can't say what Shadow knew or didn't know. But night before last, he came in my dreams again and told me to meet in the woods. I went. The others were there," he said, stealing a glance at his companions. "Shadow told us Walker had seen us change, and had to be stopped. He told us where to go. We were to take Walker and bring him to Shadow."

"Where were you in the woods? Could you take us there?"

Kenny's eyes went wide, and he shook his head. "No. I mean, I can find it again, sure. But believe me, you don't want to go there." He told them the directions, and Jacob consulted a map.

"It's the same clearing we've been to," Jacob told Mitch and Anna. "Shadow must have had more troops, for backup."

"Did he promise you anything else after you caught Walker?" Mitch asked.

Kenny nodded. "Yeah. He said there was a lost treasure and he was going to find it. And when he did, he'd be able to protect us from any kind of magic."

"Did he say anything more about this 'treasure?'" Anna asked, leaning forward.

"He said it was priceless, and that we weren't to tell anyone, because there would be people who wanted to steal it," Kenny replied. He was clearly terrified—of Shadow and of the Department agents—and had decided to bare his soul if it would save his life.

"All right," Mitch said, turning to Kenny and the other prisoners. "The Department will be by to pick you up and take you for processing. I'll take your cooperation—or lack of it, in to consideration in my report," he added with a meaningful glare at Josiah and the blond man. "They'll get the silver out of you, patch you up."

"When?" Kenny asked. "This damn silver itches like sin."

"Whenever the airship gets here from New Pittsburgh. Sorry to tell you, you're not their top priority," Mitch replied with the hint of a smirk.

They left the three men tied up in one room and locked the door behind them. Then Mitch, Jacob, and Anna went out on the porch. "Della's gonna love you for sticking her with a bunch of redneck werewolves on her airship," Jacob observed.

"Della will get over it," Mitch replied. Agent Della Kennedy was one of the best airship pilots in the Department, and a frequent partner in their investigations.

"Think Kenny told you the truth?" Jacob asked.

Mitch shrugged. "I think he told us what he thinks he experienced. We didn't see them change. For all we know, this Shadow has pulled a con on all of us. He trains some wolves, and he intimidates some feeble-minded men into thinking they're wolves. Then he claims to be a powerful dark witch who can turn men into wolves. It might just be a shell game."

"Those three aren't too sharp," Anna agreed. "Maybe this Shadow is a Mesmerist. Maybe they aren't telling us everything, and he gave them a drug in their drink or some kind of ointment that made them hallucinate."

"Or not," Jacob warned. "We saw the pentacle drawn in the dirt. When Kenny said he was stabbed, Conroy—or whoever this

'Shadow' person is—might have injected them with werewolf blood."

"Or 'Shadow' might just be someone with a gift for theatrics who's playing some kind of sick game," Anna put in.

"Except that we saw wolves that should have been dead get back up, healed," Mitch persisted. "We saw that with our own eyes. And that says 'werewolf' to me."

"Is Falken actually sending Della with an airship?" Jacob asked.

Mitch grinned. "He will as soon as I send a telegram. I think he's going to want his folks to go over these guys with a fine-toothed comb. He'll get them fixed up. But they might never get out of a cell at Leavenworth if they really are able to turn into wolves."

Anna was staring out over the land, out toward the forest in the distance. "What if it's really true?" she asked quietly. "What if Shadow really can turn men into wolves and back again? Can you imagine what it must be like to be a wolf? To be free like that?"

Mitch raised an eyebrow. "I'm not sure I'd call beholden to a dark witch 'free,'" he cautioned.

Anna sighed. "No. Of course not. I meant the in-between parts. The running through the forest part, the no-rules part."

"The eating raw rabbit part," Jacob added, clearly not enthralled. "I think I'll stay human, thank you."

"What's with the gloves? New fashion statement?" Mitch asked.

"Better grip. After the close call in the woods, I'm not taking chances," Anna said.

Jacob stood watch while Mitch and Anna fixed a cold dinner from the supplies they brought. Mitch took a shift watching the prisoners while Jacob ate and then set up the portable telegraph system Adam Farber had made for them. Then they switched places, and Mitch sent his messages.

"Did you get a reply?" Jacob asked as Anna took a turn guarding the three men.

Mitch nodded. "Falken said he'll have the airship out here tomorrow morning. They'll take the prisoners off our hands, and bring us some new supplies."

"So we're staying in the field?"

Mitch gave him a look. "For as long as Falken can keep us here," he replied. "Seriously, he wants us to track down this 'Shadow' person. Whether he's a con man or a dark witch, he's causing problems. And if he is the real deal, we've got to take him out of action."

"What about Renate?" Jacob asked. Renate Thalberg was a powerful absinthe witch, and she was related to an even more powerful ancient vampire-witch. Renate had helped the Department out from time to time when interests coincided, and Mitch had remained on good terms with her, frequently asking her advice on cases.

"Haven't been able to reach her. I'll keep trying. Here's the telegram: you can read it yourself," Mitch replied, handing Jacob the telegram.

Absalom Conroy is dangerous, the message read. *He is also powerful and real. Dark witch. Possibly your "Shadow." Use extreme caution. Have obtained invitation for you three to party at Huidekoper mansion in Meadville. Conroy will be there.*

"I guess we're going to Meadville," Jacob said, hanging the telegram back. "But what are we going to wear to the party?"

"How can we go to a party if we can't even pronounce the name of the hosts?" Mitch fretted. Falken had mysteriously included evening-wear for all three of them in the wagon that came for the prisoners, and Jacob figured Renate had been in touch. "What is it again? Huey-de-koper?"

"Hy-dee-cooper," Anna corrected. "It's Dutch. And they're very, very wealthy. Made a killing in real estate. Friends with Jacob Astor. Lots of swanky friends in New York. Quite the rural aristocrats."

"What's a guy like Conroy doing around people like that?" Jacob wondered, tugging at his cravat. He doubted he would ever be comfortable in full formal dress. Mitch, of course, wore his tuxedo like he'd been born to it, and Anna was the epitome of a well-bred lady in a gown Renate had selected for her, complete with long white opera gloves.

"Walker said Conroy came from a wealthy family," Mitch replied. "Wouldn't be the first rich-son-gone-bad we've encountered."

"Dark rogue witch is a bit of a stretch," Jacob returned.

"Apparently Andreas Thalberg knows the Huidekoper family well," Mitch said.

"Of course he does," Jacob muttered. Andreas was a centuries-old vampire-witch, as well as being Renate's great-grandfather.

"Our cover story is that we're land speculators, looking for a location for a new resort hotel somewhere between Meadville and Cambridge Springs," Mitch continued. "I'm the architect, you're the financier, and Anna is the investor's daughter, representing his interests. The hooey-de-koppers—"

"Huidekopers," Anna corrected.

"Our hosts," Mitch said with a glare, "know the New Pittsburgh and New York upper crust very well, so we're all from Chicago, with the less said, the better."

"What the objective?" Jacob asked.

"Get a read on Conroy, see if we can pick up some kind of clue," Mitch replied. "I strongly doubt he's going to spill his guts at the sight of us, so we'll just have to improvise."

"Does 'improvise' mean watch the door while you pound it out of him?" Jacob asked.

Mitch rolled his eyes. "No. At least, not yet. Not at a fancy dress ball. And give me credit—even I have the sense not to go up against a dark witch without magical backup."

"News to me," Jacob said under his breath.

"And we've got rooms at the Lafayette Hotel," Mitch continued, pretending that he hadn't heard Jacob.

"No other word of what this 'treasure' is that Conroy is after or what it does?" Anna asked. She looked more enthusiastic than Jacob felt. Her eyes sparkled, and her cheeks were flushed. *Just like Mitch. They both like the thrill of the hunt.*

Mitch shook his head. "No idea. That's one of the things we're supposed to find out."

They lapsed in to silence as the carriage neared Meadville. Hans brought them in along the French Creek feeder canal, to a row of mansions overlooking the water.

"For a small town, there's some money here," Mitch said.

Hans turned the carriage into the drive of a huge, yellow-brick mansion. The home had a large, two-level half-circle columned porch on the front. Lights glittered from every window. A.C. Huidekoper's mansion was newly finished, and the family seemed intent on throwing plenty of soirees to show it off.

"Gorgeous," Anna murmured.

The columned porch graced the four-story center section of the home. Identical wings extended from each side, each two and a half stories tall. The roofline was embellished with Flemish parapets, dormers, and gables. Jacob bet the third floor was a ballroom from the movement of the people silhouetted in the windows. Set high on the hill above the canal, the mansion was easily the equal of any of the homes of New Pittsburgh's captains of industry.

Hans was dressed as a coachman, and swung down to open the carriage door for them beneath the *porte cochère*. As Jacob moved, he was aware of his revolver holstered at the small of his back beneath his tuxedo jacket. He wondered where Anna managed to hide a gun, and then decided that he probably didn't want to know.

"I'll get you moved into the Lafayette and secure the rooms, and be back for you at eleven," Hans said as they alighted from the carriage. "If you need me before then, signal." Hans wore a portable telegraph earpiece that could receive aetheric transmissions from the prototype watch on Mitch's wrist, another experimental gadget courtesy of genius Adam Farber and Tesla-Westinghouse Corporation.

New Pittsburgh with its wealth born from steel mills and factories tended to forget that elsewhere in the state, coal, lumber, railroads, and real estate created equally impressive fortunes. As they walked into the Huidekoper mansion, Jacob recognized several of the faces from among the New Pittsburgh elite, as well as industrialists from Brookville and Johnstown and shipping magnates from Erie.

"That's some fireplace," Jacob observed. A huge fireplace stood in the mansion's entryway. Its massive carved wooden mantel and surround reached from floor to ceiling. On either side of the firebox stood life-sized figures of men, draped like Greek heroes. Carved in a banner from one side of the freestanding fireplace to the other was a motif of griffins.

"Nothing but the best," Mitch murmured, sweeping into the room like he owned the place, or at least had the cash in his pocket to buy it.

A butler met them to take their coats. Jacob eased out of his carefully, mindful not to allow passers-by a glimpse of the weapon beneath his tuxedo jacket as he moved. Anna handed off her borrowed fur and eyed the guests.

"I think I see someone who might be useful," she said. "I'm going to mingle."

"I'm going to get us both tonic waters," Mitch told Jacob. Jacob tried not to look awkward as both his companions abandoned him. He accepted a canapé from a passing waiter and watched the crowd while doing his best not to seem too interested.

Meadville might be remote by the standards of Philadelphia or New Pittsburgh, but one glance told Jacob the group of people socializing in this room were no strangers to New York, London, and Paris. The gowns were the current New York fashion, as was the cut of the men's tuxes, and a glance at one of the bottles of wine the sommelier was pouring told Jacob that the vintage likely cost more than his wages for the month.

Absalom Conroy was not difficult to pick out from the crowd. He was a darkly handsome man in his thirties in a well-tailored tuxedo who had drawn a circle of admirers. Jacob was too far away to hear what was being said, but the body language of the listeners made it clear that they deferred to Conroy, hanging on his every word.

Mitch had disappeared in the line for the bar, and Anna was talking with a woman on the other side of the room, so Jacob edged closer, hoping to catch part of what Conroy was saying.

"Darwin was right, of course," Conroy was saying. "About survival being the reward to the fittest. We should heed the warning. Modern society is comfortable, but it tends to make us soft."

"I prefer to think that our inventions remove us from the savagery of brute force," one of the listeners, an older man, said. "After all, the Gatling gun and the railroad conquered the West."

"Neither worked well though for General Custer, did they?" Conroy mused. "Not when he was confronted with real warriors, and he couldn't fall back on his iron toys to save him."

"Surely you don't suggest we would be better off as primitives!"

The woman who spoke looked like she might have an attack of the vapors at the thought.

"It's the difference between a pet cat and a mountain lion, or a pet dog and a wolf," Conroy replied, looking as if he enjoyed toying with his audience. "One thrives in a zoo we call civilization. The other can hold its own against the forces of nature." Conroy's smile never slipped, but his eyes took on a zealot's intensity.

"Look around you," he said, sweeping his hand to indicate their opulent environs. "We're birds in gilded cages when we could be falcons and eagles. That's our birthright, to be the most respected predators."

"You've been reading too much of those French philosophers, my lad," the older man replied. "Noble savages and all that. A good pack of hounds can bring down a wild fox, and a rifle can take down a wolf from yards away. Seems like progress to me."

Conroy turned to look at the speaker. Something in his gaze made the man flinch. "A rifle is a coward's tool," he said in a low voice that was nearly a growl. "It's the weapon of a weakling. Bullets run out. Then how will you stand against the natural order?"

Conroy's unexpected intensity disquieted his listeners. Some drifted away, clearly uncomfortable. Others moved closer, attracted by his force of personality.

Jacob studied Absalom Conroy more closely. He had dark hair and a lithe build. His golden-flecked brown eyes had a feral hunger in them that was at odds with his polished exterior. Jacob wondered about the source of Conroy's wealth, and what part his magic played in acquiring it.

Before Conroy noticed him, Jacob drifted back into the mingling crowd. Mitch turned up at his elbow with a drink. "Here. I've been looking for you," Mitch said, handing off a glass of tonic water.

"I was just enjoying the conversation and people-watching," Jacob replied.

"I would have been back sooner, but our host buttonholed me about our new real estate projects," Mitch replied. "He's most interested in making an investment."

"How nice," Jacob responded. Perhaps Huidekoper would not be too surprised to find out the "project" was going to vanish into thin air. Such seemed the nature of the business, even when it wasn't being used as a cover story.

"Apparently we're not the only ones here with big plans," Mitch continued and took a sip of his drink. "Conroy has been talking to Huidekoper about investing in a new hunting resort up near Kane, in the Big Woods. A 'manly retreat,' Huidekoper told me, where we can shuck off our citified weakness."

"Hmm," Jacob mused. "Conroy was just going on about that a few minutes ago. I wonder if he plans to use the retreat to gain more followers, or feed the ones he has."

"Now that's interesting," Mitch said, and Jacob turned to follow his gaze. Anna was talking with Conroy, who had managed to shed his hangers-on. Conroy was responding enthusiastically to her interest, expounding at length.

"I imagine she'll come back with an earful," Jacob replied. "Did you try Renate's charm? Is there magic afoot now?" he asked in a voice low enough only Mitch could hear.

Mitch nodded. "It's glowing so brightly I had to wrap it in a kerchief. Conroy's got to be the man Walker saw. But I still don't understand what game he's playing, or why he's gone rogue."

"I somehow doubt he's one of those Muir preservationists," Jacob replied. "I can believe he'd want a hunting preserve. The only question is, who would be hunting whom?"

Jacob and Mitch drifted apart to work the room. Jacob noted that Anna spent the better part of half an hour engaging Conroy in conversation before she excused herself to speak with one of the women on the other side of the room. A string quartet played in one corner of the room. Most of the women were gathered in on one side of the ballroom, while the men, drinks, and cigars in hand, clustered near the bar. Waiters passed *hors d'oeurves* on silver platters, as well as flutes of champagne. It might make the social register, but Jacob was bored.

"I don't think I recognize you. I'm Ezra Baldwin." A distinguished-looking man in his middle years extended a hand to shake Jacob's. "I work with the bank downtown."

"Jacob Duran," Jacob replied, using his cover name. "From Chicago."

Baldwin took a sip of his whiskey. "That's quite a ways to come for a party, but I guess it's not too bad on the train." He smiled. "Meadville's not exactly New Pittsburgh, but we're not the backwoods some might tell you. Lot of history around here. French and Indian War, American Revolution, even the Civil War played out around these parts."

Jacob raised an eyebrow. "Aren't we a little far north for the Civil War? I didn't think the Grays got past Gettysburg?"

Baldwin laughed, warming to the subject. His civic pride seemed genuine, and Jacob could not help liking the man. "You ever heard of ol' John Brown—the abolitionist? Tried to stir up a slave revolt down South and the Johnny Rebs hanged him?"

Jacob nodded. "Sure."

"Well, he had a cabin just outside of Meadville. My father remembers him coming into town now and again. The Underground Railroad ran through Meadville and this whole area, taking those runaway slaves up to Canada. We had a barber in town, Richard Henderson, who hid a bunch of those slaves right here in town."

"I hope I'll have a chance to take a look around," Jacob replied. "I'm just in for a short visit."

"If you're interested in the War, there's someone you should meet," Ezra said and motioned for Jacob to follow him to where an elderly man sat in a chair along the wall, tapping his toe to the music of a string quartet.

"Mr. Bates!" Ezra said, loudly enough for the old gentleman to hear him over the music. "I've got someone who'd like to meet you."

Bates turned, and though Jacob reckoned that the man must be around eighty years old, his blue eyes were sharp and clear. "Oh, it's you, Ezra," he said, glancing at Baldwin. "What can I do for you?"

"Jacob Duran, I'd like you to meet Mr. Samuel Bates. Mr. Bates, this is Jacob Duran from Chicago, and he's interested in the Civil War history of these parts."

Ezra turned back to Jacob. "There's not a man alive in Meadville or the whole county who knows more about the War than Mr. Bates. He's written three books on it. Met ol' John Brown in the flesh, too."

Someone called to Ezra just then, and he excused himself. Bates patted a chair next to him, and Jacob sat down. Mitch and Anna had disappeared, and for the moment, Jacob had nowhere better to be. *Besides, this might be interesting. I was afraid I was going to die of boredom.*

"Yes, I met John Brown, the abolitionist, on a number of occasions," Bates said, launching into the topic with passion. "He was a good man, a family man. I was in charge of the Meadville Academy when I first came to town, and one day, John Brown came to my office to get a letter of recommendation for a tutor for his children—he had thirteen of them, you know. I sent him Isaac Brawley, one of the best teachers we had." Bates began to cough, and it took a moment for him to resume.

"Meadville was quite active in the abolition movement," he said with pride. "Have you been up to Diamond Park yet? The Independent Congregationalist Church there had a number of members who supported the cause, and some took in runaways, too. Sent a lot of soldiers to the Union from Meadville, to fight the Rebs. I wrote a book about Chancellorsville, and one about Gettysburg, and sometimes I wish I didn't know what I know about those battles. Terrible things, even for a good cause."

Bates began to cough again. "I'm going to get a fresh nip of whiskey for my cough," he said, standing. "Medicinal, you know," he added with a broad wink. "Good to talk with you. Nice to see young people taking an interest in history. Now, if you'll excuse me," he said and made his way toward the bar.

The ballroom was stuffy, and the cigar smoke was giving Jacob a headache, so he drifted toward the balcony above the columned porch, overlooking the canal. Beyond the canal lay railroad tracks, and beyond those, a steep hill that rose against the night sky. On the rise above the canal, to the left and right of the Huidekoper house, sat other stately mansions of the Meadville elite. He could see their lights through the trees and wondered if their owners were among the guests at the party.

Movement down below caught Jacob's eye. He pulled a specially-adapted monocle from his pocket. The bulky eyepiece enabled the wearer to see better in the dark. With the help of the monocle, Jacob could make out the shapes of four men patrolling the bank of the canal and the perimeter of the Huidekoper property.

Security wouldn't be amiss, given the jewelry some of the women are wearing, and the net worth of the guest list, Jacob mused. *Huidekoper might have hired some Pinkertons for the event. Then again, I wouldn't figure Meadville as a high-risk area for kidnapping or jewel thieves. So are they Huidekoper's men, or Conroy's?*

Jacob glanced behind him. Mitch and Anna were occupied, and no one else noticed he stepped away. Without stopping too long to think about it, Jacob let himself over the edge of the railing to drop onto the second-floor balcony, and from there, to the first floor. He crouched in the shadows until he was certain none of the security men had spotted him, then straightened and headed toward the canal.

His revolver was in his hand. It was a special one he chose for the situation, an 1895 Nagant, Russian. The caliber would stop a human, and the silver bullets would drop a werewolf. The suppressor would keep things private. Jacob was not sure why he had left the party or what he expected to find, but he had learned to trust his hunches, especially when they were this strong.

Carriages lined the street. Drivers dozed, waiting to take their passengers home after the party. Jacob eased around them, glancing to see if Hans was nearby. No such luck. A hedgerow separated the road from the canal. Jacob crept along it, wary of every motion. Two large men incongruously dressed in ill-fitting tuxes paused for a smoke on the other side of the bushes.

"Don't know why we don't just take them at the hotel," one of the men said and took a drag on his smoke.

"Because the boss said to wait, that's why." The cheap cigarette made Jacob's eyes water.

"Not like the boss to play nice," the first one replied. "Maybe it's the dame. Nice cut to that jib."

"Shut up, Henry. Talk like that will get you killed. Boss has his reasons. Maybe they know where to find the thing we've been lookin' for."

"Then beat it out of them and be done with it," Henry replied. "Direct. Simple. Fast."

"We do it the boss's way. End of story."

"Sure," Henry agreed. "But when it's over, I want a crack at them. For what they did at the cabin."

"Boss already said we could kill them when he was through. Be patient."

The cigarettes were nearly done, and the smoke that covered Jacob's scent would wane. Any moment now, the two might pay more attention to the smell of the night air, and that would be bad. He eased backward, slipping between two carriages, and paused to make sure he had not been followed. *I don't think Conroy would use wolves this close to witnesses. But I don't really want to take the chance that I'm wrong.*

Jacob moved stealthily across the wide front lawn, staying out of the lights at the front of the house. He wouldn't have to scale the balconies. He could walk up the stairs, with the excuse of going out for a smoke, and even have the smell on his clothes to prove it. *It just won't do to look like I've been too far away.*

"You can stop right there, Agent Drangosavich." The big man stepped out of the shadows, blocking Jacob's way. "You're too nosy for your own good. Gonna get you in trouble someday."

"No idea what you're talking about," Jacob bluffed. The man's eyes said he wasn't falling for it. "Just stepped out for some air."

"Boss said we couldn't kill all three of you," the man said in a dangerously quiet voice. "But maybe if you go missing, the others will take the hint and disappear on their own."

"Step aside." Jacob's expression was coldly neutral, but no one could mistake the threat in his voice.

"Party's over for you." The big man took a step toward him. A sound like a cork popping blended with the music and laughter from the open windows. Blood spread across the man's chest, staining his starched white shirt. He kept coming, sure of his werewolf strength. That's when the silver registered. Fiery trails of red vined across the man's face and hands and he fell to his knees, clawing at his chest. Another pop. A small crimson hole appeared in the man's forehead. Darkness hid the spray of gore behind him as he fell forward and lay still.

Jacob froze for a moment, fearing detection by either the wolf-man's comrades or Huidekoper's security men, but no one came running. *Damn. And I'm wearing a rented tuxedo.* With a sigh, Jacob grabbed the dead man's wrist and dragged him into the bushes, rolling the body beneath the shrubbery with his foot. He rubbed the soles of his feet in the slick, wet grass to clean them, and glanced down at himself, but if there was blood on his tux, it was too dark here to see. Heart still thudding, Jacob straightened his bow tie and walked back into the mansion as if nothing had happened.

Mitch made a bee-line for him as soon as he was back in the ball-room. "Where the hell have you been?" Mitch's expression never changed to match the tension in his words. Any onlookers would never have suspected the tone.

"Out for a smoke," Jacob replied.

"You don't smoke," Mitch countered. He glanced down. "You've got blood on your jacket."

"I'll fill you in later." As Mitch began to turn away, Jacob grabbed his arm. "Conroy knows who we are and why we're here. Be careful."

Mitch nodded to show he understood, then headed back into the crowd.

Raised voices drew Jacob's attention. The guests had drawn back, giving room to a portly man who was red in the face as he spoke loudly to Conroy. From the intelligence briefing they had received, Jacob recognized the speaker as George Delamater, a prominent banker.

"You go against the teachings of the church, Mr. Conroy!" Delamater scolded. "The Creator Himself decreed that man was to have dominion over all things. How dare you suggest that mankind is some sort of weak second to animals."

Conroy appeared unruffled. "I prefer to think of 'dominion' as an honorary title," he replied. "Something to be earned, not granted to be kept without effort. Look at the wars on the Continent and the wretched poor in every city. You see none of that among animals. We are capable of claiming our 'dominion' only with the help of tools. Take away those tools, and we are no longer top predator."

"Are you challenging Scripture?" Delamater looked like he might pop his buttons.

Conroy smiled. "On the contrary. Man is the 'fallen' creature. The rest of the natural world was not so foolish and remains pristine, unspoiled. Pure. Filled with the power of Creation itself."

Huidekoper was making his way toward his two guests, moving as quickly as the crowd could step aside for him. "Now what's all this about?" he chided. "This is a night for merriment. Put your differences aside, gentlemen. Leave the philosophizing for the vicar."

Huidekoper signaled a servant, who came at once with two crystal glasses of whiskey. He handed one to Conroy and one to Delamater, with a glare that silenced them both, at least for the moment.

Mitch sidled up to Jacob. "Interesting," he noted under his breath.

The quartet continued to play, but the argument seemed to drain the energy from the party. Even before the church tower bells tolled eleven, guests began making their farewells to the host and hostess and heading for the door. Jacob looked around for Anna but did not see her until they were ready to board their carriage.

"Quite an evening!" Anna said, flushed with the warmth of the ballroom as the carriage pulled away. Jacob peered out the window toward the canal, but the figures he had seen before were nowhere in sight.

Jacob recounted what he had seen from the balcony, as well as the conversations he overheard. "I heard more of the same," Mitch confirmed. "Conroy is the last of a wealthy family. He apparently took the Grand Tour and ended up staying longer than expected in Romania. Fell in love with the forests in Transylvania. When he came back, he had a new passion for the outdoors, and created a hunting club with the sons of other prominent families."

Mitch paused. "I also heard there's been a bit of scandal around the club. One of the young men was killed up in the Big Woods a few months ago. No charges filed, of course, given Conroy's connections, but there's bad blood among some of the upper crust. At least two people warned me Conroy's 'club' was nothing more than wastrel sons gone bad with too much money and freedom."

"Any ideas about the 'treasure' that the bully boys at the sanitarium mentioned?" Jacob asked.

Mitch shook his head. "That didn't seem the kind of crowd who'd be in the know on magical artifacts," he replied. "I doubt Huidekoper knows anything beyond the ledger numbers Conroy's supplied him with. If Conroy has accomplices, I don't think they were on the guest list."

"You talked with Conroy for quite a while," Jacob said, turning to Anna. "What's his version of the story?"

Anna smiled. "He can be quite charming when he wants to," she replied. "Very bright. Willful—but then I'd expect it of someone from his background. He can make quite a persuasive case for his 'retreat.'"

"Anything else?" Mitch asked, a touch of acid in his voice.

"What?" Anna retorted, picking up on his tone. "Did you expect me to cuff him at the party and garrote him until he told us his evil schemes?"

"It might have been more effective than flirting with him the entire night," Mitch snapped.

"Tell that to Falken." Anna's eyes sparked with anger. "You know what he said when he sent me on this mission? He told me to use my 'feminine wiles' to get close to the target. Forget my ranking on the target range, or the fact that I've taken every agent in New Pittsburgh to the mat in the sparring room at least once—including you, Storm. No. I'm here to seduce him into some pillow talk."

"If Falken didn't think you could handle yourself in a combat situation, he wouldn't have sent you," Jacob said.

"And Conroy did seem disposed to expound about himself when you flattered him," Mitch added.

Anna gave him a murderous glare. "How do you know he might not have warmed up just as much to you, Mitch? You're pretty, too."

Jacob held back a chuckle as Mitch reddened, only because he was certain that if he laughed, both Anna and Mitch were likely to slug him.

"The Department expects us to get what we came for, even if that means bending the law and conventional morality to do it," Jacob replied, doing his best to keep his voice neutral.

"I am not the Department's whore!" Anna's fists clenched in her lap.

"One way or the other, we're all the Department's whores," Mitch replied. "We do what we're told to do, like it or not. We say our confession on Sunday and break most of the Commandments on Monday in service to God and country. Maybe there's dispensation for us; God help our souls. Maybe not. We pay a price so they don't have to," he added, jerking his thumb at the world outside the carriage window.

Anna sat back, arms crossed, staring out the window for the rest of the ride to the Lafayette Hotel. Hans gave her a hand to alight from the carriage, and bent low so only the three of them could hear.

"There was a message from Renate on the private telegraph," Hans said. "She has a contact for you to meet tonight, a man named Ezekiel Kronin. I have the details. But you'll have to hurry. He's going to be waiting for you at midnight, and you'll want to change."

"Where?" Mitch asked.

"Greendale Cemetery," Hans replied. "Said it should be quiet this time of night."

"THAT'S WHERE WE'RE meeting the contact?" Mitch stared at the small whitewashed stone building not far inside the cemetery gate.

"I don't see the problem," Jacob replied. "It's convenient and private."

"It's the bloody receiving vault for the cemetery," Mitch countered. "You know, where they store the bodies when the ground's too cold to dig graves?"

"Then you're in luck," Jacob said. "It's not that cold out. Should be empty."

They had arrived at the rendezvous site early to get the lay of the land. Greendale Cemetery sat at the crest of the hill and the end of a road. Huge oak trees shaded the graves of the dead, and Jacob noted markers from both the Revolution and the Civil War as they scouted the area, as well as monuments of local notables among the rhododendron and mountain laurel.

A steep ravine fell off behind the cemetery, which stretched toward a copse of trees and fields on the other side. The caretaker's cottage sat just inside the stone archway entrance as if he did not want to be any closer to his charges than duty required.

The sound of church bells tolling the hour carried on the night air. "Midnight," Mitch said. "I don't see anyone."

"Let's go inside," Jacob said. "Maybe Kronin is already here."

"I'm not going to get cornered," Mitch replied.

"I'll watch from behind that marker," Anna said, pointing to a large obelisk a few feet from the receiving vault.

"And I'll stay by the door, where I can watch as well," Jacob offered. "You can do the talking."

Enough moonlight filtered through the clouds to allow them to see inside as Mitch opened the door, gun drawn. The building held what looked like bunk bed shelves on both sides and along the back. A chill ran down Jacob's spine as he realized they were meant to hold coffins, not the living.

"You do not need your weapons," a voice said from inside. "I mean you no harm."

A man stepped forward from the shadows in the back of the stone building.

Jacob stayed in the doorway, his gun at the ready, just in case. Mitch moved inside. "Kronin?" he asked.

Out of the corner of his eye, Jacob could see the man nod. Kronin was a middle-aged man with tufts of gray hair around his balding pate and a pair of wire-rimmed spectacles perched on his nose. "Agent Storm, I presume."

Mitch nodded. "What do you have for us?"

"A warning," Kronin said. "Absalom Conroy is a powerful witch. He's smart and ruthless. Local practitioners keep their distance."

"Not an option," Jacob replied. "So what do you suggest instead?"

Kronin studied him. "Caution," he replied.

"You called us out to a graveyard in the middle of the night to tell us to be careful?" Mitch asked incredulously.

Kronin raised a hand in appeasement. "I would be remiss not to warn you. He is a force to be taken seriously, and he has an advantage you don't possess."

"Magic?" Mitch's voice was skeptical

"Yes. And I believe I know what Conroy is desperate to find," Kronin said. "It is an old artifact, and if it actually exists, it would give him even greater power. He seeks the hand of glory made from the severed left hand of Peter Stumpp—a notorious German werewolf."

"Hand of glory?" Mitch repeated. "I thought those were just legends."

Kronin chuckled. "I wish that they were. But I assure you: they are very real, and capable of more damage than the old wives' tales tell. The fingers burn without being consumed, and cast a thrall over those close-by."

"From what you say, I expected more of Conroy than a means for petty thievery," Jacob said from the doorway.

"Oh, it's thievery he's after, but not petty," Kronin replied. "Conroy's already bound a daemon to his service. I don't like to think of what kind of price he had to pay. With the daemon and the hand of glory, Conroy intends to beggar the industrialists of New Pittsburgh and the world. It's energy he means to steal, and that will gain him all the gold he could ever want."

"I don't understand," Mitch pressed. Anna backed up to stand by Jacob at the door where she could hear, intrigued.

"A perpetual motion machine," Kronin said. "One that never needs fuel and never runs down. The hand of glory, burning forever, set at the heart of the biggest generator the world has ever seen, and a bound daemon to work the controls without friction or decay, kept in place by the hand's thrall. Within the engine, entropy—perhaps even time—stops. Limitless energy without the expense of coal, wood, or oil. No one else can compete. Conroy will offer the world cheap, limitless energy, and the world will repay him with power and wealth beyond even the imaginations of Carnegie and Rockefeller."

"Maxwell's demon—with a real daemon," Jacob said, and let out a low whistle of admiration.

"Then why the werewolves?" Anna asked.

"This particular hand of glory was taken from a werewolf and answers best to one of its own. Just as important, the Oligarchy of New Pittsburgh has its private armies. Frick has his Pinkertons. But they are nothing against troops of werewolves who serve their master with the devotion of a pack for its leader." Kronin's concern was clear. "You must stop him now, because if he builds his infernal machine, there will be no stopping him later."

"Where is the hand of glory?" Mitch asked. "Sounds like we need to steal it before Conroy can."

"I don't know," Kronin replied. "But I can send you to talk to someone who might. Do you know of the *Logonje*?"

"The demon-hunting Polish priests?" Jacob replied. "Yeah. We've worked together with them on some cases that required a little 'something extra,'" he added with a glance skyward.

"Go to Cambridge Springs," Kronin said. "Take a room at the Rider Hotel, and ask for Father Dubicki. If he wants to speak with you, he'll find you."

"If Stumpp's hand has been lost for such a long time, maybe we should leave it lost," Mitch said. "I don't relish having something like that sitting in a crate in the Department's warehouse."

"You don't have that luxury," Kronin replied. "My people have been watching Conroy. We think he's very close to finding the hand."

"If he's got a daemon bound to him, why can't it find the hand for him?" Anna asked.

Kronin frowned. "There are all manner of daemons, and we believe the one Conroy has bound is a spirit of obedience. Very good at carrying out specific tasks tirelessly, but not intelligent enough to run errands."

"Since 'your people' are witches, why aren't they stopping him?" Jacob questioned. "We're just government agents. You've got magic."

Kronin turned to look at Jacob, and Jacob felt a chill go down his spine as their gazes locked. "Magic is constrained in its own way. If any of our coven were to seek the hand, Conroy would know immediately. Power calls to power. The hand offers temptation to those with magic that it cannot promise to mere mortals. We might keep Conroy from acquiring it, only to see it seduce another of our number to perhaps greater evil."

"Is the hand evil?" Mitch asked.

Kronin shook his head. "Not exactly. You've heard about the corruption of absolute power? Someone without magic could not use the hand to do the same things that a witch could. The temptation is less."

"So for non-witches, it's just an ugly candle?" Jacob asked.

Kronin chuckled. "That—and a little more. A hand of glory is a thief's tool. It will put people around it to sleep and burn without going out for a mortal with the will to use it. But it's an object taken from the body of a hanged man, and the tallow is taken from that man's corpse. It is perverse, and the energy that binds it was forced on it against its will. Such tools have a reputation for turning on their owners."

"Sounds like when it comes to getting the hand of glory, we're your cat's paw," Mitch said. "What can your coven bring to this party?"

Kronin glanced at Anna and Jacob. "Is he always this rash?"

"You have no idea," Jacob replied.

Kronin regarded Mitch with dry amusement. "My coven will do all that it can to counter Conroy's magic without unduly exposing ourselves. Witches are not tolerated well, even in this century."

Mitch looked like he was about to say something when a blood-curdling howl sounded outside the small stone building. "Looks like you've got an opportunity to pony up some of that protection," Mitch muttered, drawing his gun.

More howls echoed across the cemetery. "Sounds like that wolf brought a lot of friends," Jacob observed. From somewhere nearby, they heard the crackle of lightning and saw a flash through the frosted glass of the vault's windows.

"One of yours?" Mitch asked with a glanced toward Kronin, who nodded. A second streak flared, and a wolf yipped in pain.

"We can't stay in here forever," Mitch said. "Got a plan?"

"Preferably one that doesn't involve high-powered explosives?" Jacob added.

"Some of your coven are here?" Mitch turned to face Kronin, who nodded.

"Yes. Two others. One is assuring that the caretaker does not wake and come to investigate. The other is behind the vault."

Jacob had a shotgun. Mitch and Anna had rifles. Mitch moved closer to the doorway and dug into his rucksack. He pulled out a large slingshot and several ribbed blue bottles, each about the size of a grapefruit and emblazoned with a star. "What the hell are those?" Jacob asked.

"A little something Hans modified in his spare time," Mitch said with a smile.

"Aren't those the Hardin fire extinguishers from the hotel?" Anna asked.

Mitch rolled his eyes. "Hans appropriated them for a higher purpose. The Department can replace them later." Mitch threw bandanas to Jacob and Anna and tossed one to Kronin before tying one over his mouth and nose. "Put them on." He looked to Kronin. "Now would be a good time to do whatever it is you do." Then he turned to Jacob and Anna. "Cover me."

With that, Mitch burst from the receiving vault, with Jacob and Anna laying down fire, guns blazing. Three werewolves were waiting for them. Jacob put a bullet into the throat of the nearest wolf as it leaped toward him. *That might not kill it, but the silver dust in the cartridge is going to sting a lot.*

Anna lifted the rifle to her shoulder and brought down another wolf that sprang at Jacob, barely missing his arm. Her bullet tore into the creature's shoulder, and it dropped with a sharp cry of pain.

"They've got us surrounded," Jacob warned.

Mitch loaded a blue bottle into the slingshot, pulled back, and let fly, intentionally aiming for a tree limb above the heads of three of the huge gray wolves. The glass shattered, sending down a fine silver mist that sparkled in the moonlight. As the dust settled on the werewolves, they began to yip and roll on the ground.

"Keep firing!" Mitch shouted. He fired again with the slingshot, this time shattering the bottle against a large granite monument near two more of the wolves. He turned to the right and fired once more.

The air was filled with silver dust, falling like sparkling snow. The creatures howled in pain and fury as they tried to get the silver out of their eyes and noses.

Jacob and Anna kept firing. One of the wolves approached from the back of the receiving vault and sprang for Anna, knocking her rifle from her grip. She rolled, bringing her knees into her chest so that her feet absorbed the creature's lunge. Her revolver thundered, clipping the wolf in its side. She kicked hard, throwing the werewolf's body away so she could scramble to her feet.

"Are you hurt?" Jacob asked.

"Don't think so," she answered, grabbing her rifle from the ground.

The wolves were retreating, pushed back by the silver dust. Jacob ran after them, firing their guns, while Mitch continued to lob the glass bottles filled with silver dust. Anna hung back, covering the rear. Jacob heard a growl, and a thin gray wolf sprang at him. Jacob dodged out of the way, falling over a tombstone and rolling to land on his back. The wolf leaped over the marker, and Jacob fired, taking the creature full in the chest with the shotgun blast. The force of the shot flung the body against a granite tombstone.

"Are you okay?" Mitch yelled.

"Yeah. I'm fine." Jacob got to his knees, keeping his gun trained on the wolf until he was sure it was not going to rise. Bloody remains were splattered on the marker, which read *"Richard Henderson 1801- 1880."* A pair of hands clasped in prayer with broken shackles were carved into the tombstone, with an inscription below them that was too blood-soaked and dark for Jacob to make it out.

Two of the werewolves lay still on the grass behind them, shimmering as they changed back to men with their dying breath. A wind stirred, with the receiving vault at its center. The wolves had fallen back to the edge of Mitch's range with the slingshot. Kronin stood near the vault, chanting quietly under his breath, his hands raised. The wind grew stronger, picking up the silver dust from the grass and leaves, blowing it into a sparkling cloud that rolled toward the wolves on all sides. Blasts of lightning streaked toward the lagging wolves, throwing up a shower of dirt where they touched down on the heels of the fleeing creatures. The werewolves yelped and barked as the cloud and the lightning closed in on them, then ran for the ravine.

"What are we going to do with the bodies?" Jacob demanded as Mitch strolled back toward him.

Mitch nodded toward the building. "It's a receiving vault, isn't?

Well, it can 'receive' these bodies until the Department comes to get them."

Wary of handling the bloody remains, Mitch and Jacob lifted the corpses with shovels and placed them into the stone vault. All of the wolves had changed back to human form. Two men and a woman.

"And if the caretaker looks in here tomorrow?" Anna asked.

"He won't," Kronin said. They turned to look at the witch. Two more people had joined him, a man and a woman, members of his coven.

"The spell I've used on the caretaker to sleep through the ruckus will also make him forget anything he heard—and ignore the receiving vault for twenty-four hours," the woman replied. She was slender with pale blonde hair and green eyes.

Anna nodded. "Thank you. Our people will take care of it."

Mitch signaled Hans with his watch-transmitter, and a few moments later, Jacob saw Hans and the carriage heading up the Randolph Street hill to take them back to the Lafayette Hotel.

"Thank you," Mitch said, addressing Kronin and his adepts. "We'll go see Dubicki. And we would be greatly obliged if you could please watch our backs when you can."

Kronin's lips twitched in to a slight smile. "We will protect you as much as we can," he replied. "But be careful of your wording. It is a dangerous thing to promise to be 'greatly obliged' to a witch. Such obligations have a way of coming due."

———

"WHY ARE WE meeting a priest in a posh hotel like that?" Mitch wondered aloud as the carriage neared their destination.

"Because it's public and respectable," Jacob replied. "Maybe he likes the food."

The Rider Hotel in Cambridge Springs was a grand resort in a town well-known for its mineral springs. It sat atop a hill, which gave it a commanding view. The main hotel structure was brick, rising five stories high. Large white wood porches and decorative trim graced the two lower levels. The central building rose another two stories taller with an impressive double-deck viewing porch set off with elaborate white railings and filigree.

"I was asking a man back at the Lafayette about this place," Anna said. "It just opened a few years ago. People come all the way from Chicago and New York to take the mineral springs cures here. I heard the hotel has a golf course and every room has a telephone!"

Hans brought them up to the *porte cochère* to drop them off. "Keep your ears open," Mitch said as they climbed from the carriage, with a glance to the earpiece tucked beneath Hans's ear that could receive the signal from Mitch's watch. "Just in case." Hans nodded in assent.

Anna walked between the two men as they climbed the wide, elegant front steps. The white marble stairs ascended to a grand stone archway filled with carvings and columns. To either side of the entrance, on the expansive wooden porch, guests sat in rocking chairs taking in the view.

Jacob offered Anna his arm as they climbed. She accepted, then winced. "Something wrong?" he murmured.

"I must have gotten a bruise in the fight last night," she whispered. "Nothing major."

The lobby of the Hotel Rider was in keeping with its overall grandeur. Dark wood covered the walls. Elegant arches rose from pillars to give the ceiling the effect of a gothic cathedral, and large fire-places offered guests a place to relax.

"It's huge," Anna said, looking around. "The lobby seems to go on forever."

A young man in a bellhop's uniform approached them. "Mr. Tempest?" he asked, using Mitch's cover name. Mitch nodded in acknowledgment. "There's a priest waiting for you in the parlor. He sent me to help you find the way."

Mitch and the others followed the bellhop, though they remained wary for a trap. They arrived without incident at a small sitting area set apart to allow privacy, and Mitch gave the boy a lavish tip. "Find an excuse to keep an eye on our room and not let anyone interrupt us, and I'll pay you half again as much when we finish," Mitch promised. He and the others entered the parlor and drew the glass doors shut behind him.

Father Dubicki was waiting for them. He was likely in his forties, although his long beard and the severe, black cassock he wore made him look older. "I see you made it," the priest said, rising to greet them. "I trust your journey was smooth."

"Quite," Mitch replied. "Thank you for coming."

"Do you like the hotel?" Dubicki asked, beaming with pride. "Quite the place, isn't it? The owner has been kind enough to let us use some of the rooms for our Polish high school, just until our building is completed. We have so many residents newly arrived from the Old Country. Maybe someday, we'll even have a college, God willing."

He paused and gave Mitch the once-over. "We run in unusual company; it seems," the priest continued, and motioned for them to sit. "You mentioned Father Matija?"

Jacob nodded. "We've worked with him several times in New Pittsburgh. We consider him an ally."

Dubicki gave Jacob a measured look. "Interesting. Yet you come at the introduction of Ezekiel Kronin. How is this?"

"We're with the Department of Supernatural Investigation," Mitch replied. "Trying to stop a rogue dark witch from gaining nearly unlimited power. Kronin believed you knew something about the Stumpp artifact."

Dubicki muttered something in Polish and crossed himself. "Why do you want to know about that? It's a cursed thing, best for everyone if it remains lost."

Jacob leaned forward, elbows on his knees. "I completely agree. But Absalom Conroy wants the artifact, and he's got a bound daemon and a pack of werewolves to do his bidding. And Kronin believes Conroy is getting close to finding it."

Dubicki paled but was silent for a moment. "If I had the artifact, I would have given it to the *Logonje* to destroy it," he replied. "I would not even trust such a relic to the Church, sad as it makes me to say it. The temptation is just too great."

"We don't have magic," Mitch said. "And we don't want to use the hand. We'll give it to the Department—or the *Logonje*—and let them take care of it. But I think we've got a common cause in keeping it away from Conroy."

"What can you tell us about where the artifact might be located?" Anna asked. Dubicki might be a priest, but he was also a man, and Anna's charm was not wasted. His expression softened, and his eyes warmed.

"Peter Stumpp was executed in 1589 in the Holy Roman Empire for the crime of lycanthropy and mass murder," Dubicki replied. "One of his sympathizers cut off his left hand and made it into the abomination Conroy seeks. The hand was passed among various owners over the centuries; including, some say, the Holy Roman Emperor, the British monarchy, and the Vatican. Always, it has brought those who possess it to grief."

He paused, glancing around to assure they would not be overheard. "Legend has it that the Stumpp hand was brought to the New World by a French aristocrat fleeing their bloody revolution." Dubicki raised an eyebrow. "That would be par for the artifact's history. Evil befell the aristocrat in New Orleans, and the hand was owned, for a time, by Voodoo queen Marie Laveau. After her death, we lost track of the hand until it showed up in the possession of a wealthy Georgia plantation owner right before the Civil War. Rumor has it that the artifact was stolen by a runaway slave and brought north, possibly to this area."

Dubicki sighed. "And that's where we lost the trail. This part of the state was active in the abolition movement. John Brown found support among some prominent local men for the slave revolt he planned. They were willing to give him money, but wisely decided to let him do the shooting on their behalf. Thousands of runaway slaves traveled through all the little cities around here. Any one of them might have brought the hand with them." He shrugged. "We just don't know. It may have been destroyed—there are rumors to that effect."

"Conroy seems to believe the hand is somewhere in or near Meadville," Anna pressed.

"Then he knows something I don't know," the priest said, shaking his head.

Jacob looked up. "Richard Henderson."

Mitch and the others turned to stare at him. "Who?" Mitch asked.

"When we were at the Huidekoper party, the man I was talking to decided to fill me in on local history," Jacob replied. "Richard Henderson was a barber in Meadville who was a free Black man, and he sheltered runaways on the Underground Railroad. I saw his tombstone last night at the cemetery."

"You think he might have had the hand?" Anna asked, eyes alight.

"He might not have kept the hand, but one of the runaways he hid might have had it with him and left it behind for some reason," Jacob theorized. "It's worth looking into."

Dubicki nodded. "The *Logonje* have been following up on such trails for years now. So far, they have all been dead ends."

"Conroy's not dumb," Mitch said. "If he thinks the hand is in Meadville, then he's got a reason. Maybe he turned up a clue your people missed. Or maybe his magic helped him out. But I think we'd better get back to town and do some looking around." He glanced at Dubicki. "And since Conroy doesn't play nice, we'd sure appreciate it if the *Logonje* could lend a hand."

Dubicki nodded. "I'll send two of my priests back with you. They can be ready to travel by the time you've finished your lunch. We have a few more of our brother priests near Meadville we can call in to help. You'll have our support. But we'd like a say in what happens to the hand when you find it."

Mitch coughed. "We don't actually control that, Father. We're just agents. Something like that would need to go to HQ."

Dubicki smiled. "Perhaps. But it is said that the Good Lord works in mysterious ways. Keep an open mind."

5 / ROGUE | THE UNDERGROUND
RAILROAD

"IT'S ONLY TWELVE MILES. Why does it feel like we're hell and gone from civilization?" Mitch had his rifle across his lap in the carriage, and a bag full of more altered Harden bottles, filled with silver dust.

"Because we're out in the country," Jacob replied, equally ready for trouble with his shotgun. "That means there's space between things. This is farm country—but it's still more populated than some of the places we've been."

"Maybe we should have taken the train." Anna winced as the carriage hit a bump. The road between Meadville and Cambridge Springs was rough in places where the harsh winters had broken the macadam, so Hans was forced to reduce their speed.

"There wasn't a train at convenient times," Mitch replied. "And it was too public. Too much of a chance for bloodshed if Conroy tried something to stop us."

"Where if he tries something now, it's just our blood," Jacob added in a dry tone.

"You know what I mean."

"I'd have felt better if Agent Kennedy and her airship were closer," Jacob grumbled.

"Now that would be stealthy, having an airship follow us overhead." Mitch rolled his eyes.

Jacob kept watch out of the carriage window. He had a nagging feeling that something was about to happen, and the overcast day lent itself to gloom. The road took them past farms and forests, and a few lonely houses. "Conroy might have been less inclined to make a move in public. Out here, there's no one to see except the crows."

It would be early evening when they returned to Meadville, and Mitch was chafing at the delay. "I want to figure out where Henderson hid the runaway slaves," Mitch said. "Odds are, Conroy's already got a jump on us."

Mitch shifted in his seat, bumping Anna's arm. She flinched and slid closer to the carriage wall. "Sorry," he said. "Do you need a doctor?"

She shook her head. "No. I just have a nasty bruise, and it's going to be sore for a while. I'm just happy my sleeves and gloves cover it!"

"You've been quiet," Jacob said, turning his attention to Anna. "What did you make of Father Dubicki?"

"He believes the hand is real, but I'm not certain he thinks the hand still exists," Anna replied. "So I don't know how hard his priests might have actually searched for it."

"Conroy believes in it," Mitch replied. "And he doesn't seem the sort for wild goose chases. He wouldn't be here if he didn't think he was going to find something."

Dark clouds blotted out the sun, making it feel later than it was. An old cemetery sat near the road, with crooked headstones and tall weeds, and behind it, an abandoned clapboard church. Large trees along both sides the road cast the next stretch in deep shadows. It had been quite a while since they had passed other travelers, and the eerie quiet made Jacob nervous. He glanced out the small rear window, assuring him that the two black-cloaked priests still road behind them.

"Dubicki thinks the hand—or Conroy, or both—are enough of a worry to send some of his men with us," Jacob observed.

"Maybe he just wants to make sure we turn over the hand if we find it," Mitch replied. "I'm not sure the Department would go for that."

"If Stumpp's hand has enough bad juju to corrupt people inside the

Vatican, I'm not sure a government bureaucracy would stand a chance," Jacob said. "I think we're all better off destroying the thing."

"What if it could be contained?" Anna asked. "Maybe it could be a force for good."

Mitch raised an eyebrow. "Or someone figures out how to make it into the ultimate weapon." He shook his head. "I've got to agree with Jacob. It's too much of a risk."

Jacob's eyes narrowed as he glimpsed movement in the shadows and instant before Hans snapped the reins and the carriage took off at breakneck speed. "We've got company," Jacob warned.

A dozen muscular young men stepped out from among the trees that lined the roadway. It was the perfect spot for an ambush since the trees screened the road from view. The carriage bumped and jostled, jarring Jacob's jaw hard enough to chip a tooth. Gunshots rang out, clanging against the steel plating inside the carriage walls and the bullet-proof glass, a feature of Department vehicles. Hans's cloak was also lined with steel plates, as was his hat, for just such emergencies.

"Go!" Mitch shouted. He and Jacob opened the doors on either side of the carriage simultaneously and swung out, one foot on the running boards, to fire back at their pursuers.

"Holy hell! They're keeping up with the carriage!" Jacob's shotgun blast caught one of the men in the shoulder, and the runner dropped back but did not collapse as a normal man would have done.

"They're werewolves," Mitch's voice was tight. He was one of the Army's best sharpshooters, and a trick rider as well. Now, the training that once enabled him to hit targets while standing in the stirrups of a galloping horse paid off, because, despite the jostling of the carriage, his aim was true, and his shot took one of the men through the chest.

Some of the Department's carriages were outfitted with hidden Gatling guns, but not this one. It did, however, have a rifle hole out the back, and Anna was already kneeling on the bench, squeezing off shots. Her aim was not as good as Mitch's in the bouncing vehicle, but the shots struck close enough to force the runners to keep their distance.

They could not fire at every pursuer at once, and four of the men were gaining on the carriage, almost close enough to grab hold. "Inside!" Mitch yelled. "Hans, give us a minute, then activate!" He and Jacob swung back inside and latched the doors. "Clear!" Mitch ordered, and all three of them drew up their feet from the floor and huddled into the center of the seats, careful not to touch the outer walls.

Four thuds made it clear the men were leaping onto the carriage. A loud buzz sounded, then screams. Mitch smiled as he watched the four attackers fall from the carriage, stunned from the electric jolt Hans had sent through the steel plating. Mitch grabbed the slingshot and handed the sack with the Harden bottles to Jacob.

"Keep 'em off balance, Anna," Mitch directed as Anna resumed firing through the rifle hole. "Jacob—anchor me and hand me the bottles. Let's see if we can make them think twice about getting close." Heedless of the danger, Mitch swung out of one of the doors again, with Jacob gripping his belt to keep him from falling out. Mitch aimed the slingshot and fired the fragile blue glass globes at the overhanging tree limbs. They shattered, raining down glass shards and silver dust onto the werewolves.

Even in human form, silver burned werewolves. The men dropped back, yelping in pain. Mitch dodged to the other side and aimed ahead of the carriage, where more of the men were waiting, trying to block the road. They scattered quickly when the canisters broke, trying to evade the sparkling dust that carried on the wind.

"Where the hell are the *Logonje?*" Mitch muttered. Three of the wolves were down from gunshots, though probably not permanently. The silver dust forced the rest to back off, but the shaded section of road stretched on for at least another mile, and the wolf-men had already proven they could keep pace with the carriage horses.

"Maybe the priests are dealing with those," Jacob said, jerking his head instead of pointing since one hand was holding on to Mitch and the other was braced against the carriage frame.

Ghostly shapes drifted from the shadows toward the carriage. As the figures grew closer, Jacob could make out the features of men and women. The horse shied, and Hans fought for control. "Do some-thing!" Hans yelled.

"These bottles have silver dust, not holy water!" Mitch muttered.

More ghosts emerged from the gloom, crowding into the darkened stretch, clearly intent on reaching the carriage. "What do you think they'll do if they reach us?" Anna asked, still keeping her rifle trained on the closest solid attackers.

"I don't want to find out," Jacob replied.

The silver dust had settled, so Mitch prepared to lob more of the glass grenades. "Anna! There's a black box in my rucksack. Grab it and turn it on, then turn the dial all the way to the left. Hurry!"

Anna set the rifle aside and dug through the sack for the Maxwell box. Mitch managed to get off two of the missiles before the revenants closed in. One of the ghosts reached for Mitch, and its spectral hand passed through Mitch's shoulder and chest.

Mitch gasped for breath and Jacob dragged him back into the carriage, slamming the door. "Hans! Electrify!" Jacob shouted, hauling Mitch onto the seat as he and Anna huddled away from the walls. The loud buzz accompanied the jolt of electricity that course through the steel plating, and the ghosts drew back but did not disappear. The black box in Anna's hands whined as it powered up, and she spun the dial to the left.

Outside, the ghosts gave an inhuman shriek and retreated, but something seemed to trap them inside the dark allée of trees. "I thought this was supposed to be able to dispel ghosts," Anna yelled.

"I'll bet you anything Conroy's magic is holding them here," Jacob replied.

Anna looked out the rear window. "One of the *Logonje* isn't back there anymore," Anna reported. She put the Maxwell box on the carriage seat, still turned to ultra-low, and took up her station with the rifle. Anna was shooting well, but Jacob could see she was still favoring her injured arm. He turned his attention to Mitch, who was still shaking uncontrollably and struggling for breath. Jacob loosened Mitch's tie and collar and laid him on the floor of the coach.

"He's cold as ice," Jacob said, and grabbed Mitch's wrist, feeling for a pulse. "Heartbeat's irregular. Damn." He glared at Mitch. "Hang on. We'll get out of this."

A knock from Han's direction brought Jacob and Anna to the windows. One priest rode behind them, closing fast. Another had circled around and managed to get in front, riding toward them. Both of the black-clad men rode standing in their stirrups, holding aloft something that glowed with a golden light. The light flared, forcing both Jacob and Anna to shade their eyes.

The glow from the priests' relics blasted the ghosts, tearing holes in their gray forms wherever the beams struck. An otherworldly howl of pain and fury rang out. The ghosts were burning up, yet something held them in place when even the dead might well flee. The wolf-men were taking no chances and had disappeared into the tree line.

The golden light grew blindingly bright. Jacob felt a new tension in the air, as if the magic of the *Logonje* warred with a similar power for dominance. In the next instance, the ghosts vanished and a breath later, the golden glow winked out.

"Get us out of here!" Jacob shouted to Hans. Their driver slowed the breakneck speed of the horses but kept up a brisk pace. Fortunately, the road was better here, and that made the carriage ride tolerable.

"The priests are behind us again," Anna reported as Jacob returned his attention to Mitch.

"How are you feeling?" Jacob asked as he helped Mitch sit up.

Mitch was pale, and his skin was clammy. His eyes were wide and dilated, and he was far more pale than usual. "I'm not sure," he managed. "What happened?"

"Nothing much. A ghost just stuck its arm through your chest," Jacob replied. He dug out the flask Mitch carried in his rucksack and handed it to his partner, who took a sizeable swig.

"One minute, I was shooting the slingshot," Mitch said, his voice distant. "And the next... there was some other presence in my body, and I wasn't quite there." He shuddered. "It was like something was trying to push my soul out and stop my heart. For an instant, I think it did. I was somewhere else... like a nightmare, but I swear it was real."

Jacob handed him the flask, and Mitch was rattled enough to take another shot. Color was starting to come back to his skin, and his hands were no longer shaking. "What happened?" Mitch asked.

Jacob filled him in.

"Are they gone?" Mitch's voice was starting to regain its usual timbre, but he still looked like death warmed over.

Anna checked the windows. "Yeah. No ghosts, no creepy men. Both priests are behind us again."

Mitch closed his eyes and slumped against the upholstery. "Let's hope that's all the excitement for a while. I don't think I'd be much good in a fight right now."

"I doubt that was an accident," Jacob said, his voice tight with anger. "Conroy's worried we found something out from the *Logonje*, and he's determined to get the hand of glory before we do. There's got to be a way to find it before he does."

"Conroy's already thrown magic, ghosts, and werewolves at us," Anna said, looking out the windows. "What else could he possibly do?"

"Don't ask that question," Jacob replied. "It never ends well."

———

"WHAT MAKES YOU think the *Logonje* haven't already been here?" Jacob said as he, Mitch, and Anna tramped around the ruins of an old tannery.

"Maybe they have been—and missed something," Mitch replied. "If Father Dubicki is right and the Stumpp hand of glory came north with a runaway slave, then the logical place to look first is John Brown's old homestead." He went back to humming the tune of the *Battle Hymn of the Republic*. Even without him singing, Jacob could hear the familiar words.

John Brown's body lies a-moldering in the grave. His soul is marching on.

"Would you stop humming that!" Jacob snapped. "I'll never be able to get it out of my head."

Mitch grinned. "Just setting the scene," he replied, and immediately resumed humming.

Jacob sighed.

"What exactly are we looking for?" Anna asked. They had dressed for hiking since the homestead was long abandoned. All that remained of the tannery was the stone foundation, and even less was left of the family's wooden house. She kicked at the leaves and debris with her boot.

"An idea. A clue. John Brown was active with the Underground Railroad when he lived here," Mitch replied. "Even though it was about thirty years before the Civil War. Hundreds of slaves probably passed through here on the way to Canada."

"Where did he hide them?" Anna asked. "Are we looking for tunnels? Anything in the buildings is gone."

Mitch stood with his hands on his hips and looked around. New Richmond was a small hamlet outside of Meadville, barely noticeable without a map. "We're pretty far north," Mitch said. "I can't imagine that he needed to go to the trouble of digging tunnels to hide them. They probably slept in the barn over the tannery until they moved on."

"Hey, Mitch." Jacob waved him over and pointed to the ground near the tannery ruins. "We're not the only ones to come through here recently," Jacob noted. "It rained the day we got to Meadville. These footprints have to be recent."

The print of a man's shoe was clear in the dried mud. "The grass looks trampled over there," Anna said, pointing toward the ground near the foundation.

Mitch followed Anna, but Jacob remained near the footprint, carefully studying the wall in front of him. He pressed on the stones and looked for openings between them, but saw nothing. Just as he was going to turn away, an irregular shape in the bottom row of stone blocks caught his eye. He bent down for a closer look.

Someone had carved crude shapes into the stone. The marks looked old, and the rock around them was dark with dirt and moss. Jacob squinted to make out the carvings on one of the smaller stones. *An upright fish. The letter "i." A cross.* He made a note of the markings in the small journal he carried in his pocket. The stone did not appear to be cemented into place. Frowning, he jiggled the rock loose and grabbed a stick, poking it into the hole. *Empty.* He sighed and straightened. *Might just be kids leaving a mark. Or maybe a religious message one of the slaves put there. Nothing for us.*

"Find something?" Mitch asked as Jacob walked over to where they stood.

Jacob shook his head. "You?"

"Someone's been busy," Anna observed. Beneath a copse of trees at the edge of the meadow lay several recently dug up graves.

"Full or empty?" Jacob asked, leaning forward for a better look.

"Nothing left but a few bits of wood and bone," Mitch replied. "My bet is that some of the runaways died here, and Brown gave them a decent burial."

"Conroy's pretty determined, if he's gone to grave robbing," Jacob said.

"I think we can be sure he's determined." Anna circled the hastily-excavated old graves. "And right now, I bet he's mad as hell."

"Unless he found what he's looking for," Mitch said.

Jacob shook his head. "I don't think so. This dirt looks like it was turned up a few days ago. Conroy wouldn't have bothered coming after us if he had found the hand of glory. He'd have high-tailed it back to New Pittsburgh to start getting filthy rich."

Anna picked her way over to the far side of the graves, where a broken stone marker lay in the weeds. "Come look at this," she said. Mitch and Jacob joined her. The lettering was faint, but Anna rubbed some dirt into the faded markings to make them reasonable.

"Lambs of God," she read aloud. "Psalm 119:115."

"Thy word is a lamp unto my feet and a light unto my path," Jacob said, then realized the other two agents were staring at him. "What? Didn't either of you go to catechism?"

"The marker probably isn't related," Mitch said, muttering a curse in frustration. "It's a perfectly reasonable verse to put on a tombstone. And I doubt they'd bury something as useful as a light that never went out and that could stop time for a moment."

"Probably not," Anna replied, disappointment clear in her voice. "Then again, John Brown died years before the Civil War. Maybe the hand wasn't even in this area yet. Maybe it came later."

Mitch sighed. "We're wasting time. Conroy's ahead of us. Let's get back to Meadville and see if we can retrace Richard Henderson's tracks. He brought slaves through closer to the war."

To Jacob's relief, the journey to Meadville was uneventful. If the *Logonje* or any of Kronin's coven had followed them to New Richmond and back, they had remained hidden. But as soon as they got to their rooms at the Lafayette Hotel, Jacob knew something was wrong.

"Watch out," he warned Mitch, throwing an arm in front of him as they neared the door to Mitch's room, which was ajar.

Mitch nodded and drew his revolver. Anna was right behind him. Jacob pulled his gun as well, and they advanced on the doorway. Mitch burst through the opening, gun ready. The room was empty, but it was obvious that someone had visited while they were gone.

Their suitcases were overturned, and clothing was strewn around the room. The bed was stripped, and the mattress was off-kilter, indicating someone had searched beneath it. Down feathers covered everything, and the remains of the pillows had been slit and emptied. Drawers lay where they were tossed after their contents had been dumped.

"Someone's giving us more credit than we're due," Jacob said, shaking his head as he looked over the damage. He went through the connecting door and found his room equally trashed. "They're thorough."

Anna disappeared long enough to check her room. "Same here," she said.

Mitch grimaced and began to pick up his things. "Other than the pillows, it doesn't look like anything else was destroyed," he said. "As if I'd put that relic in my pillow!"

"Can you tell if anything's been taken?"

Mitch sighed and shook his head. "Not until I clean up. But we didn't acquire anything for someone to steal. Everything we've got is up here," he said, tapping his forehead.

"Conroy doesn't know that," Jacob countered. "And if he thinks we know something important, it's going to force his hand."

They ordered dinner to their rooms. Anna intercepted the room service cart, preventing the waiter from seeing into their ransacked quarters. It took two hours to clean up the mess, partly because Mitch insisted on running scans with all of Adam Farber's prototype equipment before allowing them to touch anything.

"So after all that, we still don't know any more than we did before," Jacob said, finishing off the dinner on his tray and leaning back in his chair. "According to your scans, it wasn't magic that trashed our rooms, or ghosts. That leaves old-fashioned muscle—guys who are probably werewolves in their spare time."

Anna had begged off early to finish cleaning up and recover from a headache. "Do you think she's all right?" Jacob asked. "She hasn't been herself for the last couple of days."

Mitch rolled his eyes. "It's probably that carriage ride from Cambridge Springs. Felt like I'd been dragged over a washboard ass-first. Had a headache all day yesterday myself."

Jacob finished his tea. "She's still favoring her arm after the fight. I tried to get her to see a doctor, but she says she's fine."

Mitch pulled out a flask and poured some whiskey for each of them. "Then take the lady at her word. She's fine. Since when do we run a case where we don't get banged around and bruised up?"

Jacob collected the dishes on the service cart and rang for a waiter. The young man who appeared had a small bundle under one arm. "This came for you just now," he said, handing the package to Jacob. "Gentleman who left it said I was to deliver it in person, and so I have." Jacob tipped the man, and went back into their rooms, studying the handwritten addresses on the brown paper wrapping.

"Something from Falken?" Mitch asked.

Jacob shook his head. "No. It's addressed to me, and it's from the man I chatted with at the Huidekoper party." He shook the package. "Feels like a book."

Jacob ripped the paper away to reveal and cloth-bound book with a blue linen cover. "*A History of Meadville*," he read aloud. Inside the front cover was a card.

"*I hope you'll find land that suits your project here in Meadville. If you need help with financing, I'll be glad to help you work with the bank,*" he read. "It's signed Ezra Baldwin."

"Mighty neighborly," Mitch said.

Jacob carried the book into his room and laid it on the nightstand. "Actually, I might do a little reading before I turn in," he said. "I didn't sleep well last night."

"We're chasing a dark rogue witch and a pack of werewolves around cemeteries looking for a hand of glory to keep it away from a daemon," Mitch replied. "I can't imagine why that might give anyone bad dreams."

"We struck out today," Jacob said, settling back into his chair. "What next?"

Mitch took another sip of whiskey. "That man in town who was part of the Underground Railroad—"

"Richard Henderson," Jacob supplied.

"We go looking for anything we can find about where he lived, where his barber shop was, where he went to church. Conroy is sure the Stumpp hand is somewhere in town. We've got to find it first."

"Nothing." Mitch sat back on his heels and looked at Jacob and Anna. They were in the basement of the Arch Street home that had once belonged to Richard Henderson. The modest clapboard house had a large cellar, all the better for hiding runaway slaves.

"Maybe it's here, and just not in the basement," Anna suggested.

"We've been through all the rooms, checked the backs of the cupboards, tapped for loose floorboards and false rooms," Jacob said. "Good thing Hans was able to get off a telegram sending the owners to New Pittsburgh in a hurry. I'd hate to have to explain why we're rooting through their cabinets."

"You spent a lot of time looking at the walls," Mitch said. "Find anything?"

Jacob shrugged. "Tally marks, likely made by someone who had to wait for transport. A few religious symbols. Some loose bricks that might have had something behind them long ago, but from the cobwebs, nothing's been taken out recently."

"I'm certain Conroy's already been here," Mitch said, gritting his teeth in frustration. "Some of the dirt's been disturbed recently, and you can see where things have been moved. I wager whoever owns this place hasn't been down here in years."

"Well if Conroy was here, I don't think he got what he came for,"

Jacob replied. "Although I wouldn't be surprised if he's got people watching us."

"So the werewolves are watching us, and the witches are watching them, being watched by the *Logonje*?" Mitch said. "While we do all the work. And they'll all want us to hand over the relic as soon as we find it. Fat chance of that."

"Maybe we'll have more luck at the church. It's just across the street," Anna said with as much hopefulness as she could muster.

Despite how cool it was in the basement, she looked flushed and pale, though she brushed off Jacob's concern. *She's an agent, doing a tough job in a man's world. She doesn't want to look weak. But I still don't think she's well.*

"It's Tuesday," Mitch said. "So maybe we'll be lucky, and the congregation won't be around."

They slipped out of the Henderson house through the back door, careful to lock up and leave no trace. The night was quiet, and few people were about, given the hour. Mitch pointed toward the white Bethel A.M.E. Zion church on the other side of the street, and the three of them made their way through the shadows toward its back door.

A glance at the cornerstone told Jacob that the white wooden church had been built decades before the Civil War. "It's the right age," he murmured, as Mitch picked the lock. The door swung open, and they found themselves in a basement room painted and furnished to be a gathering space. Long tables lined up in rows, and a kitchen had been installed at the far end of the basement. Folding chairs leaned against one side of the room. The walls extended above ground level, and narrow windows let in enough moonlight for them to navigate.

"This doesn't look promising," Jacob said, glancing around. "Hard to believe something like the hand would have been overlooked in a room that gets a lot of use."

"I bet there are other rooms," Mitch said, clearly not ready to give up easily. "Look around. Open doors. Maybe there's a furnace room, or an old sub-basement, or someplace with water pipes."

The three agents split up. Jacob headed through the kitchen and found a door that led to a pump room. He turned on Farber's electric torch and had a look around. The pipes looked original to the building. A musty, moldy smell told Jacob that there was a leak somewhere, and had been for a while. He ducked beneath a wide pipe, looking for any likely hiding places. The stone walls of the building's foundation had not been covered over, and Jacob felt across the rough rock for anything loose or removable. Smudges on the dust covering the nearest pipe let him know someone else had been here recently.

Discouraged, Jacob was about to go back to the main room when he spotted an odd mark on a rock about knee-high in the wall. He bent down, and found the same unusual markings he had seen at the John Brown tannery ruin: a fish standing on its tail and a lower-case letter "i." The stone wobbled. He caught his breath, hoping for a discovery. But when he shone the electric light into the small open space where the stone had been, there was nothing. With a sigh, he replaced the rock and rejoined his companions.

"Nothing," he said. "Although someone's been in the pump room recently. Didn't look like anything's been taken. How about for you?" he asked Mitch and Anna. They both shook their heads.

"I found the furnace room, but no secret hiding places, and no artifact," Mitch said.

"I even checked the floor of the coat closet and had a look in the janitor's room," Anna added. "Nothing."

They locked up and headed back toward their hotel. It was dark outside, but not so late that someone might wonder at them taking a stroll once they were back on Chestnut Street. Hans had been shadowing them, and he emerged from an alley several paces behind them. "Do you think the *Logonje* are around? Or Kronin's people?"

Mitch shrugged. "I doubt Conroy or his wolves are going to make a move on us in the park."

I wish I was as sure about that as you are, Jacob thought. *If Conroy hasn't beaten us to the relic, he's going to be getting pretty antsy. I'm not certain that patience is his strong suit.*

Chestnut Street's shops were closed. Even the marquee at the new Academy Theater was dark. Mist gave a halo to the glowing streetlights as they walked back toward the Delamater Block and their hotel.

"Where else could it be?" Jacob mused. "There might have been other stations on the Underground Railroad, but they were secret—that was the whole point. So who knows how many cellars in town sheltered runaways? The relic could be in any of them."

"We're missing something," Mitch replied. "It's going to turn out to be obvious—something we should have seen earlier, and something Conroy is going to kick himself for missing."

Anna stumbled on an uneven sidewalk slab. Jacob grabbed her arm to steady her. She was warm, even through her sleeve. "Are you certain you won't see a doctor?" he said.

She shook her head. "I'm all right. I think I'll have the kitchen send up a bag of ice for my arm. It's got an ugly bruise. I'm planning to turn in early."

"Why not have them send up some tea and chicken soup along with the ice?" Mitch added, concerned. "Take it easy. We'll let you know if anything comes up."

To Jacob's relief, their rooms were as they left them. "Nice to see Conroy hasn't been back."

"Why bother? We don't know anything." Mitch dropped into a chair, scowling. "I just know we're missing something."

"I'd like to take another look at Henderson's grave, up at Greendale," Jacob said. "I tripped over it the night we chased off the werewolves, but that wasn't really the right time to study it. If we go in daylight, maybe Conroy and his wolves won't be quite so bold."

"I've got plenty of Hardin bottles left," Mitch said. "And Hans is staying busy making more—with some new, nasty surprises—just in case."

Jacob gave him a look. "What happens if the hotel catches on fire and you've 'appropriated' all their fire extinguishers?" The blue bottles that worked so well for dousing the werewolves with silver dust were normally filled with a fire retardant solution, and the bottles' long necks and fragile glass made it ideal for someone to lob the "grenade" into the fire to put out the flames.

"We had a pressing government need," Mitch replied. "They'll just have to be extra careful until we're done."

Jacob had brought the book Ezra Baldwin sent and settled into a chair. Mitch rang for a waiter, who returned with a cheese plate, bread, and a bottle of whiskey.

"You know Falken is going to review our expenses, don't you?" Jacob said as Mitch handed him a glass.

"We're technically off duty," Mitch replied, swallowing a piece of cheese and pouring a glass for himself. "We can always claim it was medicinal."

Jacob looked up sharply. "What did you say?" Mitch repeated himself. "Medicinal," Jacob muttered. "That's what the old man at the Huidekoper party said."

"I have no idea what you're talking about."

"When we were at the Huidekoper party, the same fellow who gave me this book and told me about Richard Henderson took me over to meet an old man, Samuel Bates," Jacob said, "Bates actually met John Brown, and he said that there's a church on the Diamond that was very supportive of the Underground Railroad."

"You've lost me," Mitch said. "Do you want to dig up Henderson's grave, or break into another church to find the relic?"

"Neither, I hope," Jacob said. "I do want to take another look at Henderson's tombstone, but I was planning to let him rest in peace. If we can talk to Bates, he might have an idea of where the relic could be hidden."

Mitch looked skeptical. "It's a long shot."

"Do you have a better idea?"

Mitch sighed. "No. Let's hope it pans out. It's all we've got."

"I'll go let Anna know," Jacob said. He stepped out into the hallway and walked over to Anna's room, knocking at the door. When no reply came, he knocked again.

"Anna? Are you all right?" He called quietly, leaning toward the door.

"I'm fine." Anna's voice came from behind him, and Jacob jumped, startled. "I went down to the front desk to put in my order for tea and ice. Figured it might be faster that way. Did you need something?"

Jacob passed along the plan for the next day. "I'll see you at breakfast," Anna replied, as Jacob stepped away from her door. "Sleep well."

———

GREENDALE CEMETERY IN the bright light of day was a much more welcoming place. "I'd love to see it when the rhododendrons are in bloom," Jacob mused as they walked away from the carriage amid the trees and monuments.

"I wonder if anyone's opened the receiving vault yet?" Mitch said.

"Don't go asking for trouble," Anna warned.

Jacob had placed a call to Samuel Bates right after breakfast and received an invitation to tea that afternoon. In the meantime, Jacob and the others had a few more leads to track down.

Jacob was too intent on retracing his steps to join in on their banter. "I went this way," he muttered to himself, heading off toward the cemetery's older headstones. "And then we zig-zagged—ah ha!" he cried out. "I found it!"

Jacob knelt next to the tombstone as Mitch and Anna joined him. He leaned closer to study the inscription. "I saw the clasped hands with the broken chains that night," Jacob said, wiping away dirt with his handkerchief. "But I didn't notice the candle next to them."

"You think that's important?" Mitch asked.

"Maybe," Jacob said. He pushed the grass away, struggling to read a faint inscription at the bottom of the marker. "Exodus 13:21," he said.

"What? You don't remember it off-hand from catechism?" Mitch ribbed.

Jacob rolled his eyes. "I'll have to look that one up."

"It doesn't look as if the grave's been dug up by anyone," Anna observed. "That's probably a good thing."

"Let's leave it that way—at least for now," Jacob said, straightening. He turned to Mitch. "Do you have that amulet Renate Thalberg gave you? The one that can sense magic?"

Mitch nodded and drew out a pendant on a chain from his vest pocket. He stood over the grave, then walked slowly around the stone and the length of the plot. "Nothing," he said, as the pendant remained dull.

"Do you think we could talk our way into that church down on the Diamond?" Jacob asked. "I have a theory I want to test."

Mitch grinned. "You know me. Silver-tongued devil."

"And modest, too." Anna grinned.

"Let's go," Jacob said. So far, they had seen no sign of Conroy or his wolves. If the werewolves had followed them to the cemetery, the wolf-men were well hidden. *Then again, I don't see the* Logonje *or any of Kronin's people. So maybe they all decided to sleep in and let us do the legwork.*

Less than half an hour later, they were inside the Independent Congregationalist Church without the need of a lock pick, thanks to Mitch.

"Church Facilities Inspector is a new one, even for you," Jacob muttered under his breath as they made their way down to the basement.

"It worked," Mitch said with a shrug. "That fine lady in the front office wants to make sure they don't get any demerits."

"What are you looking for?" Anna asked.

"There's a link here, between the relic and Henderson and all of these places," Jacob said. He pulled out his journal and showed them the drawings he had made. "I thought this was an upright fish with a lower-case letter 'i,'" he told them. "Then I saw the carving again on Henderson's tombstone. I think it's a symbol—praying hands and a candle. A hand and a candle," he repeated. "It's been in four places so far—at the tannery, in Henderson's basement, in the cellar of the AME Zion church, and I'm betting it will be here, too."

"But where's the relic?" Anna pressed.

"I think at one time or another, it was hidden in those four spots—and marked with the symbol," Jacob said. "It's not the kind of thing you carry around with you. They might have hidden it in between journeys. And over time, it got moved from one place to another. Find the symbol, and we find another place where it might still be."

294

"Why here?" Mitch asked.

"Huidekoper's relatives gave money to build this church, way back when," Jacob said. "I found that out in the book Ezra Baldwin gave me. "Bates told me the church was a big supporter of the Underground Railroad. And get this—John Brown used to let the Congregationalists hold their meetings in the upstairs of his tannery, before they had a church."

"Let's get to work," Mitch replied.

They split up again, and this time it was Anna who found the symbol, on the raw stone wall behind the furnace. "Empty—again," Jacob sighed as they searched the small cavity behind the rock and replaced it.

"Do you think Conroy beat us to it?" Anna asked.

Mitch shook his head. "It didn't look like anyone had been in there in a long while. I think this time, we found a link he didn't know about. Not that it did us much good."

"Maybe we'll find out more from Samuel Bates," Anna said.

"Let's hope so," Jacob said. "And I've already warned Hans that he'll need to guard the old man once we leave. I don't want to lead Conroy to him."

"Isn't Hans supposed to be guarding us?" Mitch asked, raising an eyebrow.

"We've got the *Logonje* and the witches, remember?"

"Ah yes, the invisible bodyguards," Mitch replied. "I feel better now."

———

SAMUEL BATES MET them at the door. "Come in, come in. I don't get as many visitors as I used to. There's tea in the kitchen and shortbread. Let's go there—it's warmer."

Once they all had hot tea and he had put out a plate of cookies, Bates finally settled into a chair at the table. "So you want to know more about the Civil War?"

Jacob leaned forward. "We're particularly interested in Richard Henderson."

"Ah yes. He was a quite important in the Underground Railroad. Had a barber shop here in town. Active in his church."

"Were there ever any… tall tales… told about Henderson or his trips with the runaway slaves?" Jacob asked, trying to figure out how to broach the subject.

Bates chuckled. "You mean the Hand of Moses."

Jacob and the others leaned closer. "What's that?" Mitch asked.

Bates grinned. "As tall tales go, it's a hum-dinger. You ever go to Sunday School, and hear the story about Moses leading the Children of Israel out of the wilderness? Says in the book of Exodus that God led them with a pillar of cloud by day, and a pillar of fire by night, so they wouldn't stray from the path."

"And Henderson had a pillar of fire?" Anna asked.

Bates shook his head. "Nope. Slavers would have seen that. They say he had something better, the hand of Moses himself, with the fire of God that never burned out. The slaves he brought north said it was a miracle, like that lamp in the temple in the Old Testament that never ran out of oil." He took a bite of shortbread and washed it down with tea.

"Those slaves, they knew their Bible. And Moses, leading his people out of Egypt slavery, he was a hero to them. Sing about him in all their songs."

"Where did they get the Hand of Moses?" Jacob asked.

Bates set his cup down. "Well now, no one knows for sure. Some say John Brown had it first. If he did, he shouldn't have given it up when he went down to Harper's Ferry. Might have done him some good. I didn't know Richard Henderson well, but I met him a time or two when I was working on the books, talked to him about the old days. He clammed up when I asked about the Hand, and I don't blame him. Not everyone would think something like that was proper Christian."

"Do you believe it was real?" Anna asked.

Bates nodded. "Yes, I do. I don't know how such a thing could be, or how Moses's hand got all the way over here from the Holy Land, but there was a cook who worked for my parents, a free Colored woman. She had escaped with some of Henderson's people before the War. When I was writing those books, I found her—she was old then—and I got her talking. She told me that she saw the Hand of Moses burning bright the night they all came up from Virginia."

He paused, remembering. "It stuck in my mind because it was so strange. She said that the hand was old and shriveled, and the candle had melted into the fingers, but it burned with a true light that never went out." He smiled. "I never really wanted to find out the truth. It didn't matter, and the story was too good to spoil."

"What happened to the Hand, when Henderson died?" Anna asked.

Bates took another sip of tea. "No one knows," he said, leaning back in his chair. "Of course, Richard Henderson passed away fifteen years after the War was over. No more Underground Railroad. So he hadn't needed the Hand in a long time. I imagine that it's wherever they hid it the last time they used it before the War ended."

They chatted for a while after that, and Jacob was impressed with Bates' knowledge, both about Meadville's history and about the Civil War. He walked them to the door when they left. "I'm glad Ezra introduced us. Thank you for stopping by."

Hans discreetly remained where he could watch the house as Jacob and the others left. "Well, we've got more evidence that the Stumpp hand is real," Mitch said. "And Henderson thought it was from Moses. Huh."

"Let's just hope we didn't lead Conroy right to Bates," Jacob said. "We might know more about the hand, but we don't know where to find it."

They took their supper in the hotel dining room. "I don't know where else to look," Mitch confessed. "From what Bates told us, there were Underground Railroad safe houses all over this area, and half of them have been forgotten by now. We could look forever."

"Conroy doesn't know either, or he'd have it and be gone by now," Jacob said. But whatever gave him the clue that sent him here; it's solid enough for him to stick with it. We've just missed something—and the first one who figures it out will get the hand."

After dinner, they headed back to their rooms. Anna was anxious to put ice on her arm, while Jacob wanted to examine the book Ezra had given him. Mitch laid out several hands of solitaire, a habit Jacob knew meant his partner was frustrated and trying to take his mind off the case.

"... *as a free man and business owner, Richard Henderson deter-mined to avail himself of the education he had been denied as a young man, and to obtain the best education possible for his children. He engaged the services of Isaac Brawley, a well-regarded teacher at the Meadville Academy, the same tutor employed by George Delamater for his son, Thomas...*" Jacob read silently to himself then bolted to his feet. "That's it!"

Mitch laid down two cards and looked up. "What?"

Jacob read Mitch the passage from the book and glowered as Mitch looked at him, nonplussed. "So?" Mitch said.

"Don't you get it? Where are we?" Jacob prompted.

"The Lafayette Hotel."

Jacob shook his head. "That's not what I mean. What's this building called?"

Mitch looked back to his cards. "How should I know?"

"It's the Delamater Block," Jacob replied. "Named for George Delamater. Richard Henderson and George Delamater hired the same tutor for their sons. Bates mentioned Isaac Brawley—remember? Spoke well of him. Want to bet he had hard-core Union sympathies as well? Lots of White folks were part of the Underground Railroad and the abolition movement. It couldn't have operated without them. Maybe Brawley was one of them—we know Delamater thought well of John Brown's politics, even if he thought the actions were rash."

"You think the hand is here? In the hotel?"

Jacob nodded. A victorious grin touched his lips. "I do. If not the hotel, the larger building. Henderson might never have set foot here. Brawley could have hidden it for him. What better place than in the city's showplace business center?"

Mitch turned away from his cards and gave a thoughtful nod. "You could be onto something. Let's get Anna and go have a look around."

Anna begged off with a bad headache, leaving Jacob and Mitch on their own. They slipped down a back staircase, happy the most of the staff were occupied in the dining room or off duty for the evening.

Once they descended below the lobby, the stairwell was clearly designed for workers, not guests. The walls were whitewashed stone, the railing was a pipe fixed into concrete, and the lower levels stretched into mechanical rooms that ran the length of the building, wide open except for the pillars that supported the floors above.

"It could be anywhere down here," Mitch said. The huge boilers that ran the steam heat for the hotel and businesses above looked like a maze of pipes.

"If Isaac hid it, he probably didn't do a lot of crawling around," Jacob ventured. "He wouldn't want to get dirty, and he wouldn't want to get caught down here. I'll go left; you go right. We know the code— look for the markings I showed you. I'll bet money that this time, we'll find a secret compartment and it won't be empty."

Several rows of naked Edison lights dimly illuminated the mechanical room. They lit the equipment enough for the workers to see the gauges but left the edge of the room in shadow. Jacob and Mitch walked to the back of the room and worked their way forward.

"Find anything?" Mitch called out.

"Not yet," Jacob returned. A large water pipe cut across his path. The name of the manufacturer, "Jordan," was molded into the pipe.

"I wonder," Jacob muttered to himself as he carefully stepped over the pipe. *Moses. Bible verses. Henderson was very religious—and I bet Brawley was, too. So where would you find the light to get to the Promised Land? Across the "river Jordan."*

Sure enough, marked on a wobbly stone waist-high in the wall was the now-familiar mark of the praying hands and candle. Jacob maneuvered the rock out of the wall and set it carefully aside, using the electric torch to peer into the darkness.

Inside the hole was a canvas bag. "I've got something!" Jacob bent over and carefully drew out the parcel. The bag was stained and dirty, beginning to rot in the moist atmosphere of the boiler room, but inside was a stiff object that had the contours of a mummified human hand.

Mitch had joined him and was looking over his shoulder excitedly. "That's it?"

Jacob nodded. "Yeah, I think so. Let's wait to pull it out of the bag until we're up in the room. I'm in no hurry to touch it."

They were nearly to the exit when four figures emerged to block their way, and four others slipped from behind the equipment to box them in.

"Hold it right there. Drop your weapons." Anna's voice was as cold as the steel of the gun she leveled at their heads. Absalom Conroy stood beside her, with two men Jacob recognized from the encounter on the road to Cambridge Springs.

"What the hell, Anna?" Mitch demanded. "What are you doing with Conroy?"

"Drop your guns, or you won't live to find out," Anna repeated.

"I'd do as the lady says, or you'll regret it," Conroy said, amused. "If you choose to fight, realize that once my men change, they can't always control the wolf-mind easily. No telling how many of the guests upstairs might die."

With a muttered curse, Mitch laid his gun on the floor. Jacob did the same a moment later. "Take their watches," Anna said. "They're transmitters."

"Put your watches and the bag on the ground—carefully—and take two steps back," Conroy ordered.

Jacob leveled a murderous glare at Anna but did as he was told. He stepped backward and into the grip of one of the wolf-men who pinned his upper arms while a second man cuffed Jacob's hands behind him. Two more of Conroy's soldiers were doing the same to Mitch, whose expression silently promised them a slow and painful death.

"Why?" Mitch snapped, staring at Anna. "You're betraying your government, the Department—and your partners. What did Conroy offer you?"

"Safety," Anna replied, though her gun never wavered, still pointed right at Mitch's head. "Once I shift, the Department won't want me anymore—and the two of you would likely be the ones they'd send to hunt me down."

"Your arm." Jacob looked up. "You didn't get bruised in the fight at the cemetery—you got scratched. That's why you wouldn't see a doctor."

Anna shook her head. "No, I got scratched in the fight at the cabin, the day Keller got hurt. I couldn't tell you. I wasn't sure at first that it would matter, but then I knew things weren't right. Once I knew for sure, I made a deal with Conroy. I've been working with him since we came north."

"That night you said you were coming back from ordering tea and ice—you'd connected with Conroy," Jacob accused.

"I had no choice," Anna said. "Not after I saw what happened to Keller. Do you know what the Department would do to me if they didn't kill me outright? Put me in a lab somewhere and 'study' me. I'm not going to let them do that."

"We'll talk to Falken on your behalf," Mitch said. "I've never seen him do wrong by a wounded agent. Even Keller—he's being cared for in protective custody."

"I'm not wounded!" Anna's voice rose. "I'm changed—permanently. And 'protective' custody is still a cage. No thanks."

"Not just changed—enhanced," Conroy added. "The Department isn't completely sure how to handle its female agents. It won't know what to do with one who can fight, hunt, and track better than any man. I, on the other hand, know how to recognize and appreciate talent."

Eight guns were trained on them, aimed to kill. Between the weapons and the wolves' natural strength and agility, Jacob knew he and Mitch stood no chance in a fight at close quarters, even with their revolvers. Two of Conroy's men gathered up their guns and patted them down for hidden weapons, then picked up the bag with the hand and carried it to Conroy.

"Are you going to stand by and watch him shoot us, Anna?" Mitch asked. "Or will he make you pull the trigger yourself to prove your loyalty?" There was no mistaking the bitterness in his tone.

"Happily, neither," Conroy replied as his wolves forced Jacob and

Mitch toward the pipes and chained them to the equipment. "I've planted charges down here that will take out the whole block. We'll do the civilized thing and pull the fire alarm in advance so that everyone can get out." He glanced toward their chains. "Well, almost everyone."

"There really was no other choice," Anna said as Conroy's men filed to the door. "I'm sorry."

"Save it for the court martial," Mitch muttered.

Conroy was the last one out, turning the lights off as they went. Jacob and Mitch were alone in the dark, listening to the hiss and gurgle of the boilers.

"If those charges go off and blow the boilers, it's going to put a crater in the middle of Meadville," Jacob said. "And it doesn't help that you stole most of the fire extinguishers."

"I've got a plan," Mitch said. "Can you reach my belt? I need you to unbuckle it."

Jacob raised an eyebrow. "Excuse me?"

Mitch rolled his eyes. "There's a lock pick in the buckle."

It took some maneuvering, but Jacob managed to work the buckle and get it into Mitch's hands without dropping it. Mitch pulled the pick from the buckle and quickly had them out of the cuffs. "Conroy knew we couldn't just go after him if we did get free. We've got to stop that bomb."

"And Hans is guarding Bates. He's got the Harden bottles and the carriage. We've got no way to reach him without the watches, or Agent Kennedy and the airship."

Mitch had the lights back on and was examining the detonator. "How fast do you think you could get up to our room and come back with the gear bag? If it's more than eight minutes, don't bother: the upstairs will come to us."

The fire alarm blared. "The stairs will be packed," Jacob said. He saw a service elevator. "I'll give it a shot."

Jacob sprinted toward the manual elevator, while Mitch hunkered next to the detonator. It seemed to take forever to get upstairs, fight the tide of panicked guests in the corridor, grab their bag from the room and return. Jacob dodged into the service elevator in the now-deserted hallway and let the gears slip, taking him down in a dangerously fast descent that he slowed only at the last minute.

"Throw me the EMF reader," Mitch said. "Conroy rigged three bombs down here. I'm betting our lives that Adam Farber is better at gadgets than Conroy. With luck, the EMF box will disrupt the impulses and stop the detonations. This better work—we don't have time for a second try." He turned on the experimental prototype, and the box whined as it powered up. Mitch cranked it to its highest setting and placed it near the three detonators.

"Take cover!" he yelled, as he grabbed the bag of equipment and dodged out of the way, dragging Jacob with him behind one of the huge stone pillars.

The EMF reader reached a crescendo as the detonator contraption clicked down to the final count. Jacob and Mitch crouched, covering their heads. *Really not the way I want to die...*

The detonators reached "zero." Nothing happened. After a few seconds, Jacob opened his eyes to reassure himself that he was still alive.

"Was that it?" Jacob asked, barely breathing.

"Unless there are other units I didn't find," Mitch replied.

A sparkling cloud appeared from nowhere, cutting them off from the back of the basement. *Click. Screech. Pfft.*

"I think you might have missed something," Jacob said, as two of the boilers blew. Bricks pelted the iridescent curtain, and hot steam billowed, but the cloud contained it, absorbing the force of the explosion.

Jacob flung open the door into the alley, and they tumbled out. Kronin stood in the shadows, one hand outstretched toward the hotel.

"You did something... with magic, to keep us from getting blown up," Jacob said.

Kronin nodded. "Your efforts, while ingenious, would not have sufficed for all of the bombs Conroy planted."

"Glad to be in one piece. Thanks for that," Jacob replied. "But we've got to stop Conroy from getting the Hand of Glory to New Pittsburgh."

"He's got a private train," Kronin replied, sounding as though it was a strain to deflect his concentration enough to speak. My people followed him, but we can't fight him until he's away from the city. Too many innocent targets."

Mitch swore. "We need horses."

"There are two waiting and saddled in the stable at the end of the block," Kronin said with difficulty. "I came to warn you, and arrived too late."

"Thanks," Mitch said and clapped Jacob on the shoulder. "Come on!"

They found the horses as Kronin said. Mitch retrieved their rifles from the bag to replace the revolvers Conroy had taken, and they swung up to the saddles, riding hard for the station. When they arrived, they found the stationmaster dead in his office. The private train was gone.

"Let's hope the *Logonje* or Kronin's people have something up their sleeves," Mitch said as they rode along the tracks. "We can't chase him on horseback all the way to New Pittsburgh."

"There it is!" Jacob said, pointing. They caught sight of the back of a passenger car being pulled by an engine just beyond the edge of the city, as the homes and businesses gave way to farm fields. The train tracks passed under two upcoming trestles about a mile apart as the track ran in a ravine with sharply sloping banks. As the engine cleared the first trestle, explosions sounded on the rails ahead, and a wall of fire rose up across the tracks.

The train's brakes squealed, and sparks flew from the wheels as the engine slowed, trying to avoid running into the wall of flames. The explosions continued, as more plumes of fire rose from the night sky.

"Those look like the bombs I made with the Harden bottles!" Mitch said as they rode for the train, which had all but come to a stop. "I filled some of them with coil oil and wicks to light and throw. But how…"

The train was in between the trestles, barely moving. As Mitch and Jacob rode beneath the first trestle, glowing eyes appeared in the vestibule of the rear car. Four large wolves leaped from the slowly rolling train car and ran toward them.

Mitch and Jacob opened fire. The wolves had the advantage in the darkness since the flames up ahead were the only light. Their shots missed, and the wolves closed in.

Something whizzed past Jacob's ear from overhead, and an instant later he heard glass shatter a few feet in front of him. More projectiles rained down, thrown from the trestle behind them, exploding in a hail of glass shards and liquid between them and the wolves.

The wolves yipped and growled in pain where the water splashed them, and drew back, unwilling to step into the wet gravel and touch the mixture.

"You've got a clear shot!" Hans's voice rang out from the trestle just behind them.

"Thanks!" Jacob yelled. He shouldered his rifle and fired at the wolves. "What did you put in those bottles?" he asked Mitch.

"Colloidal silver and holy water," Mitch said, as he took aim and fired again, wounding one of the wolves in the shoulder.

Two of the wolves sprang into the air, leaping over the puddles of water. Mitch squeezed the trigger and dropped one of the wolves with a shot to the chest. Jacob's shot felled the other wolf with a bullet between the eyes. Hans pelted more bottles at the remaining wolves, spraying them with the noxious mixture that forced them back.

"If Hans is throwing those bottles, who's dropping the firebombs?" Jacob wondered aloud as two more wolves jumped from the train.

"No idea. But we aren't going to be able to hold the engine back forever," Mitch muttered, eyeing the wolves as they prowled just out of range.

"You have proven most inconvenient." Absalom Conroy stood on the vestibule platform. "But we have an appointment to keep." He spread his hands in a sharp gesture, and an invisible force swept Mitch and Jacob from their saddles, knocking them to the ground and tearing their rifles from their grip. The horses reared in panic and ran.

Conroy's magic kept Mitch and Jacob pinned as he turned, and another gesture extinguished the fire. "I should have made certain you were dead at the hotel. I won't make that mistake again." The pressure doubled from the unseen force, making it hard to breathe, pressing them against the ground.

Golden light flared from the banks of the ravine, focused on Conroy from four points. Conroy shouted in rage as he struck back with blue streaks of lightning that crackled from his hands, but although the glow wavered, it kept him in its light.

The Logonje*? Or Kronin's coven—or both?*

Abruptly, the pressure lifted, and Jacob could breathe again. His relief was short-lived, as a wolf's growl close at hand sent a chill down his spine. Three wolves had leaped over the silver-water barrier, and they were only feet away. Mitch rolled toward where his rifle lay, but a shot from the back of the train car kicked up gravel between his hand and the weapon.

Anna had a rifle of her own trained on them. "Don't fight. They'll make your end quick."

"To hell with that," Mitch snapped. One wolf prowled toward him, head down and hackles raised, while another headed for Jacob. The third wolf moved between them, ready to back the others up. *Wolves with human intelligence. This isn't going to go well.*

Shots rang out from overhead. Hans kept Anna pinned down, forcing her back into the train car. He fired at Conroy, but the bullets froze in mid-air and dropped to the ground before they reached him.

"Leave him to the witches!" Mitch shouted. "Keep Anna away from that door!"

Mitch and Jacob exchanged a glance. Mitch dove toward his rifle and Jacob lunged to one side, narrowly avoiding the wolf that sprang toward him. Mitch's shot took the wolf in the belly, and it dropped to the ground. Jacob grabbed his weapon, but his shot missed.

The ravine had become a war zone. More of the firebombs fell in front of the train, raising a new sheet of flames to deter the engineer from moving forward. Blue lightning and golden arcs of light pierced the gloom as Conroy fought black-clad figures Jacob figured for the *Logonje*. Yet Kronin's coven was also surely present, as the train seemed to strain against invisible bonds that kept it from trying to rush through the wall of fire, and as Jacob took another shot at the wolves that harried them, it appeared the were-creatures had difficulty holding their form.

"I think Kronin's people are messing with the shifters," Mitch yelled. "Keep firing!"

One of the wolves was in mid-leap when its body convulsed and dropped to the ground. Sinew stretched and bones adjusting unsettlingly as the large wolf became a naked man. Jacob could see where the liquid silver raised burns on the creature's skin. A second wolf-man fell, landing on his hands and knees, human once more.

"Surrender or die." Mitch brought his rifle against the temple of the closest werewolf. The man snarled and lunged for the barrel of the gun. Mitch's bullet took him through the chest, throwing his body backward so that he lay face-up on the gravel.

"Your turn," Jacob growled, bringing his gun just behind the other man's ear. The werewolf twisted and sprang at him. Jacob shot, point-blank, tearing a hole in the creature's rib cage.

"We've got to get inside the train," Mitch said. "We need the Hand —and we've got to deal with Anna."

Conroy still battled the *Logonje* and witches, but the strain was beginning to show. The protective scrim of magic he held around himself as a shield flickered wildly, and it was obvious from the new burns and gashes on Conroy's body that the shield had already failed more than once. The train was no longer moving, but Jacob was certain there were more of Conroy's men—and wolves—aboard, as well as Anna.

First, they had to get past the magical battle to even reach the train. "This way," Mitch hissed, leading them out around to one side, staying to the shadows to avoid being seen from anyone inside the passenger car, and frequently ducking as Conroy traded blasts with the witches and priests. Jacob was certain a few of the torrents singed his hair, though Mitch continued on without even flinching as the power surged overhead, terrifyingly close.

Jacob and Mitch separated when they neared the front of the train. Jacob headed for the engine, only to find Samuel Bates holding the engineer hostage with a shotgun in one hand and a Harden bottle in the other.

"We were just having a little chat," Bates said with a smile. "Go ahead and tie him up. I still have a few of the bombs handy, if you need them."

Jacob hurried to bind the engineer and raised an eyebrow at Bates. "That was you on the bridge, with the firebombs?"

Bates's laugh was a wheezy cackle. "I haven't had this much fun in a long while."

Jacob took the Harden bottles and headed for the passenger car. Conroy's battle with the witches continued at the other end of the train, with Anna and her comrades moving from window to window, shooting whenever they had a target. Mitch was outside, returning their fire, dodging and running.

Jacob lit the fuse on one of the Harden bottle-bombs, shot out the window in the vestibule door and threw the bomb inside, then dove to the ground and covered his head with his arms. The bottle exploded, and the opulent velvet upholstery and draperies inside the car caught fire like dry tinder.

That left Anna and the others the choice of trying to crowd past Conroy and his magical battle at the end of the car or crawling out the ruined windows.

"You're under arrest!" Mitch barked. "Climb out the window and surrender."

Jacob saw a shadow at the nearest window and raised his rifle. Just as he was about to pull the trigger, he heard another blast and staggered as a bullet tore into his left arm.

A barrage of shots forced Jacob and Mitch to take cover behind boxes of crates on the siding. The gunfire kept them pinned down as the two men and Anna climbed through the window. Anna had a revolver and the bag with the hand of glory.

Jacob glanced at his arm. His sleeve was bloody, and it hurt like hell, but he could still flex his hand. He popped up and took a shot at the nearest of Conroy's men, striking him in the right shoulder.

Mitch's shot got the other man in the head. Anna fired off a shot and ran for the rear of the train to join forces with Conroy. *If he uses the Hand against us, that could turn the tide.*

Mitch stepped out of hiding, blocking Anna's path. Jacob heard a shot. Anna was cradling her bloody right arm, and she had dropped the revolver, though the bag was still clutched in her left hand. Mitch's rifle was pointed at her chest. In all their years together, Jacob had never seen that expression on Mitch's face, and he hoped he never did again.

"Get the cuffs on her," Mitch said tonelessly. "We'll see to a doctor later."

"I will not go back!" Anna howled and sprang at Mitch with the same ferocity as the wolves that had attacked them. A gun fired. Anna stiffened, and then dropped to the ground as blood spread across her chest and back. She was already dead when she fell. Mitch looked from her body to his rifle in horror.

"That's not possible," he stammered. "I didn't fire."

"You didn't," Jacob said. "I did." *So you wouldn't have to. Because I wasn't sure you would.*

The train car was engulfed in flames. Conroy fought on, though even he had to know he could not win.

"Give up!" Mitch shouted, holding the bag aloft. "We have the hand of glory. You're finished."

A dark shape ghosted across the moon overhead, sending a shadow across the fight. As the airship came into view, a hail of bullets laid down straight, deadly lines in the dirt, cutting down the last several werewolves as they fled.

"This is the United States Government," Agent Della Kennedy's voice echoed from the airship's bullhorn. "Surrender or die."

Conroy's protective magic strained against the onslaught levied against him. One side of his face was badly burned, and his clothing was charred and bloodied. His right hand was blackened and shriveled, as if the magic he channeled through it was more than flesh and blood could bear. But he heard Mitch's shout, and pivoted, loosing a blast of blue-white fire right at Mitch.

Shots fired. Mitch yelped and dove aside. Conroy stood for a few seconds as if the bullet through his forehead and the shot through his chest had not quite registered. Then he wobbled and fell backward, into the fiery train car. The flames surged, blowing out the remaining windows and sending pieces of the car flying as it exploded, Conroy's last assault.

Jacob looked up to see a section of the iron train car flying straight at him. *This is it.* He braced himself to die. A foot above his head, the air rippled and shimmered, and an unseen hand tossed the heavy section of metal aside as if it were paper. Father Dubicki stepped out from the shadows.

"You're welcome," the priest said with a tired smile, taking in Jacob's astonishment.

Mitch got to his feet, one arm blistered and red from Conroy's lightning. Dubicki gave him the once-over. "You're lucky. He could have incinerated you on the spot if he'd have caught you square with that bolt."

"Thanks," Mitch said. "I'll sleep so much better knowing that." He still clutched the bag in one hand.

Two priests and several of Kronin's men kept guard on the burning passenger car. Samuel Bates came walking toward them, grinning ear to ear. "Don't forget to collect that fellow from the engine. He's a little worried, what with the fire and all."

Hans rushed up, still carrying his rifle and the last of a bag of Harden bottles full of silver and holy water. Mitch cut him off before he could ask. "Anna didn't make it," Mitch said in a tight voice. "And there's a prisoner in the engine room. We need to bring the prisoner and Anna's body back to headquarters."

"Take this," Hans said, handing Mitch his transmitter watch. "Agent Kennedy is waiting to hear from you. I called in some backup, but it took her a while to get here." With that, Hans walked briskly toward the front of the train.

Kronin himself had joined the fight at some point, and now he stood next to Dubicki. "You managed to save the Stumpp hand. Very good. My coven will guard it carefully to avoid a repeat of this kind of problem."

Father Dubicki fixed Kronin with a glare. "Such an artifact is best protected by the Church."

"Because that worked so well the last time?"

Dubicki's eyes narrowed. "Conroy was one of yours, wasn't he?"

"A witch, yes. But not of my coven."

Mitch watched them argue. "Our orders were to stop Conroy from getting his hands on whatever-it-was he was after. They said nothing about who should get the hand after the fight was done."

"And you think the government would be the best guardian of such a powerful, seductive item?" Dubicki questioned.

"I think it's caused enough problems," Mitch replied. "Which is why there's only one alternative." He lobbed the hand of glory into the flames. "Della!" he yelled into the transmitter watch, "shoot the train car!"

Dubicki's eyes went wide. Kronin croaked out a denial seconds too late. The inferno flared as the hand caught fire, blazing with new intensity. The five mummified fingers burned white-hot, and for an instant, Jacob swore that time stood still between one breath and the next. Then almost at the same second, Dubicki and Kronin sent a blast of their own power into the flames, to make certain of the cremation of both Conroy and the hand of glory. Overhead in the airship, Agent Della Kennedy loosed a Ketchum grenade into the blaze. Almost as an afterthought, Mitch lobbed the last Harden bottle at the ruined coach and turned his back as the explosion roared.

"Falken is going to have our heads for this when he finds out," Jacob muttered.

Mitch's jaw was set. "Let him try. We did what we were sent to do. We won. But this time, winning came at too high a price." He toggled the transmitter key. "Ready for pickup," he told Kennedy. "Time to go home."

BONUS

GHOST WOLF

"GO BACK WHERE YOU CAME FROM." Just for emphasis, the speaker slapped a length of lead pipe against his palm. "We don't need your type. Damn Pollacks and Ruskies."

Six men blocked the sidewalk in a shadowed section between streetlights. They were young and out for trouble. The four men whose path they blocked were older and weary from working swing shift in the foundries and ironworks along Carson Street. Their faces were streaked with soot, hair lank with sweat. Just another block and the steep tracks of the Monongahela Incline would take them up Coal Hill to their homes.

"Leave us," one of the workers said. "We have no quarrel with you. Be gone."

"Funny—that's what we'd like you to do. Be gone," the tough replied, and his friends laughed mirthlessly. They were strong, young men, not much over twenty years old, with muscles built from unloading shipping crates or working in the steel mills. The leader wore his blond hair shaved close to his head, and a scar through one eyebrow and a notch in an ear gave him the look of a junkyard dog.

"Go back the hell to where you came from." He advanced, holding his pipe like a weapon. The gang of men behind him produced chains, cut-down two-by-fours, and brass knuckles. "Or we'll send you there in a box."

The section of the city was deserted at this hour. To one side stretched the rail yards, empty and quiet. On the other side was the steep slope of Coal Hill, overgrown with gangly trees and scrub brush, littered with trash. The streetlight overhead was broken, creating a dark area between lights.

"We don't want trouble." The speaker was the oldest of the workers, and in his youth, he had been as strong and brash as the bald young man with the pipe. Twenty-five years of hard, dangerous work and uncertain fortune had left their mark. His dark hair was graying and thin, and his features were as much a testimony to his heritage as his accent. The men behind him eyed the toughs warily, holding the lidded metal buckets they used to carry their lunches like weapons. The unmistakable click of switchblades opening upped the ante.

"Then you should have stayed where you belong." With that, the toughs surged forward. The workers swung their heavy buckets to keep the attackers at bay, and from the pockets of their jackets produced hammers, knives, and wrenches to defend themselves.

A wolf's howl echoed down the dark, empty street. There was a flash of gray, a *snick* like sharp teeth snapping together, and a blur of motion. One of the toughs went flying into the underbrush, hitting hard against the hillside. A gray figure interposed itself between the workers and the toughs. The figure's face was hidden beneath a wolf's head, and a cape made from a wolf's pelt fell partway down the figure's back. The wolf's eyes glowed red.

"What the hell?" the gang leader muttered and swung hard at the gray figure's head with his length of pipe. The fighter dodged away with inhuman speed and grace, landing a roundhouse punch with one furred fist that broke the gang leader's jaw with an audible *crack* and sent him sprawling.

Two of the ruffians dove for the gray fighter, pummeling him with their fists and brass knuckles, to no effect. He stayed a step ahead of them, turning on his attackers with a snarl. Sharp claws extended from the gray fighter's fists, and one swipe laid open one of the attackers from shoulder to hip, slicing easily through his jacket and shirt and raising four bloody slashes. One of the toughs tried to flank the gray creature, but it slapped him away with a powerful backhand that slashed across the man's face and sent him tumbling.

Emboldened by this unexpected champion, the older men whooped and dove into the fight, taking down three of the gang members with craftiness and experience more than brute force.

The last of the ruffians ran away, toward the Mon Incline. Five of the troublemakers were down for the count in bloody heaps, while the four older workers generally appeared no worse for the wear than a few split lips and blackened eyes. The gray creature howled and set off after the fleeing tough like a streak, catching him easily and hoisting him with one clawed hand thrust through the collar of his jacket.

"Go to hell!" the tough shouted, kicking and swinging at the gray man-beast, who held him at arm's distance before hoisting the ruffian up and looping his jacket collar through one of the uprights of a tall iron fence.

The gray creature turned back to where the workers stared, still holding their makeshift weapons as if afraid their savior might turn on them. Sirens were already sounding, getting closer.

"Get out of here," the creature rasped. Then it turned and bounded away, running upright like a man but impossibly fast. The creature leapt up to the steel braces that supported the Mon Incline as one of the funicular cars began to clatter up the mountain, and in another jump landed easily on the top of the car. It paused just long enough for them to see its silhouette in the moonlight, part man and part beast, and to give another feral howl before it vanished into the shadows.

———

IN A QUIET neighborhood atop Coal Hill, a figure slipped quietly through the shadows, finding its way to a ramshackle spring house that stood in disrepair in the stretch of woods behind a two-story stone home. The gray man glanced furtively from side to side and then, assured he had not been seen, let himself into the spring house and closed the door behind him. He knew his way in the dark from here. Off to the right, he heard the trickle of water in the cistern. To the left, halfway down the wall, a wooden panel covered with stones slipped out of place, and he crawled backward into a tunnel barely wider than his shoulders. He fit the panel back where it had been and shuffled on his hands and knees until the passage widened and he could crouch. The press of a button activated the red eyes in his helmet, enough light to make his way down the tunnel to where it became a room.

He lit a kerosene lantern from the table on one side of the room and sat down heavily on a wooden chair. "I'm getting too old for this shit," he muttered in Polish.

Off came the furred reinforced gauntlets, and then the cloak and wolf skull helmet. He laid them carefully on the table, then eased out of the specially-built boots. He set aside the shaped buffalo horn that made the wolf-like howl. Finally, he unbuckled himself from the wood-and-metal exoskeleton. Then he set aside his cloak and shouldered out of the backpack of compressed gas cartridges the cloak and costume concealed. Some of the outfit Piotr had put together himself, but the ingenious pieces, the ones that gave him almost magical abilities, had been the covert gift of a local inventor who was one of the few to know Piotr's secret identity.

He looked up as a door opened on the far side of the room. Mrs. Szabo hustled in, bearing a pot of hot coffee and a chunk of ice wrapped in a dishcloth. "Busy night, Piotr?" she asked, taking in his disheveled appearance.

"Too many busy nights," he muttered. "Always the cops show up too late, when the fight is over, or they don't care who started it, and they just come to rough people up." He swore under his breath, then blushed. "Sorry," he said.

Mrs. Szabo waved off the apology. "No harm done. You should have heard my Oskar cuss when he thought I wasn't around." She sighed, looking at the bruises that were beginning to purple. "Let me have a look at you. There's supper in the oven upstairs once we get you cleaned up."

"No matter how many nights I go out, there's more to do, and always a fight somewhere I didn't stop," Piotr said tiredly.

Mrs. Szabo clucked her tongue at him. "Enough of that. You're a hero, even if Ghost Wolf gets all the credit. Every fight you break up is lives saved, and families that won't go hungry with their men out of work because they got busted up by ruffians." She winked conspiratorially. "Ghost Wolf is becoming a legend. I've heard that just the name is enough to scare off some troublemakers."

"If the name alone scared off more people, I wouldn't get so banged up," Piotr replied.

Piotr winced as Mrs. Szabo daubed at the scrapes and bruises. The ice felt good. His special suit had blunted the killing blows and deflected the worst of the damage, but beneath the disguise, he was still flesh and blood.

"What happened?" she asked, liberally applying the homemade salve she kept on hand for the aftermath of his nightly excursions. Piotr told her, sparing her any details that were unlikely to be in the newspaper, just in case the police ever came to call.

"God bless you," she said and took a break from bandaging up his injuries to hand him a steaming cup of black coffee. "Those rough boys would have killed those men," she added. "Just like my Oskar."

We make an odd pair, Piotr thought, sipping the strong coffee. Mrs. Szabo was old enough to be his mother and determined enough to stand behind his cause. He was in his thirties, scarred from a life of hard work, first with traveling carnivals back in Poland, and then taking whatever work he could find in America: day labor, steel mill, longshoreman. As a younger man, he'd been a carnival magician and acrobat and then a bare-knuckles fighter, anything to make enough to keep body and soul together. Now, those skills helped him protect his fellow immigrants, so no one else had to lose a beloved husband to roving gangs.

"You're going to have some bad bruises," she fussed, being as gentle as possible though her touch made him catch his breath. "Bruised ribs," she added, shaking her head. "Oh—that's a deep cut. I'll have to stitch up you and your outfit." She kept up a running narrative as she cleaned and bandaged his wounds and wrapped his ribs in strips from torn bedsheets. Her poultice smelled of herbs and tea, and Piotr knew from experience it took out the soreness and kept cuts from going sour. He gritted his teeth as she took black sewing thread, waved her needle through the flame to cleanse it, and set to closing up the gash on his arm.

"When this is all over, and you're back in your room, you should have a slug of that whiskey you keep under the bed," she said sagely, with a sly sideways glance that let him know she was onto his secrets. "Oskar always preferred vodka."

Mrs. Szabo was a thin woman old enough to be his mother. Her ropy muscles and long, skinny legs made him think of the scrawny chickens back home in the farm towns outside Warsaw. Like those chickens, Mrs. Szabo was a tough bird, capable of taking care of herself in a strange country when the gangs left her widowed, and her children grew up and moved away from New Pittsburgh's smoky valleys.

She'd found him one night, after one of his more disastrous fights. That was before he had his new, improved equipment, when he was just an over-the-hill former prize-fighter with a doomed one-man war against the immigrant-hating gangs that roved the city's streets. When he awoke, he had discovered himself here, in a room once used to hide escaped slaves, beneath the old stone house. She told him that she had seen him fight off a gang so a group of boys from the neighborhood could get home safely. There had been no one to do that for Oskar. Since then, she had been part landlady, part fussy aunt, and part co-conspirator.

"I was careful," Piotr said. "No one followed me."

Mrs. Szabo nodded. "Good." She was nearly done, with a neat row of stitches to show for her work, a testimony to her skill as an expert seamstress. Tonight, he had fought the Irish to protect the Poles. But just as many times, the situations were reversed, and if it was Poles beating up Irish workers, he stepped in, too. That meant both sides equally hated and loved the Ghost Wolf, and he was just as likely to get killed by one side as the other. His goal was a corridor of safe passage through the Birmingham and Limerick neighborhoods and up to the top of Coal Hill. It was a never-ending battle.

"I heard them talking down at the market, about the Ghost Wolf," she added, refilling his coffee cup. "The tales get taller with the telling. Some think he's a real wolf, or a werewolf, come from the old country to protect us. A few think he's a demon, and they cross themselves when they speak his name, but in the next breath, they say they're glad he protects their men. The rest seem to think he really is a ghost." She grinned. "I know exactly what the Ghost Wolf is," she added. "Hungry."

"*Dziękuję*," he said when she gathered her things and turned back to the stairs.

"You're welcome." She gathered her skirts. "Hurry up. You don't want the stew to burn. Leave the outfit down here. I'll come back tonight and patch it."

EARLY THE NEXT morning, Piotr Janacek was back at work, mop and bucket in hand. The pawn shop on Liberty Avenue was shabby, but the offices on the next two floors were in much better shape. He made a point of speaking broken English at work, knowing that most people would assume his understanding of the language would be just as limited. They would be wrong. While his English was heavily accented, he spoke, read, and understood it fluently. He had long ago realized the benefits of being underestimated, especially when it came to eluding suspicion as a masked vigilante.

"*Dzien dobry*." Piotr looked up as Agent Jacob Drangosavich greeted him. Tall and broad-shouldered, with a long face and pale blue eyes, Drangosavich looked like most of the men down at the mill, except for his business suit. Drangosavich's Polish carried a hint of a Croatian accent, but Piotr appreciated the gesture.

"Good morning," Piotr replied in Polish. "Beautiful day today."

Drangosavich's gaze lingered for a few seconds on the bruise on

Piotr's cheek. "It's nothing," Piotr said, ducking his head. "Walked into a door in the dark."

"Take care," Drangosavich said, though from his eyes Piotr was uncertain the agent had believed his excuse.

It had taken Piotr less than a week on his new job to realize that the pawn shop was not what it seemed, nor were most of the people who came and went through the store. *Spies,* he thought. Those had been common enough back in Poland. It was easy enough to listen as he mopped and swept, or to read the notes jotted on the blackboard in the conference room. *Government agents*, he realized. *Secret agents who look for ghosts.* That intrigued him, though he was careful not to appear to be interested for fear the agents might become suspicious.

"Is the coffee ready? Adam hasn't had a cup in at least an hour." Agent Mitch Storm strode toward Piotr with his usual confident swagger. Storm was shorter than Drangosavich, with dark hair and a five o'clock shadow despite being clean-shaven. He was handsome and cocky and probably had raised plenty of hell in his younger days.

"Coffee is making, sir," Piotr replied. Then he spotted the guest behind Storm and ducked his head, wishing he could become invisible.

Adam Farber, the young genius inventor from Tesla-Westinghouse, was headed his way. Tall and lanky, with sandy brown hair and wire-rimmed glasses slightly askew, Farber looked as if he'd already had enough coffee to be twitchy. To Piotr's relief, Farber swept past him, joking with Storm, as if he had not noticed the janitor in the shadows. But for a split second, Piotr saw recognition in Farber's eyes. Only to be expected, since Farber had built Piotr's wolf-suit exoskeleton.

When the men were past, Piotr let out a breath he hadn't realized he had been holding and moved his bucket down the hallway. He had already learned that the heating ducts carried sound through the building in strange ways. If he timed his work right, he could find tasks that kept him in hearing range for most of the agents' meeting. And with Adam Farber involved, Piotr was very interested to find out what was going on.

After some chit-chat in the small kitchen, Storm, Farber, and Drangosavich made their way to the conference room. Piotr noticed that

Farber had his cup in one hand and the entire pot of coffee in the other. They closed the conference room door behind them, and its pane of frosted glass kept Piotr from seeing what they were doing, but he suspected they would leave the half-erased chalkboard for him to clean, as usual.

No one else was in the office space at the moment, so Piotr could move about as he wished, so long as he kept up the appearance of doing his job. He pushed his broom down the hall and got out some brass polish to work on a light fixture near one of the best grates for eavesdropping.

"Since when does the Department of Supernatural Investigation get involved with hooligans?" Farber asked.

"It's not the hooligans we're interested in," Storm replied. "It's the ghost."

"Actually, it's both," Drangosavich put in. "The ghost—if there is one—on principle, since that's what we do. But HQ has every department on alert. The hooligan gangs are getting out of hand. HQ is worried there could be a turf war, maybe even a bombing, if this anti-immigrant talk goes much further."

"From what I read in the paper, the Ghost Wolf seemed to have the gangs on the run," Farber said off-handedly.

"Which is why we haven't investigated before this," Storm said. "But we've heard from our informants that the Rail Rats gang has been trying to hire a witch to take care of this 'ghost wolf.' So while the police and the guys from the Department of Justice are worried about a bomb that could take down a city block, we're more worried about a witch who could—oh, I don't know—open up a portal to Hell or put a curse on the whole south side of the city."

"Mitch exaggerates—as usual," Drangosavich replied with a sigh. "But the danger is real and growing. People spoiling for a fight are taking it out on the city's newest residents. There've been a lot of ugly incidents, and the police aren't always as quick to step in as we'd like. Or they're just as bad as the troublemakers, and the immigrants end up deciding they have to form gangs of their own for protection because they don't trust the police or the politicians to help them."

"And they would be right about that," Storm added. "The Oligarchy is making plenty of hay on the notion that foreigners should go home." He snorted. "Good for votes. So we can't expect any support from the Oligarchy, the cops they own or the politicians they pay for."

"And that drives your problem underground," Farber noted.

"Exactly," Drangosavich said. "So what do you have for us?"

Piotr clumped along the hall with his bucket, making sure he made enough noise so that they knew he was hard at work. He moved to another good listening post, and pulled out a wrench to fiddle with the radiator.

There was a *thump* like something had been placed on a table. "I've re-tooled the Maxwell box a bit, just for this," Farber said. "If your 'ghost wolf' really is a ghost, and you decide you want him to keep his distance, the box will do it. But," he said, pausing for emphasis, "if you intend to call ghosts, I'd have a care about where I did it. The venom these gangs are spewing isn't new. It's been around since before the War, even though New Pittsburgh couldn't run its factories and mills without the immigrants the gangs are bashing. Choose the wrong location, and you might rouse ghosts that join the fight on the gang's side."

"Then maybe we pick our battlefield," Drangosavich mused. "If we want the ghosts on our side, then we force a showdown in Birmingham, near St. Adalbert's, instead of in Limerick near St. Malachy. Dead Poles will be more friendly to the cause, I warrant, than dead Irish."

"Most of the attacks have been down toward the Limerick neighborhood," Mitch mused. "Typical. The new kids off the boat get beat up by the last bunch to get off the boat, who got beat up by the previous bunch."

"There's been retaliation by the Poles, too," Drangosavich pointed out. "The Ghost Wolf seems to put an end to the fights, regardless of who starts them."

"What about the *Logonje*?" Farber asked. Piotr frowned. That was a phrase he had only heard whispered, a group of demon-fighting Polish priests he wasn't even sure were more than a myth.

"We've already alerted them. They're looking into the possibility of a real magical threat. If they think the stakes are high enough, they'll get involved. If not... we're on our own," Mitch replied.

Piotr had cleaned the glass on a nearby door until it shone, then got his mop and started to work on the floor. He would have to move out of earshot soon. It was dangerous to linger, but the information he gained made him loathe to leave.

Another sound, like metal sliding across wood. "Here's the new and improved EMF locator box," Farber said, sounding like a proud papa. "I've tweaked it a bit. Been following the work of a daring young man, William Duane, at the University of Pennsylvania and Harvard. I won't bore you with the details, but it has to do with whether we're made up of light or particles." Farber's voice was alive with curiosity.

"Anyhow... I started thinking about science and magic, like those waves and tiny particles. Maybe it's not either/or. Maybe it's both, and they're just on different frequencies. So I've been tinkering."

"Can it block magic?" Storm asked.

"No," Farber replied. "But it can... phase out a small space." He sighed. "It's hard to explain without doing the math. But imagine that you could put a bubble around someone in a rainstorm. They wouldn't get wet, although it was raining all around them. Now make that bubble a really fragile energy field and the rain is magic."

"So you can block magic," Drangosavich repeated.

"Not really," Farber said. "But whoever has this gadget can elude it for a very short period of time. Seconds, maybe. I haven't fully field tested it—"

"Have you tested it at all?" Storm pressed.

Farber cleared his throat. "Renate and I went a few rounds. It worked—mostly."

"You're overwhelming me with confidence," Storm said drily. "Anything else?"

"Not yet, but I'm always working on something new," Farber replied, seemingly immune to Storm's tone.

The sound of chairs pushing back from the table was Piotr's cue to move far down the hallway, where no one might suspect he had been listening. *At this rate, the floor will shine like a mirror,* he thought.

Storm, Farber, and Drangosavich joked with each other as they emerged from the conference room and headed for the door. To Piotr's surprise, Farber bumped him as he passed, and Piotr felt a bit of paper slip into his pocket. He steeled himself to keep his expression neutral.

"Sorry," Farber muttered, but he met Piotr's gaze intently, a signal to have a look at the paper when Piotr was in private. Then the two agents and the inventor were gone, leaving Piotr alone with his mop and bucket.

He reached into his pocket and withdrew a receipt for tailoring. He frowned, then read the address. The receipt was for a man's suit, and the seamstress was Mrs. O. Szabo. An additional note was hastily scrawled in a man's neat handwriting. *Pick up alterations. 8 pm tonight.*

Piotr put the note carefully into his shirt pocket, where it would not be dislodged. *That means Farber will be by the house. I wonder what he's got for me. This should be interesting.*

———

MRS. SZABO, LIKE many widows, took in borders and sewed and washed other people's laundry in order to make ends meet. Piotr rented a room that had belonged to one of his landlady's sons. A river pilot paid rent on the second bedroom so it would be available when he came through town. Most of the time, it sat empty. Piotr's rent included breakfast and dinner plus a sandwich for lunch. He helped out whenever he could with chores and repairs. It was his opinion that Mrs. Szabo worked too hard, but he knew better than to say so out loud.

Meals were served in the kitchen because the small dining room had been turned into a sewing room. The room got good light and was suitable to host customers who came for a fitting or to drop off their mending. Wash tubs and a mangle for laundry were down in the basement, as well as the flat irons. Piotr finished washing dishes as Mrs.

Szabo put the leftovers in the icebox, wrapping his sandwich for the next day in waxed paper.

The tapping at the back door made Piotr look up. Clients came through the front door, and hardly anyone came around back. Mrs. Szabo lifted the blind and then opened the door with a wide smile. "Miska! What a surprise!"

Miska Kovach seemed to fill the doorway. Tall and muscular, it wasn't hard to believe he was a former army rifleman, now a private security chief. "Brought you some of mama's *pörkölt*," he said with a grin. "She makes too much."

"Ohh," Mrs. Szabo said appreciatively. "It'll be dinner tomorrow!" She quickly wrapped up a dozen of the cookies she had just baked and pushed the package into Miska's hands. "Here. Tell her I said 'thank you.'"

Miska chuckled. "She likes your cookies so much; I think this might be a plot." Then he glanced toward Piotr. "Big night?" he asked, raising an eyebrow.

Piotr nodded. "Yeah. For what it's worth." Miska had connected him with Adam Farber, though neither would say just how the unlikely pair knew each other.

"It's worth a lot," Miska replied. "Just keep yourself in one piece."

A knock at the front door came just as Piotr finished cleaning up. "I'd better go," Miska said. "Remember—stay safe. Leave the martyrs to the Church."

Mrs. Szabo went to greet the visitor as Piotr closed the back door behind Miska. Customers dropped off washing or mending throughout the day, nearly until bedtime. The frequent comings and goings were good cover for Piotr's exploits.

"Mr. Farber—so good to see you," Mrs. Szabo greeted the newcomer. "Will you share a cup of tea with us?" She did not wait for an answer before she bustled in to get the kettle and the tea tray, which Piotr had readied.

Piotr followed her into the sewing room. Farber grinned. "Hadn't expected to run into you downtown," he said. "Don't worry—your secret is safe with me." At that, he lifted a large carpet bag onto Mrs.

Szabo's worktable. He removed a tangle of shirts for mending and laundry, which he set to one side. "The usual," he said with a tired smile. Mrs. Szabo nodded.

"I'll have them back to you next week. Now, let me get you some of those cookies I just baked." Mrs. Szabo retreated to the kitchen. The clatter of dishes did not fool Piotr in the least. He was certain his landlady was listening.

Farber reached into the bottom of the bag and withdrew a few strange objects from the carpet bag. "These are for you," Farber said, pushing the items toward Piotr. One was a metal box with a dial and two buttons. The second item was a man's vest. At first glance, it appeared to be made of many layers of silk. When Piotr looked more closely, he could see that the silk had a thin coating of metal.

"What are they?" he asked.

"Added protection," Farber replied. "I know I can't talk you out of what you're doing, so I thought I might keep you a little safer." Farber held the box up.

"This is completely experimental," Farber warned. "But it's worked well in trials. It might be of help if someone tries to jinx you, but it won't hold off a strong witch for more than a few seconds, if that, and it won't stop a big blast of power."

He handed the box to Piotr. "It works off a battery," Farber continued. "That means you've probably got one usage before the battery drains. I couldn't make it last longer without making it heavier and bigger."

"It's good," Piotr replied. "And the vest? Rather fancy." He chuckled.

Farber grinned. "It's not for show. Silk is woven very tightly. The strands are tight enough that on occasion, a silk pocket kerchief has stopped a small bullet." Piotr raised an eyebrow, impressed. "There are thirty layers of silk in that vest," Farber continued. "It's not armor, but it's a lot better than nothing, and you should be able to move easily with it, unlike metal plates."

"Why does it shine?" Piotr asked, holding up the vest and turning it in his hands to catch the light, which reflected more than could be accounted for by the silk's luster.

"Because each layer has a light coat of aluminum," Farber replied. "Something I'm playing around with. Ideally, I'd like to coat the silk before it's woven, but there wasn't time."

Piotr nodded. "Thank you."

Farber fixed him with a look. "Mitch and Jacob—the two agents I was with this morning—think the situation is going to get worse. Don't take foolish chances. One man can't stop an army."

Piotr lifted his head and squared his shoulders. "No. But in my country, a handful of men have stopped armies by being fast and clever."

Farber clapped him on the shoulder. "Then take care. And good luck."

Just then, Mrs. Szabo bustled back in with a package of cookies wrapped in cloth and tied with string. "Here," she said, thrusting the bundle into Farber's hands. "I baked these just this afternoon. Fatten you up," she said with a motherly smile. "And your mending. It's done. I checked all the buttons too; made sure they were on tightly. No extra charge."

Farber thanked Mrs. Szabo profusely as he slipped the payment into her hand, gave a nod to Piotr, and then left, carrying the carpet bag filled with freshly laundered and mended clothing. Piotr closed the door behind Farber, then moved to take the vest and box down to the hidden room.

"There's talk at the fishmonger's about the gangs," Mrs. Szabo said. "Problems are getting out of hand. Too many incidents in too many places for even the Ghost Wolf to take care of them all, they say."

Which is exactly what the government agents also said, Piotr thought. "And what else are people saying?"

Mrs. Szabo shrugged, but Piotr could tell she was worried. "Depends on who you talk to. Mrs. Baczkowski at the market says that the Irish might bring in more ruffians from Boston or New York to cause our boys problems. And at the butchers, I overheard the men saying that if the gangs get out of hand, the mill owners might call the Pinkertons on them." After the bloodshed of the Braddock riots and the Pullman strike a few years back, New Pittsburgh's steelworkers feared having private security forces or even the army brought in to put down trouble.

Not good. Not good at all. The Pinkertons come in and split heads open. That's all they know how to do, Piotr thought. *Half the cops are Irish, and the other half belongs to the fat-cat mill owners who pay them. They'll be no help.*

Piotr mustered a smile. "Maybe we can stop it before it gets that far," he said, more confidently than he felt. "Farber's friends, the government agents, they sounded like they might help."

Mrs. Szabo sighed and looked suddenly older. "I wish I believed such things, but I don't anymore. Not after all I've seen." She shook her head. "It is the history of our people for others to try to take things from us. Only when we stand up to them ourselves does it stop. Counting on help from outsiders is a fool's errand." She paused. "Stay here. I have something for you."

Piotr waited as Mrs. Szabo went up to her room. When she came down a few minutes later, she had a piece of folded fabric in her hands. She stopped in the kitchen long enough to retrieve a salt shaker and brought both items to him.

"I found this in the attic," she said, handing him the folded cloth. Piotr unwrapped it to find a faded belt embroidered with strange symbols and words. "It's a *ladanki*. Belonged to my grandfather. He said it had protective magic. I tried to get Oskar to wear it, but he didn't think such things were 'Christian.'" It went without saying that Oskar had forfeited the belt's protection for piety, and had not survived.

"I want you to have it," Mrs. Szabo said. "Wear it in good health. And take this," she said, thrusting the salt shaker into his hand.

"Salt?"

She nodded. "The old women in the village where I grew up believed salt kept away evil spirits and bad magic. The *ladanki* and the salt together may help you, if there really are witches about."

Piotr accepted the gift with thanks, wrapping the belt around his waist beneath his shirt and dropping the salt shaker into a pocket of the jacket he pulled from a hook near the door. "I'm going out for a bit," he said as he headed toward the kitchen and the door to the secret room. "Not to fight. Just to clear my head." He glanced back over his shoulder. "Don't worry."

She made the sign of the cross. "Of course I worry." Then she muttered a phrase Piotr remembered his grandmother saying, a warding against evil.

Piotr headed out, pulling his jacket up against the evening chill. He headed down the block to Luczak's Bar, where most of the men in his neighborhood spent their evenings. The air was heavy with the aromas of roast pork, stuffed cabbage, and beets, mixed with cigarette smoke and the smell of dark Polish beer. He shouldered through the crowd to the bar. In the back corner, he heard the shouts of men playing darts and betting on dice.

"Gimme a beer," he said in Polish, no one else was speaking English.

Marek, the bartender, slid a lager his way and collected the coins Piotr put down on the bar. "Haven't seen you in here in a while."

Piotr shrugged. "Working. You know."

Marek nodded. "Yeah. I know." He eyed the bruise on Piotr's face. "Trouble?"

"Nothing important. Took a shortcut; got slugged by someone looking for a fight." Technically true. His mask and outfit could not completely protect him from the hazards of his nightly excursions, and the frequent bruises, black eyes, and split lips were one reason he did not show up at Luczak's more often.

Piotr took a sip of his beer and looked around. Luczak's wasn't as crowded as usual. He said as much to Marek.

"It's the Irish," Marek replied, adding a curse. "Damn gangs. It's got so people don't like to go out at night." He laughed. "But not these guys. They're not going to let any damn Irishmen get between them and a good beer."

Piotr sat at the bar for over an hour nursing his beer. He listened to the conversations around him. Much of it was trivial. But even among the bets on sports teams and racehorses, the vulgar jokes and the tall tales, it didn't take long to pick out comments that let Piotr know the ruffian gangs were never far from the bar patrons' thoughts.

"Dead rabbits." The phrase caught Piotr's attention, and he kept from turning around with effort. He had the feeling the man wasn't talking about game hunting or picking up stew meat for dinner.

"... big in Boston. Even the cops can't shut them down," the voice was saying.

"Boston's a long way from here," another man replied.

The first speaker gave a bark of a laugh. "You know the Irish. Every one of them Micks is related to all the others. Mark my words, those Muckers'll come here if one of their Paddy friends calls for them. There's gonna be blood." The two men moved on, and the cheers from the dart game in the back drowned out the rest of their conversation. All he gleaned from the rest of the conversations was that feelings were mixed about the Ghost Wolf, since the mysterious vigilante had trounced Polish gangs as often as he attacked Irish ruffians.

"... he's a menace. Whatever he is, he needs to get out of the way and let us settle this with the Micks our way, once and for all."

"... takes balls to do that. My wife thinks he's a hero for making the streets a little safer. Me, I think he must be nuts..."

Piotr finished his beer, tuning out the idle gossip. His thoughts went back to the comments he heard earlier. *Plenty of Irish in Boston,* Piotr thought. *Big city, big gangs. Could "Dead Rabbits" be a gang name?* Piotr didn't have a way to find out, but the Ghost Wolf did.

———

THE GHOST WOLF hunkered on the rooftops, just a shadow in the night. The part of town they called Limerick was dangerous for anyone who wasn't Irish. Small, dirty houses huddled not far enough from the soot-belching rail yards of the P&LE Railroad, a world away from the palatial concourse where swells caught trains to and from much fancier places.

Limerick and its Irishmen were at the bottom of Coal Hill, where the Polish settled. The Irish had come first and claimed New Pittsburgh as their own. Now it was the Poles' turn to be strangers in a strange land, and the Irish weren't about to give up what they had gained with sweat and blood to a new crop of broad-backed men eager to work for whatever wages the mill owners and factory men would pay. *Play one group off against the other, and they never realize that the man in the middle is picking their pockets equally,* Piotr thought.

The exoskeleton Farber created enhanced his natural agility. He prowled like an alley cat, staying in the shadows, watching his prey. He'd had the men in his sights for a while. Not all of his nightly runs ended in fights. That was only when there was no helping it, when gangs of armed men stalked through the night, looking for victims. On the other nights, Piotr did reconnaissance, like his father who had been a sniper in the army before he joined the carnival.

His father had been part gypsy, *Polska Roma*, and hadn't been above picking a few pockets when necessary to keep food on the table. Piotr didn't hold with thieving, but he had his father's eye for a mark, his quick reflexes, and his ability to deflect attention until the strike was made. They served him well in his one-man war.

The Irish boys were drunk. Liquor made them mean. More than once, Piotr had smelled the stink of cheap whiskey as he fought ruffians still sober enough to go looking for easy prey to harass. But this night, the men staggered home without bothering anyone. Piotr sighed in relief. He had a more important quarry in mind.

It was hardly fair to call most of the ruffians on New Pittsburgh's streets "gangs." They were usually groups of friends, neighbors, or co-workers who went looking for trouble. The Ghost Wolf ensured they found more than they had expected. But the majority of the fights he broke up were spur-of-the-moment spitefulness.

So far, both the loosely organized Polish and Irish criminal gangs had stayed out of the fights, sticking to making money off making book and selling cheap whiskey. But if they got into a battle over who owned the sidewalks of the South Side, it was likely to end in disaster for both sides especially if the Pinkertons or the Army got called in to put down the unrest.

Not if I can stop it.

Tonight, the hunters were about to become the hunted.

Piotr stifled a cough. New Pittsburgh's skies were dark with coal smoke at all hours of the day. It was worst at night when the air was still, and the soot and fumes of the mills hung heavy, almost blotting out the moon. He glanced around, getting his bearings, and saw that he was near the Duquesne Incline, in a part of Limerick where only a fool would venture if he wasn't Irish.

Guess that makes me a fool, Piotr thought grimly, not the first time he had come to that conclusion.

Talk of bringing in Irish gang members from Boston worried Piotr. So he made his way to a building he had been watching for a while, a coal company's headquarters near the P & LE tracks that Sean Brennan, the Crime Boss of Limerick, had taken for his own.

Lights were on in the old building, dimmed by worn, stained blinds. The streetlights near the building did not work, something Piotr doubted was an accident. Farber had made him special goggles that let him see better at night, and he spotted four guards despite the deep shadows. The trick would be to get close enough to hear what was going. He hadn't made up his mind yet about fighting. That decision would come later when he knew his enemy's plan and had a counter-strategy.

The coal company had left behind a mess. That worked in Piotr's favor. Even without his exoskeleton, he could have climbed the rusting equipment and piles of rubble easily, but with his equipment, he could jump farther and move faster. He went over the heads of the guards and made it to the building's roof. From there, he let himself down on a rope-and-pulley he had built for just these kinds of occasions. It allowed him to descend noiselessly and if necessary, ascend much faster than he could go hand-over-hand.

Darkness hid him, and his gray outfit blended with the shadows. The old windows were high off the ground, keeping him well above the guards' line of sight. If he gave them no reason to look up, they were unlikely to see him. Holding his breath, Piotr edged as close as he dared to the window.

Sean Brennan, the Crime Boss of Limerick, sat behind a mahogany desk that was in much better shape than the building he had chosen for his headquarters. With him were two other men Piotr recognized as Jamie MacCabe, Brennan's bodyguard, and Cian Maguaran, a slim, dark-haired man with the look of a Traveler whom many claimed was a warlock.

"Of course I don't want the damn Dead Rabbits in New Pittsburgh," Brennan said. "Just like the bloody live rabbits—first you've got two of them, and then they take over." He lit a cigar and shuffled through a folder on his desk. "But the idea of a proper gang from Boston coming here to bash some heads together is enough to put those Oligarchy bastards on pins and needles. All we've got to do is spread the word, provide a little provocation, and wham!" he said, slapping one hand against his desktop. "All the little vermin show up to fight, and the Pinkertons do our work for us."

"You want the Pinkertons?" MacCabe said incredulously.

Maguaran chuckled. "He wants them to pull the trigger for us. Let the Oligarchy pay the 'exterminator.' Get rid of the rabble."

Except that the Pinkertons will take the Poles down too. And when everything's done burning, and they mop up the blood, Brennan's political machine will own Birmingham as well as Limerick, and probably Coal Hill and all the South Side.

Piotr shimmied up the rope and squatted on the roof, taking in the lay of the land around Brennan's headquarters. He was watching the movements of the guards, planning his next steps. *Ginning up my nerve, because this is a lot bigger than scaring off some half-drunk hooligans.*

There was no way to alert Storm and Drangosavich without admitting to his—highly illegal—alter-ego as Ghost Wolf. If the government didn't put him in jail, he'd be dead in a day on the street from reprisals from both sides. It would take too long to warn Farber. And if he went home and did nothing, Brennan would provoke enough unrest —maybe even stage a riot—and the Pinkertons would end it with a bloodbath. Much as Piotr hated the ruffians, wholesale slaughter was worse.

And there was no one to stop it except him.

He drew a deep breath, muttered a curse, said a prayer, and made a decision. *First things first. Get rid of the guards.*

The Ghost Wolf was known for showing up out of nowhere, running off the hooligans, and disappearing into the night. Taking prisoners wasn't part of the plan. But he'd had an inkling that tonight might require different tactics, and so he had brought a small pack with him with handy objects, just in case. Rope, lock-picking tools, other useful items. Not for the first time, he questioned his decision to forego a knife or gun. *I may be a vigilante, but I'm not a murderer. At least, not yet.*

The first guard never knew what hit him. The Ghost Wolf bounded from the depths of the shadows, and a single swing of Piotr's blackjack laid the guard out before he could make a sound. Piotr dragged him behind a piece of rusted machinery, bound and gagged him for good measure, and resumed the hunt. The second guard fell just as easily, and Piotr trussed him up and hid him with his companion.

Something made the third guard wary. Piotr used the man's suspicions to his advantage, luring him into the shadows with the ping of a few pebbles thrown against old equipment.

"Who's out there?" the guard called.

"No one's there," the fourth guard mocked. "You're just daft."

"I swear, I heard something," the third man insisted. He moved a few steps toward the shadows, then paused to look over his shoulder.

The fourth guard had vanished.

Piotr wrestled the downed guard out of the way and circled the last of Brennan's protectors. He could see indecision in the man's face, fear that his colleagues might be playing a prank on him, or that calling for back-up might look like weakness, versus the reasonable impulse to yell for help.

In that moment of indecision, Piotr vaulted from the darkness, slamming the guard to the ground, following up the tackle with a smack of the blackjack. The guard went limp. "Still breathing," Piotr muttered. "Don't envy you the headache."

He finished tying up and gagging the last two guards, watching over his shoulder to assure that he had not been spotted. If the rumors about Brennan's man Maguaran were correct, then it would take more than speed and acrobatics to get past the thick-necked bodyguard and a warlock.

Piotr fingered the "magic" belt for good luck. He listened beneath the window for a few seconds, making sure that Brennan and the others had not moved. Then he slipped around to the back of the building. It took only a moment to jimmy the basement door lock and find the electrical panel, then pull down the lever and plunge the building and grounds into darkness.

He froze, listening. Brennan and his allies were right overhead. MacCabe shouted to the guards, but no one answered. Silently, Piotr slipped out of the basement and circled the building, staying to the shadows. He was already in the hallway when MacCabe warily peered from the room. Piotr used the exoskeleton's added strength to grab MacCabe by the shoulders and pull him abruptly into the darkened corridor, simultaneously turning him so that the bodyguard's gun pointed away.

Before MacCabe fully realized what was going on, Piotr leaped, and the steel toe of his boot caught MacCabe under the jaw. The bodyguard went down like a sack of potatoes.

From inside Brennan's office, Piotr heard the sound of a revolver's hammer being cocked. Maguaran began to chant.

Too late to turn back now.

Piotr grabbed MacCabe's gun. He knew how to shoot; he just preferred not to, if there was another way. Then he leveraged his exoskeleton to haul MacCabe to his feet and push the big man's unconscious form into the doorway.

Six shots rang out as Brennan unloaded his bullets into the lumbering shadow. A flash of white light and a shout in a language Piotr guessed was Gaelic sent the smell of smoke and burning cloth into the air as a blast of power struck MacCabe square in the chest. As

MacCabe's body slumped to the ground, Piotr hunched beside the doorway, shooting out one of the large windows with a crash of breaking glass and then the other.

In the instant when Brennan and Maguaran turned their weapons toward the windows, expecting a threat from outside, the Ghost Wolf lunged and dove. He came up shooting, intentionally taking a line of fire across the room to force the crime boss and the warlock to scramble for cover.

Maguaran was the first to make a move, lobbing what appeared to be a ball of green fire right at the spot where the Ghost Wolf had been seconds before.

Maguaran might have magic, but Piotr had technology. The special goggles Farber had made for him let him see although the room was almost pitch dark. He had discarded the empty gun, and the blackjack was in one hand and Farber's little box in the other.

Propelled by the gas cartridge that ran the exoskeleton, the Ghost Wolf sprang for the warlock in the darkness. Green fire flashed toward him. Piotr pressed the button on the box, felt a second's disorientation, and realized the fire had missed him. The *ladanki* belt pulsed once with a soft, golden light. Before Maguaran could recoup, Piotr slammed the warlock to the floor, pressing the magical belt against the small of the magic-user's back and giving the button on Farber's box another push, just for good measure. The air around him crackled with power both electrical and magical. Piotr cracked his blackjack against Maguaran's skull and dove out of the way in case Brennan had a second gun.

He rolled and came up right beside Brennan, swinging his weighted, metal-clawed gauntlets. One swipe slashed down across the crime boss's face, opening four deep, bloody slits and nearly blinding him in one eye. Brennan cursed and fell back a step. Light flashed, a force struck Piotr in the chest, and he staggered.

Brennan clutched a Derringer, his hold-out gun, its shot spent at close range. Piotr swung his blackjack. Brennan managed to block him, clamping down on Piotr's wrist with an iron grip.

"You should be dead," Brennan growled.

"And you should be in jail." Piotr bent his knees and pushed off.

The exoskeleton vaulted him toward the ceiling, taking an unprepared Brennan with him. Piotr ducked, but he yanked on Brennan hard, slamming the crime boss's head against the ceiling. The apparatus cushioned Piotr's landing, but he let Brennan fall hard, and as his enemy stumbled, Piotr brought the blackjack down with a satisfying crack.

Only then did Piotr take in what had happened. He clutched at his chest. The small caliber bullet had torn through the gray cloth of his costume, slowed by the silk of the vest beneath. But his ribs felt as if they had cracked with the impact, and warm blood trickled down his belly.

First, I'm going to get what I came for. Piotr had sized up his options and made preparations before he launched his attack. Now, speed was of the essence. It was only a matter of time before more of Brennan's men showed up. Piotr had no desire to leave Brennan and Maguaran for the local cops, who were likely to be on Brennan's pay. He gasped with pain as he dragged first Brennan than Maguaran to the back door, and went back to grab files from Brennan's desk to make sure the two men were fully incriminated.

He had hog-tied both men, gagging and blindfolding them for good measure. Swearing under his breath, he hauled them with the last of his strength to the large wooden crate that sat in a boxcar ready to leave the yard with the midnight train. Only his exoskeleton enabled Piotr to heft first Brennan and then Maguaran into the crate. He watched them both to make sure they were still unconscious, dropped the files from the desk in with them, then dumped salt over Maguaran, just in case.

Piotr gritted his teeth as he nailed the wooden crate shut. He had marked the shipping recipient when he prepared the crate. In the distance, he heard a train's whistle. In a few hours, the rail spur would bustle with the night shift. With luck, it would give him enough time to get home.

Piotr stuck to the darkest shadows, limping away from the coal company. After many a successful fight, the Ghost Wolf had triumphantly ridden atop one of Coal Hill's inclines, but tonight, Piotr was too injured to execute the necessary acrobatics. In his disguise, he dared not be seen by passers-by, so riding in the passenger compartment of the incline was out of the question. That left the long trek up the switchbacks of Indian Trail, a winding route that made its way up the steep slope of Coal Hill.

Piotr had always considered Indian Trail beyond the territory he patrolled as the Ghost Wolf. But he had heard rumors that forest spirits wrecked their own particular vengeance on anyone who tried to prey on the weary souls who climbed the dark, winding trails. As Piotr forced himself onward, he was certain eyes watched him from the shadows beneath the trees.

I've got to get shelter before daylight, he thought, pushing himself on. *I don't dare be caught dressed as the Ghost Wolf. And more to the point, I'm bleeding.* The silk vest was soaked with blood, and fire lanced his chest with every movement, every breath. The vest might have stopped Brennan's bullet from putting a big hole in him, but the slug had done damage, nonetheless.

Piotr's breath was labored, loud in the still night. He was injured and many blocks away from home, in enemy territory. And while he had put an end to Brennan's scheme, Piotr wondered if the price had been his own life.

There were no railings along Indian Trail and no markers. Piotr stumbled, nearly falling. He was certain that he heard footsteps behind him and equally sure he had no fight left in him. No streetlights marked the trail. It was an old path, and the factory workers and mill hunks who climbed this trail knew to carry a lantern for the trek home.

It was too early for the night shift to be getting off, too late for the swing shift. That meant no one else had good reason to be on Indian Trail unless they were looking for trouble. Piotr gasped as he caught his boot on a root and nearly fell. The exoskeleton was keeping him upright, helping to bear some of his weight, giving him a spring in his step to counter his exhaustion. But the compressed air tanks were nearly empty, and when they were spent, Piotr knew he would not be able to go on.

If the cops don't get me, the Micks will.

He reached a place on the trail where the tree canopy opened up to the sky. Moonlight filtered down, and he saw three men not far behind him, gaining fast. Piotr tried to pick up his pace, but the world spun, and he pitched head-long onto the trail. The men were running now. Maybe they had recognized him and saw their chance to capture or kill the Ghost Wolf. Piotr had heard that there was a bounty, put on his head by ruffians with a grudge. He gritted his teeth and tried to rise, just as four new shadows emerged from the trees. A sound like thunder made his ears ring. His pursuers cried out in fear, and their running footsteps receded. Piotr struggled to reach his knees, knowing he needed to defend himself from this new threat or at least escape into the woods, but even the exoskeleton could not keep him from collapse. *I'm a dead man.*

———

PIOTR WOKE SLOWLY. First, he realized that he wasn't dead. Then he gingerly moved his wrists and ankles, fearing police shackles. When he realized that he was not chained, he panicked as it dawned on him that someone had removed both his Ghost Wolf outfit and the exoskeleton. He opened his eyes and found himself in a small room that held a bed, a small desk, and a chair. A crucifix hung over the door.

When he tried to sit up, his ribs protested. Piotr's chest was neatly taped, with fresh bandages that smelled of herbal poultice. A homespun nightshirt replaced his clothing, but as he took in his surroundings, he realized with relief that the exoskeleton leaned against the wall behind the door, and the rest of his outfit lay on the desk, next to a pitcher and a glass.

Just as Piotr was thinking about trying to get to the pitcher for a drink, the door opened. A woman in a nun's habit entered and looked him up and down like a boys' school matron. She was in her middle years, plump and round-faced, with a solid build and broad hands that suggested a life of hard work.

"I see you're awake." Her voice had a strong Irish lilt, and Piotr's heart sank. Her lips quirked as if she guessed his thoughts.

"Relax. You're safe here, Pole or Irish." She paused, and he thought he saw a glimpse of mischief in her eyes. "And for the famed Ghost Wolf, you have the best room our poor cloister has to offer."

"You were on the trail? The ones who saved me?"

The nun nodded. "Aye. Did you think the Ghost Wolf was the only one trying to make sure our young men stay in one piece on their way home from work? We watch over Indian Trail since it comes out just below our cloister house. Sister Aideen had a vision in which the Holy Mother herself sent us to protect the trail, and so we have taken it as our calling."

"That noise... did you *shoot* those men who were following me?" Piotr knew it was probably impolite—not to mention unwise—to ask so many questions of his rescuer, but he had no idea what he had just gotten himself into.

The nun laughed. "Rock salt," she replied. "Stings like the devil, but won't put much of a hole in them." She sobered as she regarded him. "Unlike the bullet we dug out of you," she added, raising an eyebrow.

"It was a busy night," Piotr said. He had no desire to add to his sins by lying to a nun, but since he had acquired that bullet from two Irishmen, he thought it best to say as little as possible, here in an Irish convent. "Where am I?"

"You're in the cloister of the Sisters of Saint Athracht," she replied. "And I am Sister Muread."

"What do you intend to do with me?" Piotr asked, deciding it was better to get to the meat of the matter.

Sister Muread gave him a quizzical look as if he might still be addled from his injuries. "Heal you and send you on your way, with the blessings of the Saints and the Holy Mother," she replied.

"But I'm... not Irish."

This time, Sister Muread chuckled. "Sure'n your not, that's true. An' we know the stories of the Ghost Wolf, even up here, how he stops our boys fighting with your boys, which is as the Good Lord would have it. So you're welcome here, Sir Wolf, under our protection, 'til you can safely go home."

"Thank you," he said, managing a wan smile. "I'm grateful to you and the Sisters."

"We've found some fresh clothing for you," Sister Muread said. "Come nightfall, you can put your other items into a sack and throw a sheet over the larger pieces," she added with a nod toward the exoskeleton. "Our groundskeeper can take you in the wagon where you need to go."

"How long was I out?" Piotr asked.

"Just a day," Sister Muread replied. "Our healer dosed you with medicine to help you sleep, and cleaned your wound, bound up your ribs. With a good meal in you, you should be mostly mended."

I've missed a day of work, Piotr thought. *I might have saved the South Side, but I've probably lost my job.*

———

WITH A HEAVY heart and aching ribs, Piotr went in to work the following day. He had spent the prior evening reassuring Mrs. Szabo that he was fine, and feeling very guilty since she had stayed up all of the previous night waiting for him, worried sick, and had gone out looking for him. Now, a different kind of worry gnawed at him, but he squared his shoulders and entered the pawn shop by the back door, as he always did.

"Piotr! Where have you been?" Agent Drangosavich was the first to spot him.

Piotr doffed his cap and looked down. "Apologies, sir. I fix things for my landlady, and I fall from ladder. Knocked out." He tapped his knuckles against his temple. "But I have a hard head. Good as new."

He steeled himself, waiting to be fired. "Good to have you back," Drangosavich said. "Probably for the best you weren't around yesterday. Damndest thing. A box showed up at headquarters with two men inside. Troublemakers—from New Pittsburgh. Made for a busy day with the brass trying to figure out how they got to Washington, D.C. Lots of people in and out of here, and now there's dirt tracked all over

343

the hallway." He gave Piotr a sidelong glance. "You'll take care of that right away?"

Piotr grinned. "Oh yes, sir. Don't you worry. I'll get it done." He went to fetch his mop and bucket, sensing that Drangosavich watched him walk away. But if the agent suspected anything, he chose to save it for another day.

Good to know the railroad runs on schedule, Piotr thought. *I'd have hated for that box to get lost.*

THE PATENTED TROLL

ONCE UPON A TIME, in a world of gears and steam, there lived an inventor. Now this was no ordinary dreamer. This was an inventor of clockwork creatures so amazing that they could learn tasks and follow orders. He developed all kinds of mechanical wonders, each more ambitious than the last, all beyond the limits of what others had considered possible.

The brilliant inventor's fame grew, and people came from all around the world to see his amazing creations. Some of his clockwork creatures had the shape of men, but they could work for days at a time and never required sleep or food. Others resembled dogs, but the steel and steam dogs could hunt for a week and never lose the scent of their quarry. His iron horses were a wonder to behold, powerful and regal, stallions that could run as fast as a train. Audiences swooned at the beauty of his mechanical falcons and aluminum eagles, with cameras for eyes that beheld the world beneath them.

But all too soon, the inventor came to the attention of those who could not appreciate his clockwork creatures for their elegant beauty and saw in them only a means to create profit and inflict pain.

"Sell us your fantastic creatures," the men from the army said to the inventor. "We will make you a hero! Your steel dogs will run enemy soldiers to ground, and your iron horses will trample the enemy under their hooves."

"Sell us your amazing inventions," the men who ran the factories said to the inventor. "We will make you rich! Armies of your mechanical men will run our factories, men that require no pay and no sleep, who never feel pain and cannot die, and we will work them until they fall apart."

"Sell us your clockwork monsters," the criminals said. "You will be powerful! With control of such creatures, we can best our rivals and eliminate anyone who stands in our way. We will rule the world!"

Now the inventor had never imagined such horrors when he created his mechanical wonders. He had a brilliant mind, but he was childlike when it came to the darkness of the human heart. When he saw what others wanted to do with his creations, he refused their offers in horror.

"I will never sell my fabulous animals and mechanical men to help you kill and enslave and destroy!" the inventor said. "They were created to improve the world, not to make it a place of bloodshed."

But powerful and greedy men do not listen to the likes of a poor inventor. And so they broke into his laboratory and stole his wonderful creatures and his clockwork men, and they beat the inventor senseless and left him for dead. "If you will not accept money, fame, or power, then you are a fool," the men said. "We are going to change the world."

And change the world they did. The inventor did not die, though he was badly injured. Some days, he wished he had perished, because it broke his heart to see what the men who stole his mechanical creatures made of them. Governments waged war without end, pitting clockwork soldiers on iron horses against each other in battles that never ended, fighting men that could not bleed. Steel dogs killed without remorse, wiping out villages and farms in their path. Criminals used mechanical monsters to terrorize cities and hunt down anyone who opposed them until no one was safe.

Factories filled with metal men worked around the clock, belching smoke and sending flames into the night sky. Outside their gates, the human workers and their families starved, their labor no longer needed.

The inventor saw all of this and wept. "I have brought this on the world. I have failed my precious creatures, and let them be enslaved. If anyone discovers that I am still alive, the powerful and greedy men will take me prisoner and make me invent more horrors for them. I cannot let that happen."

So the inventor went away, to a secret place only he knew existed. On an island in the middle of the deep woods far away from cities or towns, he had built himself a cabin and a workshop. Not all of his beautiful steam creatures had been lost to the profiteers, because he had already begun to move them, slowly and secretly, to his sanctuary in the forest. He had planted a garden to grow his food, and he had outfitted his laboratory with all the tools and materials he might need, intending to spend his old age tinkering. He planned his escape, and slipped away one night, making certain to take with him or destroy any of his notes that might be used to exploit his inventions. But in his hurry, he forgot one of his notebooks.

And so it was that when the cities fell, and the skies burned, the inventor was far away, living with his beloved clockwork creatures. Smoke carried on the wind from the conflagrations, and the night trembled with thunder from the explosions that lit the horizon with false sunsets. The inventor sobbed for his part in the destruction, and none of his fabulous animals could console him.

"I must never let anyone misuse my creatures again," the inventor said. His island had a single, wooden bridge that connected it to the mainland, since its shores were steep and rocky and unfit for a boat to land. To protect himself, the inventor built a large, powerful mechanical man with a broad chest and thick arms and legs.

"I will call you 'Troll,'" the inventor told his creation. "You will stand guard over this bridge and keep away any intruders."

Troll did as he was told. Like all of the inventor's creatures, Troll was able to learn tasks and follow orders. He watched the animals in the forest, and they watched him. When he made no move to hunt or hurt them, the birds and rabbits, foxes and bear cubs dared to come closer. Troll watched them jump and play, and saw them tend their young. It occupied his circuits while he waited.

Sometimes, the inventor would come across the bridge with one of his mechanical dogs to visit Troll and check on his gears and wiring. The inventor was scarred from the attack that nearly killed him, and he walked with a cane. When the inventor visited, he would talk to Troll of this and that. Troll learned the words, and when he was alone, he would speak to the animals, and they would bark and howl in return.

Years went by. Troll saw the animals in the forest find mates, give birth, grow old, and die. Troll never changed. The mechanical dogs that came with the inventor never changed, either, but the inventor grayed with every turn of the seasons. His visits, once frequent, came less and less often. After a while, the inventor did not come at all.

Twenty years went by. Troll counted the winters and summers to pass the time, though he did not change. He looked across the bridge for signs of the inventor or his dogs, but nothing stirred. Troll did not have instructions to go back across the bridge, so he stayed where he was. Generations of birds and animals took him for part of the forest. They ran across his broad shoulders and perched on his head. Troll learned to make their songs and noises, and they considered him one of their own. But always, Troll waited for his inventor to return.

———

FAR AWAY, IN the ruins of what was once a vast city, a young man named Tad spent his time tinkering with bits of metal. He scavenged the pieces he found in old buildings and garbage dumps, and took what he needed from the rusted hulks of long-silenced factories and huge, broken machines.

"I have no money and no prospects, and barely enough food to eat," Tad said to himself. "But with a few tools and some old junk, I can amuse myself and pass the time."

Tad had no family and few friends. He spent his time searching for food and materials, exploring the wreckage of the buildings destroyed in the long-ago war. Sometimes he found books, and Tad taught himself many things. He liked numbers the most, because some of the books showed him how numbers could help him build wonderful things.

One day, Tad found a room in an old, deserted building that was full of strange equipment, disassembled and badly damaged. He moved his few belongings into the room so he could examine the odd tools that had been left behind and read the books that were filled with drawings and numbers.

At first, Tad tinkered with making small clocks and little machines. He built a mechanical mouse, and then a clockwork cat to go with it. As he learned more, he built a steel dog he called Gear and a donkey he named Trouble. Now he was not alone.

Though the war had long been over, the city and its streets were still not safe. Wild animals walked the ruined boulevards, and gangs of desperate men were a law unto themselves. Tad ventured out from his hiding place only when he needed food, or water, or equipment. He dreamed of going somewhere with all of his mechanical animals where he could build new wonders and not be afraid.

One day, Tad found a notebook that had fallen behind a bookshelf. No one else had found it in all the long years, and its hiding place had protected it from the elements. The pages were yellowed, and the ink was faded, but Tad discovered the most wondrous drawings he had ever seen.

"I must find the person who wrote these notes," Tad said to Gear, who wagged his steel tail. "But where could he have gone?"

Then Tad found a piece of a map stuffed into the back of the notebook. He knew where there was a building full of a lot of old books, and he took the fragment with him, daring to go searching for a clue to where the inventor might have gone. Many of the old books had burned in the great fire, and others had been damaged by time and water, but Tad finally found a map that matched the fragment in the notebook.

"This is where we're going to go," he told Gear. "This is where we'll find the inventor."

Then Tad realized how far away the place on the map was, and he grew sad. "The road is long and dangerous. I'll need a way to protect us on the journey."

So Tad built a large metal man. The metal man moved with springs and gears like his other inventions, and he could see and hear and speak. Tad called him "Billy." Billy had room to carry Tad inside his big, broad chest. Tad could also see through Billy's eyes and speak through Billy's mouth.

"Cat can scratch, and Gear can bite. Mouse can run, and Trouble can kick. Now Billy can protect us, too," Tad told his creations. "We're ready for our adventure."

So Tad packed up his few possessions and took his mechanical creatures and struck out to seek his fortune. He carried Mouse in his pocket as he rode within the mechanical man and Cat and Gear walked alongside Trouble and Billy. Soon, they left the city behind. Tad had a compass and a supply of candles, and he had learned how to trap rats and rabbits for food. He had a knife to protect himself and to cut wood for a fire, and he had enough bits of metal and tools to fix anything that might go wrong with his clockwork companions.

Tad and his mechanical menagerie walked for many, many days. By now, the ruins of the big cities were far away. They passed abandoned homes and farms fallen in to disrepair. All of the people were gone. The weather grew colder as they went north, and by the end of the summer, they had found the forest on Tad's map. On they walked, deeper and deeper into the woods.

Tad had never seen a forest, except in books. He marveled at the smells and sounds, and feared the noises he heard in the night. Animals were all around them, watching from a distance. By now, Tad had learned which plants and berries and nuts were good for eating, so he did not have to harm any of the forest creatures. They followed Tad and his companions at a distance, as if they were curious to see where they were going.

"There it is!" Tad stopped Billy on a rise overlooking a large lake. In the distance, he could see a few buildings on an island and a long wooden bridge. "That must be where the inventor lives!"

So Tad and the others headed for the bridge. Cat and Mouse played chase with each other. Gear wagged his tail and pranced. Trouble picked up his plodding pace. But when they reached the bridge, Troll was waiting.

"You cannot pass." Troll's voice was metallic and scratchy.

"We've come to see the inventor," Tad said, still riding inside Billy's big chest.

"No one can cross," Troll warned.

Just then, Mouse scampered around Troll's feet. Troll reached down and picked up the mechanical rodent, holding Mouse in his big metal palm. "Nice," Troll said. He let Mouse down, and immediately Mouse ran toward the bridge with Cat right behind him.

"You cannot pass!" Troll warned, but it was too late. Cat and Mouse were already halfway across the bridge.

"Don't worry about them," Tad said through Billy's mouth. "They won't cause any harm. The inventor has clockwork animals of his own, doesn't he? Maybe they would like company."

Troll had not seen the inventor or his mechanical dogs for a long time. The clockwork dog with this newcomer looked like one of the inventor's favorites.

"That's my dog, Gear," Tad said. "He's very friendly."

Troll threw a stick like the inventor had taught him. Gear brought it back and wagged his steel tail. Again and again, Troll threw and Gear fetched. While Troll and Gear played, Trouble edged closer to the bridge. Before Troll could stop him, Trouble ran across the bridge after Cat and Mouse.

"You cannot pass!" Troll called after him, but it was too late. Cat and Mouse were on the island, and Trouble was most of the way across the bridge.

"Gear can get them to come back," Tad said. "I'll send him after them." Gear followed Cat and Mouse and Trouble across the old wooden bridge.

Troll stood between Tad and the bridge. "You cannot pass!"

Tad was still inside Billy. Billy and Troll were nearly the same size. But while Billy was shiny and new, Troll was weathered and stained. His metal was dented in places, and Tad saw a few spots of rust. He looked at the weathered old bridge and at Troll and knew that the inventor must be dead.

"You've been guarding this bridge a long time," Tad said.

"A very long time."

"Have you seen beyond the hillside?" Tad asked. "The forest is very big and filled with beautiful things. There are waterfalls and ponds and flowers and animals."

As they stood there, the forest creatures came closer. A bird landed on Troll's shoulder, and a squirrel skittered across his big metal feet. "Your friends could show you where they live," Tad said. "It isn't far. I will guard the bridge for you."

"You cannot cross!"

"I'll stay right here until you get back," Tad promised. "And when you return, I'll keep you company, and so will Cat and Mouse and Gear and Trouble."

"Stay?" It had been a long, long time since Troll had company.

"Yes. I'll stay and guard the bridge. Go and see the animals. I'll be here when you come back."

The rabbits and squirrels seemed to understand, because they headed up the ridge, and stopped to see if Troll would follow. Troll took one step and then another, and looked back uncertainly. Billy waved, still standing at the end of the bridge. No one would pass. And so Troll followed his animal companions, up the rise and over the ridge.

When Troll was out of sight, Tad climbed out of Billy and closed the metal body back up again. "Stay here, and keep Troll company," he told Billy.

"Stay?" Billy asked. Tad had taught him to follow instructions and do many tasks during their long journey, but Billy had never been away from Tad before.

"Yes. Here with Troll. Help him guard the bridge." Then Tad hurried across the bridge, leaving Billy on the other side, to keep watch.

Cat, Mouse, Gear, and Trouble were waiting for Tad. Together, they explored the island. There was an overgrown plot for growing vegetables and plenty of fresh water. A barn held more crates of parts and tools than Tad had ever seen. Tad found several mechanical dogs that had wound down, and when he turned their keys, the dogs and Gear played a game of chase.

The cabin was tidy and comfortable, with a fireplace and a stove and a table with chairs. Shelves of books lined the walls, and there were lanterns to read by and a bed to sleep in, along with a trunk full of clothing that was close to Tad's size.

On the floor, Tad found the inventor's body, shriveled to mere bones. It made him very sad that he could not talk to the man whose notes had inspired him. But as he looked around the cabin, he realized that the walls were filled with new drawings and numbers, plans for all kinds of wondrous creatures the inventor had not lived to create.

"I will pick up where you left off," Tad promised. "I will build your dreams and take care of your inventions." He looked at his companions. "We're home now."

After a while, when Troll had followed his animal companions to see the forest, he headed back to his bridge. There stood Billy, just as promised. And for the first time in many years, smoke rose from the chimney of the inventor's cabin. Mechanical dogs chased and barked on the far shore.

The inventor waved to him from the window of the cottage. Troll settled into his place at the end of the bridge, next to Billy. All was as it should be.

IRON & BLOOD (EXCERPT)

"THIS WOULD HAVE BEEN SIMPLER if we'd done it my way." The slender woman lifted her chin defiantly. Dark ringlets framed her face, and her violet eyes sparkled. Her black wool traveling suit was nipped in at the waist, making the bustle in the back more pronounced. Her voice was starting to rise.

"Your way involved dynamite. We wanted to remain discreet." Jake Desmet tugged at the collar of his suit coat and tried to look nonchalant.

"We'd have been done by now." Veronique LeClercq fixed Jake with a glare. "Rick's taking forever to make the deal."

Jake took a deep breath and counted backward from five. His cousin's impatience was nothing new, nor was her penchant for more adventure than he fancied. And the dynamite had been a joke—maybe. "Nicki, be patient! Rick's good at this sort of thing. We've got to be delicate about this."

Jake hoped that passersby would take them for spatting siblings. While their disagreement was real, it was no accident that they were standing where they could keep an eye on the corridor in each direction. Jake smoothed a wavy lock of brown hair out of his eyes. Much as he hated to admit it, Nicki was right. Rick was taking a long time, and the delay was likely to cause trouble.

"Remind me again why you and Rick didn't just steal the damn urn?" Nicki's voice had dropped. "It would have been better than standing here like targets."

"One: I've got no desire to see the inside of Queen Victoria's dungeons for theft."

"Oh, piffle. Queens don't have dungeons anymore," Nicki said with a dismissive gesture.

"Two: The urn is very valuable to our client. It might be dangerous. We don't need to take additional risks." Jake could see Nicki's faint smile, which meant she wasn't really hearing a word he was saying.

"Tsk. If the urn is that dangerous, why hasn't it harmed the fellow who thinks he owns it? Eaten him, maybe, or sucked out his soul?" She was clearly relishing the argument, a pattern that hadn't changed since childhood.

"Andreas impressed on us that it could be dangerous, but he didn't say how," Jake responded. "Rick and I take him seriously when he says things like that." Jake focused on keeping his breathing regular. He'd been awakened in the night by a nightmare, and had had a sickening feeling of impending doom ever since. He'd told Rick and Nicki, but couldn't give them more details, just a gut feeling. Unfortunately, Jake's gut feelings were right more often than not.

"Just because your client is a centuries-old vampire-witch with a tendency for drama doesn't mean he's always right."

Andreas isn't the only one with a fondness for drama, Jake thought. Just as he was about to respond, the door opened. Out stepped a good-looking, young blond man in an impeccably tailored Savile Row suit with a bulky bundle, wrapped in oilcloth and tied up with twine, under one arm. Rick Brand was smiling broadly, and shaking the hand of a man who was hidden to Jake by the door. Their pleasantries suggested a meeting gone well.

Jake let out a breath he hadn't realized he'd been holding as he saw his friend safely back with them. The door closed and the smile disappeared from Rick's face as he strode toward them. His mouth became a grim line, and his sky-blue eyes flashed a warning. "Let's make a quick

355

exit before the seller changes his mind," he murmured as he passed Jake and Nicki, forcing them to keep up.

They strode three abreast down the corridor, as fast as they could go without breaking into a run. Their footsteps echoed on the tile, mocking their desire for stealth. A black carriage awaited them at the curb. Jake gave the driver a hard stare, assuring himself that no substitution had been made. He kept back a pace, watching the street for danger, as Nicki climbed into the carriage, surrounded by her voluminous skirts.

Just as Jake started toward the cab, he caught a glimpse of movement and alerted Rick. Three burly men rounded a corner on the right and headed toward them at a dead run, while from the left, four more brawny strangers stepped out of an alleyway and started in their direction.

"Get in, get in!" Rick gave Nicki an ungentlemanly shove. Her protest was muffled. Rick swung up, handing off the wrapped urn to Nicki as he ducked into the carriage. "Come on, Jake." Jake already had a Colt Peacemaker in his hand, and was not surprised to see Nicki withdraw a pearl-handled derringer from her purse.

"Go!" Jake shouted, jumping for the doorway of the carriage. His foot had barely landed on the running board before the carriage lurched forward and the horses took off like the start of the Royal Ascot.

A shot splintered the rear left corner of the carriage. "I thought you said this coach was bulletproof," Nicki snapped.

"Part of it is," Jake said, ducking out of the carriage door long enough to size up their pursuers and get off a warning shot. Jake saw more men entering a waiting carriage down a side street.

"Only part?" Nicki's voice rose a few notes.

Rick opened his door, clinging to the carriage frame as he squeezed off two shots from his Remington revolver. An answering shot zinged past, putting a hole in the door just above his head.

"The carriage body is steel-reinforced," Jake said, before repeating Rick's move on the opposite side of the vehicle. "About to the height of the top of your head."

Nicki ducked. "Why not all of it?"

"Trade-off, weight and speed," Jake replied, getting off another shot through the narrowly opened carriage door.

The carriage careened onto two wheels, taking the corner at break-neck speed as the pursuing carriage struggled to keep pace. Several of their pursuers' shots missed their marks, clattering against the brick walls of the buildings lining the road. Pedestrians and carts scrambled to get out of the way of the two carriages. Their driver had long been in the employ of Rick's father, and was one of the best in London, having survived more than one run like this. Still, as the carriage bumped and jostled, throwing them from side to side, Jake could not help wishing he were already safely back home in New Pittsburgh.

"Nearly there," Rick muttered under his breath, and Jake wondered if his friend had been counting the turns. Another volley of gunfire sounded around them, but this time, it seemed to come from every direction. Jake threw Nicki to the floor on top of the urn and dove to cover her with his body as Rick sank as low as he could into the seat.

A bullet tore through the top of the carriage, just missing the edge of the steel reinforcement. Several more clanged against the body of the carriage, leaving depressions in the metal. The shots were near-misses, despite their driver's efforts to keep their pursuers at bay.

Pinned between his chest and the urn, Nicki was muttering curses in French. Jake met Rick's gaze. "Why do our buying trips always end like this?"

Rick shot him his best crooked grin. "Because our usual business isn't business as usual," he replied, looking as unruffled as if he had just finished a cricket match back at Eton.

Jake kept his head down. There was good reason why the import/export company owned by his father and Rick's father employed ex-military sharpshooters for its drivers and secured former cavalry horses for its carriages. This sort of thing happened far too often.

"I thought they weren't supposed to be able to follow us," Nicki grumbled.

"Obviously, they're not as stupid as we took them for," Jake returned.

"I rather prefer dimwitted henchmen," Nicki muttered. "And I'll thank the two of you to mind not to sit on me. It's hard enough to breathe in this corset."

A few more twists and turns through the narrow streets, and the carriage finally slowed to a more acceptable pace. Another hail of gunfire sounded close at hand, then silence.

"Do you think we've lost them?" Nicki asked.

Jake shrugged. "Either that, or they ran out of ammunition."

———

The carriage slowed to a halt. Rick and Jake exchanged a wary glance, rising carefully, guns at the ready. A sharp rap came at the carriage door. "Safe to come out now, guv," a familiar voice said.

Jake cautiously peered around the edge of the battered door, the Peacemaker still in his hand. Behind him, Rick also had his gun at the ready, and Nicki was struggling with her mass of skirts as she climbed off of the carriage floor. Jake's heart was still pounding, but his gun hand was steady. They had arrived in a walled private garden, where they were hidden, at least for the moment, from prying eyes.

"We've got a fresh carriage and a change of horses," their driver said. "Throw them off the scent. Standard operating procedure." He gestured toward a small, elegant carriage that looked like something a fine lady might use for a day of shopping. "Don't you worry," the driver went on, at Jake's skeptical expression. "It's reinforced, like the other one. A bit faster and lighter too, just in case they pick up the trail." Jake cast a backward glance at their carriage. The passenger compartment was peppered with marks where bullets had struck.

The driver waved them on. "Hurry now and get in the new coach. Then we'll send this carriage on—in the other direction. That should get rid of the blighters, and keep them away from the warehouse. Wouldn't do for them to catch up to us, or know too much about what Brand and Desmet does."

Jake, Rick, and Nicki moved at a run to the new carriage, keeping the bundle with the precious urn safely between them. They climbed inside and the carriage took off, drawn by different colored horses than the original coach and with a driver wearing a brand new cloak and hat.

The next time the carriage stopped, it stood in the middle of a loading area for a large, featureless warehouse. At least a score of brawny men greeted the carriage, most holding shotguns that were agreeably pointed toward the ground.

"All clear," the driver announced.

"Thanks for that," Jake said, opening the door and swinging down. To his relief, the area around the warehouse did not appear to have been the scene of any recent fighting.

"Think nothing of it, Mr. Desmet," the driver said with a broad grin. He shifted, and his dark cape gave a tell-tale jingle. "I was glad of the metal plates in my cloak and hat, that's for certain."

"Good to know," said Jake with a laugh. Behind him, Rick helped Nicki down from the carriage as if they were alighting at the opera.

"Guess that 'gut feeling' of yours was right again, Jake," Nicki said. "Now can you get it to be more specific about when and where?" She paused, as her gaze swept over the large warehouse. "Is that building one of yours?"

The driver bowed low and made a sweeping gesture with his hat. "Another fine warehouse of Brand and Desmet, m'lady."

All across Europe—and increasingly throughout the United States —warehouses were emblazoned with the 'Brand and Desmet' name. George Brand and Thomas Desmet—fathers to Rick and Jake—had built their import/export firm into an amazing, if decorously low-key, success story. Discretion was a necessity, given their clientele. Museums on both sides of the Atlantic hired them to bring back the relics of antiquity for their collections. Aristocrats in Europe and the rising elite in the States retained the Brand and Desmet Company to outfit their country houses, or to buy back treasures sold off or gambled away. Hard-to-find antiquities, rare objects, valuable pieces with unusual provenance—Brand and Desmet had built its fortune by acquiring these items for clients for whom money was no object.

Jake had long ago gotten over being star-struck by the names of their clients: dukes, earls, and lords in Europe; Carnegies, Vanderbilts, Goulds, Morgans, and the like in America. But he had not yet grown completely comfortable with their other customers, the ones who came by night to arrange more 'unusual' requests, like the immortal for whom they had retrieved the ancient urn and nearly been killed for their trouble.

People say that everything has its price. Mostly, Jake found that to be true. But sometimes, when a piece's ownership or provenance was in dispute and a buyer was insistent, successful acquisition had more to do with having a fast airship, good aim, cash for bribes, and a monetary relationship with customs officials. Those were the situations in which Brand and Desmet had earned a solid, if hush-hush, word of mouth reputation in the highest society circles. The rest of the import/export business was a well-maintained cover story.

"It's rather plain, isn't it?" Nicki asked. At first, Jake thought she was talking about the urn, but then he realized that she was staring at the unmarked warehouse.

Rick chuckled, his blood still rushing from the fight. "There's a reason for that. It's not just a warehouse, Nicki. It's also a hangar. Best to keep a low profile."

There was a hiss of steam, a whir of gears, and the muffled clank of chains. The sloped roof of the warehouse opened like the lid of a box and a large steel door slid back in the side of the warehouse, revealing just a glimpse of the private airship inside and a flurry of activity. Jake thrust his hands into his pockets, enjoying the show that he and Rick had seen before, but which was leaving Nicki, for once, almost speechless.

"*Mon Dieu!*" Nicki murmured.

"I had your things brought from the hotel and stowed aboard, as you requested, sir," the driver said. "Looks to be a good idea, since there were sure to be more of those blighters watching your lodging."

"Very good," Rick said, as unruffled as if a valet had just brought him his riding horse. "We'd best get going before any more of our 'friends' catch up with us."

"Mr. Desmet!"

Jake looked toward the warehouse, where one of the office clerks was running toward them.

"Mr. Desmet!" The clerk was out of breath when he reached them and his suit was rumpled. "I'm glad I caught you before you got aboard. Mr. Cooper asked to see you. He said it was important."

Jake shot a puzzled glance toward Rick, who shrugged. "Don't look at me. I wasn't expecting anything."

That wasn't entirely true. That sixth sense Nicki joked about was right more often than not, and all day, the expectation of bad news had hung over Jake. He feared he was about to discover why.

"Maybe Harold caught wind of what happened in town," Rick said with a meaningful glance. A telegram certainly could have reached their London office manager while Jake and the others were making their wild escape.

"Or maybe he's got an update on our next appointment," Jake replied, making an effort to keep the worry out of his voice. "Our Paris contact may have needed a bit more time to get the artifact, and our man in Krakow doesn't run on a strict London style schedule. There could be a delay there."

"No way to know until you go talk to Harold," Rick said. "But you know how he goes on a bit. We need to get into the air and out of here before our 'friends' show up."

"I'll make it brief—and warn him to watch out for trouble," Jake promised, striding off toward the office next to the warehouse.

The office building was a two-story Georgian-style affair, under-stated yet dignified. It was all that remained of an old city estate belonging to a minor aristocrat who had owned this land long before the property was parceled off for other uses. Though converted to business use, the offices still had the feel of a stately residence, with beautiful woodwork, embellished plaster ceilings, and fine furnishings. It was every bit as grand as the New York office, and it was the standard the New Pittsburgh office had been designed to emulate.

The office building was unusually quiet when Jake entered. The grand home's entranceway remained a foyer, with the rooms to either side of the sweeping stairway given over to the use of the clerks, and the upper floors reserved for a meeting room, storage, and the office of their London manager, Harold Cooper.

Usually, Jake enjoyed seeing Harold. Although he looked like the quintessential British accountant, he was quick with a joke and whip-smart when it came to business. A former officer in Her Majesty's Army, Harold could hold his own on the occasions, like today, when the work got dicey. But he was also just as comfortable lifting a pint at the pub over a game of darts as he was reviewing ledgers and contracts.

"Mr. Cooper's waiting for you upstairs," the receptionist said, but for once, she did not greet Jake with her usual smile. In fact, she seemed to take pains to avoid meeting his eyes.

A leaden feeling grew in Jake's stomach as he climbed the stairs. He knocked once at Harold's half-open door. "Come in," a voice called.

"Your clerk said you needed to see me," Jake said, popping his head around the door. "Can we make it quick? We had a rather rushed departure from town. It would be good to get on to Krakow as soon as we can lift off."

"I'm afraid there's been a change of plans," Harold said. The manager was ten years older than Jake, and while he was still in his mid-thirties, his dark hair had begun to gray at the temples, something he jokingly blamed on Jake and Rick. Now he looked somber, and Jake's sense of foreboding grew. Jake sat down slowly, and Harold reached across the desk, extending a folded paper toward Jake.

"This telegram came through an hour ago," Harold said. "I'm sorry."

Jake stared at the piece of paper in his hands, reading and rereading it as if the words might change their meaning. It took a moment for him to find his voice, and he blinked as his vision swam, then he crumpled the paper in his fist. "Father's dead?"

He met Harold's gaze. "How can George be sure it was murder?"

Harold shook his head, and Jake saw loss in his eyes. Harold had worked with Brand and Desmet for over a decade, and his loyalty was absolute. "George sent a second telegram to me with the news, and instructions to have your ship ready to return to New Pittsburgh immediately. I've got another crew preparing to go on to Paris and Krakow, and we've got your airship prepped to make the Atlantic crossing."

It was all too much for Jake to take in. Part of him wanted to believe that if he just discarded the crumpled paper in his hand, it would negate the message and return the world to its prior order. But the truth was, the world had changed, and he would never see his father again.

"Ruffians chased us through London," Jake said, focusing on the immediate danger to avoid thinking about his pain. His voice was constricted as he fought for control. "We don't dare linger— they could show up at any moment."

Harold nodded. "The airship is ready. Rick and Miss LeClercq should be onboard by now. I asked Brant to give them the news. I thought that might be a little easier on you." Brant Livingston was Harold's long-time secretary, a thoroughly capable man with an almost encyclopedic knowledge of art and, occasionally, a fondness for ribald humor.

"Then I'd better get going," Jake said, putting on a good front with effort. He met Harold's gaze. "Someone just tried to kill us, and now this. I'm going to get to the bottom of it."

"Just be careful, Jake," Harold cautioned. "Someone out there wants something badly enough to commit murder, and if they didn't get it from Thomas, they're going to keep coming after you and Rick."

Jake closed his fist around the telegram. "That's what I'm counting on."

END

Continue the adventure in *Iron & Blood: A Jake Desmet Adventure*

AFTERWORD

PITTSBURGH, PENNSYLVANIA IS a real place, but we have embellished, a bit, around the edges. We grew up in small towns a few hours north of Pittsburgh, went to college near the city, and lived in Pittsburgh for ten years. Two of our children were born in Pittsburgh, and we worked for Pittsburgh-based companies. We visit the area frequently since we still have close family living nearby. It's one of our favorite cities, and we always enjoy a visit to the "Burgh."

In the late 1800s, Pittsburgh really was the nation's industrial epicenter, quite deserving of a steampunk legacy, since steam powered the factories of legendary industrialists like Andrew Carnegie and Henry Clay Frick. In the Gilded Age, Pittsburgh was also home to more than its share of Robber Barons, men whose inventiveness shaped our modern world and whose rapacity and desire to live large were breathtaking, even by today's standards. And in case you wondered, history reports that Nikola Tesla and George Westinghouse did work together for a time… what if they had taken their partnership further? Thereby hangs the tale.

New Pittsburgh is a fictional construct. While many of the places mentioned in *Iron & Blood*, and the *Storm & Fury Adventures* (and some of the historical figures) are real, we've also invented people, places, and things and taken liberties with key events to create a raw around-the-edges Gilded Age true to the city's frontier heritage. Historians may notice that we've fudged a few details here and there. Please forgive us in the name of entertainment.

Gail Z. Martin is the author of the new epic fantasy novel *Scourge: A Novel of Darkhurst* (Solaris Books). Other recent books include *Shadow and Flame* (Orbit Books) which is Book Four in the Ascendant Kingdoms Saga following: *Ice Forged, Reign of Ash, War of Shadows*; and The Shadowed Path, a collection of Jonmarc Vahanian Adventures short stories. Her Deadly Curiosities urban fantasy series set in Charleston, SC with *Deadly Curiosities, Vendetta*, and *Tangled Web* plus *Trifles and Folly* and *Trifles and Folly 2*, a collection of related short stories and novellas. She is also author of The Chronicles of The Necromancer series (*The Summoner, The Blood King, Dark Haven, Dark Lady's Chosen*) from Solaris Books and The Fallen Kings Cycle (*The Sworn, The Dread*) from Orbit Books. Gail writes three series of ebook short stories: The Jonmarc Vahanian Adventures, the Deadly Curiosities Adventures, and the Blaine McFadden Adventures. Her work has appeared in over 35 US/UK anthologies. Newest anthologies include: *Journeys, In a Cat's Eye*, and *Baker Street Irregulars*.

Larry N. Martin is the author of *Salvage Rat*, coming in 2018, co-author of the Steampunk series *Iron and Blood: The Jake Desmet Adventures* with Gail Z. Martin and a series of related short stories: *The Storm & Fury Adventures* set in the Jake Desmet universe. These short stories also appear in the anthologies *Cinched: Imagination Unbound, The Side of Good/The Side of Evil, Clockwork Universe: Steampunk vs. Aliens* and *Weird Wild West* with more to come. Larry and Gail also have a new urban fantasy, monster hunter series with Falstaff Books: *Spells, Salt, & Steel* in the New Templars universe.

Be among the first to hear the news! Please join us on social media:@GailZMartin or @LNMartinAuthor on Twitter, The Winter Kingdoms on Facebook, blogs at DisquietingVisions.com, and at our JakeDesmet.com home page. You can also find Gail on Goodreads, and be part of the monthly book discussions!

The following stories featured in this collection were first published in the anthologies as noted.

- Airship Down – Originally featured in *Clockwork Universe: Steampunk vs. Aliens* from Zombies Need Brains, LLC
- Lagniappe – Originally featured in *Cinched: Imagination Unbound* from Falstaff Media
- Ruin Creek – Originally featured in *The Weird Wild West* from eSpec Books
- The Hunt – Originally featured in *Alien Artifacts* from Zombies Need Brains, LLC
- Ghost Wolf – Originally featured in *Side of Good / Side of Evil* from eSpec Books
- The Patented Troll – Originally featured in *Gaslight & Grimm* from eSpec Books

ALSO BY GAIL Z. MARTIN & LARRY N. MARTIN

If you'd like to know more about the authors and other works, check out their website at www.JakeDesmet.com.

Jake Desmet Adventures

Iron & Blood

Spells, Salt, & Steel: New Templars

Spells, Salt, & Steel

Open Season

Other books by Gail Z. Martin

Darkhurst

Scourge

Vengeance

Ascendant Kingdoms

Ice Forged

Reign of Ash

War of Shadows

Shadow and Flame

Chronicles of the Necromancer / Fallen Kings Cycle

The Summoner